PRAISE FOR *AT THE BOTTOM OF THE GARDEN*

"All the elegance and all the venom, like one of E. Nesbit's supernatural stories served with a side of arsenic."
—GRADY HENDRIX, *New York Times* bestselling author of *Witchcraft for Wayward Girls*

"Camilla Bruce tills the macabre for all of its Edward Gorey glory, cultivating one gorgeously morbid gothic novel that's just as gleeful as it is gashly-crumb. At the bottom of this particular garden you will find a wicked sense of humor that harkens back to the best of Roald Dahl's *Tales of the Unexpected,* with all its vicious thorns intact."
—CLAY McLEOD CHAPMAN, author of *What Kind of Mother* and *Ghost Eaters*

"Camilla Bruce writes dark fantasy like no one else out there. A gothic masterpiece, *At the Bottom of the Garden* is a propulsive novel with gorgeous prose and incredible characters you won't soon forget. You'll never look at the wicked stepmothers of fairy tales quite the same way again. Put this book at the top of your TBR pile immediately; you won't regret it."
—GWENDOLYN KISTE, Bram Stoker Award–winning author of *Reluctant Immortals* and *The Haunting of Velkwood*

"Wonderful spooky, rich in intrigue and full of surprise, *At the Bottom of the Garden* is the excellent Camilla Bruce at her absolute best."
—LAIRD HUNT, author of *In the House in the Dark of the Woods*

"Bruce's unique cast of characters is both charming and terrifying. A young synesthetic musician, an even younger sensitive, a murderous aunt, and a houseful of furious ghosts—it's all here! A delightful read."
—LOUISA MORGAN, author of *A Secret History of Witches*

The Witch in the Well

"A startling and original plot is woven around a cast of gleefully unpleasant characters—I was gripped from the very first page."
—LUCIE MCKNIGHT HARDY, author of *Water Shall Refuse Them*

"A compelling, creepy story of angst, obsessions and lost friendship."
—*BookPage*

"Bruce masterfully plays with perceptions of reality, truth, and magic. It's a uniquely told and riveting read."
—*BuzzFeed*

"[This is] a superb folk horror tale that delivers an imaginative feminist take on the historical persecution of witches through the conflicting viewpoints of three complex and at times believably unlikeable female protagonists."
—*Toronto Star*

All the Blood We Share

"Chilling, terrifying, utterly addictive . . . a beautifully written, spellbinding read."
—KAREN COLES, author of *The Asylum*

"A horrifyingly realistic view into the minds of a serial killing family that really tormented the old West."
—*BuzzFeed*

"A riveting portrait of the dark side of the American dream."
—*Publishers Weekly* (starred review)

BY CAMILLA BRUCE

You Let Me In
In the Garden of Spite
The Witch in the Well
All the Blood We Share
At the Bottom of the Garden

AT THE
BOTTOM
OF THE
GARDEN

AT THE BOTTOM OF THE GARDEN

CAMILLA BRUCE

NEW YORK

Published in the United States by Del Rey,
an imprint of Random House, a division of
Penguin Random House LLC, New York.

DEL REY and the CIRCLE colophon are registered trademarks
of Penguin Random House LLC.

LIBRARY OF CONGRESS CATALOGING-IN-PUBLICATION DATA
Names: Bruce, Camilla, author.
Title: At the bottom of the garden: a novel / Camilla Bruce.
Description: New York: Del Rey, 2025.
Identifiers: LCCN 2024037743 (print) | LCCN 2024037744 (ebook) |
ISBN 9780593724958 (trade paperback) | ISBN 9780593724965 (ebook)
Subjects: LCGFT: Gothic fiction. | Novels.
Classification: LCC PR9144.9.B78 A92 2025 (print) |
LCC PR9144.9.B78 (ebook) | DDC 813/.6—dc23/eng/20241025
LC record available at https://lccn.loc.gov/2024037743
LC ebook record available at https://lccn.loc.gov/2024037744

Printed in the United States of America on acid-free paper

randomhousebooks.com

2 4 6 8 9 7 5 3 1

Book design by Alexis Flynn
Title page illustration: stock.adobe.com/erika8213

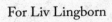
For Liv Lingborn

AT THE
BOTTOM
OF THE
GARDEN

CLARA

1

I wanted to say no, of course. Every sane woman would have said no. I had finally reached a point in my life where things were somewhat settled. I had the house, the garden, and a well-stocked wine cellar. I had a mostly reliable housekeeper and a lovely, big jewelry box crammed with sparkling rocks. I had new dreams, too—*plans*—that had bloomed forth in my aging heart long after I had deemed that dried-up organ satisfied.

All I needed to make the dream of my legacy come true was a sizable influx of cash.

That was why I did not immediately hang up on Miss Feely when she called and disturbed my otherwise excellent breakfast of hard-boiled eggs and an assortment of melon balls; why I did not merely snort at her request and call for Dina to come and whisk the phone away again. Instead, I played for time, knowing only too well what kind of wealth my late half brother had inherited. Wealth that he, in my opinion, did nothing but squander on "adventures" and foolishness. He was always blessed, that one—touched by a golden finger at birth and wandered through life as if bad things could never happen to him. He was just that *special*—so *beyond* us mere mortals.

Until he wasn't, of course.

"Miss Feely, are you telling me there's no other option for the girls?" I asked, incredulous. "Surely on Amanda's side . . . ?" I didn't even care if the busybody on the other end learned just how little I knew about my late sister-in-law. "We weren't close," I felt obliged to clarify nevertheless. "I suppose you could call me and my half brother estranged, though there was no bad blood between us." None that *he* knew of, anyway.

"Mrs. Webb sadly had no one left," the woman on the other end replied. "As far as we can determine, you are the girls' closest living relative—you *did* know that your brother had passed?" She sounded aghast all of a sudden, terrified that she had blindsided me and become the bearer of terrible news.

"Of course." How could I *not* know? It had even been in the news: *The search continues for missing couple, now presumed dead on K2.* The press seemed to be unable to decide whether the incident was more tragic or romantic, given that the two of them had climbed the mountain as an anniversary celebration. Personally, I couldn't help but think of it as justice: Icarus flying too high at last. It was nothing more than he deserved. "I sent flowers to the memorial."

"I'm sure the girls were grateful." Miss Feely sounded an itsy bit terse. "As I mentioned, they are living at home with Lucia, the nanny, for now, but that needs to change going forward."

"Why?" My free hand toyed with a linen napkin.

"An employee is not a substitute for parental care, Mrs. Woods. Besides, the will is very clear: Mr. and Mrs. Webb wanted the children to go to their closest living relative—"

"What about foster care? Or an orphanage?"

"Well, that would be a last resort, and hopefully unnecessary." Miss Feely did her best to poke at my conscience. "You have to understand, Mrs. Woods, that these girls are very vulnerable, not only because of their age and circumstances, but because of what they stand to inherit—"

"Yes." I cut her off. "How much is that exactly?"

Miss Feely seemed to think for a moment before suggesting an amount that made my withered heart twitch with delight. "It's hard to tell exactly with a fortune this size. A lot of it is invested and tied up in bonds," she noted.

I did my very best to sound unfazed, though it truly was a struggle. "In that case, I assume I wouldn't take them for nothing?"

Miss Feely went quiet for a moment. "The bulk of the inheritance will come to the girls when they turn eighteen—if they are still living, that is. Otherwise it will all go to charity." It shouldn't have stung but it did. Even though I knew better than to expect anything from my brother, the callousness of the stipulation ached like a two-day-old bruise. Charities were well and good, but what about *me*, his own sister?

Miss Feely gave me a second to process the unfortunate news before offering a touch of hope. "But there is a clause . . ."

"Yes?" My fingers drummed lightly on the polished oak of the table.

"Well, in the event that Mr. and Mrs. Webb were to die before the children came of age, there is a clause that stipulates what each child will need to live and get a good education—"

"Yes?"

"It will be paid in monthly installments to the guardian."

"Is that so?" I stopped my drumming and pressed the heavy black receiver tightly to my ear. "How much are we talking about, Miss Feely?"

Her answer left me grinning like the cat that got the cream, and my old heart sped up its pace. Maybe there was still hope for my grand plan, despite my dwindling fortune. It wasn't that I hadn't coveted my brother's ample assets before—far from it. I had just not envisioned coming by them in quite such a roundabout way.

"How old are they now?" I asked. Though I had made it my business to stay informed, the girls' exact ages had escaped me, being of so little consequence.

"Lily is fourteen; Violet is nine."

"Good," I said, although it wasn't exactly ideal, with Lily being only four years away from her inheritance. At least they weren't toddlers, with all that entailed. Perhaps they were even quiet kids with impeccable table manners. They were recently bereft, too, so would

6 CAMILLA BRUCE

likely be sad and cry a lot. That was fine by me. I much preferred a little crying to ear-shattering shouts of joy.

"The guardian would also have to act in the girls' place when it comes to managing their fortune, together with Mr. Skye." She was referring to my brother's lawyer—Miss Feely's own employer. "Lily is very mature for her age, but we cannot expect her to know much about money. She will need the guidance of a steady hand—"

"Of course," I readily agreed. A nice feeling had started spreading through my body: a tingling sensation, like lust, or even love. I belatedly recognized the feeling as relief. Here was the answer—the thing that I needed. Surely Mr. Skye could be persuaded to steer some of the fortune my way? I did, after all, have a brilliant proposal. "I'll take them," I told Miss Feely.

"Well." She sounded perplexed. "Don't you want to meet them first?"

I experienced a surge of annoyance. "This is *why* you called me," I reminded her. "You wanted me to take the girls."

"Yes, but—I suppose, since you don't know them, there should perhaps be some consideration—"

"You should be grateful, Miss Feely. My nieces are *blessed* to have a capable aunt to take care of them, with a big house and soft beds waiting. Not all orphans are as lucky."

"Of course not." Miss Feely quickly composed herself.

"I'll be there tomorrow," I assured her. "Tell them to expect me by dinnertime." Now that I had realized what this stroke of luck could mean for me, I was eager to strike at once, before the chance scuttled off and disappeared. This was a windfall, and I'd better make it work in order to secure my legacy.

"That's quite soon." Miss Feely sounded surprised. "It is a long trip," she saw fit to remind me.

"I may not live in a big city like my brother and his family do— did—but this *is* the seventies after all, and we have access to an excellent airport. Ivory Springs may be a small town by some standards, but it isn't primitive." Not quite, anyway.

"No, of course not," Miss Feely hurried to say. "I suppose I will see you tomorrow, then."

"Yes, Miss Feely, I guess you will." I wore a wide grin as I hung up the phone.

Still, I should have said no. Any sane woman would have—but not me, no . . . I marched ahead toward my own doom like a witless, grinning fool.

LILY

2

It was raining on the day she came. I was happy to notice that I noticed, since it had been hard for me to care about normal things ever
since we learned that Mama and Papa weren't coming back. Not even
their bodies had come back yet. They were still up there, on the mountain.

I hated that place with all my heart.

It had been a stupid thing to do in the first place, climbing the
"savage mountain." I hadn't known that people called it that until
after the fact, when the newspaper wrote about what had happened to
my parents. If I had known earlier, I probably would have protested
the trip even more than I did, because who even wants to go to a
mountain that has "savage" in its name? I didn't know that before they
left, though, and it probably wouldn't have made a difference even if I
had. Papa would have wanted to go anyway; that was just how he was.
He could never do anything normal. "We want to celebrate our fifteen years in a most spectacular way," he had said, but honestly, it
wasn't *they* who had wanted it but *him*. Mama would probably have
been just as satisfied with a trip to somewhere warm, or even just a
dinner at the place that had her favorite orange ice cream—she hadn't
even climbed that much after I was born—but Papa always had to

make everything *extraordinary*. It wasn't even because he had wanted to impress someone with his bravery or prove himself somehow. When I asked him about it once, he said that it was just so he'd know that he had done it. He kept the memories of his adventures like precious pearls on a string, he said, and wore them like an invisible wreath of accomplishments. It made him feel alive, I think.

But then, of course, it killed him.

And now there was Aunt Clara, whom Violet and I had barely known existed. The only times I had heard her name mentioned were when Mama and Papa discussed what to get her for Christmas, even though we never got anything in return. When I asked Mama about it, she said that we had so little family left that it was important to take care of the few that we had, even if it was thankless. I thought that was sweet but not very smart. "You'll understand when you get older," she had said, but I still doubted it.

On the day when Aunt Clara arrived, I wished that I was just a little bit older. If only I had been eighteen, Violet and I could have stayed in the house, and nothing more would have to change. *I* could have taken care of my sister. Instead, we had to *prepare to leave,* as Miss Feely had said. We didn't *have* to sell the house, she continued, but maybe it was for the best? Whatever we decided—together with our new guardian—she encouraged us to pack up our clothes and toys and photographs, so we would feel at home at Aunt Clara's. Neither of us wanted to go, though. We wanted to stay at home, where we belonged.

Miss Feely wore a cheerful face when she arrived that day, an hour or so ahead of Aunt Clara, but the joy didn't show in her eyes. "You'll see," she said, as she settled in on our buttercup-yellow living room couch. A pile of Mama's unread books was still balancing on the side table. "As soon as your aunt arrives, I'm sure that everything will feel better." Just as the words came tumbling out of her mouth, a lime-green flame flickered on the skin of her round wrist, and I blinked quickly, several times, to make it go away. Lime green wasn't good at all. It meant lying or doubt, and I really needed to trust her just then.

"It's what Mama and Papa wanted," I replied, although I didn't think it was *Aunt Clara* they had had in mind when they set up the will. They had been "slow in updating the document," Mr. Skye had told us, and now all our other relatives were gone.

"This way you are sure to stay together." Miss Feely pushed her horn-rimmed glasses farther up her nose, and no more flames appeared on her skin. "Once there are arrangements outside of the family, all bets are off. You are very lucky," she added, and smoothed down the fabric of her dark blue pencil skirt.

"What about the rest of our things?" I was sitting in the soft wingback leather chair where Papa used to relax in the evenings. It still smelled a little of his aftershave: a sweet, minty scent.

"That is, of course, something that must be dealt with." Miss Feely's gaze drifted to the family portrait that hung on the wall, and I couldn't help but follow her gaze, even though I knew exactly what I would see: Mama standing there in her sky-blue dress, which looked beautiful against her brown hair and golden complexion; Papa, next to her, wearing a sharp gray suit, his dark hair as precise as if cut with a ruler. Both Violet and I wore white dresses in the picture and had pale blue ribbons in our hair. Violet's ribbon was about to come undone, as seemed to happen with any knot on her body. She had lost both her front teeth when the picture was taken but still smiled at the camera without any shame. Her small, freckled face was framed by frizzy clouds of brown hair. I looked strangely proper next to her, with my single braid falling straight behind the ribbon and my smile looking almost shy. I had been twelve then, and happy.

Now I was fourteen and full of pain.

Miss Feely spoke again. "Perhaps your aunt could help you pack up the belongings and send them to storage? That way it would be easier if you decided to sell. I also know of a couple of wonderful charities that would love to take your parents' clothes—"

"I know." I cut her off while swallowing bile. Talking about endings only made me dread my aunt's arrival more. Again, I remembered the Christmas gifts: the silk shawls and butterfly brooches that Aunt Clara never thanked us for—but maybe she just wasn't a Christmas person.

The front door opened and then slammed shut, as Violet and our nanny, Lucia, came back from their walk. I could hear them talking and laughing in the hallway, then the smacking sound when Violet pulled off her rain boots. Lucia rummaged around in the umbrella stand and then clattered with the clothes hangers as she hung their coats to dry.

Violet didn't wait for her but raced across the floor and peeked her head around the doorframe. "Is she here yet?" Her brown eyes were wide with excitement; her unruly hair had curled in the rain. "Has Aunt Clara come to get us yet?"

"No, not yet," I replied, rolling my eyes. She *did* have eyes of her own and could see that for herself.

"She will be here soon, though. I can *feel* her," my sister continued chattering. "Can't you feel her, too, Lily? She's moving through the streets."

"Oh, sure." I snorted and rolled my eyes again. "I can *absolutely* feel her."

Violet gave me a bright smile. "See? Everything will be fine now," she said, as if trying to convince me—and herself.

"Of course," I croaked, but inside I felt sick.

When Violet's face had vanished from the open door and I could hear her feet drumming up the stairs, I turned to Miss Feely again. "I'm only worried because I don't think Aunt Clara liked Papa very much."

"She assured me there was no bad blood." Miss Feely sounded calm. "Sometimes people just drift apart. There doesn't have to be any animosity involved."

"No," I agreed, although sometimes there was.

Miss Feely caught and held my gaze. "Remember, Lily, this is what your parents wanted," she said, repeating my own words back to me. "And you can always reach out if need be. You know our office hours."

I felt a little grateful to her for saying that, although I didn't really know what good it would do.

As soon as the proper papers were signed, we would belong to Aunt Clara.

CLARA

3

It was raining horribly when I landed in the city, and it did not ease up. When the taxi pulled up in front of my late brother's fancy town house, the downpour was so bad that I had to open my umbrella just to make it to the front door. I looked up at the brick façade for a moment, counting stories and windows, as I always did when admiring my brother's home.

The door itself was pristine and white, the wooden core enclosed within a smooth lacquer shell. Someone had hung a wreath on it, crammed with dried greenery. At first, I thought it was because of the deaths, that it warned of the sorrow inside, but then I noticed how all the other town houses surrounding me had similar ornaments on their doors and realized it was merely a token of conformity. Still, the collection of dead foliage made me feel somehow uncomfortable—as if warning me to think twice before entering the abode. I undoubtedly should have listened to that sense of foreboding, but instead I brushed it off, lifted my finger to the brass button, and pushed.

A deep chime reverberated through the house before me.

The woman who came to answer the door was young. She wore her dark hair up in a perky little ponytail and had donned a puff-sleeved blouse that would have looked better on a ten-year-old, so I figured she had to be the nanny.

"Lucia, I presume." I held out my hand, still glove clad, and the young woman squeezed it briefly while sporting an insecure smile. She looked anywhere but at me, I noted.

"Yes," she confirmed. "You must be the girls' aunt."

"I am," I replied, serving her a brief smile. "Clarabelle Woods." I offered my name as the nanny stepped aside to let me into the hallway. It was about high time, too, as my poor black fur coat had soaked up the rain like a sponge and felt heavier by the minute.

My feet touched marble the very moment I stepped inside. Black and white tiles were laid out before me. The wallpaper was a risqué robin's-egg blue. To my surprise, I noted how the walls were lined with coat- and shoe racks, and how a musty scent of wet outerwear permeated the air. The whole room was a strange mixture of affluence and down-to-earth practicality—like someone ashamed to have an excess of cash.

I wriggled out of my coat and tried to hand it to the nanny, but she just gave me a strange look and motioned to a free clothes hanger. I rolled my eyes but went on with it, thinking how my housekeeper, Dina, would never be so rude. Then I removed my hat and my gloves to reveal the sparkling stones on my fingers.

"They are all waiting for you in the living room," Lucia informed me with a smile, then lowered her voice a little. "I think they are very excited to meet you—especially Violet. It has been such a hard time for them."

"Uh-huh," I agreed, forcing my lips into a smile of my own.

"The two of them need to feel safe and cared for . . ." the nanny prattled on.

"Of course." I placed a hand on her shoulder and pretended not to feel her wince. "Let's go and meet them, then, shall we?"

The living room, it turned out, was through the door to our right. It was spacious and well furnished, though the decorator seemed to have preferred a limited palette of yellow and gold. Two of the walls had built-in bookshelves, and above the white marble mantelpiece hung a family portrait in an ornate frame. I saw the picture before I saw the girls. It could not be helped because *he* was there, sporting his usual smug smile. Benjamin Webb: the meal ticket, the golden boy, captured in glass and brass. As a teenager I had often prayed to never have to see that face again, and when that hadn't worked, I knitted a doll that looked somewhat like him and threw it into the fire. It seemed that someone had listened at last, and the irony of the situation didn't escape me. Now it was *his* daughters who were to pay *my* way, just as he himself had paved the way for our mother.

I quickly turned my gaze on the group of people huddled around the coffee table. All three of them had risen from their seats and were looking at me with varying degrees of curiosity—and even a little suspicion, I noticed, before straightening my back and widening my smile.

"Oh, girls," I said, and pressed my hands to my black satin blouse. "Oh, girls. What a terrible, terrible thing to have happened!" I crossed the honey-colored carpet in a few quick strides and stretched my arms out before me; my pretty diamonds caught the light and glittered like ice crusts on my fingers. "How sad it is for us to meet again under such horrible circumstances!"

The elder girl's face instantly turned bewildered, knowing full well that we had never met. It didn't matter, though, since the performance wasn't for her, but for the gray-haired lady standing between my new charges: Miss Feely, in the flesh. She turned out to be just as drab as I had imagined, with a head crowned with lead-colored curls and a perfectly pressed blue skirt and jacket. Whether she was taken in by my performance was honestly hard to tell. Her round face displayed a degree of relief, but whether that was due to seeing me so appropriately moved or because she just wanted to unload the girls, I really couldn't say.

"Oh, Violet." I grabbed the younger girl by the shoulder, then caught her chin in my free hand and tilted her face up to inspect her. She wasn't much of a violet. Maybe more like a thistle, with a crown of bushy hair and clothes that hung haphazardly on her body. "Look at you," I cooed. "How old are you now? Nine? Ten? What a beautiful little girl you are!"

"I'm nine," she burst out, and her brown eyes went wide. She had the same golden flecks around the pupils as Ben, and his ugly tooth gap, too. She even had his freckles, though his had faded with time. I let the girl go as if she was made of fire.

Better to look at her sister, then, who appeared much more like Amanda: slim and lean with golden-blond hair. *Her* eyes were a pale blue, and there was not so much as a freckle in sight.

"Lily," I uttered. "My dearest girl! How hard it must have been for you to shoulder all of this alone . . ." I made as if I was about to cry by twisting my lips and swallowing hard. "If I hadn't been just out of surgery, I would have come here at once, of course." Again, I was speaking mostly for Miss Feely's benefit, worried that the dull woman would suddenly find a reason to object to the arrangement, but it was for Lily, too, I realized, seeing how the blue of her eyes turned icier by the second. She was clearly brighter than anticipated, which could become a problem—or a challenge—depending on how things panned out.

"It's good to see you, Aunt Clara," the girl replied with an uncertain smile, while blinking several times as if struggling to adjust her vision. Her hands were folded over her stomach, and her fingertips were very callused.

"Let us all sit down and have some tea." Miss Feely gave me a cool smile. "We are all very grateful that you could come on such short notice, Mrs. Woods—"

"Oh, please, call me Clara." I sat down in an empty wingback chair and pressed my hands to my chest again. "How could I *not* come?" I turned a stern gaze on Miss Feely. "You should have telephoned me *ages* ago! I had no idea that the girls were both bereft and alone. I always assumed that Amanda's family—"

"Aunt Sarah died three years ago in a car crash, and Grandma Fiona died last year," Lily interrupted. "If not, we would have gone to her."

"Yes! I just assumed that Amanda's mother—"

"Well, we didn't know about you before Lily mentioned your name." Some defensiveness had come into Miss Feely's voice.

I looked at Lily, sitting there before me on the yellow couch. She looked straight back at me, clever as a fox. Foster care was clearly not something she wanted for herself and her sister. Perhaps she even worried that the two of them would be separated. I saved that little nugget of information for later.

"Oh, don't worry about it." I waved my hand airily. "The important thing is that Lily had the good sense to make you aware of me. God only knows what would have happened to them if you hadn't made that call." I served Miss Feely my sweetest smile.

"Where did you have surgery?" Ben's eyes peered curiously at me across the marble tabletop. Violet sat so close to her sister on the couch that you couldn't squeeze as much as a dime between them.

"On my hip," I explained. "It was an old injury—"

"Really?" The little girl sounded puzzled, and her gaze darted between me and Lily. She tugged at the latter's shirtsleeve, but the older girl gently shook her off. For a moment, my heart picked up its pace. Could it be that she saw through my lie?

Surely not. How could she?

"Yes, it was all very painful," I muttered.

A horrible clattering by the room's other door preceded the tea's arrival and saved me from further scrutiny. Apparently, Lucia *could* be used for other things than child minding, but she was clearly not very good at it. Tiny teacups and sugar lumps danced around on the silver tray as she moved toward the table with all the grace of a buffalo. Then came the haphazard shelling out of fragile china and the sloppy pouring of a scaldingly hot oolong. Finally, there was a selection of undoubtedly stale jam-filled tarts. Perhaps Lucia ought to keep to the child minding after all.

"So, Mrs. Woods," Miss Feely said when the storm had settled and we were all waiting for the tea to cool down. "I realize how this must have come as a shock to you—"

"Yes," I replied. "But a welcome one, of course. I'm *honored* to be able to help in my nieces' hour of distress."

"Still, you are perhaps not prepared?" She lowered her head a little, and the horn-rimmed glasses made her look rather menacing. "You have no children of your own, do you, Mrs. Woods?"

"Sadly, no," I lamented. "That blessing has not been bestowed upon me."

"You are a widow?" She arched an eyebrow.

"Not to my knowledge." I assumed a mournful expression; I had some experience with this particular question. "My husband vanished nearly ten years ago."

"So, you are . . . divorced?" The other eyebrow joined the first.

"No, Miss Feely. He did, in fact, vanish. No one knows where he is." I picked up a strawberry tart and daintily bit into the crust. The girls both watched me wide-eyed.

"Did someone look for him?" Miss Feely sounded incredulous.

"Of course! It was quite the manhunt—at first. Then the police found out that his mistress, Ellie Anderson, had disappeared on the same day, and no one looked much after that." I gave them all a tremulous smile, as if to say that I was bravely trying to not care. "They are probably living the high life somewhere. I would have preferred to have a proper divorce, but then, it was a long time ago and I have come to terms with it. The house and the money were mine anyway, so I didn't really lose much from his betrayal—except for a husband, of course." I laughed to take the edge off my words. "I have missed having my own family for quite some time, so perhaps that is why I am so very grateful to have this opportunity—though I would of course have preferred for it to have happened under less tragic circumstances," I hastened to add.

"I appreciate your honesty," Miss Feely said, although she did look a little pale. She had probably not expected to be exposed to such a sordid tale over tea. "We *are* grateful, of course, that you are willing to take in the girls. It's bound to be a great change for you."

"Oh, I'm not worried. It is the least I can do for my own flesh and blood, and it *is* what my late brother wanted." I gave the girls a soft smile and Lily replied with something like a sneer. "I have a big, empty house, Miss Feely, just waiting for someone to fill its rooms with life. For the longest time, I considered adoption." I gave the woman a pointed look. "But it's hard when you are a single woman and your husband's whereabouts are unknown. Now, however, it seems that fate has intervened." I grabbed a soft napkin from the silver tray and pressed it to the corner of my eye. "Yes." I gave a decisive nod. "It was fate—or God—for sure."

"That is a lovely sentiment, Mrs. Woods." Miss Feely picked up a tart. "A lovely sentiment indeed." I could see that she was moved, and a feeling of victory spread through my body like lazy molasses.

"Can I see the scar from your surgery?" Violet asked, and the victorious feeling instantly dispersed. Beside her, the older girl blinked repeatedly again, as if I was some spectacle she struggled to comprehend.

"Perhaps later," I replied, suddenly sullen. Although I knew it was highly irrational, I couldn't help but feel Ben's gaze on my neck as he peered down from the family portrait.

There was nothing he could do now, though. Nothing at all.

He was finally—utterly—dead!

✦ VIOLET ✦

4

I didn't want our last day at home to end, so I brushed my teeth as slowly as I could while looking at my face in the mirror above the basin. Some toothpaste foamed around my mouth and made me look as if I had rabies. I pulled a rabies face in the mirror, with the yellow toothbrush still sticking out between my lips.

"Stop stalling, Violet." Lily came in from her room to the left. "It will happen if you like it or not, and time won't move slower even if you do." Lily tried to sound like Mama when she said it, copying her voice. I think it made her feel better, as if Mama was still around. But it didn't help me, because I *knew* that it was Lily. And no matter how good she was, she never sounded exactly like Mama.

I took out the toothbrush to say, "I have rabies, Lily."

"You don't have rabies, Violet. You're just being messy."

"What color am I now?" I asked, while filling my blue plastic cup with water.

Lily looked at me in the mirror. "You know I never see your color."

"What about Aunt Clara?" I asked next, before rinsing and spitting. "She must be very green, I think. Lime green as in liar."

"Why do you say that?" Lily had taken her own toothbrush out of the cabinet. It was red like a strawberry, or the color of Mama's climbing parka. Behind her in the mirror I could see the pink marble walls and the claw-foot bathtub. I knew every vein in the marble above the tub, having traced them with my finger while happily splashing around, pretending to be a blowfish or a mermaid.

"Because she never had anything done to her hip," I said. "I didn't *feel* it, Lily. There was nothing there."

"Well, maybe you felt wrong." Lily shrugged, but I could tell from her stiff face that she believed me and didn't like our aunt one bit. "It will be fine, Violet," she murmured while squeezing toothpaste onto the brush. "This way, we will be together, and that is all that matters. And in four years I'll be old enough to take care of us myself."

"If we live that long." I rinsed and spat again.

"Violet!" Her brow had knitted up. "That's a horrible thing to say—*of course* we will live that long. Why would you *say* something like that?"

I shrugged. It didn't feel that bad to me. "I can just *feel* that maybe we won't."

"Oh, Violet." Lily threw her arms around me and held me close, which was strange since I wasn't sad or anything. "Do you miss Mama and Papa that badly?" she asked. "They would have wanted for us to live and be happy—"

"I know that," I said—or tried to say—but my face was pressed against Lily's blue pajama top and my mouth was muffled by fabric. "It's just a feeling. It doesn't have to happen."

Lily let me go and took a step back, looking at my face all the while. For some reason, her eyes were wet with tears. "Maybe your feeling is *wrong*," she said.

"It never was before." I shrugged, thinking of Aunt Clara's hip again. "I don't think it would be so bad if we died. It's not scary, Lily. It's dark and warm, like going to sleep in a giant bed, full of pillows and blankets and lots of stuffed animals—and maybe some real animals, too." Lily had always loved animals.

"We are not going to *die*, Violet." Now she sounded annoyed again, even though I had just tried to make her feel better.

"Okay," I said, but the feeling still tickled at me. It had come flying in as soon as Aunt Clara stepped inside the house, settling in my stomach like a badly burned pancake. "Her feet are red," I murmured, because that was what I felt, even though I didn't know exactly what it meant.

"Whose feet?" Lily looked very upset, which was not what I had wanted at all. She stood before me on the bathroom floor and held my shoulders with both hands, looking into my eyes. Her brow was still wrinkled up, and I wanted to lift my hand to smooth it out, but I knew it wouldn't help.

"Aunt Clara's," I told her with a sigh. "It's like she's leaving smudges of red when she walks. Even if I don't see it, I just *feel* it," I tried to explain.

Lily shook her head. "There's nothing wrong with Aunt Clara, Violet. There *can't* be, because we need her." Now her eyes looked scared again.

"Just because you want her to be right, it—"

"Violet, no!" Her hold of my shoulders tightened a little. "It's all going to be fine, don't you see? We're going to live with Aunt Clara for a while, and then we will come back here and everything will be good again."

"Okay," I repeated, because I wanted it to be true, and because I didn't want Lily to be upset. It seemed to work, too, because her brow finally smoothed out, and she had a smile on her lips. I could feel it, too, when her shoulders slumped and she loosened her grip on mine.

"And no more talk of dying," she said before letting me go. "I know it *feels* like dying in a way, leaving this house behind, but it won't be forever, I promise. We just have to be brave—as brave as *they* were— and then it will be fine in the end."

No matter how many times she said it, though, I could tell that she wasn't so sure.

"Do you want to say good night to Mama and Papa?" Lily asked after she was done with brushing my hair. We were both sitting on my bed, between my shelves full of toys. Some of them were old enough that I didn't play with them anymore, but looking at them still comforted me at night. They reminded me of when it was Mama who used to sit next to me and "tease the tangles out." I *could* do it myself, but Lily insisted that we should do things the way we did before, even if two of us were gone. I *felt* that it was important to her, and so I went along.

"Sure," I replied, and folded my hands, even though it wasn't a prayer exactly. We both closed our eyes and I saw it at once—it just sprang into my mind: the snowy mountain, with the wind whipping up shrouds of white. A flash of red where Mama lay, and a glimpse of Papa's boot.

"Good night, Mama," Lily started, although it wasn't night yet on K2. "It's our last night at home now, and we're about to go to bed."

"Good night, Papa," I continued. "We promise to behave and be good to Aunt Clara, even though we never saw her before you died. Lily says that we must give her a chance, so I will."

"We will be fine," Lily said again, this time to our parents.

"Sweet dreams, Mama and Papa," I finished.

I could hear Lily sniffling softly beside me, but I wasn't ready to come back yet. I just kept sitting there with my eyes closed and my hands folded, staring at the mountain. A rope hung down the mountain wall, and a piece of an ice pick stuck up from the snow. It hadn't been there before, so the wind must have dug it out.

"It is so cold up there, you wouldn't believe it," I told Lily. "It's colder than you can even imagine."

"You don't know that," she muttered, still sniffling.

"But I *do* know," I insisted, because it was the truth. "And now it's snowing, too—big, fat flakes of snow. It's going to cover them up again." Which wasn't good at all, because then they wouldn't ever be found.

"Stop imagining things," Lily said in a small voice. "You're just tormenting yourself."

"I'm not imagining *anything*," I told her, still with my eyes closed.

"You can't see K2," she said. "It's thousands of miles away."

"Just because *you* can't see K2, it doesn't mean that I can't," I replied. "You can see colors that I can't, so maybe I can see something *you* can't, too."

"*No one* can see K2 from here, Violet."

"So maybe I'm the first."

"No, you're just imagining," she insisted, which only made her seem stubborn.

"I know what imagining feels like," I said. "I'm not *stupid*, Lily."

"Of course not—"

"If I say that it's snowing on K2, it *is*."

She finally gave up. "Sure, sure." If my eyes had been open, I probably would have seen her brow all knitted up again.

Inside my head, behind my closed eyelids, something new was happening. A dark shape came flying through the snowdrift, not bothered at all by the wind. It landed just by the red of Mama's parka and looked at me with clever eyes.

It was a bird—a raven. At first, I was confused, since I had never seen a bird on K2 before, but it didn't feel like a stranger to me, and when it opened its beak and croaked, I felt that it knew me, too.

CLARA

5

After the girls and their nanny had gone to sleep and Miss Feely was safely out the door, I walked the town house's dark hallways by myself. It was indeed a moment of triumph. I had imagined doing this so many times before, and had even fallen into the slightly shameful habit of passing by the house on my trips to the city, just to stand outside and look at it, somewhat disguised by large sunglasses and a hat. I would imagine what it was like inside, what riches were to be found. I had often fantasized about what would happen if my brother and *all* of his family were to perish on one of his "daring adventures," and wondered if those riches would maybe land in my lap. There was no one closer to inherit, after all—not by blood, anyway.

Now that Miss Feely had shattered my delusion by letting me know that all the money would have gone to charity, I felt somewhat stupid for having dreamt of it at all. But back in those days, I had been hopeful—wistful—and kept my fingers crossed for swift and sudden deaths.

Only half of my prayers had been answered.

Sometimes, on those little excursions of mine, I would even sneak up behind the house and enter the long, narrow garden through the latched gate, just so I could get closer to the windows and steal a peek inside. I always went during daylight hours, since I knew that Amanda and the girls would likely not be at home. It was harder to gauge my brother, though, who often spent his days just lounging about the house. I was very careful, however, and was never observed, to my knowledge. On one particularly memorable occasion, I found the large garden shed unlocked and made my way inside. Ben kept many of his toys in there: water skis, parachutes, kayaks, and climbing gear. I took my time going through it all, making slight adjustments: cutting a rope, scratching a side, removing tiny safety pins. Nothing much, really, and it would probably be discovered during rigid safety checks—although I did have a faint hope, at the time, that perhaps my brother, so full of himself, would think sabotage so unlikely that he maybe wouldn't go through it all with a fine-tooth comb, but opted to jump or ski or climb without ever noticing my small adjustments.

A woman is allowed her dreams.

So, all of that considered, it brought me immense satisfaction to walk the town house's rooms at last, even if the access came with the price of child-rearing and bothersome lawyers and paperwork. I wasn't there just for the novelty, though, but had brought a notebook with me to copy out the signature on any piece of hanging art I could find, in order to have their value appraised later. I also made crude drawings of the china and folk art littering the spacious downstairs, in case they were worth something. I felt as giddy as a girl in a candy store as I walked around, eyes peeled. It was a treasure trove of valuables just sitting there, waiting for someone to sweep it up.

And why shouldn't that someone be me? I certainly deserved it—and more.

Finally, I penetrated the inner sanctum—the heart of it all—the master bedroom. It looked as if someone had poured a jar of honey out in there. Everything was shimmering, golden and soft yellow: the bedspread, the curtains, the abundance of silk pillows. The woodwork, too, held a dark honey shade, gleaming and polished to perfection. Amanda clearly had a preference. The air in there still kept a memory of the pair: rose and oolong tea for her, and sweet mint for him. He had worn that same scent since he was fifteen.

There was art in the bedroom as well, and I quickly added the pieces to my list, but that was not the main reason why I was there. I had to look for a while before I found it, digging through closets full of shimmering silk and soft velvet, bespoke suits and ironed shirts. But I finally came upon it, just lying there in a vanity drawer: Amanda's jewelry box.

It was a modest thing made of carved wood. The lid displayed an abundance of plums and leaves, skillfully teased from the grain. The box didn't even have a lock on it, so sure were they that their wealth was safe, and that nothing—and no one—could touch it.

Clearly, they had been wrong.

I opened it with awe—and no small sense of victory—to behold the glory within: rings, brooches, pendants, and bracelets; faceted stones in an array of colors, some of them worth a fortune. I turned on a small brass lamp with a golden glass shade standing on the vanity's shiny surface, just so I could hold the pieces up to the light and admire their sparkle and shine. Some of it was old, I realized, when I recognized a strand of pearls as the ones my mother wore around the house when the day wasn't special enough for diamonds. I had always imagined that those would go to *me*, but no—here they were, deep in Amanda's jewelry box. I found said diamonds, too, when I had dug deep enough. Clearly all my mother's finery had ended up with Amanda, while *I* hadn't seen a dime.

And there *it* was, too—the apple of discord—the one thing that had sent me running from my brother, never to look back: Amanda's engagement ring, formerly my mother's wedding ring, precious enough that my sister-in-law had not dared to bring it along to K2. It was an exquisite pink diamond the size of a pinky nail, surrounded by paler siblings. I had always loved that ring, its blushing ice-cold beauty, and my mother had known that well. That was why it had been such a betrayal when Iris gave the ring to Ben instead—he who had inherited his father's fortune by then and could have bought as many rings as he liked. That one ring, though, it could have been mine, if only Iris had chosen differently.

Their engagement party was the very last time I had seen Ben and his bride before they died.

I quickly pocketed the ring and the rest of my mother's diamonds before making my way back to the guest room. Maybe there was a list somewhere detailing all the pieces that Amanda had owned, but surely no one would notice—at least not for a while—that some of it was missing. Miss Feely had said they would deposit the jewels and crate the art, but maybe they wouldn't look too hard. And even if they *did* discover the theft, no one would suspect *me*, the girls' selfless and loving aunt.

I was determined to bleed my brother's corpse dry—starting with my mother's diamonds.

Needless to say, I was *jubilant* the next day when I brought my new charges with me to the airport. Not only because of what I had accomplished the night before, but also in anticipation of what was to come. I felt as if I was transporting a cache of gold—albeit a chattering one.

"What is your house like?" Violet asked while the taxi slid through the quiet neighborhood of town houses and neatly pruned trees.

"Oh, it is big," I answered, and it wasn't entirely a lie. Compared to the house I first grew up in, Crescent Hill was a castle, and I clearly remembered admiring its size the first time I set foot in there. "It's not as modern as the house you're used to, but that's the charm of old places."

"Grandma Fiona lived in an old house," Lily noted from the other end of the back seat. "It was a big farmhouse, and the floorboards creaked when you walked on them."

"Well, isn't that novel." I had to fight not to roll my eyes. "I suppose it had mice as well?"

"Yes, it did, in winter," Lily replied. Her voice was muffled by the pink scarf she had insisted on wrapping several times around her neck, fearing she would catch a cold. Both of the girls were bundled up like small bears in woolen coats and knitted mittens, even though it was April and spring was in the air. Lily clearly took her responsibility as the eldest very seriously, which I supposed was a good thing. They had to be awfully warm, though. I myself had folded up my fur coat and kept it in my lap.

"Well, there are no mice at *my* house," I assured them. "I won't tolerate vermin and have traps set out all year round."

"Do you ever catch any?" Violet asked.

"All the time. Sometimes they are still alive when I get to them, and Dina has to drown them in a water bucket."

Lily was appalled. "Couldn't you just let them loose outside?"

Violet didn't seem to mind dead mice but peered at me with curious eyes.

"They would just come back again," I answered. "It's the way of vermin."

We then drove in blissful silence for a while before Lily asked, "How far is it from your house to the school?"

"Not far, although I have to take you in the car. Unless you would prefer bicycles?"

"Isn't there a school bus?"

My finely painted eyebrows arched upward.

"No, not where I live. It's a little bit outside of town, but I'm sure we will find a solution." Anything for my little nuggets of gold. "It's nothing you have to worry about right now anyhow. With your situation being what it is, you won't have to enroll until fall." We had all agreed on that—me, Miss Feely, and Mr. Skye. I, for one, was utterly relieved not to have to face that particular institution just yet, and all the bad memories that swirled around the place.

"Is it a good school?" Lily persisted. "Because if it's not, boarding school—"

"Oh, the local school is fine," I interrupted. "Everybody says so," and boarding school was expensive. If I could manage to get my hands on their whole fortune, I would rather it be as intact as possible. "You should at least give it a try." I leaned over and gave Lily my very best smile.

"Of course." Appropriately chastised, Lily leaned back in the seat again. Her restless fingers were toying with a pair of fluffy earmuffs in her lap, as white as her woolen coat.

"I *have* to continue to play, though. Do you think that's possible there?" She had made a great fuss about her violin before we left, worrying that air travel would somehow damage the instrument. "Do they have good music teachers in Ivory Springs?"

"I'm sure we can scramble one up," I muttered.

"I'm really serious about my playing." Her cool gaze had gained some fire. "Mama says—said—I could become good enough to maybe give concerts one day, or play in a big orchestra." Her voice took on a soft timbre when she painted her glorious future in words, and Miss Feely *had* mentioned a wish expressed in the will about the girl continuing her music education. Ben and Amanda had clearly held some aspirations for her. Not that it mattered, of course.

"We'll see what we can do, but you have to understand that things are different now, and adjustments have to be made." I couldn't conjure a skilled teacher out of thin air, and Ivory Springs wasn't known for its flourishing cultural scene.

The girl looked a little stung by my words and leaned back in the seat. I honestly wished that she would give up the music altogether—not because I didn't have an ear for it, but because I *did*, and nothing in this world aggrieved me more than an amateur butchering the masters.

"Are there any children where you live?" Now it was Violet who had questions.

"Oh, I don't have many neighbors, and those who live closest to me are elderly. I'm sure you'll befriend several of the young boys and girls in town, though, once you start school."

"Will we have our own rooms in your house?" The girl was relentless.

"Of course you will—one each!" Did she think I was going to place them on the floor?

"Do you have any pets?" Lily asked; her cold gaze held a tiny spark of fire. She was clearly hoping for a feline companion or some such.

"No, but there are quite a few animals around."

"The mice?" She looked at me with horror and the little spark died in her eyes.

I smiled, thinking of my home décor. "Other animals, too."

"We had a dog before," Violet volunteered. "Her name was Goldie and she was really old. When she passed away, Lily cried and cried—"

"She was my best friend." Lily sounded stung. "Wouldn't you be crying if your best friend died?"

"Yes," Violet agreed. "But I told you she was all right."

Lily snorted. "How would you even know?"

"Why are you wearing all those diamond rings?" Violet had let her gaze be snagged by the stacks of jewels on my fingers.

"Because they are beautiful. Don't you agree?" I eyed the girl, who nodded slowly, still staring at my hands.

"Mama and Papa had a plan for our education." Lily returned to what seemed to be her favorite subject. "I really think boarding school—"

I cut her off. "Well, your parents are no longer around to make those decisions."

Another stricken expression appeared on the young girl's face, just as I had hoped. It was better if she learned right away that I wouldn't spoil them like their parents had.

I didn't owe my nieces *anything*—but they surely owed *me* a great deal.

"This is a difficult situation for all of us," I continued, adding a little warmth to my voice. "We all have to do our best, and at least you two are together."

"It's what our parents wanted," Lily said in a hollow voice. She blinked her eyes rapidly again, just as she had done the night before. At first, I thought she was fighting back tears, but that seemed not to be the case, as she was fine again the next moment. Maybe it was just her nerves.

"Yes, it was," I replied, though I did have my doubts. Benjamin really should have updated his will after his mother-in-law's passing. It was only just, though, that things had turned out this way. Finally, it was my time to blossom, and I could certainly endure a few questions to make it happen.

"Lucia will probably miss us," said Violet.

"Lucia will be paid to care for other children now," I replied. It was nothing but the truth, and these girls clearly knew nothing of the world.

"She said she would *never* forget us," Violet insisted, which was probably not a lie on the young nanny's part. Who could ever forget the spectacle of their parents' demise?

"Do you have a job, Aunt Clara?" The next question came from Lily, who had obviously recovered from our little tiff.

"I have independent means," I replied, though that was barely true anymore. Years of indulging my passion had seen my fortune dwindling, and it didn't much matter if they had been sound investments. "I have training as a nurse," I continued. "Your grandpapa paid for my education." To get me out of the house, but I didn't mention that part. "It was very generous of him." I felt a little sick as I said it.

"We never met him." Violet sounded sad, though that regret was most certainly misplaced.

"He was old already by the time he married Iris," I noted. Benjamin had been about Lily's age when his father died. Iris had still been vital, though, for many years after, monitoring her golden boy closely.

"Do you miss being a nurse?" Lily asked next, and I felt the first pangs of a headache coming on.

"Not particularly, no. I have other interests now."

"Like what?" Violet looked up at me again, her eyes too close for comfort. I noted how the knot of her red scarf had come entirely undone, and one of her shoelaces, too.

"Oh, I dabble in this and that." I didn't want to share my plan just yet. It was bold enough that it could make the older girl suspicious of my motivations.

It was better for now if they saw me as just their kind and selfless aunt, who had taken them into her home out of nothing but the goodness of her heart.

❧ VIOLET ❧
6

Everything was happening so fast. One moment, we were in the house we had lived in all our lives, and the next we were in a place where the pretty streets we were used to were gone, and there were only bumpy dirt roads running between farms and fields, and sometimes thick dark woods. There was a town, too, but it wasn't much more than a few streets of stores that seemed to sell mostly animal feed and tractor parts.

Aunt Clara had parked her car at the airport, and on our way to Ivory Springs, I realized she was probably what Mama had called a "reckless driver." I sat in the back with Lily and squeezed her hand every time the car made a turn. When Aunt Clara said we were "soon there," I heard Lily let out her breath.

Aunt Clara's house wasn't what I had imagined in my head. Because of the way she had talked about it, I had thought it was as big as the town house, but when we came up the steep, narrow driveway, I could tell that I had been wrong. The house wasn't large but normal-sized. It was old and run-down and looked a bit strange.

"It's *blue*," I whispered to Lily. If Aunt Clara heard me, she pretended not to, and just sat there with her curled blond hair forced in place by lots of little hairpins. She had stacks of diamond rings on every one of her fingers, except for the thumbs. Her lips in the rear-view mirror were thin and painted red.

"The house isn't blue exactly," Lily whispered back to me. "It's more like teal, don't you think?"

"It's *cyan*." Aunt Clara's sharp voice sounded in the air. "I had it painted myself when I inherited the place."

"It's very beautiful," Lily said, even though she didn't mean it. She just wanted Aunt Clara to like us. "It's just not common in our old neighborhood."

"No," she replied as the car stopped on the gravel outside the big front door. "That is *why* I picked the color. Who would want a house just like everybody else's?"

I absolutely agreed with Aunt Clara, despite what Lily thought. I *liked* the cyan walls. It made the house look different—like a parrot in a flock of crows.

"All right." Aunt Clara opened the creaking car door and stretched out all her long limbs until she stood upright, draped in her black fur coat. "Come along, girls." She opened the door next to me, letting in a chilly breeze. "Welcome to Crescent Hill—your new home!"

I looked up at the house again as we shuffled around the station wagon to get our suitcases and Gertrud—Lily's violin—from the trunk. The cyan paint flaked from the gables, showing us the gray wood underneath. The climbing roses grew wild and were crowding the stained-glass windows on the ground floor. Above the black front door, a crescent-shaped window shone red in the light from the set-ting sun. Big oak trees grew everywhere around the house, and empty flowerpots were stacked by the house wall, next to a couple of empty oil drums that looked burned on the inside. The wooden stairs to the door had a few slats missing, and I wondered if we would have to jump across to make it to the top.

Just when we had unloaded the luggage—all the suitcases we had brought belonged to a yellow set Mama had left behind in her closet—the door to the house opened and a small, thin woman stepped out onto the top of the stairs. I figured it had to be Dina, the housekeeper. She seemed friendly as she came down the steps—

sidestepping the holes—wearing an orange-and-brown-striped dress and carved bone earrings shaped like whales. Her dark, graying hair was gathered in a bun at the back of her head.

"Welcome, girls," she said when her feet were safely down on the gravel. Her voice was very light and sounded young for someone who was not. "You must be Violet." She bent a little at the waist to look me in the eyes, which made me like her at once, just for that.

"I am," I said, and shook her hand, which was warm and dry and felt strong.

"I am Dina." She reached for our largest suitcase. "Let me help you with that," she said, and hoisted it up in the air, using only one hand.

"Lily, I presume?" The housekeeper reached out her free hand to my sister.

"Yes." She shook the housekeeper's hand, and I could tell that she liked Dina, too, by the way she smiled.

"I hope you're hungry." Dina turned away and started moving back toward the stairs, carrying the suitcase as if it weighed nothing. "I have fresh rolls, honey, and jam," she continued as she started to climb.

"Oh, good." I was so hungry that my stomach ached just from thinking about it. We hadn't eaten anything since the plane.

"Something lighter, too, I hope," Aunt Clara's voice snapped in the air. "A little salmon, maybe? Cucumber sandwiches?" When Dina didn't reply right away, she said it again in a louder voice.

"Of course, Mrs. Woods." Dina didn't turn her head to look at Aunt Clara, just answered over her shoulder. Her voice was much colder than when she had spoken to us, so I didn't think she liked Aunt Clara much either.

"Come along, girls." Aunt Clara lifted her own purple suitcase and followed Dina inside. Lily and I exchanged a look before gathering up the rest of our luggage and following her up the stairs, both of us careful not to stumble on the ruined steps.

The house looked even stranger on the inside. In the hall, there was a set of winding stairs made of carved dark wood, and two glass chandeliers hanging from the ceiling with several of the light bulbs missing. It was the rest of the room that made me feel like my heart had stopped, though. There were so many animals. I saw an elk, a fox, and a bear, and even a chimpanzee, hanging from a ledge high up on the wall—and they were all talking to me! Not with words, but like a quiet whisper or hush drifting through the air, and some of them had tendrils of smoke swirling around their bodies. The smoke was reaching out toward me, wanting me to come closer. Without even thinking about it, I reached out a hand to touch a swaying ribbon that came from the bear. I wasn't afraid at all. It reminded me of Goldie, and how she had always wanted to lick our faces when we had been gone.

"Look, Lily," I said, when the smoke had curled up my arm to touch the edge of my scarf. When the smoke reached my cheek, it tickled and I laughed.

Lily gave me a dark look. "They're not funny," she snapped.

"They're not bad just because they're dead," I said, just as the smoke from the chimpanzee landed on my head. They touched only me, though, I noticed. They didn't even try to touch the others, and Lily was looking at me as if I had done something wrong.

"What?" I asked, before figuring that Lily probably didn't see the smoke either, just like she didn't see K2. Just like I couldn't see the colors Lily saw burning on people's skin.

The smoke was one of those *things*.

Aunt Clara dropped her suitcase to the scuffed wooden floor and looked at the animals, too. "They were here when I moved in, and I still haven't figured out how to get rid of them."

"Isn't there an attic where they could go?" Lily asked with a grimace. She didn't like dead things. I wound my fingers with the bear's smoky tendril to keep it from my face—it just tickled too much—while pretending to scratch my ear. The bear felt like trees, moss, and a clear, cold spring, but it was faint, like the memory of a dream after you have woken up.

"Oh, sure," Aunt Clara replied to my sister, "but it's already crammed with the old woman's knickknacks—and it is *off-limits*! Do you hear?" She turned her gaze on both of us, and Lily and I quickly nodded. "Good." Aunt Clara pulled off her gloves and shook out of the fur coat. "The basement as well," she continued. "Completely and utterly *off-limits!*" Her green eyes fell on us again, her red lips curved down at the edges. "It's not safe down there," she said.

"Who is the old woman?" Lily asked, and I wondered about that, too. She had come drifting out of an open door and stood behind Aunt Clara's back, smiling at me, but she didn't speak or come any closer. I was still looking at the bear, the elk, and all the curling ribbons of smoke, though, so I didn't pay much attention to her. I smiled at the chimpanzee on the wall and gave a secret little wave to the fox by the umbrella stand.

"Who?" Aunt Clara looked at Lily.

"You said 'the old woman's' things were in the attic, so who is the old woman?" Lily asked again, and now I *did* pay attention, because, clearly, Lily couldn't see her either. I looked at the old woman again and saw that she was very pale and wore something that looked like a nightgown. When she caught me staring, she lifted a gnarled hand as if to say hi.

"That would be Cecilia Lawrence—she used to live here before." Something clever had come into Aunt Clara's voice. "She willed this house to me, along with everything she owned."

"Really?" Lily sounded surprised. "Why did she do that?"

"Because I was her live-in nurse," Aunt Clara replied. "I washed her aging body, fed her three times each day, and made sure that she took her medication on time. Sometimes good deeds pay off."

"Didn't she have any family?" Lily asked, and the old woman, too, started listening to them, cocking her head slightly.

"None that mattered," Aunt Clara replied. "Cecilia wanted her assets to go to the one who had *been* there for her during her last, terrible illness."

"And that was you?" Lily barely looked up when Dina took her coat. Her gaze was glued to Aunt Clara and I wondered what *she* saw dancing on our aunt's skin.

"That was me." Aunt Clara nodded, sounding proud. Behind her, the old woman—who had seemed so friendly and kind before— sneered. Then she took a few steps back and seemed to *melt* straight into the wall. I had never seen anything like it before and couldn't help but gawk. I stood there staring at the place she had vanished until Lily noticed and poked me in the back, thinking I was rude.

We left the suitcases behind in the hall so Aunt Clara could give us a tour of the house. All the rooms on the ground floor were dark and full of shadows because of the stained glass and the branches that covered it. Dina went before us to turn on the lights, but that didn't help very much.

"Cecilia's father—an avid hunter—built the place," Aunt Clara told us when we walked into the living room. "They thought this town would flourish back then, since they had found gold." The room around us was full of overstuffed chairs and couches—all of them green—and throw pillows with flowers embroidered on them. There were lots of colorful glass lamps, which were nice, and four large wooden bookcases, which was good for Lily because she liked to read. Heavy-looking curtains of green velvet hung in the windows. There were animals in there as well: A finch sat frozen in a golden cage that hung from a chain in the ceiling, and a snake had been turned into a lamp, holding the bulb in its open mouth. The lampshade balancing on top of it was made from snakeskin, too. Even though the snake was in pieces, it had smoke coming off it, too, reaching out for me as I walked by. I wondered why it did that—if the animals *wanted* something from me. It wasn't just the tendrils either. I felt a nudging in my brain—as if my head was a window and the animals kept throwing pebbles at it to make me look. Yes, they definitely wanted something.

"What happened?" Lily asked Aunt Clara. She was better than me at being polite. "Wasn't there any gold after all?"

"Oh, there was." Aunt Clara shrugged. "But not much of it. Cecilia's father opened a mine, but it was soon closed again. The ore wasn't prevalent enough for such an enterprise. By then he had built this house, though, for his family to live in. Besides him, there was his wife, two daughters, and a maid who lived in the attic, as Cecilia told it." She looked back over her shoulder to make sure that we were still following. "The family didn't stay, of course, but they kept Crescent

Hill as a summerhouse—and as a place to die. Cecilia's sister came here first—she had cancer—then Cecilia herself when her heart failed. She was the only one left by then, and childless."

She continued to talk as we walked into the dining room, where a long table filled up most of the floor. It had a white table runner on top of it, and several silver candelabras with half-burned candles. The chairs around the table had dark blue seats, and the curtains in the windows were blue, too. A big moose head hung on the wall between two of the dark windows, and just below it stood the old woman. She looked all sweet and kind again and had folded her hands over her belly, on top of the pink nightgown. When she noticed me looking, she smiled at me and winked, as if we had a secret. Above her on the wall, the moose head shot tendrils of smoke out in the air, reaching almost all the way across the room. I suddenly felt a little dizzy and was happy when we decided to continue to another part of the house.

Next there was a solarium—although Aunt Clara called it a "winter garden"—with lots of wicker furniture, a taxidermy parrot, potted palms, and a broken piano. The large windows in there only had stained-glass tiles at the top and the bottom. There was also a bathroom with a pink basin and a brown floor, but the best room by far was the kitchen. It had a blue-checked floor and white-painted cupboards and counters. Lace curtains hung in windows that were *not* stained but clear as water, letting us see the garden on the back side of the house. Although it didn't look like there had been a gardener visiting for a while, I liked the look of it. It had gnarled plum and apple trees and a dry fountain with a green-stained horse rising from the middle. There was an old overgrown pavilion, too, sticking up from the wizened grass. And there was something else down there, too! Just at the bottom of the garden, where the lawn became woods, a man was walking back and forth, wearing what looked like a suit. Looking at him made me nervous, even a little sick, and I shifted my gaze. I *felt* right away that the man was one of the *things*.

I turned back to the kitchen and the food laid out on the table— a small basket heaped with fresh rolls, and glass jars filled with berry jams, shining like bright jewels—and slumped down in a chair. No one had said that I could, but I didn't care if it was rude; I just really needed to sit down. Even while I sat, it felt as though the room was spinning a little around me, and I had to swallow hard so as not to throw up.

"It looks like our little one is hungry." Aunt Clara's voice was cheery, but I didn't trust it at all. It was like she was just pretending to be nice, and there were too many *things* going on in her house. I could *feel* it even now, that her feet were red.

"It's been *ages* since we ate on the plane," Lily defended me.

"Indeed, it has," Aunt Clara agreed. "I usually take my meals in the dining room, but you can take yours in here if you like." I was very happy to hear her say that, since I liked the kitchen much better. I also wasn't sorry when she left us shortly after to go and eat her fish. The kitchen seemed even cozier once Aunt Clara was out the door.

I only had to make sure not to look out the window.

LILY

7

While eating the delicious rolls, we learned that Dina was there from nine in the morning until six every night. "Mrs. Woods is not a morning person and has her breakfast at ten, which may be a little late for you two, but I'm sure you are able to fend for yourselves?"

"Of course," we both said at once, while devouring the food. It really *had* been a long time since the last time we ate. Violet seemed to have lost her appetite, though, and kept staring at the wall while slowly chewing pieces of food. She looked a little pale, too, and I worried that she was coming down with something. That would not have been a good start to our new life.

"It may in fact be best if you take your meals in here," Dina continued, with a quick glance in the direction of the dining room door. "She is particular about her food and says the scent of butter and gravy makes her ill. To be honest, I think that she is just trying to avoid temptation. She is so very thin, you know, and not in a healthy way ... You must never let her convince you to change your diet." Dina gave us both a stern look.

"Why does she want to be so thin?" Violet asked. She had a smear of strawberry red on her freckled cheek.

"Some women just do," said Dina. "It's like an obsession with them."

"Maybe she wants to look pretty," I suggested.

Violet shrugged and Dina chuckled. "Your grandma was perhaps the same way? I have seen her pictures . . ."

"We never knew Grandma Iris," I replied. "She died before we were born." I did remember how thin and tall she looked in the family albums, though. Just like Aunt Clara did now.

"Well, then I hope that ill-advised family trait ends with you two," said Dina. "It's so good to see someone *enjoy* food in this house again." Dina looked a little golden just then—she had a faint misty halo—and since gold meant love, I knew that she really meant it.

"Who enjoyed food here before?" Violet asked.

"Oh, there was *Mr.* Woods, of course. He had a healthy appetite—and Miss Lawrence, before she got too sick to enjoy much of anything."

"I didn't know that you had been here that long," I noted, thinking of how sad it had to be for a friendly woman like Dina to be working in this lonely house all her life.

"I came with Miss Lawrence," Dina explained, "then I fell in love with my husband. We own a small farm not far from here." She buttered up a roll while speaking. "It's been convenient for me to work so close to home." A little lime green had come into her gold, though, which made me think that it maybe wasn't the whole truth.

It was late by the time we hauled our luggage up the winding stairs to settle into our new rooms. Even though it was dark, I could still make out some of the carvings in the wood: some type of animal—bears, maybe?—and grapevines heavy with smooth, round fruits.

The hallway upstairs was narrow and dark; several framed paintings hung on the walls between the six matched doors. The wallpaper was burgundy with small golden leaves on it. It looked very old and had loosened in several places.

Dina showed us into our rooms with a pride that told me that she was the one who had made them up for us. My room—"the owl room"—was pretty small and narrow, with blue-painted walls and white curtains. There was a sturdy brass bed with a thick duvet, heaped with pale blue pillows, and a white writing desk perched in a corner. At the end of the room towered a large white dresser, and there was a bookcase, too, crammed with old mystery novels that made me want to sit down and read at once. It was a cozy room, and I told Dina that—although inwardly I swore to get rid of the large taxidermy owl that scowled at me from the top of the dresser as soon as I possibly could. I still placed Gertrud next to it, though, because it was the safest place in there.

Violet's room—"the raven room"—was opposite mine. It had rose-colored walls and an oak bed. Her dresser looked a lot like Mama's at home, so I knew it had to be walnut. Instead of an owl, she had a raven; it sat on a smooth gray tree branch, with its wings spilled out and its beak wide open. I hated it on sight, but Violet seemed to like it, and even paused by the dresser to stroke its feathers.

"Aren't you pretty," she said, smiling. She had always liked ravens and crows and was obviously delighted to find one in her room.

"Pretty *dead*," I said, and stepped back outside to the hallway.

"Your rooms used to belong to the Lawrence girls," Dina said with a sad kind of smile when we were all done inspecting and had gathered back in the hallway. "I hope you don't mind me telling you that."

"No, of course not." I liked the idea that other girls had lived in the rooms before us, even if they had grown old and died. It was a nice story, in a way, that they had lived long enough for their hair to turn gray and their bones to turn brittle. "Where does Aunt Clara sleep?" I looked at the other doors that lined the burgundy corridor.

"Over there." Dina pointed, looking a little wary. "I can show you if you like, but I wouldn't go in there if I were you. She *does* like her privacy."

She turned and moved quietly down the hallway, with us following closely; a thick black runner rug muffled our steps. With an almost frightened look over her shoulder, she turned the knob and opened the door to the last room on the right.

It was very purple; that was the first thing I noticed. The walls were all coated in a deep, dark shade. It was also much bigger than our rooms and had an elegant vanity, a couple of black velvet chairs, and a pair of ornate wardrobes that looked like antiques. There were pictures on the walls, but of diamonds instead of people: Dozens of stones glittered inside heavy silver frames. Against the wall to our right stood a massive black brass bed, made up with purple satin, under the watchful gaze of a green mamba that curled on the wall above the headboard. I grimaced when I saw the snake—not because it was a snake, but because it was so dead.

Dina chuckled when she saw my reaction and closed the door again. "It *is* fairly hideous," she said. "Mr. Lawrence brought in all the animals, and Mrs. Woods has no idea how to get rid of them."

I silently swore, in that very moment, to make it my personal mission to help Aunt Clara get rid of her dead.

There was a bathroom as well, next to Violet's room. Everything was apricot in there: the bathtub, the tiles, and even the toilet. Even *I* turned a soft shade of apricot in the mirror. It was clean, though, and everything seemed to be working. The other two doors were the entrance to the attic—though it was locked—and, to our surprise, a small elevator, which had been used to transport Miss Lawrence and her sister when they were sick.

"Don't play with it," said Dina. "It hasn't been in use since Miss Lawrence died, and I'm not sure if it even works anymore."

Dina left us after that, as she had to get home to her husband, Joe. She told us where to find food in the morning and then went for the stairs. As she descended the first step, she turned around and said, "You are unlikely to see Mrs. Woods again tonight. I can hear that she has entered her 'opera and wine' part of the evening. It's best not to disturb her then."

I didn't like how serious she sounded, but I was too tired to truly care. Now that Dina had made me notice, I could hear it, though: a faint sound of music rising from below. It was *Carmen,* one of my favorites, and I had seen it many times with Mama and Papa. A small part of me hoped that maybe Aunt Clara would take me as well, and that opera maybe could be a thing we shared between us—but then I thought maybe not, since I had seen how annoyed she was when I talked about my playing.

"You have everything you need, don't you?" Dina asked. She wet her lips with the tip of her tongue and wrung her hands in front of her body. Pink flames erupted on her fingers, so I knew that she was worried. "Maybe I should—"

"No, we'll be fine," I said, even though I *did* feel a little lost. "We're just going to go to sleep; you don't have to worry about us." I did my best to give her a convincing smile, and it seemed to work, too, because she *did* go then, leaving us alone with Aunt Clara.

When I had unpacked what little I had brought with me, and visited the apricot bathroom to change into my pajamas and brush my teeth, I found my hairbrush, crossed the hallway, and opened the door to Violet's room. She was already sitting on her bed in her nightgown, the last one Mama had bought for her. It had ribbons and lots of laces—something Violet usually hated since the knots came undone all the time, and which they had been fighting about. But ever since Mama had died, she had worn it every night and had to be bribed with cookies to let Lucia wash it once in a while.

"Are you ready?" I asked her, and Violet nodded. She had become quiet again, like she had been when we ate.

"Tell me if it hurts too bad," I told her, before seating myself behind her to try to make sense of her massive hair. She nodded again but still didn't say anything.

"It's just for now," I told her to try to make her feel better. My hands and the brush were hard at work, untangling the tangles. "In just four short years I'll be eighteen and we can stay wherever we want—even go back home." She nodded a third time but still didn't say anything. My stomach started to hurt.

"Do you want me to sleep in here tonight?" I asked in a final attempt to figure out what was bothering her. I really started to worry that she maybe was coming down with the flu.

"Yes," she replied, but in a very small voice, and I suddenly remembered how she had always hated the first night in a strange bed. It had been a problem on every family vacation. Mama and Papa would have remembered that, but I had completely forgotten.

"You should have said something," I scolded her lightly. "This isn't the time to be brave—or any braver than you already are. You have to tell me if something is bothering you, Violet." With a little effort, I finished the brushing, and then we lay down under her duvet, side by side. I reached over and turned off the light, leaving the room in blue darkness.

"There's a woman downstairs," Violet whispered as soon as it was dark.

"Yes," I whispered back, confused. "Aunt Clara is listening to music."

"No, a *different* woman," she replied, "downstairs in the hall, and in the dining room, too, right under the moose. She looked kind."

"I didn't see any woman," I said, since that was the truth, but a cold ripple ran down my spine anyway.

"I thought so. I figured you would have said something if you did." Violet gave a deep sigh. "She was very pale and didn't look so great. I'm pretty sure she was dead."

"Violet," I scolded, "you shouldn't be making stuff up. Things are bad enough already."

"I'm *not*," Violet protested. "She was there, even if you didn't see her." If my sister had been someone else, I could maybe have seen flames on her skin to decide if she was lying or not, but it didn't work that way with Violet. I never saw any flames on her. I didn't like her talking about ghosts, though, since just thinking about them made me feel cold all over. "I didn't mind seeing her," she said. "I don't think she was dangerous or anything, not like—"

"Well, you *didn't* see her," I replied. "Ghosts aren't *real*, Violet."

"But you see colors all the time." She turned over to face me in the darkness. "I don't see them, but I always, always believe you."

"I don't even believe it myself," I scoffed, and wondered if it had been such a great idea to tell Violet what I saw.

The colors were something that had started happening just after Mama and Papa died: Suddenly flames would appear on people's skin for no reason. And it wasn't just the flames either, because the colors were all different feelings, and I would know—without knowing how—just what the different shades meant. It was like the knowing just appeared in my head.

They didn't mean what I thought they would, though. Before, I had always thought that pink was a romantic color, for instance, but the pink flames meant fear and had nothing to do with hearts and kisses. Sometimes they did match, though—like I had always thought that red looked angry, and that was true for the flames as well. But I had never thought that lime green meant lying, or that blue flames meant that someone was in pain.

At first, the colors had been something good—something that could take Violet's mind off what had happened to our parents—and she would ask me all the time what color this or that person had, especially if we were somewhere crowded, like the park. Sometimes I didn't see any colors but would pretend to just to make her happy. But if my seeing things made *her* think she was seeing *ghosts*, maybe I should have kept it to myself.

"Perhaps we just have poor eyes in our family," I muttered. "Maybe I should see a doctor."

"Oh, I don't think a doctor could help you with that." Violet sounded rueful. "It's just the way we are now—different."

"But we *don't* see ghosts," I decided. "And maybe the colors will disappear in time." It was what I hoped for, anyway, and if I blinked quickly many times in a row, they *did* disappear, too—for a while. "What do you make of Aunt Clara?" I asked. "She's a little strange, but I think she wants to help us."

Violet didn't reply at first, but then she said, "I still don't think she had any surgery done."

"Why?" I asked, although I knew Violet was right; Aunt Clara had been lime green when she said it.

"I don't *feel* it," Violet explained. "When Koko removed her tonsils, I *felt* it."

"You can't feel another person's pain, Violet." Koko had been Mama's best friend, but she had gone to India just before K2, and we hadn't been able to reach her since the accident. I thought maybe she was in a monastery somewhere, but Violet kept insisting that she was dead, that she had met some bad men on the road. I thought she only said that because of what had happened to our parents, that she felt as if nothing was safe anymore. I still had a tiny bit of hope that someday Koko would come back and help us.

"But I *do* feel it," Violet insisted, "and Aunt Clara didn't have any surgery done."

"Well, maybe she was just embarrassed that she didn't come to the memorial." I didn't really think so, though. Embarrassment was a dark shade of yellow, like mustard, while Aunt Clara had only been liar's green.

"I have *always* felt things, Lily. You know that." Violet sounded offended beside me. "But it is different now—it's more than before, and all the time."

Everything inside me screamed no, because everything was so scary right now and I needed Violet to be okay, at least for the next four years. But for my inner eye, old memories came drifting in: Violet in the bathtub at home, no older than three, staring at a fixed point in the air; laughing and cocking her head, as if someone had done something funny to amuse her. Then the shock on Mama's face when she noticed, which slowly turned to delight.

"What are you seeing, my little pea? Has someone come to visit you?"

Then, after Goldie died, how sure Violet had been that our dog was all right.

No. I pushed the thought away. It *couldn't* be true. I wouldn't *let* it be true.

We had more than enough to deal with as it was.

CLARA

8

I never wanted children—had never felt that urge—and, having had my nieces around for a couple of days, I remembered why. I had been so intent on bringing them home with me that I had given little thought to what to do with them once I had them. I suppose I thought I could put them up in rooms and then go about my days as I always had, leaving it to Dina to deal with their needs, but that was not to be.

Instead, I was barraged with a torrent of questions. Young, fresh-faced Lily certainly had demands in spades: *Aunt Clara, when will we visit our new school? Aunt Clara, have you found a new music teacher yet? Aunt Clara, can our friends come to visit? Aunt Clara, when can we go to the city to visit our friends? Aunt Clara, could we get some newer books—or a downstairs TV? Aunt Clara, is there any news about our parents' bodies yet? Aunt Clara, can we sometimes eat something other than soup? Please, Aunt Clara, can't we get rid of the dead animals?*

The only thing that—surprisingly—did not bring me as much grief as anticipated was Lily's playing. She was quite advanced for her age, and honestly fairly good. So as long as she kept the instrument in her room, I did not much mind her practicing. I did not share her parents' ambition, however; the girl was much too spoiled and wouldn't last more than a week in the competitive jungle of the music world. In that sense, it was a waste of time. On the other hand, it kept her occupied and out of my hair for a while, and it was a welcome respite from her constant nagging.

When all the questions got to be too much for me, I reminded myself of the money that was already trickling my way, and of the substantial assets the girls represented, which I felt sure I would be able to take a big bite of, if only I played my cards right. The town house, for instance. As their guardian, I would be well within my rights to see to a quick and efficient sale. The money ought to go into the girls' trust, of course, but maybe there was a way around that? I also vaguely remembered my sister-in-law speaking of a lake house at their engagement party. Did the place belong to her? Could it be sold? The easiest thing, however, would be if I could persuade Mr. Skye to invest the girls' money in my company directly, and I felt confident I could make a strong case. Surely Mr. Skye would see the wisdom in keeping the girls' guardian happy and prosperous—keep the money in the family, so to speak.

I had already asked Mr. Skye for a comprehensive list of the girls' assets and had planned another trip to the city to see if there was more that could be pilfered from the house that was *not* on said list. My brother had been careless by nature—his failure to update his will proved as much—so perhaps he hadn't bothered to keep track of every piece of art he bought either. I also kept dreaming of another cache of jewels hidden away in a secret wall safe or some such—or the deeds to a newly purchased property that no one even knew about. Benjamin had been rich enough that he easily could have bought a condo on the beach, only to forget about it all the next day when something new and exciting had caught his attention.

Or perhaps that was what I wanted to believe.

It was certainly far more satisfying to plan my legacy and dream of future riches than to have to fend off the actual girls, who seemed to be everywhere I looked, their voices always in the air. I had imagined them to be sad and quiet, but as it turned out, the pair of them had an unfortunate zest for life that not even bereavement could deprive them of. Especially the youngest. Violet was a loud sort, always peeking her head around corners and noticing every detail: *How come you always drink wine at night, Aunt Clara? Why is there a snake over your bed? Do you have to curl your hair every day, or were you born with hair like that? How old were you when you met Mr. Woods? Why don't you want to work, Aunt Clara? Are you always alone in the dining room? How come you never came to our birthdays?*

It truly was insufferable, and it chased me upstairs many a night to sit at my vanity and clean my diamonds—a habit of mine when I was upset—instead of having to answer more of her impertinent questions. Better to touch white gold, to hold the stones up to the light and watch them glitter and gleam. Iris's diamonds from Amanda's jewelry box only added to an already vast collection. I remembered how and when I purchased each and every one of them: what I wore on that day; what the stores smelled like; the sight of the ice-cold stones before me—beauties all—lying next to their siblings on velvet trays, safe behind thick glass. The satisfaction of pointing and choosing, and having the little darling placed in a box and wrapped up. I had rings and necklaces, chokers and bracelets, and even a tiara in a black satin box. I rarely had occasion to use it, but the joy of owning it was more than enough. I suppose you could call me a serious collector.

It was also where I would make my mark.

I had met an excellent jewelry designer, Isabella Roux, at a fair a few years back. I often went to such events to look at what was to come. Most of them were wholesale only, but I had forged some papers, and no one had ever questioned my legitimacy. Isabella and I had shared several glasses of a dry, tart champagne at the bar and found that we had similar tastes. We had kept in touch ever since, and slowly this idea had emerged in me that perhaps I should have my own jewelry line—my *own* glittering brand: Clarabelle Diamonds. The idea had seemed so right, so utterly unavoidable.

What better legacy was there to be had than the kind that lasted forever?

Isabella was certainly on board, but she had warned me about the costs, of which the raw materials themselves were the greatest by far.

I had faced worse hardships, though, and had assured her that I would find a way—and now I *had*, somewhat. The girls' monthly stipend was a very good start—enough that we could start buying stones for the collection. And if I could persuade Mr. Skye to invest, we could buy *all* that we needed.

Oh, how I longed for that to happen.

I knew very well *why* I had developed this fondness for sparkling rocks. In the beginning, it had been all about spite—a childish notion to prove my mother wrong. Though Iris had been almost as fond of the pretty stones as me, so perhaps I would not have liked them as much if it hadn't been for her. Still . . .

"You will never have fine things in life," she had told me once, when I was about fifteen. "You will never have furs or cars or a diamond necklace, unless you commit to bettering yourself."

It had always bothered me how she had died without ever seeing my collection, and now it bothered me even more that she would never get to see the birth of Clarabelle Diamonds. Not because I thought it would have made her proud—that was not the type of relationship we had—but because I knew how it would have aggrieved her. And she certainly deserved that and more.

Iris had not always been so high-and-mighty herself, though few who met her later in life could see through the excellent façade that she had crafted for herself. That was why she never much cared to have *me* around, preferring to keep our correspondence to a postcard every now and then. I never complained about this arrangement, but it didn't mean I didn't think about her—pretty Iris—every day. I suppose that's how it is when you are burdened with a bad mother. It becomes like a disease; it flowers and rots inside you like a tumor of hatred that never goes away.

Her rejection was harder than *any* diamond.

It didn't help one tiny bit that I knew just *why* Iris loathed me so. I was the only one who remembered what she had been before—and she did not want to be reminded of the days when it was just her, me, and Father on the farm.

I never truly blamed her for that.

She was a different creature back then, and so was I. The place wasn't much: just a patch of dirt with enough soil to yield a crop, and just enough space for some pigs to shuffle around and roll in the dust. That was what we had most of: dust. It settled everywhere and coated everything. It tasted gritty: chalky and impure. Whenever we had been foolish enough to hang our sheets out to dry, they had taken on a sheen of gray by the time we got them back inside.

The house was as bad as you could imagine—only four rooms with very little in them: beds in the bedrooms, a table in the kitchen, and a few patched armchairs in the living room for resting. There were a few cupboards, too, and a chest of drawers. A filthy rug on the floor where the dog used to lie. And that was all. Brown-checked curtains hung in the windows and turned more sun bleached every year. It truly was a sad and hopeless place, but it was all Ivan North had had to offer Iris Bull when he accidentally knocked her up after far too many drinks down by the river.

An event that Iris would lament until the day he died.

I always knew that I was an unwanted child. Iris told me so, often, while sitting by the tiny, scarred kitchen table, where she hadn't even bothered to add a little tablecloth or a jar of wildflowers, as most of the poor housewives on the surrounding farms would do. No, Iris delved into her misery with all that she had, and cursed be the one to suggest that she could do something herself to make things better. She always thought it was a great injustice that she had been roped into this life of toil and poverty, even though she had made the choice herself.

I'm sure she could have gotten rid of me if she had truly wanted—if not by going to a doctor, then by using a little parsley or some such—but Iris was a coward when it came to bodily pain, and maybe she even liked Ivan North back then. He was tall and broad and had a scruffiness to him that some women found attractive. I suppose he had "allure," if that is a word that can be used about a man. What he did not have, though, was money—or the inclination to redeem that flaw.

"I was meant to *be* someone!" Iris would cry to me when Ivan was out, and only she, I, and the whiskey bottle were at home. "I was meant to *make* something of myself!" Her hand would shake when she topped up her glass. "It was never supposed to be like this. It was my fate to *soar,* Clara. *Soar!*"

As a child, I always worried that Iris would leave us. That she would one day pack up her small wardrobe of thin cotton dresses and leave me and Father behind. Looking back, it doesn't make much sense, as I loathed my mother even then. Perhaps Father and I *would* have been better off without her. But that, I suppose, is how children are: They cling to the people they know, no matter how toxic they are. Some never grow out of it either, but keep chasing those who do them harm even as adults.

Iris never left, though—or at least not in the way I expected her to. Probably she was too afraid. Although he was usually a lamb, my father had a mean streak when he drank too much—which happened more and more frequently as I grew up. Iris would often emerge from their drunken battles with a cut lip or a bruise and hatred burning in her green eyes. I never blamed my father for it—at least not back then. I knew how insufferable Iris could be, how her loathing smarted. I suppose I thought she deserved every single slap for being so very mean.

When it got to be too bad between them, I would be sent to my aunt for a few days. Aunt Laura was just as tall and slim as Mother, but her face was lined and always looked tired. She had five children of her own, all of them younger than me, and it showed. While my mother's cotton candy hair framed her face like a halo, Aunt Laura kept whatever was left of her own golden crown hidden under a headscarf.

She didn't like Iris much either.

"She always had a way about her," Aunt Laura said. "She always thought she was better than everyone else, that she was *special*." She said the last word as if it tasted foul. "Even from when she was as small as a rabbit, she would climb up on a chair to preen and pose in front of the mirror, or pretend to be a princess, dressing up in lace curtains."

I didn't mind how crowded it was in Aunt Laura's house. To me, it felt quiet. And at least I didn't have to lie in my bed at night and listen to the insults being hurtled back and forth in my parents' bedroom. How my mother told my father that he—and I—had ruined her life, or hear his meaty fists land on her flesh as he let loose his anger.

I couldn't fathom why she couldn't keep her mouth shut, why she always had to cause a stir, provoke him as she did with all her insults. If only she could be quiet, I thought, Father would behave himself and be the lamb that I knew him to be.

We had a bond, he and I, that Iris never shared. Because such work was beneath her, it was I who accompanied my father to feed the pigs and sow the field, mend the fences, and paint the barn. I even accompanied him when he went fishing in the creek or hunting around the farm. We were similar, my father and I—both of us the quiet type—and we shared a companionable silence as we worked. We had an easy way around each other that just didn't require many words. I handed him the nails before he thought to ask for them, and he showed me where to use the hammer by pointing to the spot. I suppose deep down I felt sorry for him—for the sad and ugly thing his life had turned out to be.

The change arrived when I was nine, though it happened so slowly that I barely noticed at first. Iris had started working summers at a hotel that had been built not far from where we lived. She did it to help with our terrible finances, but she seemed to like it, too. She got to leave the farm in the morning and put on a pale blue maid's outfit, which suited her hair and complexion well. The hotel—*the resort*, as she called it—was a magnet for rich tycoons who came to fish and hunt and lounge about. She liked that, too, of course, being around the wealthy. Her mood brightened considerably when the hotel was "in season," and she even brought home treats some nights: pieces of glistening fish or a slab of leftover cream cake. Father and I didn't much complain either, as it was a relief to have Iris gone so much.

Little did we know—although we really *should* have known—that she had met a man there: one with a wallet fat enough that she found him worth her while. Otis Webb was a businessman with big investments in oil and iron. He was also an aging and childless widower, which suited Iris just fine. For three years, they indulged in their summer affair, with Father and me none the wiser. But of course it couldn't last.

I don't know who saw fit to tell Ivan about his wife's adventures, but it could have been any one of our neighbors. None of them liked Iris either. Whatever quarrels my parents had had before, they were nothing compared to the weeks that followed. Both of them drank heavily. Ivan would refuse to let her go to work, and she would scream in reply, chasing him through the small house with an upturned bottle as a weapon. Then he would get a hold of her and all hell broke loose. Eventually the sheriff arrived on our doorstep, having been called in by a passing neighbor. Neither of my parents was arrested, but Iris had to go to the doctor to get stitches, and while she was there, she somehow managed to call her lover. Otis had then arrived, only to be spotted by Ivan, and apparently things had gotten even worse after that. I don't know exactly what transpired between the three of them, as I had been sent to Aunt Laura's by then.

It was she who told me the news two days later, as I sat in her kitchen with the kids. "You have to go home to your mother, Clara. It's Ivan . . . His heart gave out." And that was the end of their quarrel.

We had barely had time to bury my father before Otis was there, driving himself out to the farm in his black Cadillac. When the car returned to the city, Iris and I were in it, along with a cotton dress or two—but there was no reason to "bring all the rags," as Iris said. Her new man would see that we had everything we needed.

To be fair to Otis, he *did* keep that promise. He married Iris, too, and gave her the life she had always felt she deserved. I was told to forget about the farm, and Father, and the booze—to forget about Aunt Laura, too, and all my little cousins. Then Benjamin came along when I was fourteen. He was the meal ticket, the golden boy, and how could I ever compete with that? I would forever be the inconvenient daughter; a hair in the chilled soup; a spot on the linen. The only one who remembered, who *knew*.

It was no wonder, really, that Iris could never love me.

I will never forget what she said to me on the night my father died, as I lay there weeping on the bed. "It's for the best, Clara, just you wait and see." Later she would say, "I took care of us, didn't I? I pulled myself up by the bootstraps and made everything all right." Then she would don her satin dress and wear diamonds around her neck, lift long-stemmed glasses of champagne and eat canapés with caviar.

She had taken care of it.

If nothing else, though, my mother taught me to survive. She taught me how nothing is holy when it comes to fending for oneself—and that I had done, in abundance. I did it still, by taking in the girls and mining whatever I could from them. It was Mother's way—*Iris's* way. It might seem cruel to others, but who needs a heart when there are diamonds to be had, beautiful and eternal? The only love that is ever worth having is the one that won't bring you pain.

Mother taught me that as well.

I sometimes saw a little of Iris in Lily—in her unpleasant direct-ness and insufferable entitlement. It was akin to having a slice of my mother back, and I did not like it one bit. There was something about the way she held her head, and the way a smile always seemed to tug at the corners of her mouth. I could barely believe that the girl had never actually met my mother. It seemed strange to me that such traits could travel by blood alone. She looked just like Iris when flick-ing her hair away from her shoulders, and when her nose wrinkled up if she didn't get her way . . .

It was fine, though—it was. I had dealt with Iris *herself* before, and compared to her grandmother, Lily was merely a speck of dust in the sunlight: annoying, but nothing much to think about.

Or so I thought at the time.

LILY

9

Before our parents took their last anniversary trip and we landed on Crescent Hill, Violet and I had lived ordinary lives. It shouldn't have been possible since our father had so much money, but it was what my mother insisted on, having come from a normal family herself. Papa used to call her his anchor and his voice of reason. Too bad that he didn't listen in the end, but insisted on climbing that mountain.

I suppose Mama did it for love.

Violet and I *were* lucky in certain ways: We never had to go hungry, we went to a very good school, and I had the best music teachers they could find. But Mama always made sure that we knew just how lucky we were. She often talked about the responsibilities we had as heirs—about how important it was to share. She should know all about that, since she worked with charities herself, raising money for children in need all over the world. She said the money was what she had found *least* attractive about Papa when they first met at a fundraising event. I don't think she ever enjoyed being rich.

Mama's family came from the mountains and had made cider and jams and jellies for a living, growing all the pears, apples, and plums themselves. Violet and I always loved to visit Grandma Fiona on the farm and hear stories about how it had been when she was a girl—the picking and peeling and boiling that went on. The cider house at the edge of her property still smelled of sweet apples. By the time Mama was grown, though, they didn't make anything anymore. Grandma Fiona said that the family business had gone bankrupt. She still lived in the farmhouse, however, white and cozy, and some of the orchards were still there, if overgrown. It just wasn't her land anymore, and most of what had been hers before had been turned into pastures for cows. I know Papa asked her once if she wanted him to buy it back for her, but she said no. It was a closed chapter.

I didn't think Mama should be so bothered by marrying a man who had money. Grandma Iris had done the same thing, and Papa had said that she thought it was a blessing. "She *flourished* after she met your granddad," he said to me once. "She used to tell me that she never had a full night's sleep before she married him." I thought that I could see it, too, when looking at pictures of Grandma Iris; she always looked so happy. She was always smiling and her eyes sparkled almost as much as the jewels around her neck.

Aunt Clara looked very much like Grandma Iris—although her nose was larger, and her mouth a little wrong, and Aunt Clara didn't smile much, but often wore a frown. While Grandma Iris had preferred designer clothes—and collected them, too, Papa said—Aunt Clara wore much cheaper brands: flowery dresses of rayon and two-piece sets in solid purple. Once in a while, she wore black. She always, always wore diamonds, though—on her fingers, in her ears, and around her spindly neck.

Before, Violet and I had lots of friends, and we were with them all the time. In the mornings, my best friend, Marie, would knock on our kitchen door, and we would eat breakfast together before Lucia took us and Violet to school. In the afternoons—unless it was a violin day—I used to do homework with Marie, and often Ingrid and Michelle as well. If we were at my house, Lucia would make us sandwiches and serve them on a tray, together with a pitcher of sweet iced tea. When the schoolwork was done, we would gossip and laugh and draw in each other's books until it was time for me to do scales.

Violet, too, had two best friends: a girl called Anna and a boy called Marcus. The three of them liked to play outdoors, and especially in the garden. All three were members of a drama club for children, and sometimes they rehearsed on the patio, among colorful flowers in the summer and blazing leaves in fall. The winter before K2, Papa helped them build a stage of snow and even carried out work lamps so they could play long into the night. Anna's and Marcus's parents came to watch, and Mama and Koko made mulled wine for the grown-ups and hot chocolate for me, so we had something warm to drink during the performance.

There were no friends for us at Crescent Hill. All we had there was each other and our stationery, and we both wrote copious and longing letters home, while begging Aunt Clara to let us go visit. She wasn't all that eager, though.

"It will only upset you," she said. "It's better to focus on the here and now. You will find new friends in *no* time."

She meant when we entered the local school in the fall—a place we hadn't even seen yet. Aunt Clara had *sworn* to Miss Feely that we would visit the school right away, but so far it hadn't happened. I asked her about it every day, but she never gave me a good answer, just sat there with lime-green flames all over her skin. "It's too soon," she would say. "You need more time to come to terms with what has happened before you start looking to the future."

Mama and Papa had always said that the key to a happy life was a good education. Whether the local school counted as good or not, I didn't know yet, but I wanted to go there and talk to the teachers so that I could get a sense of it. If I didn't think it would be good enough, I had decided to talk to Mr. Skye and insist on boarding school for us both. I knew that was what my parents would have wanted. The decision would have to be made soon, though, if we were to be ready by the fall, but as long as I hadn't seen the local school, I couldn't decide either way. It really was very infuriating.

I would sometimes complain to Dina about it, when we had lunch together in the kitchen—soup mostly, it was always soup, unless we begged her for an omelet. It was Dina who made our days at Crescent Hill a little brighter. She was always calm and kind, and I liked her even more for not pretending that our aunt was a wonderful person. It was as if we were in cahoots, and we all knew the truth between us.

We didn't have to see Aunt Clara very often, though. The fact that we didn't eat together suited me just fine, since I would rather not spend my meals looking at Aunt Clara picking a piece of fish apart, or scare myself by thinking of the lady ghost in the dining room. I knew Violet went to "see her" sometimes, as if she were visiting a neighbor, and would find her sitting on a chair in there while her eyes moved through the empty air. I never saw anything, though, except maybe for a thin red mist that flitted across the floor before it disappeared. I would always chase Violet out of the room since I didn't like the idea of my sister spending time with ghosts—imagined or not, especially since Violet didn't look so good, but was pale and had dark shadows under her eyes that never seemed to go away. I thought maybe she lay awake at night thinking about the lady ghost. I pretended not to listen when Violet told me how the woman was sad or sometimes that she was angry. It was much cozier in the kitchen anyway, where the sunlight streamed in through the windows, and the food was good, even if it was the same every day.

It was Aunt Clara who had decided on the soup, to pack as many nutrients as possible into one meal. She figured herself very smart, I suppose, for coming up with that plan. For dinner, it was the same thing, only by then the soup had turned into stew. I really craved a green salad but figured it was rude to ask. I sometimes wondered if the food really was sufficient, though, since Violet was so pale. I thought maybe she was lacking in iron and knew that if Mama and Papa had been alive, they would have taken Violet to see a doctor. Aunt Clara wasn't like them, though, and when I suggested taking her, she just said that a little paleness was to be expected in times of grief.

Every day after lunch, I homeschooled Violet for a few hours so she wouldn't fall behind. I had called and asked her teacher at our former school for the curriculum, and then ordered the books through Mr. Skye, to make sure that I got it right. I wasn't worried about myself since my grades had always been good, but Violet had been struggling and I really wanted to help her. We read books together, too, so Violet could become a stronger reader, and I liked that the best, as it reminded me of how Mama and I would read books to each other before—mostly mystery novels, but a little romance, too. We would read every other chapter aloud to each other and then talk about who the murderer could be before we switched. I had loved doing that with her.

Violet and I did our tutoring in secret, though, as I didn't want Aunt Clara to know and get the idea that we didn't *need* a real school and insist on homeschooling instead. This, too, was something that happened in the kitchen and had nothing to do with our aunt. While Dina chopped and fried and baked, I taught my little sister about measurements, old Egypt, planets, and stars.

Every night, after dinner, I would go up to the owl room to play my violin for *at least* two hours. Sometimes Violet came with me to lie on my bed and draw or dance around on the floor while I practiced scales and went through my pieces, but mostly I was alone. I always started with a gavotte, then I would move on to "The Lark Ascending" or Sonata no. 2 in G minor, or sometimes "The Swan" from *The Carnival of the Animals.*

I had fallen a little behind for a while, after K2, but once I had started again, I wished that I had never stopped. It was as if the world itself fell away while I was playing, and I could almost forget where I was and everything that had happened. I could even—almost—forget how angry I was that Aunt Clara hadn't found a new music teacher yet. I knew I was good, but I wanted to be so much better. And although I tried, I couldn't play tricky pieces like the Devil's Trill Sonata, which I really wanted to do. I knew I needed a teacher.

At the end of each session came the best part. It was something Mama had taught me to do when I was stuck on a piece or angry that my fingers didn't move faster, but now I did it every time because it felt so good. I would unbraid my hair and take off my socks. If I wore clothes with strings or ribbons on them, I undid them, too, which took a while, because they were always so tight on me. Then I stood with Gertrud, wide-legged, my feet naked against the floorboards,

and played. I didn't look at any sheet music or try to play a particular
piece, but just played whatever I wanted to. What came out then was
usually wilder than any of the *real* music in my books, but it felt better
than any chocolate cake I had ever tasted. I felt like the strongest
person in the world when playing like that, and it seemed as though
the air itself had colors then, and I didn't mind but just let them all
come without blinking them away, until it was as if I was standing in
the middle of a dancing rainbow. Sometimes it even felt like there
were waves crashing through me and lifting me up, and I wouldn't
have been surprised at all if my feet had suddenly risen off the floor.

When I was all done, I wiped down Gertrud and the bow, checked
her strings, and put her back in the case. Gertrud still lived next to the
taxidermy owl on the dresser, but the dead bird didn't bother me so
much anymore, since I had hidden it under a pillowcase. I wished that
I could have a *real* owl instead, one whose eyes weren't made of glass.

On Fridays, we went with Dina to the supermarket, and it was the
highlight of our week. It felt so strange to be out among other people;
to see the brightly lit aisles at the store and hear the chatter of families
deciding on green or red apples. Saturday was Dina's half day off, and
on Sundays she was entirely gone. We hated that day the most. Although she always left soup for us to reheat, and even a little treat
from time to time, it still wasn't the same without her in the kitchen.

What Aunt Clara did with her days was honestly hard to say.
Sometimes she would jump in her big beige diesel-guzzling station
wagon and be gone all day. Other times she would stay in her room,
where she kept a TV, and only come down to eat. From the sounds
that escaped her room, it seemed that she preferred romantic TV
shows, or nature programs about lions and zebras. She *did* have visi-
tors sometimes: women she knew from her nursing days. They would
sit in the winter garden and drink tea or wine and talk about their
youth. Every once in a while, Aunt Clara would go into the city, "on
business"—whatever that meant—and be gone overnight. No one
stayed with us then, and I had trouble sleeping, worrying about everything that could go wrong. I used to tell myself, while lying awake in
the dark, that this was better than foster care, by far. That this way, at

least, Violet and I were together. But that didn't mean that it wasn't hard.

Crescent Hill wasn't very large, though, so we couldn't entirely avoid Aunt Clara. Unless we wanted to spend the night in our rooms or the kitchen, we had to use the living room, and Aunt Clara was usually there after dinner, listening to opera and sipping wine while her diamonds sparkled and shone on her fingers. It could have been a good time for us to get to know each other—and I knew Violet, too, pined for that, at first—but whenever I tried to talk to her, she would say things that hurt me—especially about our parents, and particularly about Papa. I would like to think that she wasn't being cruel on purpose, or that she was speaking without thinking, but there were lemon-colored flames dancing on her skin when she said it, which meant that she felt gleeful, so maybe she just liked being mean.

Once, when I mentioned K2, she said, "I suppose that's what happens when you are used to having more than you can spend; you never truly grow up, but remain a man-child for the rest of your life, treating your wife like a mother. I guess it's charming to some . . ."

Another time she said, "It is the privilege of those who have never faced true hardships to go on reckless 'adventures.' I suppose they want to impress their peers who have also never known pain or danger. Those of us who have truly struggled in life would never needlessly risk our own safety, because we know that bad things can—and *will*—happen. But I suppose Benjamin learned that, too, in the end."

The worst thing she ever said, though, was, "It's not very unusual, really, losing one's parents young. In fact, you have no guarantee they will last all through your childhood, and it's the privilege of the spoiled to take such things for granted. In the *real* world, you are not so special."

I just couldn't understand why she wanted to take something so big and hard and make it into something so small and unimportant. Violet and I weren't spoiled—and we *were* pretty special.

And none of our friends back home had ever lost a parent.

Aunt Clara was nothing like Mama and Papa, and it bothered me mostly for Violet, since she was only nine, but it bothered me for *me*, as well. I suppose it was the small things we missed the most, like being tucked in at night and kissed in the morning, or the way someone would notice if our sleeves were too short, or if we hadn't washed our hair. Not even Dina noticed these things, and so we were left on our own.

VIOLET

10

I knew that Lily worried about me, wondering if I was sick. She complained a lot that I was too pale and tried to make me eat all the time, even if I didn't feel hungry. She said that I was dark around the eyes, too, and tried to make Aunt Clara take me to the doctor, just in case I had an iron deficiency, but that wasn't why my eyes had dark circles. I knew exactly why I looked like I did: I didn't sleep at night.

I wasn't tossing and turning and thinking about Mama and Papa, like I had done right after K2, but I had discovered that I could get a lot more done at Crescent Hill if I used the night. First of all, it was quiet, so no one interrupted me or told me that I didn't see what I saw, which I absolutely did. I knew that Lily was scared, but it was still really annoying when she kept telling me that what I said wasn't true—especially since she knew that it was but had just decided not to believe me because it made things easier for her. At night, though, when I was alone, I could spend as much time as I wanted with the animals, and with the old lady, too. I would go from room to room and let the smoky tendrils touch me. Sometimes it tickled, but mostly it felt like a draft of air. Sometimes they came with feelings, like being outside in the wilderness, or swimming in a stream. Sometimes I felt the jungle, too, spreading out around me, with scents and colors and lots of green.

What I felt depended on the animal, and I liked spending time with the bear, the fox, and the raven in my room the most, because they reminded me of the woods around the lake house, where Mama, Lily, and I used to go berry picking. When I closed my eyes and let their smoke touch me, I remembered the scent of the thick moss and the raindrops gathering on the spruce branches. I remembered the taste of ripe berries, too, the sweet pangs of flavor in my mouth and, later, how we would put the berries in a large pot with sugar and make jam. Fresh bread with butter and jam was the best thing I knew when I was little.

I still didn't know what the animals wanted from me, though, or why they reached out for me every time I came into a room, but the pebbles in my brain became louder all the time, and I thought that if only I spent some time around them, sooner or later I'd figure out what it was they wanted me to do.

The old woman was different. After the first day, I only ever saw her in the dining room, where she seemed to stay almost all the time. She didn't say anything, but just shuffled around and smiled and winked. She seemed very friendly except for when she was not. Sometimes, when I went in there, she just stood frozen under the moose head with her mouth wide open, as if she were screaming, although there was no sound. She looked very, very scary when she was like that: Her eyes stared into nothing and her skin looked very blue. When I looked into her open mouth, all I could see was black.

The woman didn't have any smoke, and she was also different from the animals in that she wasn't mounted on a branch or hanging on a wall. She could move around mostly as she wanted, as if her smoke had become solid somehow, making her look like she had in life. I wasn't stupid, so I figured she must be Cecilia Lawrence, who had gifted the house to Aunt Clara. It could be Miss Lawrence's sister, too, but I didn't think so, because every time my aunt was in the same room as the ghost, the old woman would pull a face or become very ugly. I didn't think Miss Lawrence's sister had ever met Aunt Clara, but Miss Lawrence had, and maybe she wasn't happy with what my aunt had done—or *not* done—to the house.

I wondered if the old woman, too, wanted something from me.

The one who definitely wanted something was the man at the bottom of the garden. Every time I went outside or looked out the window, he was there, waving his arms and shouting, even though I never heard a sound. He looked very scary: His cheek was bloody and his shirt was ripped. When I squinted from the kitchen window, I could see that his legs seemed to be stuck in some sort of dark mass. It came down from his belly and reminded me of thick glue, but I thought it maybe could be a very thick smoke, like the one that came out of the animals. There was something about the man, though, that I didn't like at all. Maybe it was just that he was so angry. It didn't feel safe to go down to him—even if I realized that he was in pain, and Mama had always said that we should help people in need. I tried to avoid looking at him because of that. I wanted to help, I *did*, but he scared me too much, walking back and forth like he did, stuck to his black cloud. The animals—and the woman—were much easier. They didn't scare me at all. Instead, they felt like friends almost, that were there just for me. They made me miss my friends back home a little less.

I really wished that I knew what they wanted, though.

It was on one of those nights, when I had come back to my room and crawled into my bed, that the best thing happened. Just as I closed my eyes, I heard a knocking on the window above me. At first, I thought of the man and shuddered. Then I thought it could be a tree branch. But then, when the knocking never stopped, I decided to look, just to know for sure, since I wouldn't be able to sleep anyway with the knocking going on.

I would never have guessed what I saw when I lifted the curtain away. There was a bird out there—a big raven. It was too big to land on the ledge outside the window, but it flew toward the glass, poking it with its beak whenever it came close enough. I laughed when I saw it, not afraid at all. I knew at once, without knowing how, that it was the same bird that I had seen when I visited K2. I opened the window and the raven flew inside, landing on the bed's footboard, where it curved its talons around the wood and started picking at its feathers.

I sat up in the bed with the duvet pooling around me, just looking at it, thinking it was the most beautiful creature I had ever seen.

"Who are you?" I whispered, though I didn't expect it to answer, which made me even more surprised when it did. It didn't speak with its beak like in a cartoon, but sort of whispered the answer into my head. Not with words, exactly, but more like a *knowing*—like the answer was suddenly just there.

Irpa, she said.

"What do you—? Is that your name? Irpa?" I asked, and the raven said yes.

"Hi, Irpa," I said, and cocked my head. Irpa cocked her head back and I laughed. "I'm pleased to meet you," I said, reaching out a hand and pretending to shake hers in the air. "Where do you come from?" I asked her.

She replied with lots of images that I didn't understand. There was darkness and dirt, but air and light, too—and a mossy clearing full of bones.

"What are you here for?" I asked her next, when the pictures had disappeared.

This time, the answer was very clear. It was a feeling, not an image, but I knew that she had come to be with me. She said that we *belonged* together.

"Oh, good." I let out my breath and laughed again, because I was so happy. Irpa said she was going to be my friend and help me, which was something I definitely needed, since Lily didn't want to talk about the things that bothered me the most—like the man and the fact that our aunt had red feet.

When I woke up the next morning, Irpa was still there, but when I came up after lunch to get my schoolbooks, she was gone. I had left the window open, so it wasn't a great mystery, but I worried all day that I wouldn't see her again. She did come back, though, as soon as I had gone to bed, and I let her inside. She followed me downstairs when I went on my midnight walk through the house, flying before me down the stairs and perching on the furniture. It was even nicer to say hi to the animals when I had someone else with me. She wasn't like the other animals on Crescent Hill, and not like the old woman either. Irpa was something altogether different, and even if a part of me knew that maybe I *should* be afraid of her, I wasn't. Already on the first night, she felt like a part of me—like an arm or a leg, or the freckles on my nose. It was as if I had *always* known her.

She made things easier, too, because Irpa *knew* things. The first time we went to visit the bear together, she told me right away that the animal wasn't supposed to be here anymore. It was gone, she said—and by "gone" she meant dead—and had been gone for a very long time, but something of it was lingering behind, like a *footprint*. It would be better for the bear if it was whole and strong again. She told me this by showing me a sick bear in the woods, whose fur was matted and gray, and then showing me the same bear happy and healthy, lumbering along. She said the bear couldn't be happy like that again before it had gotten back what it lost. After that, she made me sit on the green couch for a long time and just listen to the lamp snake until the patter of pebbles in my brain finally made sense. Suddenly—as fast and as bright as a flash of lightning—I knew that the snake was asking me to help it be gone. I almost laughed when it happened, because I was so happy to finally hear it clearly.

It was easy after that: Whenever I passed by an animal, I could feel the *asking* inside me as clear as my own feelings and thoughts. Suddenly, it was so obvious to me what they wanted to say that it seemed weird that I hadn't properly heard it before.

They all asked for the same thing, though: to be gone from Crescent Hill.

When I took Irpa to see the old woman, she landed before her on the table, puffed out her chest, and spread her wings. The lady took a step back as if she was scared, or at least a bit nervous, but she didn't take her eyes off the raven.

Irpa said in my head that the old woman, too, was sick, but sicker than the bear. She hadn't gone anywhere at all, even though she *was* dead.

"Why?" I asked her, standing by the table and looking at the two of them: the woman and the bird, who were still staring at each other. Irpa showed me in my head that the woman, too, was stuck to the floor, even though the black cloud wasn't as big as the one the man outside walked around in. It came out from under the skirt of her nightgown, and Irpa showed me in a lightning-quick flash how it came pouring out of the old woman's belly button. She also showed me a grassy field full of dead ravens, where I could see how some of them left their bodies and flew away, while others just sat there on top of their bodies. Without really knowing how, I suddenly knew that it was different for everyone, depending on who they were. Some just left—like Mama and Papa—while others stayed behind for a while, not really knowing what had happened to them. And then there were some that *wouldn't* leave, and those were the ones that Irpa called sick. Not sick in the body like a disease, but sick in the soul, somehow.

"But why?" I asked again, looking at the woman, who pulled a face like she was in pain.

Irpa, being a bird, couldn't always explain everything, but she showed me fire and a sword, so I knew that she meant that they were angry, or that there was something violent going on that had made them sick. Just the thought of it made me shudder and feel cold. Who could ever be violent to that sweet old woman? And what had made her angry enough to stay?

I swore there and then that I would help her—no matter what it took.

We helped all the animals the next night, walking between them with a candle I had taken from the dining room, a huge box of matches, and a small tray with a hunk of bread and some salt from the kitchen. I also had a pitcher of water and a drinking glass. I didn't know exactly why I needed all that, but as soon as they *asked* me, I just *knew* what to do. I knew it the same way that I knew how to breathe, or to scratch my nose when it itched. It was as if I had really known all the time but had forgotten that I did. I also knew that since all that was left of the animals were footprints, it wouldn't be hard to help them. It would just be like using an eraser on pencil scribblings to make them go away, only the eraser was my candle and bread.

When we arrived at each animal, I ripped off some bread and placed it on the floor, before pouring a little salt from the silver salt-shaker on top of it and setting a glass of water beside it. Then I stood before the dead animal with the candle and wished with all my might that what was left of them would go to be with the rest of them, wherever that might be. I said words, too—a little verse that just arrived in my head: *Dear Mr. Bear, I wish for you to go home now. Bread for your soul, salt for your spirit, bread for your soul, salt for your spirit, bread for your soul, salt for your spirit* . . . I would say the same words over and over again until the candle flame went out without my doing anything to make it happen, and when the tendrils of smoke disappeared, the animals were just stuffing, glass, and fur, and the asking in my head was gone. Every time it happened a ripple of joy ran through my body, because I knew that the animal would be whole and healthy again.

The bread on the floor didn't look so good after, though, but had grown a layer of green mold. I didn't know what to do with it, so I stuffed the moldy pieces down in some of the flowerpots that littered the house, hoping that Dina wouldn't notice. Perhaps it would even be *good* for the plants—or that was what I hoped for. The water I had poured in the glass had entirely disappeared.

While we made the rounds downstairs, I wondered if the reason why some of the animals stayed was because they had been taxidermized, and Irpa said that it wasn't unusual for something to remain when an animal was shot or stabbed to death. She showed me a rotting bull in my head, so I figured it meant that they usually went away when the body was gone, but for the animals at Crescent Hill, that had never entirely happened. I asked her if Aunt Clara's fur coat, too, had something of the animals left in it, but Irpa said it wasn't as common if the animal didn't look like it had in life anymore, which was a relief, since all my shoes were made of leather.

It was a good thing to help the animals, though. It felt *right* in a way I hadn't felt before. I couldn't do anything to help the old woman, though—or at least that was what Irpa said.

She had to *ask*, Irpa told me. Just like the animals had.

I couldn't do anything at all before she *asked*.

CLARA

11

When the girls had been with me for some weeks, I put on my best purple two-piece and went back to the town house with a camera in my suitcase. It wasn't *just* my desire to document my brother's riches that had spurred me on; I was running out of time.

I had called Mr. Skye the day before to discuss a possible investment in Clarabelle Diamonds. I had prepared a speech and been ready to do whatever it took to persuade the man to decide in my favor.

"My brother would have liked the idea of the money doing good for the family," I said. "I have a top-notch designer already doing the work and an excellent jeweler at my disposal. It would benefit the girls, too, of course. Not only would they live even more comfortably than they do now, but they would have a good role model in the home. Female business owners are still rare, Mr. Skye, but surely we want my nieces to see that it can be done."

"Of course, Mrs. Woods," he had said, but sounded distracted. "It's just that the late Mrs. Webb had a few stipulations as to what the money could be invested in. The diamond business, as you may know, is not a very ethical one. The stones are mined with no concern for the workers—"

"Well, I'm sure we can find 'ethical stones,'" I cut him off, although I honestly had no idea how to do that, and it sounded horribly expensive. Plus, it would also be a hassle to replace the stones I had already bought.

"Well, perhaps if you brought assurances—but honestly, Mrs. Woods, the directions from the late Mrs. Webb are very clear, and the diamond business falls far short of what she envisioned. You would have known this already if you had read the paperwork I sent you."

My cheeks flushed red—as if I had had time to read the thousands of pages that he had sent me after I became the guardian. It was an unreasonable request, and I told him as much. "Getting the girls settled has been my number one priority, Mr. Skye, and the most important by far, as I'm sure you agree."

"Absolutely. And perhaps, for the time being, that is also where your focus should be. Building a new business takes a lot of time and effort."

I had to bite my tongue not to say something nasty—or ask him if he would have shared the same advice if the girls' guardian had been a man. But then again it was a *woman* who had gotten me in trouble this time and utterly curtailed my plan with her *ethical* considerations. It never ceased to astonish me what lengths Amanda had gone to in order to be able to live with the fact that she was filthy rich.

My disdain for my sister-in-law didn't solve my problem, though, and I just couldn't find it in me to beg. Mr. Skye was someone I needed to keep me afloat, if only by sending me a check once a month.

"Perhaps you are right," I said between gritted teeth, while my mind was spinning with numbers, trying to calculate how long I had to wait to see my dream come true with only the girls' stipend to rely on. The answer was far too long.

"When the girls come of age, they are free to make their own choices, of course. Perhaps it would be a better time for you to start your business then."

"Of course," I muttered, while tasting the bitter defeat on my tongue. Four years to wait was a long time, too—and even if I did, I had no guarantee that Lily would just hand me the money. She *was* Amanda's daughter after all.

Mr. Skye also informed me that they had hired a company to bring all the art and other valuables out of the town house and put them in storage. Thus far, they had kept a night guard on the property in addition to the burglar alarm, but that was not a very economical solution, so the move would be happening next week. Though smarting from this most recent defeat, I decided to seize the opportunity to canvass the assets before everything was gone and thought a visit at noon, when no one was around, would give me ample time to do my business.

I didn't mention it to the girls, of course, as I knew they would like nothing more than to join me, and that was out of the question. Even I would find it hard to spin a convincing lie as to why I was photographing their parents' art collection, so they remained oblivious.

I was met at the airport by my friend Sebastian Swift, a jewel appraiser I had known for a long time. Sebastian looked like a proper gentleman, with graying hair that was white at the temples and a chic little mustache. He always wore three-piece suits in shades of gray, and his long and angular face was tanned. The only area where his elegance ever gave way to whimsy was in the bold colors he chose for his bow ties. The one he had opted to use that day was a stark and vibrant green to match the color of my eyes.

He greeted me with hands almost as bejeweled as my own. Though while I stayed faithful to my diamonds, he carried black onyx and smoky quartz among the more glittering rocks. He pressed a pair of soft lips to my cheek before guiding me to his car.

On our way to the town house, we fell into our usual easy way around each other, and, as it always was with Sebastian, I never knew how much I had missed him until we were together again.

"It's a nice thing that you are doing, getting your nieces' valuables appraised," he said with his hands on the wheel. "Though I'm surprised that the insurance company hasn't already done it—or their lawyer."

"Oh, they have, but my brother was an easygoing sort, so I just want to make sure that *everything* is appraised. He was never good at looking after his belongings." I still had a scar on my calf from an ill-fated encounter with one of his toy cars.

"I'm flattered that you asked *me,* though. I'm sure they have their own people—"

"I only trust you, you know that." I smiled. "Besides, why pass up the opportunity to see you when I can?"

"Well, there is that." He cocked his head slightly, and one of his eyebrows climbed a little. "We don't see each other nearly enough."

"I know," I replied, suddenly a little hot and bothered. I opened the window just a crack. "Work before pleasure, though."

"Clearly. Your nieces are lucky to have such a dedicated aunt, who knows a little something about managing a fortune."

"Yes, aren't they just." I laughed to smooth out the sarcasm. "They are a handful, though. I'm not as free to do as I please—"

"You could maybe tell them about me," he interrupted, and he didn't sound playful anymore. His gaze was glued to the windshield. "I would love to meet them, you know that. I'm sure they are extraordinary children, just like their aunt."

"Of course they are," I said automatically. "But they are also very vulnerable right now, so I would like to keep their lives simple and easy for a time, and not introduce new pieces to the chessboard—"

"I am hardly a *new* piece, though, Clara." I sighed when I heard the edge of bitterness in his voice. "How long have we done this? Ten years?"

"And I hope we will *continue* to do it for decades more," I assured him. "You know how it's been hard for me, ever since Timmy—"

"I know." Now it was he who sighed. "Still, I think ten years is ample time to prove that I am trustworthy."

"It *is,*" I assured him, "and you *will* meet the girls in time—just not yet." How could I ever explain to him that it was the same thing that had brought us together that also kept us apart: that I found it hard to trust a man whose love for diamonds nearly rivaled my own. There was no way he would understand, not without my explaining it all, and that I could never do. "Please, let's not argue," I begged him. "We have so little time."

"Of course." His features softened at once, and he gave me a brief look. "It has been a trying time for you, I know."

"Yes," I agreed. "It *has* been hard since Ben and Amanda died—and what a horrible way to go! I can't help but think about them still stuck on that mountain." I made a point of turning my head and gazing sadly at the horizon.

"At least you're taking good care of their daughters, and that means something," he said. I suppose he was trying to comfort me, but the only thing he accomplished was to make my old dry heart twitch with pain. I hated this side of Sebastian; he had a way of prodding my resolve. Perhaps it was the woman he *thought* I was that came haunting me whenever he was around.

A woman I had never been, and certainly never would become.

I was relieved when we arrived at the town house and could leave the conversation behind. I opened the door with the key I had gotten from Mr. Skye when the guardianship was transferred and disarmed the alarm. Then I brought Sebastian with me on an adventure through the rooms, my camera clicking constantly. Sebastian was content to just admire and sigh and compliment my late brother's tastes.

"It wasn't him, though," I said, when we had entered the dining room, where the lilac wallpaper showcased an array of pastel flowers. "It was all Amanda. She was a sensitive soul, always going on about the importance of art and things that grow. It was surprising, to be honest, that Ben fell for a woman like her. I always imagined him ending up with someone from the same background as us." I had conveniently never told Sebastian how I had not even been mentioned in my mother's will.

"She worked, didn't she?" Sebastian asked about Amanda.

"She did, yes, with a global charity. She always had a bleeding heart, that one—always ready to save the world." The shutter went off as I captured another painting, this one showing an orchard in moonlight.

"Do the girls take after her?" Sebastian came up beside me—to admire the painting, it seemed.

I thought about it for a moment. "The elder girl is more restrained, but the younger has her mother's abandon."

"She is the one who plays?" Sebastian had been kind enough to go shopping for some horribly expensive violin strings when Lily was in need. They had arrived in a beautiful package together with two bags of lavender toffee, one for each of the girls; he knew well that I didn't eat candy. I never mentioned to my charges where the toffee came from, though.

"Lily, the eldest, is the one who plays," I answered, "and quite beautifully, I must admit. Violet hasn't honed any of her talents yet, though I'm sure that she has several."

"You should take Lily to the city, then—to a concert," he suggested.

"Oh, I will." The camera clicked again, committing a fetching vase to film. "But not just yet. As I said, they have been struggling."

"Of course," he said again, almost annoyingly patient with me.

I had saved the best for last, just to marinate in the sweet anticipation, but as the moment approached, I found myself getting more and more giddy.

"Come on," I said, when the last downstairs art piece had been photographed. "Let's go appraise some jewels."

I didn't even pretend that I did not know where they were, after we had climbed the stairs and entered the rose-, tea-, and mint-scented bedroom. No, I went to the drawer at once and pulled out the carved jewelry box, placing it on top of Amanda's vanity. The opulent plums that were carved on the box's lid reflected the soft light from the little lamp, making them appear like globes of gold. I held my breath when I opened it up, revealing the sparkles and shine within to Sebastian's hungry gaze.

"Oh," he exclaimed, "that is quite a dragon's hoard." He came closer to look over my shoulder, while his long, elegant fingers dipped down to toy with an emerald ring.

"Yes, isn't it just." I sighed with longing and lifted a sapphire pendant. "Some of these designs are highly unusual—there's a lot of flowers."

"Yes," he agreed. "They're not classic at all, but maybe worth even more just because of it? I suppose they would have bought them directly from designers . . ."

"Undoubtedly." I laughed with joy as I filled my hand with jewels and gold and let them drizzle down on the vanity's polished walnut top. I noticed how some of the pieces were tangled together; Amanda had clearly not taken very good care of her treasure. I supposed she would rather have worn wildflowers and apple blossoms around her slender neck.

"Ah, nothing brightens the mood as much as shiny metals and stones, does it?" Sebastian's smile was as bright as my own.

"No, there's nothing like it," I purred, and turned my head to steal a kiss from his lips.

"Your nieces are two lucky young ladies," he continued, which certainly diminished my mood somewhat, but I did take comfort in my hope that, somehow—someday—all of this would be mine.

I rose from the chair and patted the upholstery. "Do what you do best," I whispered. "Tell me what these babies are worth."

Sebastian chuckled as he took the vacated seat and flicked a small magnifying glass out of his breast pocket. He pulled the little lamp closer, then picked a small ruby ring to start. I seated myself upon the golden bedspread with my notebook in my lap and my pen poised, ready to take down numbers. All the while I was thinking of how the contents of the wooden jewelry box could one day be traded for money to buy even more beautiful jewels to embed into Isabella's designs. Clarabelle Diamonds was so close but yet so far—though not *impossible* in the least.

Sebastian started naming approximate values. Now and then he would comment upon a flaw in a stone or discard a piece completely. I wrote down every number and chuckled again when I saw how the list grew. This was indeed a fortune!

When he had made it about a quarter of the way through the box, I couldn't stand it any longer. The excitement and the numbers had become too much for me.

"Come here, Glitter Bear," I whispered, and pushed the notebook down on the floor.

"What?" Sebastian looked over his shoulder, still holding the magnifying glass in front of his left eye. "Here?" He looked perplexed when he saw the expression on my face. "Is that appropriate, Clara?"

"Don't you want to?" I teased him, and stretched out on the bedspread.

"Of course I do." He sounded flustered, and a little extra color had come into his cheeks. "But should we really—"

"We won't be *in* the bed," I told him. "We'll stay on top, just here." I patted the golden satin. "Benjamin wouldn't have minded at all. He always just wanted me to be happy."

Sebastian took another moment, but then his hands were at the green bow tie, loosening it with eager fingers. I suppose the jewels had snuck into his blood, too, whipping it to a frenzy.

"Oh, Clara," he moaned, as he fell down next to me on the bed and kicked off his shoes.

"Oh, Glitter Bear," I purred, and pulled him close to me. Our lips locked in heat and passion. "Call me by my name," I gasped when our lips finally parted. "Call me by my *true* name."

"Clarabelle Diamonds." His voice was strained with want. "Clarabelle Diamonds, forever and ever!"

VIOLET

12

When the air grew warmer in May, Lily and I spent more time outside. We hadn't been in the woods yet, even though they grew thick around the garden. Dina said they were "inhospitable," but they looked just fine to me. I hoped that we could go out there soon, since I didn't like the garden much because of the man who walked there.

Lily loved the garden, though, and wanted to go there all the time, saying that the sunshine was good for us, and the fresh air, too, and all the green. She only said that because she didn't see what I saw; Lily only ever saw colors. I thought about telling her about the man many times, but I knew she would just pretend not to believe me, or even get mad at me for seeing him. It was impossible *not* to see him, though, every time we went out there—his angry plodding and silent shouting; the way that he waved with his arms to make me look.

I couldn't forget that he was there, no matter how much I tried, but the pavilion felt safe because of the angle; I couldn't see him at all from inside the thorny thicket that covered the walls. I made up a game where I ran an apothecary, and while gathering different twigs and leaves and sorting them into piles on the built-in bench, I could almost forget him for a while. I gave all the plants new names and pretended that they could help with different things. Lily had to be the customers, and her pockets were full of gravel, which was what we used as money.

"Hello, Miss Apothecary. I have a terrible back pain today," she would say as she came into the pavilion.

"Oh, well, I am sorry to hear that, Mrs. Baker. It sounds like you need some afroksiala to ease that," I replied. "Steep it in hot water and drink it every night. Don't take too much, though, because then you'll die."

I think Lily thought the game was childish, but she liked it anyway. Maybe she, too, needed to forget about all the things that made her angry or afraid. She even helped me smuggle out some empty wine bottles from the kitchen, so I could make tonics of rainwater and leaves. Sometimes, she got so into the game that she, too, started making things up. We even argued about what the plants could do.

"These leaves can help with headaches but also make your eyes bleed," I would say. "If you eat too much of it, you will lose *all* your blood."

"No." Lily shook her head. "They will make your eyesight stronger, not weaker, and it's *good* for the blood."

Or I would say, "These flowers will make your liver fail if you aren't careful."

And she would say, "They don't work like that at all. They can make fever go away."

Even though I didn't like the garden as much as Lily, I did like to see how spring changed it. Though all the flower beds were very overgrown, some new, green things still came up through the dirt, and flower buds appeared on the rose vines. Lily said that the plants, too, had flames sometimes, but that they were mostly white, so I guess they didn't feel much, since white meant peace and calm. There were birds in the garden as well, filling the air with happy songs. It should have been the best place to be on Crescent Hill—but because of *him*, it wasn't. I almost told Lily about him once, when I caught her staring down at where he was. When I asked her about it, she said that there was something on the ground down there, something red that moved around like tiny fish. I thought that maybe it was him she saw—or his colors, anyway—but by the time I had opened my mouth to say something, Lily had already walked off. She didn't like to see the colors, while I wished that I could see them, too, since it seemed like a very good trick to be able to see what people felt.

I suppose I hadn't thought that things would change, though. I suppose I had thought we would just continue on like that—him walking and hollering, and me pretending not to see him—but that isn't what happened.

The day had started out better than most. Aunt Clara had been busy with two of her friends, who had arrived that same morning in a large, bulky car and parked it in front of the house. Dina had carried tea and sandwiches into the winter garden and then sent us in there to "say hello," as we always did when Aunt Clara had guests. I could never tell the ladies apart. They all looked the same to me, with stiff hair lacquered in place, rayon dresses with funny patterns, and brightly painted lips. Some of them were nurses—or used to be nurses—and they wore a little less jewelry than the other friends. All of them seemed to think Aunt Clara was the nicest person alive for letting us live at Crescent Hill.

I didn't know exactly why we had to "say hello," but everything always happened in the same way. First, we would come in and say our names to the ladies while taking their soft, dry hands. Then they would coo and sigh for a bit—perhaps ask us a few questions, or tell us how sorry they were about K2—before we were let out again. Aunt Clara would sometimes ask Lily to play for the guests, which I don't think she minded much, but she always chose an easy piece that wasn't very long.

We could see them from the garden that day, or at least flashes of their moving heads, through the web of thorny branches that covered the winter garden walls. We saw the dead parrot in there, too: a glimpse of bright red feathers. I knew that the parrot was free now; all of it was gone from Crescent Hill, which made me feel happy and warm all over. It was what I thought about while we walked around and picked old oak leaves off the ground to use in the apothecary.

"They will make the blood run thicker; sometimes it clogs everything up," I said, just as something happened—or not—down at the bottom of the garden. I had looked up to see him standing there—not walking or shouting, just standing and staring with wild eyes. A sudden breeze moved through the woods, making a rustling sound.

"What is it?" Lily said beside me. "What are you looking at, Violet?"

"The man down there." It just came tumbling out of me. I suppose I was too worried by his change in behavior to be careful. He had never stopped like that before—never stared at me like that.

"I don't see any—"

"Hush, be quiet!" Something was going on in my head. It was like when Irpa spoke to me, but different. Maybe more like the animals—but, no, not that either. It was as if someone was poking at my brain, as if there was something inside there that wasn't me.

"Okay," Lily muttered, and shifted on the ground. "Where is he?"

I lifted a finger and pointed to the middle of the crescent, even though I knew she couldn't see him.

"No." She shook her head. "There's no one there, Violet. You're imagining again." She sighed loudly and shifted on the ground again, but this time I couldn't pretend like he wasn't there, because he was in my head now, pushing and poking.

"But he *is*," I insisted. "He has ruined clothes and a wound on his face." I showed her with my hand, trailing it down her cheek. "He is *always* down there, Lily, walking around in black glue, only this time he is standing still, just looking at me."

"You're making it up," she said. "You're only saying it because *I* saw the red tadpoles down there."

"I'm *not*," I replied, feeling angry—almost as angry as the man was. "I would never make up someone like that! I would only make up nice people who didn't have any wounds at all. I even think his clothes are burned."

"Stop lying," Lily said again, but her voice was shivering now, so I knew she didn't really think I was. Inside my head, something was building. It felt as if something was about to explode. I fell to my knees and heaved for breath while Lily cried out beside me.

And then, in my head, he *asked*.

LILY
13

Violet didn't want to go to the garden at all after she nearly fainted, just shaking her head whenever I asked. I was a little worried about it, but then I thought she had just scared herself by pretending to see the hurt man. I didn't like how she pulled away from me, though, and chose to spend her time alone in the raven room rather than with me and Dina in the kitchen. When I went to check on her, I would usually find her kneeling on the bed with her elbows propped up on the windowsill, staring out at the garden.

After a whole week had passed in that way, I finally asked, "Are you looking for the man you saw before?"

She gave me a quick glance over her shoulder. "I am looking *at* the man."

I looked outside as well but of course couldn't see anything.

"What is he doing?" I really wanted her to keep talking. Whatever it was she thought she saw, it hadn't sounded very nice, and I didn't want her to feel like she was alone with it.

"He is shouting something," Violet said, "but he has no voice."

"That's too bad," I offered.

"Yes, isn't it just," she muttered. "The old lady never tries to talk to me, but this one *really* wants to."

"Why are you up here and not down there, then?" I pointed through the window to the overgrown lawn below.

"*You* would only come out," she said. "You *never* leave me alone."

Clearly, *I* was the problem, and not the dead man in the flower bed. "Are you angry with me?" I asked.

"Why does it matter?" She shrugged. "You just call me a liar all the time."

"No, Violet. No!" I climbed onto the bed with her. "Whatever it is you think you see—"

"You're doing it *again*!" Her eyes flashed with anger. "If you truly believed me, you wouldn't say things like that! I *never* say that your colors aren't real!"

"Oh, Violet . . . It's just hard, you know, because I can't see him myself."

"Well, I can't see colors, but I don't pretend like they don't exist!"

"Maybe it's just my eyes—" I protested.

"Or maybe you're just stupid." She gave me a scorching look.

"I'm sorry, Violet." I put a hand on her shoulder. "I really, truly am."

"Then prove it," said my sister.

"What? How?" My stomach started hurting. I just knew that whatever came next would be bad.

"Come out to the garden with me, tonight, after midnight." She looked very serious when she said it; her dark eyes shone when she looked at me.

"Why can't we go now?" There was nothing stopping us.

"No, it must be tonight, after Aunt Clara has gone to sleep." She nodded as if to say that this was the only way.

"Sure," I answered, despite the stomachache. "But why—?"

"Just say that you will come," she begged. "Or do you want me to go out there on my own?"

"No, of course not." It was a horrible idea. Maybe a bear would come out of the woods and eat her—or maybe she would feel sick again, like the last time we were out there. "Why, though, Violet? What are we going to do in the garden?"

"I don't know yet." She shrugged. "But I'll figure it out."

I worried all afternoon, just trying to think of ways to make Violet change her mind, but I couldn't think of anything that wouldn't make her upset with me again. I absolutely didn't want to be out in the garden at night, but I definitely couldn't let her go by herself either. I even considered telling Aunt Clara about Violet's plan, but something told me that would only make things worse. So, at a quarter past midnight, I was there, in the hallway outside Violet's door, with a flashlight in my hand, hoping that she had forgotten the whole thing and fallen asleep.

Sadly, she had not. She came out just a few minutes later, wearing her usual favorite nightgown and a pair of knitted blue socks on her feet. The smile on her face when she saw me almost made everything all right.

Violet whipped out a flashlight of her own, then pressed a finger to her lips to warn me to be quiet before we started toward the stairs. I tiptoed after her through the dark hallway, our feet shuffling against the thick rug, until we arrived at the landing and started the descent to the ground floor. The stairs were thankfully sturdy, and kind enough not to make a sound.

I had thought that we would go straight for our coats, but Violet didn't pause in the hall. She continued toward the kitchen instead. I quickly turned to follow her lead, almost crashing into the poor dead elk in the process. I couldn't ask Violet why she was going to the kitchen since we were still trying to be quiet, but I felt relieved. I thought that maybe she had changed her mind at the last minute and just wanted something to eat instead.

At first, it looked as if I was right, since she did go to the refrigerator and open the heavy door. A cool yellow light spilled out on the floor, making the slim beams of our flashlights pointless. I didn't know what she was looking for, so I just watched as my sister rummaged through the food. All the while I was listening to the house, searching the night's quiet for signs that Aunt Clara had heard us and was on her way down. It didn't seem that she had, though. She *was* a very heavy sleeper, and Dina had even let it slip that Aunt Clara sometimes took sleeping pills.

Finally, Violet seemed to have found what she was looking for and rose with several items clutched to her chest. I could see the Styrofoam tray of tomorrow's beef, and a parcel wrapped in butcher paper that I knew was a piece of liver for one of Aunt Clara's meat days. There was also a bottle of chilled cider and a lidded plastic bowl with the last of yesterday's chicken; bones mostly, and other things that didn't go in the stew. Dina used it to make broth for our soups.

I almost said something then, wanting Violet to at least return the liver, but then she nodded toward the door and started moving. She had abandoned her own flashlight on the kitchen table, so mine was the only source of light as we moved into the hall. I gingerly got our coats out of the closet, and we both slipped on our shoes before I opened the front door as quietly as I could, still carrying our coats.

The air outside was cool and crisp, smelling of dirt and fresh greenery. I still didn't want to go, but as surprised as I was by Violet's food theft, I was curious, too. I wanted to see what she did with it. Could it be for the apothecary? I also figured that since Aunt Clara got some money from our being there, the food belonged as much to us as to her.

I walked first as we entered the dark garden, since I had the light. I could hear Violet behind me, the crunching in the leaves as we moved away from the house and toward the pavilion. When I thought we were far enough away from the glinting windows of Crescent Hill that our voices couldn't be heard, I finally asked in a whisper, "Violet, what are we doing out here? Where are you taking the food?"

"To the bottom of the garden," she replied, and my stomach started aching again.

"To *the man*?" I couldn't believe it. "Why?"

"I think he's terribly hungry," said Violet. "He needs meat and bones and something sweet if he's going to break free."

"*Free?*" I shuddered, from both fear and cold this time.

"From the flower bed," said Violet.

"The man is stuck in the flower bed?"

"Uh-huh."

If she hadn't been so angry with me before, I would have stopped her—said something to chase her back into the house. Instead, I bit my tongue and swallowed my feelings until we finally reached the crescent of flower beds and Violet put down the stolen food.

"Here." I handed her the blue coat and quickly pulled on my own as well.

Violet smiled while she put on her coat, but she didn't say anything else. She put her hand in the left pocket and pulled out something long and white. It took me a moment to recognize one of the half-burned candles from the dining room table. She had a matchbook, too, and held it up to show me.

"I took it before," she said with pride.

"We have the flashlight already," I muttered, though I somehow already knew by then that whatever she needed the candle for, it had nothing to do with light.

She stuck the candle down in the wet ground, just in front of the flower bed at the center of the crescent, and struck a match. She failed, twice, before I decided to help her.

"Here, let me." I took the matchbook from her and struck one redheaded match. The flame ignited with a hiss. "*The man* is hungry, huh?" I muttered while guiding the flame to the wick.

Once the candle flame was strong and steady, Violet started on the food. She unwrapped all of it and placed the meats around the candle. The beef and the liver glistened in the candlelight, and the chicken bones looked like polished sticks. Violet had pilfered a corkscrew, too, and used it to open the cider bottle. Then she very carefully poured it all out on the meat and the ground surrounding it. She left the empty bottle down in the grass.

"What now?" I whispered, though we were far from the house. "Is he eating?" I didn't like the look of the "meal" one bit. It seemed to me that, as soon as the food had touched the ground, it had become filthy, somehow—in a way that had nothing to do with dirt.

Violet didn't answer my question. Instead she started praying—or so I thought at first. "Dear man in the garden," she started, "please take this meat and cider I have brought to you. Flesh for your flesh, bone for your bones, sugar for your spirit. Flesh for your flesh, bone for your bones, sugar for your spirit, flesh for your flesh, bone for your bones, sugar for your spirit . . ." She started repeating the same words over and over again. By her feet, the candle flickered wildly, although I couldn't feel any draft in the air. She said the same words so many times that it became a rhythm—one that grew faster and wilder by the minute. "Flesh for your flesh, bone for your bones, sugar for your spirit, flesh for your flesh, bone for your bones, sugar for your spirit . . ."

I wanted to interrupt when she started swaying on her feet but somehow couldn't bring myself to break the eerie rhythm. Instead, I took a step forward so I stood right behind her and held out my arms in case she fell. My heart was racing wildly, and the red tadpoles were back, squirming now, around the meal on the ground.

Finally—suddenly—the candle went out, and Violet stopped chanting. I had dropped my flashlight to the ground, and it lay there, shining its light into the tangled lawn. I grabbed it before checking on Violet.

I put a hand on her shoulder and she slowly turned around. The sight of her face made a pang go off in my chest; she looked so very tired. She smiled at me, though, in her usual way, so I thought that she was all right.

"What was all that for?" I asked her.

"I don't know yet," she replied. "I just know that it had to be done."

CLARA

14

Something had changed. I knew it the moment I woke up in my bed, under the watchful eye of my taxidermy snake. I couldn't say what it was, as my room looked just as it always did, faintly illuminated by a rude ray of sunshine that had snuck in between the heavy curtains. Yesterday's clothes lay piled on the floor, waiting for Dina to pick them up, and the empty wineglass sat perched upon my nightstand, keeping Isabella Roux's sketches in place.

Everything looked just as it should, but still, as I rose from the bed to slip on my silk robe and draw my morning bath, something felt utterly and unmistakably *wrong*. Perhaps it was the scent: something moist and wet, like dirt after a rainfall, or the oppressive feeling I got while making my way to the door. It made me think that someone was in the room with me, watching me cross the floor. I didn't like it at all.

Dina had already set the table in the dining room when I came downstairs: Neatly sculpted melon balls lay on a plate, next to a couple of eggs in their shells. She had offered to peel them for me once, but I rather liked the feeling of the shells being crushed under my hand as I rolled them across the linen napkin.

I had to cross the living room to get to my food, though, and that, of course, was a trial, because my nieces were there, dressed in nice flowery dresses, draped on each side of the couch. They both looked up from their books and scowled at me as I passed them, and I thought that this was highly unfair, seeing how I had *just* relented and bought them a new TV. I sighed, wondering what fresh demands they were going to serve me today.

I much preferred my melon balls.

I had almost finished one egg when the first little missile was fired. Lily had come into the dining room so silently that I hadn't even noticed and parked herself within my eyesight.

"Aunt Clara," she said in her clear, no-nonsense voice that I so dearly had come to loathe, "why can't we come with you the next time you go to the city? It would be good for Violet to get away from the house for a little while—and me, too. We used to travel all the time, before—"

"Dearest Lily," I drawled, while balancing a glistening red melon ball on a spoon. "I am not traveling for amusement, but to attend to business. There's no time to go sightseeing or—"

"Maybe we could bring Dina?" she suggested. "She won't have anyone to cook for here at home, so maybe she could come along."

I picked a fresh napkin from the table and used it to fan myself, although the air in the room was fairly cool. My teeth were at work, devouring juicy melon flesh. "Lily, I would rather not discuss this with you so early in the morning. You should at least let me finish my breakfast in peace."

I always did my best to evade her when she brought me her concerns. The fact of the matter was that I didn't *want* to bring them to the city with me; that was *my* time with Sebastian. Neither did I want the hassle of a visit to the town house, and I *certainly* didn't want to chaperone them around to see friends.

Why couldn't the two of them just be happy and content at Crescent Hill, where I knew where they were at all times?

With their money so securely locked away, my nieces were quickly starting to feel more like a curse than a blessing, and I had even started to long for when school began in the fall. It would certainly keep them out of the way for a large portion of the day—but then they would make new friends, and those friends would have parents, and then there would be teachers, and before you knew it, *everyone* would have their nose in my business. A boarding school, as Lily so often suggested, might be the better option, but then they were expensive, and the money coming in was better spent on beautiful stones.

"Won't you at least think about it, Aunt Clara?" the insolent girl insisted while doing that peculiar blinking again. "I really think it would be good for us to see something other than Crescent Hill—"

I raised an eyebrow. "Is that so? Don't you find the accommodations to your liking?"

"Of course we do, Aunt Clara, you *know* that we are grateful." Her eyes went wide as she spoke, and her voice rose in pitch. She had folded her hands in front of her body—the calluses on her fingers were *very* thick—and her braid hung neatly over her shoulder. She was the very picture of an obedient young lady, but I, of course, knew better. She had a will of steel behind that angelic exterior, and there was nothing else to do but smack it down.

I sighed and put the napkin down on the tablecloth. "It really would be very unfortunate if we cannot make this work, Lily. I would like nothing more than to honor my late brother's wishes, but if you cannot settle in here—"

"But I can! We are!" Her eyes flashed with both fear and regret, and I grimaced to hide a satisfied smile. "We wouldn't want to be anywhere but here, Aunt Clara." She fidgeted. "It's just that Violet misses her friends a lot, and I'm a little worried." She lowered her voice as she said that last part, although her sister in the other room had to be hard of hearing not to pick up the words.

"Oh?" I arched my other eyebrow. "I think Violet is doing just fine." Unlike my niece, I did *not* lower my voice, and Lily's face turned a shade paler as she glanced at the open door.

"Maybe we can take some walks?" she suggested next. "Maybe Dina can take us to the woods?"

"Sure," I said. "Why not?" The woods around my house were desperately unfriendly, wild, and without as much as a single hiking trail, but if it would keep my nieces away from the house for a few hours—and stop the relentless whining—why not? "You can ask Dina." I poured myself some hot coffee, lifted the cup to my lips, and blew on it. "I won't let you go visiting your old friends yet, though—or visit the school." I quickly intercepted whatever other pleas she had in store. "It's too soon. You're still grieving." The coffee was extremely hot, but I drank it down anyway.

"Of course, Aunt Clara." She sounded just a tiny bit terse. "Maybe it will help, a hike in the woods."

That matter settled, I was finally able to finish my breakfast in peace, but I still didn't feel right. I just couldn't shake the feeling that someone was standing right behind me, looking over my shoulder, as I opened my mail—mostly bills—and skimmed its contents. I couldn't properly relax at all and didn't even finish all my melon balls.

It was a Friday, so the girls left with Dina before lunch to do the weekly shopping. It was a relief. I had a budding headache that just wouldn't go away no matter how many painkillers I swallowed. I found a box of secret chocolates in one of my hiding places—this particular one behind a set of encyclopedias on the bookshelf—opened a fresh bottle of wine, and dragged myself up the winding stairs to my room, where I turned on the TV and settled down upon the bedspread. I pulled open the pale blue ribbon that sealed the chocolate box, lifted off the lid, and found my favorite: apricot meringue. Then I poured myself a small glass of wine and brought out Isabella's sketches. They were for our first collection—and they were wonderful. My toes curled with delight as my finger traced a necklace with a pear-shaped pendant; a marquise-cut stone in a slim ring; a simple but elegant bracelet . . . At the top of the pages was written in an elegant hand: *Clarabelle Diamonds.*

The first stones had already arrived at Isabella's studio, and soon the production would begin in earnest. It would all just be a bud dying on the vine, though, if I couldn't find a way to pay for manufacturing, distribution, and presentation. The wholesale was of lesser concern; I planned to handle it myself, seeing how I clearly was the best spokesperson for the brand. In fact, I believed I would excel at sales, and as soon as the jewelers saw my collection, it wouldn't take much to sway them anyway.

I did, after all, have excellent taste.

The TV filled the air with its hapless chatter as I lay there on the bed, dreaming about the future, about the jewels that would carry my name. The smell was still there, though, even stronger than before: soft dirt and rotting leaves, and the rancid stench of meat gone bad.

Suddenly, the sound from the TV was gone. I looked over, and the dark screen glared right back at me. I sighed and got to my feet, then padded across to turn it back on. The same mindless game show rerun as before instantly filled the screen, while bouts of hysterical laughter streamed out in the air. I went back to the bed and had just lain down when the very same thing happened again. There was a sudden silence and the screen was black. Feeling a little annoyed, I got up once more and repeated the procedure—even gave the useless contraption a hard slap to make it behave. My attempt at discipline didn't seem to have an effect, however, as the TV turned itself off again as soon as my feet were off the floor.

I gave up after that and remained lying on the bed. I found another chocolate in the box: coconut crème. I was still licking chocolate from my fingers when the lights started blinking. First it was just the lamp on my nightstand: an antique one made of brass, with a purple satin shade. Every other second it would give a quick, sharp blink. I instantly thought of the bulb, of course, or the ancient wiring, but then the glass-enclosed overhead light started blinking as well.

I got up again and rushed to the door, only to find that the hallway was the same. All the bulbs in the golden wall sconces blinked, making it look as if there were fireworks going off out there. One of the girls had left the bathroom door open, and even in there it went on, blinking in a sickly shade of apricot. There was a sound, too, accompanying the madness: a soft hissing noise that slowly increased in volume.

Just when I had decided to brave the blinking hallway and go for the stairs, a loud bang from behind made me startle and spin around. At first, I couldn't see anything out of the ordinary except for the blinking, but then the door on one of my wardrobes suddenly sprang open, entirely of its own accord. It opened wide on well-oiled hinges and gaped toward me like a maw before suddenly slamming shut again.

Then its twin door opened in the same way, and then the two doors on my other wardrobe—and suddenly all the doors were opening and closing, slamming shut with increasing speed. The hissing sound had reached an almost unbearably loud frequency by then, and the headache that had somewhat subsided came back with a vengeance. Just then, as I watched the bedlam unfolding, my half-full wineglass on the nightstand toppled over—entirely by itself—and hit Isabella's precious sketches in a torrent of red.

"Oh no!" I cried, and before I even had time to think, I ran into the room with the blinking lights and the slamming doors and the hissing sound—just to save my dream.

"Oh no," I muttered again as I lifted the wine-stained pages and made to assess the damage. I could tell already, despite the blinking lights, that at least the top page—the one with the necklace—was utterly ruined.

Then the blinking stopped. The noise was gone. The dresser doors stopped moving. Even the dreadful smell abated.

But I knew without a doubt that someone was standing right behind me.

Slowly—very slowly—I turned around, with the ruined pages held up before me like a shield. I saw his feet first, then the singed hem of his black pants, then his equally burned white shirt. Finally, I lifted my gaze to the wound on his cheek, slowly dripping red.

"You!" I gasped, appalled.

LILY

15

We were surprised to find Aunt Clara in the living room when we came back from the supermarket. She was lying on the green velvet couch, pressing an ice pack to her head. She had closed all the curtains, too, which made the whole room look gloomy. What really made the scene strange, though, was the way she kept staring up at the ceiling. Her eyes weren't moving even an inch when Violet and I came into the room.

She looked like she had seen a ghost.

"Hi, Aunt Clara." Violet sounded perky, but her worried gaze kept darting in my direction. "We're back from shopping," she declared. "And yes, we helped Dina put away all the groceries in the kitchen." She climbed onto an overstuffed recliner. "We got beef and cheese and celery and—"

"Aunt Clara, are you ill?" I interrupted her. I was still standing just inside the door, unsure if I should call for Dina. "Do you have another headache?" Though if she did, why wasn't she in her room? She usually hid away in there whenever one of her wine and opera nights had gotten out of hand and made her temples pound the next morning. "Do you want me to ask Dina to bring you some aspirin?"

"No," Aunt Clara growled, finally showing signs of life. She shifted a little and the couch's springs creaked, while the diamonds on her fingers glittered. "I must have taken half a dozen already," she muttered.

"Does it hurt very much?" Violet leaned forward and gave our aunt a concerned look. I had been worried about Violet ever since the chanting in the garden, but she seemed to be doing just fine. Even before I had made my way downstairs that morning, she had admitted to Dina that she had taken the food but had said it was to feed a fox she had seen through her bedroom window. I came into the kitchen just as she said it and was too surprised to even say a word when I sat down to eat my oatmeal. I hadn't known that my sister could lie like that.

Dina, of course, had bought the story straight away and had even promised not to tell Aunt Clara. She had probably thought it was a sweet thing for Violet to do. We could buy new meat, she had said, on our trip to the supermarket.

I wasn't sure if I liked that Violet lied so easily, though. Not because of the lying itself, but because it made her harder to trust. I suddenly felt like I didn't know the first thing about what was going on in her head. And as for our trip outside the night before, *I* seemed to be the one who was rattled.

Aunt Clara groaned and sat up slowly. Her eyes were bleary when she looked at us. "Why are you two even in here?" she snapped. "Don't you have anything better to do than to gawk at a woman in pain?"

"Shouldn't you go upstairs?" I replied. "It's quieter there, and you can be alone."

"No." The word shot out of her mouth like a bullet. "I'm perfectly fine where I am, thanks."

"But then Violet and I don't have anywhere to be," I protested. "We were going to watch TV later—" Just then, I noticed several small pink flames crowding together on her hands and forearms. "You're *afraid* to go up there," I blurted.

"I certainly am not." Aunt Clara shot me a glare. "I just prefer the living room—for now."

When Violet and I retreated to the kitchen, we learned that Dina had her own theory as to what was wrong with our aunt. "It happens when women reach a *certain age*," she told us while chopping carrots for our soup. "They become a little peculiar and prone to all kinds of problems. I'm sure she wants to stay down here because her bed is sticky and wet."

"Because she has *peed*?" Violet's eyes went wide.

"No." Dina chuckled. "Because she has been sweating something awful. I remember when Miss Lawrence went through the same thing . . . all the windows in the house had to be open all the time."

"Why was that?" I asked.

"Because she was so hot." Dina nodded and pursed her lips; the bone whales in her earlobes danced. "I suppose I'm up next, and I can't say I'm looking much forward to it."

"Why do you do it, then?" Violet had snatched a few slices of carrot from the chopping board and munched on them while she spoke.

"It happens to all women as they age," Dina told us. "There really isn't much to do about it."

"Does it give you headaches?" I asked with my heart in my throat. I had barely gotten used to having my period, and now some other horrible female thing had been revealed to me. It didn't explain Aunt Clara's fear, though.

"I suppose it could," Dina replied. "Though in your aunt's case I think *that* might have just as much to do with the merlot."

"We were going to watch TV," Violet said sulkily.

"Perhaps you can play cards in the winter garden instead?"

We tiptoed through the living room so we wouldn't disturb Aunt Clara. Violet carried the pack of cards. When we arrived, we pulled the double glass doors shut behind us before climbing onto the wicker chairs between the potted palms. We did play for a while, but we both kept a close eye on the doors to the living room and listened intently for sounds. Aunt Clara tended to stick to her habits, so her doing something different was unsettling to us both.

"What color is she?" Violet asked.

"Pink," I muttered.

"Pink means fear," Violet said, proud to remember what I had told her.

"Stop it." I sighed. "It doesn't matter what my stupid eyes see. Maybe the color doesn't *mean* anything."

"No." Violet gave me a pointed look. "I think it does, and you *know* it."

When the light bulbs in the ceiling blinked, none of us thought much about it at first. It was raining and blowing outside, so I suppose we both thought it was the wind. They kept on blinking, though, and it was very annoying—not because it wasn't light enough outside for us to see, but because it made it hard to concentrate. Then there was a hissing sound in the air, and I guess I thought that, too, was the wind at first.

Then we heard Aunt Clara scream.

Both Violet and I were out of our chairs at once, the playing cards scattered around our feet as we rushed for the door.

"Aunt Clara," Violet shouted before we had even entered the living room. It was a firework of blinking lights in there, and the air was filled with an even louder hissing. Aunt Clara sat on the couch, hugging a moss-green pillow. Her gaze darted from side to side as the wild blinking continued.

While Violet and I stood frozen by the glass doors, the books on the bookshelves started moving by themselves. Huge leather-bound volumes wriggled free from the tightly packed rows and either tumbled to the floor or shot into the air. A book on flowers barely missed Aunt Clara's head, while a book full of hiking maps hit the blinking snake lamp and thankfully killed the bulb. Another volume flew straight across the room and smacked into the wall not far from where we stood. I saw tadpoles again, too—just flashes of red as they rushed across the Persian rugs.

It was *dangerous*, I realized with a start. Dangerous and *crazy!*

"Dina!" I shouted over the insistent hissing. "Dina!" I called again, with my heart in my throat. Then I pushed Violet back through the glass doors and told her to stay put. I braved the living room with my arms held up in front of me, sidestepping the tadpoles as well as I could, while making my way toward the kitchen. Aunt Clara, too, was on her feet by then, still armed with the pillow, and then Dina finally arrived and rushed into the room, wide-eyed and pale.

"What on earth is going on in here?" she cried, before a volume of Dostoyevsky nearly took her ear off.

"It's bedlam!" Aunt Clara cried. "Bedlam!"

"Watch out!" I cried to Dina as *Religious Verses for the Home* came hurtling through the air. Both Aunt Clara and I were on the move by then, aiming for the safety of the hall, where Dina had already re-treated. She had found herself a sturdy black umbrella and held it up like a baseball bat, ready if another book came flying. So far, the chaos seemed to be limited to the living room, though.

The three of us huddled together in the hall and watched as the shelves slowly emptied: All the novels were already on the floor, and even the heaviest encyclopedia wriggled free and tumbled down in a flurry of small brown paper cups—the kind you find in chocolate boxes. All the while, the lights kept blinking, making me feel dizzy.

"Mrs. Woods, you're hurt," Dina exclaimed, and I followed her gaze to see a red mark on my aunt's high forehead. It almost matched the color of the pink flames that danced all over her skin.

She brushed Dina off. "Nothing to worry about. It was only a very slim volume."

Across the room, I noticed how Violet stood behind the double doors with her hands pressed to the clear glass. Her eyes were very large as she watched the flying books and the blinking lights, but she was smiling, too, as if she found it thrilling.

Swallowing my annoyance, I called to her. "Step back from the glass, Violet, it isn't safe!" She really should have heard me, as the glass doors were old and thin, but she didn't move an inch, so she either couldn't or *wouldn't* listen. I only hoped that an encyclopedia didn't fly across the room and crush the glass in front of her nose.

Suddenly, everything went quiet. The lights stopped blinking and the noise was gone. If it hadn't been for the books that lay scattered on the floor, the broken lamp, and the shards of china—small porce-lain dogs and shepherds that had been hit by the heavy missiles—it could have been another ordinary day. We all stood completely still, just looking in on the empty room for a very long time.

The first one to move was Violet, who slowly pushed the glass doors open and gingerly stepped into the room. We all held our breaths as she moved through the debris to reach us. She didn't seem very frightened herself, but made silly grimaces all through the crossing, as she tiptoed between books and sharp-edged china.

"He's gone now," she said breathlessly as she stepped into the hall; then she came to stand by my side and wrapped her arms tightly around me, as if she wanted to comfort me.

"How do you know?" Dina asked in a shivering voice. Her hands, too, were crowded with pink flames.

"I just do." Violet shrugged. "He was very angry, though."

"You don't say," Aunt Clara croaked, and inspected her rings to look for damage.

"What on earth just happened?" Dina's mouth hung open and her face still looked pale. None of us could give her an answer.

We all retreated to the kitchen, where Dina made us hot chocolate "for the shock." I suppose we all needed something to settle us. Dina even tipped a little rum into the adults' cups. Aunt Clara, who was normally never in the kitchen, had planted herself in a wooden chair and didn't leave it for the rest of the day. She just sat there, staring into the air, and accepted whatever Dina gave her: a cucumber sandwich; a warm blanket; a piece of salmon at dinnertime. Her pink flames calmed to a faint dull glow before they slowly were replaced by angry red ones.

The rest of us eventually braved the living room with brooms, plastic bags, and the vacuum cleaner. It was less scary when we did it together, but we still kept looking over our shoulders, worried that something would start moving again. At least Dina and I did; Violet was her usual happy self. She was in charge of putting the books back on the shelves and kept humming loudly while she worked.

When we were almost done and the sound of the vacuum cleaner filled the air, she came over and whispered in my ear, "It was *him*."

"It was who?" I asked, even though I somehow knew. The tadpoles had given it away.

"The man in the garden." She gave me a big smile, full of secrets and excitement.

"Don't be stupid," I hissed at her, but my heart was beating fast again, and I felt like I wanted to cry.

I saw the man from the garden myself that night. He was standing in the hallway outside Aunt Clara's room when I came out of the bathroom after brushing my teeth. I swallowed a scream and froze in place while my skin turned slick with ice-cold sweat.

He looked just like Violet had said, with clothes that looked burned and a wound on his cheek. He also had a crown of thinning blond hair, a bony nose, and thin lips that were lifted in a sneer. The ghost's skin was snow white but discolored in places; patches of blue and purple covered his hands, face, and neck. He smelled like wet dirt and rot. The wall-mounted lighting flickered, and red tadpoles squirmed around his feet.

He didn't seem to notice me as I stood there in the doorway, staring—my heart racing like crazy in my chest—but just looked right through me with cloudy blue eyes. Then he turned away, and I could see that the seeping wound on his cheek was nothing compared to the ones on his back: There were five or six of them—deep gashes of red that gaped toward me through his ripped, singed shirt.

He lifted his hand to Aunt Clara's door and knocked.

❧ VIOLET ☙
16

I had to go out to the hallway because Lily was there, and maybe not okay. I had heard her come out of the bathroom, then stop, and then the man had started making lots of noise. Not the hissing sound from before, but knocking on wood, and Lily hadn't moved at all, so she had to still be there and was probably scared. I had to tell her that the man only bothered Aunt Clara. I didn't know why that was, but I just knew, deep inside.

When I opened the door, I found my sister right outside it, her eyes glued to a spot farther down the hallway. She was wearing her blue pajamas and her mouth was half-open. Her eyes were very wide as she stared at the man who was banging on Aunt Clara's door. I didn't know why he did that, because he could just go through it, but maybe he just wanted to scare her. He did seem pretty scary, hammering on the door like that.

"Lily," I whispered. "Do you see him, too, now?" I couldn't be entirely sure that it wasn't just the sound that scared her.

Lily didn't look at me but nodded very slowly.

"He looks bad, doesn't he?" I whispered from the doorway. I couldn't help but feel happy that someone else finally saw him, even though I didn't want Lily to be scared. At least now she couldn't pretend that I didn't see what I did anymore.

"His back," Lily whispered hoarsely. "It's so bloody."

I nodded because it was true. "I don't think it was an accident."

Her head snapped in my direction. "What do you mean?"

I shrugged. "He couldn't have *fallen* to be like that. Something else must have happened to him."

Lily looked even more scared than before. "Why is he banging on Aunt Clara's door?"

I shrugged again, because I didn't know. "Maybe it was his room before?" I suggested.

"He doesn't look that old, Violet. His *suit* doesn't look that old." She gave me a frightened look and I knew what she was thinking. We were both wondering if the man was the lost Mr. Woods. At least it would explain why he was so interested in Aunt Clara. "Why do I see him now and not before?" Lily asked. "What did you *do* in the garden, Violet?"

I shrugged for a third time because I didn't know that either. I had thought that what I did would help—that he would vanish like the animals had—but instead he had started to move around and throw things. I had *tried* with the candle first. I had gone down there, all alone—even though it was scary—on the second night after he *asked*. Not even Irpa had wanted to come with me but had decided to wait inside on my bed. She didn't like the man much, and neither did I— mostly because he was so angry all the time. But he had *asked,* and the asking had stayed inside me like a headache or an itch— something that it wasn't possible to forget because it bothered me so much—and so I had taken matches, bread, salt, water, and a candle and gone outside, as close to the flower beds as I dared. When I lit the candle, the flame had shivered because I couldn't keep my hand steady, and lots of wax had dripped down on my fingers. I had looked at the man even though he was ugly, and he had been standing all quiet again, like he had done the day before. The candle never went out either, but kept burning and shivering, while he just stood there, smiling as if he thought I was stupid, until I blew out the flame and ran back inside.

It hadn't felt good at all, and the asking kept bothering me inside.

When I tried to talk to Irpa about it, she had just flapped her wings and showed me an image of the man walking away from the flower bed and up toward the house, so then I knew that he didn't want to disappear but wanted to be able to walk around. I asked Irpa if this was a good idea or not, but she just cocked her head and gave me nothing at all. Since then, I have found out that she is better at showing me what to do than telling me if it is the right thing. She can help, but she doesn't decide. I don't think Irpa worries at all if a thing is right or wrong. To her, they just *are,* which I like.

After the candle didn't work, I had spent days just thinking about it, looking at the man through the window, while the *asking* ached inside me. I knew that he wanted to walk around but didn't know how to make his feet not be stuck in the black glue. I wanted to help him, if only to stop the burn of the *asking*—and because I felt sorry for him, wandering around in the flower bed alone. It didn't seem right that he should be stuck there, bleeding and yelling, but I just didn't know what to do—until I suddenly did.

It was just like with the candle, as if something I had forgotten just came shooting into my brain. As if I had always known, somehow. It was easy after that. All I had to do was find the food and the cider and the candle and bring them with me outside.

The only thing I hadn't *known* inside me, but decided to do any-way, was to bring Lily along. It had been so scary the last time I went into the garden at night that I felt better having her there—*even* if she yelled at me and pretended that the man wasn't real.

And he *did* get loose. He could walk up to the house now and hang around, and even though I didn't like him much, I was happy to see that he could. It meant that what I did had worked, and he wasn't stuck in the flower bed anymore. I hadn't expected him to make such a mess, though—to throw all the books around—but then again it wouldn't be fair to expect that a man who had been stuck in a flower bed would come just wandering in and act all polite. Perhaps he just needed some time to get used to it, like Lily and I had needed time to get used to living at Crescent Hill. I thought that he was happy to be able to throw things around, though.

He still couldn't speak, but he had his own sound: a hissing in the air that reminded me of the noise from the TV or a radio when it didn't have a signal. When I asked Irpa about it, she showed me the man pulling something out of the air around him—some sort of energy, I assumed—which he used to be able to do stuff. He must have drawn in a lot of it, though, to be able to do all he did in the living room, and still have enough energy to bang on Aunt Clara's door.

As Lily finally stopped looking at the man and slipped into my room, closing the door behind us, I wondered if he really *was* Mr. Woods—and if so, what had happened to his clothes.

CLARA

17

It's not fair, was all I could think as I stood inside my bedroom and listened to the insistent knocking. I had long since buried the whole debacle. I had built myself up again and done whatever I could to preserve a shred of dignity.

So how could this be fair?

"Go away!" I stepped closer to the door and pressed my palms against the wood, then leaned in and whispered in my sternest voice, "You are not welcome here!"

Yet the knocking persisted.

"I am done with you!" I hissed through the door. "You are history, Timmy! You are dead!"

But my husband seemed not to hear me.

I slowly backed away and did not stop before my hip connected with the TV. Then I turned around and bent down to turn it on, hoping that other voices would drown out the knocking and that terrible hissing static, which rose and fell. I was sorely disappointed, though, as the screen showed nothing but more static. I left it on anyway, then threw myself down on the bed with a deep groan of frustration.

Of all the ways I had imagined my ill-fated marriage to come back and bite me, this had *not* been on the list. A *ghost*? It was ridiculous! And a malevolent one at that!

My forehead still hurt from the unkind assault.

"Go away," I hissed again, aimed in the direction of the door, but the insistent knocking continued. He only did it to annoy me—I knew that much. He could just as easily have come inside to slam the wardrobe doors or knock over my wine, but no. He preferred to stay out in the hallway, as useless in death as he had been in life.

"What are you going to do?" I asked the door. "*Annoy* me to death?" My voice faltered a little as I said that last part, since Timmy seemed to have grown some claws since his demise. I had a bump on my forehead to prove it.

How could I put an end to this madness—and what had spurred it on? Why was this happening *now*, just as I was about to start building my legacy? Could *that* be what had called him back? Was he truly so reluctant to see me thrive? I thought about Sebastian for a second, but we had been at it for *years,* so he could hardly be the reason for this encore.

Next I thought of the girls, as they were new additions to the household—the only thing of consequence to have changed since Timmy's days—but how could they possibly have anything to do with it? Had they perhaps gone up in the attic and played with his things? But no; I didn't think that was possible. The only one who had a key and went up there was me. I kept a box of chocolates there and would sometimes sit down in Cecilia's old rocking chair to savor a piece or two. I would certainly have noticed if someone had been there, and the layer of dust that covered his boxes had remained undisturbed ever since the girls arrived.

What then? Was it just some random occurrence? Timmy had always been a bit slow, so perhaps he had just discovered his new unfortunate circumstances. Or maybe it had to do with the alignment of the stars or some such nonsense.

I remained puzzled. And Timmy kept knocking.

"If you think this is the way to make me forget what you did, you are sorely mistaken," I called to him. "A few magic tricks are hardly enough to make *this* girl sweet!" I chuckled a little to myself, despite still feeling rattled. It was just Timmy, I told myself, and I knew that old fool like the back of my own hand. There was *no* way he was going to be allowed to keep tormenting me—even if he was dead.

"There's a time for everything, Timmy, and yours is up!" I reminded him, to no avail. My husband just kept knocking at my door. He always was a little hard of hearing.

"Time has been unkind to you," I told him next. "Death certainly hasn't done you any favors. How does Ellie feel about that? You truly look ridiculous—all blotched and ruined, and with filthy clothes . . . Have you seen yourself in the mirror lately?" I could not help but chuckle again, although I knew it made me seem like a lunatic. "I guess you really haven't," I noted, and sat up on the bed. "Well, death has made your ugly face even *uglier*, Timothy!" I shouted. In my chest my heart thumped hard and painful, and I wondered for a moment if I was about to have a stroke.

It just was not fair! What was buried was supposed to stay *dead*—although I had to admit that it rarely did. Even in that moment, my mother's voice came slithering back into my mind, as wicked and venomous as always: *Why can you never do anything right, Clara?*

It was because of her that I had married in the first place—because she had said that I never would. So, fool that I was, I had set out on a mission to prove her wrong. It sounded childish when I thought back on it—*ridiculous*, to be honest—but it was nevertheless true. Not only did I want a husband to prove my mother wrong, but I went out and *hunted* for one, sparing no expense to hitch myself to someone.

I suppose it wasn't *entirely* Iris's fault. It is how the world is, after all. If you lose in Cupid's lottery, people are prone to pity you—and I never could stand being pitied. I remember finding it highly inconvenient, however, to be burdened with society's conventions when all I ever wanted was to make my own mark upon the world. Yet conventions, I suppose, rule us all. I, for one, know I went into the world with a list in my head that was not of my making: *Money, Marriage, Mansion, Mark . . .*

The mark on the world always came last.

I had the money and the mansion already when Timmy and I met. I had to resort to a matchmaking service, as the pool of eligible bachelors in Ivory Springs was small to say the least. I even cursed fate a little bit for giving me a house in such a backwater, yet Crescent Hill was what I got, and there I would remain, as I had long since come to learn that it was unsellable for a fair price, what with it being so remote.

I remember how it was a bit exhilarating to receive the pink envelopes from the matchmaking agency, crammed with letters from possible suitors, and reading them while lying on my bed with some wine and secret chocolates. I particularly liked looking at the men's pictures and imagining myself on their arms. I wondered, too, what Iris would think of the various candidates, for there were quite a few. None of them had money, though—that was what *I* was for.

I think I settled on Timmy because he seemed so cultured in his letters, just the type to make Iris feel silly and small. He was an English major and a teacher by trade, which also suited me fine, as there was sure to be something for him to do around these parts, where knowledge is as scarce as rain in the Sahara and the schools are crying for half-decent staff. He was also flat broke, which suited me even better, and taller than me, which was a rarity.

I thought my money would be enough to keep him.

As it often is with matters of the heart, things were good at first between us. Since there are no proper hotel accommodations in this godforsaken town, he stayed with me at Crescent Hill from our very first meeting. He was meant to take one of the spare rooms, but of course, that was not how it turned out. It only took a few months before we were living together, and we really did seem to be a good fit in the beginning. Both of us were past the first blush of youth and wanted nothing but a good and fulfilling existence. We talked about books—or, he did—and diamonds—well, I did—and we both appreciated the finer things in life. Though he had nothing when we met, he came from money, and so we had that, too, in common.

I suppose I was enamored. It felt special to receive little gifts: flowers, perfume, or a nice scarf, and to find little notes on the nightstand in the mornings, wishing me a nice day. I did my best to give as good as I got and bought him little trinkets as well: some dainty little diamond cuff links, silk shirts, and a car. I couldn't wait for Iris to meet him—but of course I was disappointed on that count.

I called her a few months before the wedding. I remember how nervous I was, not entirely sure if she would even take my call. It was strange to hear her voice again after all the years of silence, and I was immediately afraid that I would lose her again; that she would feed me a line to slip away, as she had done so often in the past. She sounded just as before, only a little older. Her voice had taken on a darker timbre.

"I'm getting married, Iris," I quickly informed her. "And my fiancé and I would like to invite you—"

"Who are you getting married to?"

"Oh, he is a wonderful man. His name is Timothy Woods and he is an educated—"

"How did you manage to make that happen?"

"Oh, it was quite easy," I purred. "He simply fell in love with me."

"Nonsense." Iris laughed. "You are hardly fresh and dewy anymore. No matter what he has told you, there must be another reason."

"I'm not like you, Iris. Sometimes there are no hidden motives." I obviously chose not to mention his finances.

"You don't even believe that yourself." She was right, of course, and it annoyed me.

"Whatever the reason, will you come?" I asked.

"I'm very busy, Clara. Amanda is pregnant, as you may know, and I'm expecting my first grandchild!" At once, she was changed as if by the tap of a magical wand; her tone was all butterflies and sunshine.

"How wonderful. Congratulations," I muttered. "It's only one day, though—the wedding."

"Oh, Clara." She sighed. "You know it will never last."

"You don't *know* that," I replied. My free hand was balled up in a fist so tight that it hurt. "You cannot know that for sure!"

"Oh, believe me, Clara, I *do*."

Iris died four months later of a stroke. I did not attend her funeral.

Timmy and I had a wonderful wedding, though, small and intimate. I wore my best diamonds.

But before too long, things soured between us.

It is terrible when you wake up one day and find you have become a cliché, sister to countless hapless, sad, and angry women all through space and time. It's not the betrayal, truly, that stings, but the way it devalues your worth, both in your own eyes and others'. Society has dictated that, too: The betrayed must carry the burden of disdain, pity, and ridicule.

As if it is all their fault.

I cannot say when my husband started sleeping with Ellie Anderson, but it had to be sometime after our third anniversary. I was already an avid diamond collector at that point and was often away to attend fairs and auctions, so I suppose he took the opportunity.

It was just small signs at first: a strange floral smell in the bathroom; a smear of lipstick on his lapel in a shade I didn't wear. Once my suspicion was roused, however, and I truly started to look into it, the evidence was stark. I found notes in his pockets and dark, curly hairs in my bed. There were scratches from fingernails on his back, and a pair of ladies' gloves on the mantelpiece. They truly were sloppy—though perhaps poor old Timmy thought me so meek or desperate that I would keep him no matter what.

An afternoon spent in my car outside the schoolhouse with binoculars told me with ease just whom he was seeing. Ellie Anderson was younger than me, and pretty. Her hair was black and curly and reached all the way to her waist. She was also in hiding from a jealous ex-husband, but I didn't know that at the time. The fact would suit me fine, though, later—when the illicit pair had run away without a trace. It made sense to disappear when someone bad was on your trail.

I felt oddly empty as I drove away from the school—just a sad, aging lady, worth nothing at all. I was plagued by the sound of Iris's laughter, mocking and disdainful. I imagined the pity from my fellow citizens—people I didn't care for at all—when the affair became public knowledge. I thought I could hear the whispers already: *There goes that sad, lonely old scarecrow. There is poor Clara who cannot even hold a man. There is that dreadful divorced lady whose money wasn't even enough . . .*

But I would have shouldered that—I would have. I would have licked my wounds like a hurt lioness and continued. I would have dusted off my dignity and polished it to a shine.

If only he hadn't come for my diamonds.

It was just luck—or fate—that I found out. It was all due to a phone call that I happened to take on a day when I was supposed to be out. It was from a jewel appraiser in the city, so of course I thought it was for me at first, and it took a few awkward minutes of confusion before I realized that it was *Timmy* he wanted to talk to.

Timmy, who had no interest in jewels at all.

"What do you want my husband for?" I asked the puzzled appraiser, whom I later would come to know as Glitter Bear.

"He wanted to make an appointment to come in with some rings," he replied, much too flustered to be discreet.

"Rings, huh? What rings?" I asked.

"Diamond rings," he said. "I suppose he wanted to sell them."

It took me a moment longer to realize what this meant. Yes, my husband was going to leave me, and yes, he meant to rob me to do so. Not only would he take my dignity, but he wanted to take my darlings, too.

Of course it was the final straw.

The next morning, I told Timmy I was going to an auction in an attempt to acquire a vintage necklace; then I drove two towns over and soothed my nerves with a sundae. When I came back, I parked a little away from the house, then got out my binoculars and slowly approached Crescent Hill from the woods. It was not hard to see what was going on. The oaf had taken his mistress into the winter garden, and they were both sitting there, snug under a brown blanket that had once covered Cecilia Lawrence's bed. They had been in my wine cellar, too, and chosen a rich Amarone to set the mood. I hoped it gave them both blue teeth. They had lit candles as well, and looked as snug as could be in my winter garden, as if nothing bad could happen to them at all.

I waited until they went upstairs, as then they wouldn't see me arrive. I rightly assumed that they would be far too preoccupied with each other once the bedroom door was closed.

Next to diamonds, I am fairly certain that a woman's best friend is a well-honed ax.

It was a horrible end to a tragic misstep; I should never have gotten married at all. I could see that clearly, in hindsight. But the ending was also unnecessary. If he had only kept his sticky paws off my diamonds, none of it would have happened. As things turned out, however, it truly was nothing more than he deserved.

I sorely missed holding said diamonds, as I lay there on the bed and listened to my late husband's efforts to get my attention, but I didn't deem it safe to bring them out. I worried what would happen if he got his ghost hands on my jewelry box. Maybe he still wanted the stones.

It just wasn't fair, at all. I had gotten *rid* of the man, so *how* could this be fair?

I had put him down once before, though, and could surely do so again.

I just had to figure out how.

LILY

18

"It *is* Mr. Woods. There's no doubt about it." It was about a week after the first attack in the living room, and Dina was stirring the tomato soup we were going to have for lunch. "I would know his face anywhere, and he even came to see me last night."

"Did he?" I asked from the kitchen table. Violet wasn't down yet and I was a little relieved, since I wanted to talk to Dina by myself.

"Uh-huh." Dina nodded. "I was just laying out the fish for Mrs. Woods when the lights in here started blinking, and when I turned around, he just stood there, stock-still, staring at me with dead eyes." I knew what she meant by dead eyes. I still couldn't help but see them in my head, all cloudy and broken.

"But what is he *doing* here?" I whispered. "Didn't he disappear without a trace?"

Dina shrugged but didn't turn to look at me. She didn't say anything either.

"Maybe he wants Aunt Clara to know that he is dead?" I suggested. "But I'm sure he could have done that without being so angry."

These had been difficult days for all of us. The ghost attacked when we least expected it, and it usually was long enough between the attacks for us to start thinking that maybe he had gone away again.

Violet and I had found our own way of handling it. As soon as the lights started blinking and the hissing sound arrived, we would run to the dining room and dive under the table. No matter what the man in the garden—Mr. Woods—threw around, we were pretty safe under there. Not only was the tabletop made of sturdy oak, but Violet also believed that the dining room lady somehow protected us. My sister had even stored some pillows and a blanket under the table and had started calling it our "fort."

Aunt Clara and Dina couldn't fit with us under the table, though, and had to find other hiding places. Dina would often lock herself in the closet in the hall, while Aunt Clara ran into the pink-and-brown bathroom downstairs—although at least once the ghost had followed her inside, and there had been some terrifying moments while Dina looked for the spare key and Aunt Clara screamed. She got a bruise on her cheek after that attack, as a hard piece of soap had jumped from the dish. Another time, she got a cut on her hand from an exploding teacup. No one else had gotten hurt, though—yet.

"Maybe Mr. Woods has reason to be angry," Dina muttered from the stove. The air was slowly filling with the metallic scent of boiling tomatoes. "No one quite knows what happened between them before he disappeared. Perhaps he has unfinished business with her?"

"Maybe," I agreed, and yawned. None of us had had much sleep since Mr. Woods's return. For me, it was the idea of him pacing in the hallway that bothered me the most. He was always up there when I was about to go to bed, and even sometimes when I went upstairs to practice with Gertrud; I had never actually seen him anywhere else. He always stood outside Aunt Clara's door, knocking—although I didn't see why, as he had already proven many times over that he could go wherever he liked.

"There must be *something* we can do," I said, and thought of Violet. She was the one who had made him come, so maybe she could reverse it somehow?

"I don't know a lot about these things," Dina replied, "but it's my understanding that troublesome hauntings stop when the ghost's unresolved business has been taken care of."

"Then, what does he want?"

"Oh, I'm sure I wouldn't know." Dina sounded as dry as a twig, and a few lime-green flames leapt up on her skin. "Your aunt might, though."

"Didn't he disappear with his mistress?" I remembered what Aunt Clara had told us when we first met.

Dina nodded. "Ellie Anderson was her name. The two of them worked together at the school in town. I suppose that's one of the reasons why your aunt is reluctant to let you visit. There was a lot of gossip at the time."

I shuddered as I rose from the chair and went to the counter to help Dina slice the bread. "He looks horrible, though. I wonder what happened to him . . . all those wounds . . ."

"Yes." Dina stared down into the bubbling soup, not even bothered by the hot fumes, it seemed. "It must have been something bad." Her voice sounded strained; small pink flames had started erupting on her arms. I had stopped blinking the colors away. They felt useful to me now, since I was so scared all the time. I liked to know what people were feeling—or what I *thought* they were feeling, anyway. I had also discovered that the less I tried to ignore them, the more colors I saw. I hadn't really decided yet if this was a good thing or not.

"Isn't there anything else we can do? Sprinkle salt or hang crosses?" I had read up a little since the haunting began, but the Lawrence library didn't have many books on ghosts, just a few novels about haunted castles and family curses, which I had devoured—twice.

"I think that only works on demons," Dina replied.

"Oh." That wouldn't help, then, as Mr. Woods was clearly not that. He was just a very angry, very unhappy dead man.

"But why did Violet see him in the garden?" I asked next, careful not to give too much away. I didn't think Dina would appreciate my little sister feeding the dead.

"Now, *that*," Dina murmured while spooning hot soup into blue ceramic bowls, "is a *very* good question—" She stopped abruptly when the kitchen door opened and Aunt Clara came inside, tired-looking and wearing a tattered pink housecoat that I knew had belonged to Miss Lawrence. Her whole body seemed to be haloed in an orange glow, which meant that she was exhausted.

"What are you two gossiping about?" She strode into the middle of the room. "Is my fish ready?" she continued without waiting for an answer.

Just then, the usual flickering of the lights started, followed by the hissing sound. I threw the knife down on the counter and dove for the kitchen table, while Aunt Clara and Dina started for the door. They didn't even reach it, though, before the drawers in the counter started opening and shutting on their own, and suddenly the heavy drawer of cutlery sprang open and a shower of forks rained down on them.

"Goodness," Dina cried. She crouched down and shielded her head with her arms.

Aunt Clara decided to brave the rain and continued moving, only to be stopped by a sharp-tined fork burying itself in her forearm.

Aunt Clara screamed, and I screamed, too. From under the kitchen table, I could see a little blood dripping down on the floor tiles.

Then it was quiet.

It took us all a few seconds to realize that the attack was over— that the air was silent and the lights weren't blinking.

Dina slowly rose from the floor and watched with a grimace as Aunt Clara pulled the fork out of her arm. "I'll find the first aid kit," she said.

"Good." My aunt sounded both tired and angry; the orange glow had been replaced with flames of blue pain and red anger. She slumped down in a chair as I scrambled out of hiding.

"I'll tell you one thing." She looked at me. "Never, *ever* marry." Her gaze dropped to her bleeding arm. "That advice is yours for free."

❦ VIOLET ❧
19

After we had eaten lunch, Dina, Lily, and I went for a hike. The woods around Crescent Hill weren't really meant for hiking, but it had still become one of our favorite things to do. There weren't any real tracks—only deer trails—and lots of windfall that slowed us down, but there was also fresh air and thick moss, and lots and lots of trees. Being in the woods made me feel lighter. It was easier to laugh and talk in there, and not worry so much about Aunt Clara and the ghosts. Dina, too, seemed happier on our hikes than she was in the kitchen. She always brought a basket along in case I found something I wanted to take back, like funny-shaped rocks, twigs, or twisted roots.

Lily was in a bad mood, though, and not even the woods seemed to help. Walking beside her almost felt like walking alongside a thundercloud. When we had hiked for a while, she grabbed my arm to hold me back and let Dina get a little ahead of us.

"You have to put him back," she whispered. "He is *dangerous!*"

I shook my head; that wasn't how it worked.

"But *why*? Do you want us to get hurt? This is not a *game*, Violet!"

"He used to be stuck out there—in the flower bed. I don't want him to be stuck again," I said.

"I don't care if he is stuck. He stabbed Aunt Clara with a fork!"

"But he is only throwing them at *her*," I argued. "If we stay away from Aunt Clara, we'll be fine."

Lily went quiet for a while, thinking it over. "I suppose they didn't like each other much by the end," she muttered, and was probably right, with Mr. Woods leaving her and all. "There's no way we can avoid Aunt Clara, though. The house is too small—and just because he's aiming for her, it doesn't mean that someone else won't get hurt . . . Violet, won't you *please* put him back?"

I shook my head again. "He has as much right to be here as anyone else—"

"No, Violet, he doesn't. He is *dead*. The flames, you know—the colors . . . his are broken and squirming all over. They look like giant tadpoles. He just isn't *natural* anymore."

"That doesn't mean he doesn't *want* things," I said, since I knew for a fact that he did. He had wanted to be free from the flower bed, for one.

"Maybe not, but he is dead, so he can't have it. This isn't a game," she said again. "And I'm no detective, but I suppose that what he *wants* is for someone to find out what happened to him—who gave him those awful wounds—but even if we found who did it, they are *dangerous*, Violet. No normal person goes around hurting people like that. You have to put him back at once!" She used her annoying Mama voice again.

"Mama and Papa would have *wanted* me to find out. Something *bad* happened to Mr. Woods, and they would have *wanted* me to help him." I hadn't planned on finding out what had happened to him, but I definitely would if he *asked*.

"I don't think Mama meant *ghosts* when she told us to always be kind." Lily's nostrils flared and she lifted her chin a little. "I think she meant that we should share what we have—"

"She said to always help when we can."

Lily didn't say anything else, but just spun around and started walking fast to catch up with Dina, not even bothering to check if I kept up. I thought she was very mad at me, which was *so* unfair. All I had done was help Mr. Woods, who *really* didn't like it in the flower bed.

I didn't think I had done anything wrong.

Finally, we all met under a large oak tree that had become our usual place to take a break and tie my shoelaces. Dina gave us apples and had also brought tea, which we drank out of hard plastic cups. The sun had come out just then and filtered through the trees, making everything seem golden. Suddenly, the woods were so peaceful. While Dina and Lily sat down on a fallen trunk and closed their eyes to soak up the sun, I explored the ground around us, hoping to find some interesting bird feathers, or maybe the paw print of a bear. What I found instead was so much better, though. They were tiny little mushrooms, small and white, nestled deep down in the moss. "Look at these babies," I said to the others.

"What is it?" Lily had come to stand beside me and look over my shoulder. "Oh, Violet!" she suddenly cried out. "Don't touch them!"

"I won't," I snapped, angry and scared at the same time. "But why?"

"They are purple," she said quietly under her breath so that Dina wouldn't hear it. When I turned my head to look at her, her eyes were wide, and she had closed her hands to fists by her sides, so I figured that she was upset. Purple meant dangerous, I suddenly remembered, and a little thrill passed through my body. "What are they?" Lily asked Dina, who came sauntering over to where we were, still holding the brown teacup in her hand. She cocked her head when she looked down at the mushrooms.

"They could be just innocent button mushrooms"—she scratched her chin—"but they could also be destroying angels; we have them around here."

"What is that?" Lily sounded panicked.

"*Enormously* toxic mushrooms." Dina gave us both pointed looks. "Joe's grandmother died after eating an unhappy mushroom soup."

"They're *not* button mushrooms," Lily said, and nudged my calf with the tip of her shoe, wanting me to move away from there.

"Why are they called angels?" I asked, not moving as much as an inch.

"When they get bigger, they grow little skirts, see? Like angel wings." Dina showed with her free hand, brushing it around her hips. The basket dangled from the crook of her arm.

"These are just babies, though." I rose and wiped my hands on my thighs. "We'll visit them again when they get bigger, to see the skirts."

"No," Lily snapped. "We won't. We're out here to *forget* about death and danger, not to seek it out." I thought that was a silly thing to say, as there were few places in the world as dangerous as the woods—any fairy tale could tell you that. And I still thought I would come back to see the mushroom skirts. If Lily didn't want to, that was *her* problem.

It was late when we came back to Crescent Hill, and Aunt Clara wasn't around downstairs. We didn't hear any hissing noise or something bumping against a wall, though, so perhaps she was just sleeping upstairs.

We had decided to watch TV after dinner, but Lily took so long helping Dina with the dishes that I visited the old lady instead. We had started playing rock-paper-scissors together, not for any reason but to pass the time. I figured she was lonely in the dining room, because she was always so happy when I came to play with her—and she usually won, too, but that was just fine by me.

We had just finished our twenty-first round when Lily came in behind me. I didn't pay any attention to her, though, because something was happening with the lady. She had suddenly stopped and was just looking at me. The staring reminded me a little of Mr. Woods in the garden, which I didn't like—but then I *liked* the old woman, so I didn't mind that much when she started poking in my head.

"What are you looking at?" Lily sounded anxious.

"The old woman, of course."

"Oh, Violet," she moaned.

"I think she *wants* something."

"Violet, no! No more helping the ghosts." Lily stomped her foot so hard that I felt the floor shake a little. After Mr. Woods came back, she didn't pretend that the ghosts weren't there anymore, but she *really* didn't like them. "I'll never forgive you if you help her."

"But she's *asking*," I said. "And when they *ask*, I have to."

CLARA

20

I first learned of Cecilia Lawrence's return at breakfast, while trying to catch a particularly slippery melon ball. I was so intent on this task that I might not even have noticed the tall, pale woman who stood next to the dining room table—the very one she had called her own—if she hadn't used her gray ghostly fingers to flick the spoon right out of my hand.

I let slip a curse and was already out of my chair to fetch the stray piece of cutlery before looking up to see her standing there, wearing her old pink cotton nightgown, with her hair up in a bun. She looked a little younger—and honestly, better—than she had the last time I had seen her alive. Her pallor left much to be desired, though. It was ashen and quite ghastly. The blue half-moons under her eyes—a permanent fixture for as long as I knew her—had deepened to a solid black.

There was no doubt that the woman was dead.

"That's a mug I had *not* expected to see again," I told her, straightening up with the spoon in my hand. "What on earth compelled *you* to come back?" It had been bad enough with Timmy, and now the old hag was here? What was happening to my life? What was going on in my *house*?

Cecilia didn't seem to have heard me. She just stood there, still as a statue, looking with burning eyes at nothing at all. I blinked, twice, just to make sure that she wasn't a hallucination brought on by my anger and a profound lack of sleep.

The woman stubbornly remained, though.

"What?" I asked her. "Are you just going to stand there and watch me eat?" I added a brief laugh, which came out broken and brittle. "Well, be my guest. It's not as if I didn't have to suffer through *your* meals a thousand times."

I sat back down and wiped off the spoon with the napkin. Then I aimed for another melon ball, scooped it up, and lifted it to my lips, but she was there again at once—quick as a desert viper—and flicked the luscious melon ball off the spoon to roll across the table.

"What nonsense is this?" I rose to my feet and aimed to stare down the ghost, but she was back in her statuesque state, just staring into the wall. When I had stood there for quite some time myself, I sat down again, determined not to let her see how unsettled the whole thing had made me. But more than unnerved, I felt angry.

"What *is* this, Cecilia?" I said before even attempting the egg. "Are you trying to get back at me? Is this your way of saying that I treated you poorly?" I laughed again, and this time it came out a little stronger. "You were a demanding lady," I told her. "Nothing but a hassle . . . You just made it so *hard* to be sweet to you." Now I did embark on the egg, and put it down on the napkin. I placed my palm on top of it and applied just enough pressure. Then I started rolling it back and forth, and the eggshell gave way with satisfying cracking sounds. I looked at the ghost all the while. When the egg was all naked, white, and perfect in my hand, I gingerly lifted it to my mouth while watching Cecilia all the time.

She still got the better of me, though, and before I even knew it, she had lashed out with her wrinkled talons and whipped the egg right out of my hand.

I stared at my empty fingers, utterly surprised, then turned back to the ghost again. Cecilia stood as before, just staring at the wall. "I must say, you are a lot quicker in death than you were in life." I was begrudgingly impressed. "Is this about the porridge?" I asked, though I was no longer expecting an answer. "Or the raisin soup?" I folded the napkin over the empty eggshell. "What else was I to do, Cecilia? You wouldn't sign the papers!" I just couldn't help but berate her a little. Whatever had happened between us back then, none of it would have come to pass if she hadn't been so incredibly stubborn. "It brought me no pleasure to deny an old lady her food," I said. "*Nor* her medication," come to think of it. "If only you had signed a little sooner, those terrible weeks would never have happened, and I treated you well after that, didn't I? I cooked your broth myself and had Dina make that pudding you liked. It all worked out, don't you see?"

Cecilia didn't seem to see anything at all. Her eyes were as black and slick as oil and night, and there appeared to be a fire burning deep within them. I didn't think she was happy with me.

"And I gave you ample medication in the end," I couldn't help but point out. A smile was tugging at my lips. "*All* the medication you wanted, and then some. You should be grateful, really."

Just then, Dina arrived at the door to break up our little tête-à-tête. "Oh my goodness!" she exclaimed. "Miss Lawrence?" The water pitcher she carried promptly fell to the floor; I could feel cool droplets hit my calves even under the table.

I rolled my eyes a little. "Yes, Dina, I'm sorry to say it appears that we have acquired another *guest*."

"Oh my goodness!" the housekeeper said again, and came closer to inspect the apparition. She nearly stepped on the peeled egg. "Miss Lawrence?" she asked. "Is that you?"

Cecilia didn't answer her either.

"It seems like the afterlife has devoured whatever was left of her sparkling wit," I informed her. "Perhaps hell is overbooked and is sending people back—"

"Miss Lawrence would *never* go there!" Dina looked at her former mistress with adoration. The sight annoyed me to no end. "I'm surprised that she didn't come back with white wings attached to her shoulders."

"Well, she didn't. And we have to get rid of her."

"But why is she here? What does she want?" Dina couldn't take her eyes off the dead woman.

I shrugged. "Who knows? But she cannot stay, that's for sure."

I gave up on breakfast after that, and when I looked in on the dining room a few minutes later, Cecilia was finally gone. Since Timmy's return, I had learned a little something about the nature of ghosts, however, so I wasn't stupid enough to think it was over. I had hoped she would give it a rest for a while, though, seeing how she had so brazenly made herself known that morning, but I was sadly disappointed on that score.

It was the very same thing at lunch. I pierced a piece of fish; she whipped it off the fork. I picked up a slice of cucumber; she promptly flicked it away. Her fingers left behind a reek of upturned dirt, formaldehyde, and the chalky scent of crushed pills.

I tried so hard not to get agitated. I had learned from my encounters with Timmy that he seemed to get worse the more upset I got, so I did my best to remain calm around him, even when objects went flying. I figured the same trick would work on Cecilia, but she made it so very difficult—and my belly was aching with hunger.

It didn't make things better that Dina and the girls came in to gawk at the spectacle. They stood by the door that led to the kitchen and stared: Dina in awe, Lily appalled, and Violet seemingly thrilled. She even smiled and waved at Miss Lawrence.

I had to give up on lunch, too, and as a final indignity, when I sought the comfort of my secret chocolates in the living room, the Strawberry Passion was flicked right out of my fingers. I couldn't even have a taste of a sweet! She truly didn't mean to let me have any nourishment at all—and I could hardly begrudge her for that. In fact, I found some admiration for the old hag that I had never had in her lifetime.

Death had toughened her up.

But by dinnertime, I was starving, and—being ever the fool—I raced to the dining room as soon as the clock struck half past six. It was a meat day, too, and I had ordered Dina to serve me a fine piece of turkey on a bed of asparagus and salad greens. I had been looking forward to it all week, thinking it a fine reward for putting up with Timmy's antics.

I had barely sat down, however, before she was there, silently standing sentry. Her ugly dead face hovered above me, and it didn't take a genius to know what would happen if I dared cut into the delicious turkey breast that lay there so tantalizing on my plate.

Instead, I grabbed the food, rose, and went into the kitchen.

The happy chatter died at once when I entered the room. The rest of the household was already there, gathered around a steaming pot of turkey stew on the table. They all looked at me when I came in, clutching my plate with white-knuckled fingers.

When they were all done gawking, Dina pulled out a chair and said, "Take a seat, Mrs. Woods." So I did.

It was doubtlessly awkward, and it felt like a defeat. I had prided myself on always taking my meals in the dining room, sitting by the end of the table. I had earned that spot; it was mine to keep, but now I had been evicted, and my nieces were there to see.

While the rest of them kept chewing their stew, I stared at my plate, reluctant to touch as much as an asparagus spear.

"You have to eat *something*." Dina addressed me as if I was one of the girls. "I'm sure she'll leave you alone in here. Just try."

I gritted my teeth and grabbed the fork. It was true that there was no sign of Miss Lawrence—yet. I stabbed a little piece of raw spinach and aimed it at my mouth.

The leaf went flying.

Angry now, I went for a long green asparagus spear, but it didn't go any better. The only saving grace of the moment was that she didn't show her long-dead face but remained an invisible presence; I'm sure it was to save the others' appetite. Cecilia had always been very careful not to bother other people—unless it was me, of course.

"Here, Aunt Clara." Young Violet, to my left, leaned over and took the fork out of my hand. She stabbed another vegetable and lifted the utensil to my mouth. Her lips were curved in a gentle smile.

Slowly—nervously—I parted my lips and carefully nibbled the offered food.

It actually seemed to work.

I opened my mouth a little wider and took a bite of the asparagus. No one stole my food.

As long as Violet fed me, it seemed, Miss Lawrence would stay her hand. As soon as I tried to lift the fork myself, however, she was there, lashing out.

The indignity was unbearable. If I hadn't been so hungry, I would have marched right out of there. To be fed like a small child—or an infirm old lady!

Cecilia truly knew how to make me suffer; this was worse than any of Timmy's pathetic attacks. It didn't help that they all watched me: Violet, of course, but also Dina and Lily, the latter all but forgoing her own food to revel in my disgrace. She looked an awful lot like Iris just then, with the arrogant tilt of the head.

But I was hungry, so I ate.

When I finally retired to my room that night, I had barely had time to put my head on the pillow before Timmy started knocking at my door, accompanied by that horrid hissing. I had finally figured out *why* he knocked, after sifting through an unpleasant series of long-buried memories. He used to do this—relentlessly knock—when we had had a fight and he had been evicted from our bedroom to spend the night in the owl room instead. He never handled rejection well and would come late in the night, when his angry stewing had brought him to a place of rage, insisting that I let him back inside—as if he had a *right* to my company, and as if he could make me relent if he became a big enough nuisance.

It had been childish and pathetic and it absolutely never worked. I had stocked up on wax earplugs and kept a few bottles of wine in one of the wardrobes to get through those long and dreadful nights—but it had bothered me, it truly had . . . The knocking had been like a drilling in my head, and clearly, he remembered, even after death, just how much I despised this behavior. And clearly, just because of that, he had decided to keep it up.

Now that Cecilia, too, was back, I finally contemplated leaving. Why should I stay and suffer when I could just pack a few bags and be gone? I had gone to great lengths to be rid of the two of them, so why should I remain for their encore?

I had already lifted the phone off the hook to call Sebastian when my pride got the better of me. Timmy and Cecilia were in their current sorry state because *I* had put them there, and letting them get to me now would unravel all of my good work.

If they thought they could guilt me into a teary confession, they surely had another think coming. I was Clarabelle Diamonds—just as hard and indestructible as my beloved jewels—while they were nothing but spirits from the ashes, and I *swore* I would put them back where they belonged. I would be damned if I was to be scared or starved out of my own home!

You really would think they knew better than to mess with me by now.

LILY

21

I knew that Violet had done something even before I saw Miss Lawrence's ghost myself. I figured it out that same morning, just as Dina was done scooping melon balls for Aunt Clara's breakfast. Violet and I had already eaten by then but were both still lingering in the kitchen with our tea.

When Dina went to put the fruit back in the refrigerator, she suddenly stopped what she was doing and started rummaging in there, lifting out cheeses and pieces of cold cuts.

"That's strange," she murmured to herself. "I could have sworn . . ." I looked up just then to see how Violet's gaze was glued to the tabletop, while a deep pink color rose in her cheeks—her telltale sign of guilt.

"What did you do?" I mouthed, but she pretended not to notice.

"Have either of you girls seen the side of bacon we bought last week? Or the beef bones?"

I shook my head as I hadn't seen any of it, but I felt pretty sure who had. I glared at Violet and kicked her shin under the table. She grimaced and winced from the impact, even though I had barely touched her.

"I saw the fox again." Violet turned around in the chair to face Dina, and I was secretly impressed by how easily she lied, even though I didn't like it. "It looked *so* hungry," she went on. "I just *had* to help it."

This time, Dina was less willing to overlook the theft, though. A few annoyed flickers of red had erupted on her neck. "You have to tell me if you take anything from the refrigerator," she said as she straightened up. "Especially if it's food that you know I'm going to use for something. Now I have to take another trip to the supermarket to replace it."

"I'm sorry." Violet sounded meek. "I wouldn't have taken it if I'd had another choice."

Dina sighed and went back to the counter, carrying two eggs in the palm of her hand. The red flames abruptly disappeared. "I'm sure the fox appreciated the gesture. No wonder it comes back if you keep feeding it so well."

"Maybe it just can't find food anywhere else." Violet sounded sorry for the made-up fox.

"Maybe it's sick," Dina suggested. "Take care not to get too close."

It was just like the last time, though: meat and bones. I felt sure that if Dina had looked for it, she would have found something sweet lacking, too. I knew without a doubt that Violet had ignored me and "helped" the old lady. My whole belly ached just from thinking about living with another ghost.

As it turned out, Miss Lawrence wasn't so bad, though. Even if she was a problem for Aunt Clara, she didn't make a mess like Mr. Woods. We didn't see her often, but when we did, she just stood there in the dining room and stared. She did *look* a little frightening—her skin was very gray and her eyes were very black, and she smelled bad—but she didn't seem to be dangerous . . . to us. She wasn't really that dangerous to Aunt Clara either, although I figured it had to be hard to have to be fed by others all the time. But at least she was nothing like the *awful* Mr. Woods, with his banging and hissing and flying forks.

Miss Lawrence being back was difficult for Dina, though. On the first day, after we had all been out in the dining room to look at the new ghost, she made herself another cocoa with rum, even though it was a very hot day, and the rest of us drank iced tea.

"I'm sorry, girls," she said, and slumped down in a chair. "It just bothers me to see her like that. It was bad enough when she was sick, but this is just horrible . . ."

I gave Violet an angry look. This was all her fault. "I'm so sorry, Dina," I said. "I know that you cared about her."

"*Cared* about her?" Dina chuckled a little. "She was all the family I had, if not by blood. I had known her all of my life, you see. My mother used to work for the Lawrences," she explained, while a light blue mist formed around her, telling me she was sad. "I was with Cecilia through it all: victories and challenges, heartbreaks and joy . . . She was like a sister to me, although a much older one."

"Would you rather she hadn't come?" Violet asked, and I was a little happy to see how she didn't seem so sure of herself anymore. Maybe she, too, realized how this had been a bad idea.

"I would rather not see her a mindless ghost, yes." Dina downed her cocoa. "But I suppose that's all that she is now, forever an old lady, forever trapped in this house." She lifted a hand to wipe her tears, the blue mist pulsating gently around her like something out of the sea. "She died in there, you know—in the dining room. She was so weak by the end that we always had to be at hand, so we had the dining room set taken to the attic and put up a bed in there . . . She lasted only a couple of weeks after that, although now it does seem like she never left." Dina sounded pained.

"Maybe she didn't *want* to leave." Violet wore a stubborn expression.

"Why?" I asked, feeling angry again. "Just so she can play with Aunt Clara's food?"

"Oh, but there's a lot of resentment there." Dina sounded serious. "Your aunt was the one in charge of feeding Miss Lawrence as she grew weaker, and they had many battles over the porridge. Something must be lingering."

"She gave Aunt Clara everything she had, though, so she must have liked her well enough." Aunt Clara had told us about it many times—how grateful Miss Lawrence had been, and how generous.

"People have all sorts of reasons for picking an heir." Dina's expression turned dark. "Sometimes it's not about 'liking' someone; sometimes it's about—"

"Maybe she wants Aunt Clara's melon balls for herself," Violet suggested. "Maybe she misses fresh fruit."

Dina smiled at that. "Yes," she agreed. "Perhaps that's it."

But when Violet had gone upstairs to get her spelling book for our lesson, Dina became serious again. She looked at me for a moment across the scarred tabletop, and some silver mingled with the blue when she said, "I always found it strange that Miss Lawrence willed everything to your aunt, seeing how the two of them didn't get along . . . I suppose that's why I stayed on. It just never really sat right with me, and I wanted to know a little more . . . Then it became a habit, I suppose, being at Crescent Hill."

The words made me feel uneasy. "What do you mean?" I asked. "Why do you think Miss Lawrence did it, then?"

Dina shrugged and poured a little more rum into the dregs of her cocoa. "I probably shouldn't say anything. You are still so young . . ."

"No, please, tell me!" Suddenly, I was desperate to know.

"No, I . . ." Dina stared down into the stained cup. "Let's just say that I think Violet may be right, and that Cecilia *did* come back because she wanted to be here. That she came back for a reason." There was almost more silver than blue around her now, which meant she was telling me the truth.

"What reason do you think?" I stared at Dina open-mouthed, but suddenly she was done talking.

"Oh, I don't know, Lily. Perhaps I'm just a crazy old lady." She laughed but it sounded insincere. The silvery halo disappeared. "You'll be pleased to know, though, that my husband asked his sister, who knows a little about such things, and she told him that angry ghosts who appear out of nowhere can disappear just as quickly, too. We might not have to live with this forever."

I smiled politely, but I had my doubts, seeing how our ghosts hadn't just "appeared out of nowhere." They had appeared because *Violet* made it happen—so maybe they wouldn't disappear again until *she* made that happen as well. And that was something she refused to do, and I couldn't figure out why.

I talked to her later, while we sat with her spelling book between us on the table. M-I-S-E-R-Y, she wrote. R-E-V-E-N-G-E. Dina was upstairs just then, so we had the kitchen to ourselves.

"I'm sorry, Violet, but the ghosts are making our life here so much harder," I said between the words. "We want to make this easy on ourselves . . . It's *less* than four years. We can do this for a while, and then I'll be eighteen, and we can go back to the town house, just you and me. I don't understand why you want to make things harder by bringing back ghosts—"

"She wanted to come back," Violet insisted. "She probably figured out that I helped Mr. Woods, so she wanted to come as well, and it would have been rude not to help her when I can."

"But she isn't really back, though, Violet. She is less than what she was before. You heard it yourself, how seeing her like that upset Dina. Whatever it is you do to them, they're not as they were in life. If they were, we could have just brought Mama and Papa back and—"

"No," she interrupted. "Mama and Papa aren't here anymore, but the ghosts in this house never went anywhere." A cold ripple ran down my spine when she said it. "At least people other than me can *see* Miss Lawrence now."

"It's not useful, though. Not for any of us, and we don't know what it does to *you*. Maybe they're taking *advantage* of you." Mama and Papa had warned us many times about people taking advantage. "You are *my* responsibility now, and I just want to keep us both safe—"

Her eyes suddenly flashed with anger. "I can't help it if they *ask*."

"How do you even know if they *ask*?" So far, neither of them had said a word, to my knowledge.

"I just *feel* it," she replied, and used her index finger to tap her own temple. "In here—just like you do with the colors."

"But what exactly do they ask you for, Violet? What is it that you *do* to them to make them visible all of a sudden—and able to throw forks?"

Violet shrugged. "Nothing much. They're hungry, that's all. They need food to be able to do those things."

"Well, why didn't they just steal some of Aunt Clara's melon balls?" None of it made sense to me.

"No, *I* have to give it to them and *want* for them to be real. I don't know why it works that way." She gave another shrug.

"They aren't real, though," I pointed out. "They're both still very dead."

"Real-*er*, then." She sounded unhappy. She looked down at the table and pursed her lips. Her notebook lay open before her with the pencil discarded on a blank page.

"You said to me before that Mr. Woods was stuck in the flower bed. Why isn't he anymore?" It sounded like an accusation, as if I was grilling her, but I didn't really mean it like that. I just desperately wanted to understand.

"I don't know, exactly, but he got away from there when I fed him. Sometimes when I see them, it's like they have black glue coming out of their belly buttons." She patted her own stomach through the polka-dotted shirt. "Like it's gluing them in place. When I make them realer, the glue disappears."

"And we can see them. What was Miss Lawrence glued to?"

"The dining room floor," Violet replied. "Though the glue could stretch all the way to the hall."

"She's not glued anymore, though."

"No." Violet sounded satisfied, which annoyed me a lot.

"But how do you know what to feed them—and what to say?" I was thinking about her chanting in the garden.

"I don't know. I just *do*—like when you know what the colors mean."

"I don't *know* that I know—not for sure." I tried to reason, but Violet didn't like reason very much.

"I don't think anyone has ever seen the ghosts here before me." She sounded smug. "That's why they like me so much."

"Or it's because you give them treats and make them realer. Have you even thought that there could be a good reason nobody sees them? Maybe they aren't *supposed* to be seen. Life is for the living, in case you haven't noticed." I didn't mean to be so hard on her, but I had to let her know how I felt.

"*Someone* has to care about them," she muttered. "Think if it was you who was stuck in a flower bed for years—or if Mama and Papa were stuck on K2." That was, in fact, a *horrible* thought, and I instantly shuddered all over.

"Well, *tell me* at least, the next time someone *asks*!" I felt a little stung that she hadn't even *tried* to wake me up the night before.

"You will only yell at me," Violet said, and she was probably right.

I sighed. "I'm sorry. It's just that I *really* don't like dead things."

"I know." She gave me a look full of pity, then reached over and placed a hand on my cheek, as if she wanted to comfort me.

I didn't try to talk to Violet after that, as I knew she wouldn't listen. And after what she had said about K2, I wasn't even sure if I *wanted* her to put the ghosts back.

Maybe it *was* right to help them?

I also didn't want Violet to be angry with me, or feel that she couldn't tell me the next time someone *asked*.

How was I supposed to protect her if I wasn't even there?

I couldn't tell Dina why the ghosts had come either, since I didn't want her to be angry at Violet for bringing Miss Lawrence back. It was bad enough that she had lied about the fox. Telling Aunt Clara was also out of the question; I could only imagine how mad she would be. Maybe she'd send us away to different places.

So since I couldn't do anything else, I watched Violet like a hawk. In the following week, I made sure to know exactly where she was at all times, and even cut my sessions with Gertrud short because I was so nervous all the time. I really wanted to be there if Violet did something dangerous again, so that I could stop her. Besides my sister, none of us wanted more ghosts around the house. Miss Lawrence made Aunt Clara *livid* as the days went by, as she still couldn't eat by herself. At every meal she needed Violet's help, or her food would just go flying. Dina and I had offered to take turns, but Aunt Clara would only let Violet help her. I suppose she had her reasons for that.

It wasn't easy, though, being at Crescent Hill while Aunt Clara slammed the doors and cursed Miss Lawrence many times over. She seemed to be even more upset by the old woman's quiet attacks than she was by Mr. Woods's louder ones. He was still a problem, though, and we all had to hide at least once a day, when things went flying through the air. His latest ambush involved cooking pans and ladles, and I figured it could have done some serious damage if the kitchen-ware had hit its mark.

But even though Miss Lawrence was gentler, I didn't like either ghost and felt more certain every day that this was *not* what Mama and Papa had wanted for us.

Yet where else were we to go?

VIOLET

22

I wished I could have explained it to Lily in a way that made her see things the way I did. That I could have told her how Miss Lawrence's *asking* had been different from Mr. Woods's. It hadn't bothered me so much, for one. It had been polite, as if she really asked instead of just insisting. It had definitely been there, though, like a gentle nudging or a pull, so I knew that she absolutely had *asked*—and thankfully, because of Mr. Woods, I had already known what to do.

I hadn't said anything to Lily because I knew she wouldn't understand. She was always so afraid of things that were dead and didn't feel sorry for them at all. *I* did, though. I didn't think Miss Lawrence wanted to be glued to the dining room floor—and she looked so sweet and kind, always waving at me and smiling, but I knew that Lily wouldn't see it that way and would only yell at me and tell me not to help her, so that was why I didn't tell her.

It was as if my sister thought that people didn't matter anymore after they were dead, even though she knew that wasn't true. Mama and Papa mattered a lot—Lily always thought of what they would have done or what they would have thought—and they weren't even around anymore. The first time I went to see them on K2, just a few days after we learned that they were missing, the two of them were already gone, leaving only their shells behind. No matter how much I looked for them, flying over the snow, I couldn't *feel* them anywhere. Now that I had learned a little more about how death worked, I knew that was a *good* thing. It meant that they weren't confused or sick but had just moved on as they were supposed to. I didn't know where they went exactly, but I was happy that they weren't afraid to go there, *even* if I would have liked to have them with us still. Maybe Lily, too, would have liked that, and not been so angry at the other ghosts if Mama and Papa were ghosts, too.

At first, after Irpa and I had helped the animals, I had thought that the reason why I saw the dead was because I was going to help those who were stuck to move on or be whole, but after Mr. Woods asked and didn't go away but only became visible to everybody, I thought maybe I was meant to help them with whatever I could. It felt like a good thing to be someone they could turn to if they were stuck in glue or wanted to go. Since most people couldn't see them or feel them *ask,* I was just happy that I could.

Irpa had told me that there were lots of stuck people on the planet whom no one ever found—and others who got loose from the glue just by accident, because someone prayed for them a lot, lit a bunch of candles, or just had a barbecue in the wrong spot. Most of them just waded around in the glue, though, which didn't seem right to me at all. Irpa showed me a newborn baby with the umbilical cord growing into its belly button, and then she showed me Miss Lawrence again, with the glue coming out of her belly, and said that the cords were the same thing, somehow. But while the umbilical cord tethered the baby to the mom, the black glue—which had been silver in life—tethered the soul to the body and the world. When someone got stuck, it became black and gooey, because the soul was dead and not supposed to exist here anymore.

I didn't understand everything she told me, and because she didn't use words, just images, I might have gotten some of it wrong. It *felt* right, though—like another half-forgotten memory—and when Miss Lawrence asked, I was happy to help her. I thought maybe she would help with Mr. Woods, too—who had totally ignored me after I helped him, which I thought was rude—and maybe make him quiet down, or at least not scare Lily and Dina so much. Even though I liked the dining room fort, I didn't like that the others were so scared, or that we had to clean up after him all the time. He seemed to keep away from Miss Lawrence, though, and almost never went into the dining room.

On the night after Miss Lawrence *asked*, when everyone had gone to bed, I went down to the kitchen and searched the refrigerator again. I found some bacon and a box of beef bones, a half-eaten cream cake, two pears, and a piece of cheese that Aunt Clara had said was French and expensive, so I figured it would do. There wasn't any more cider, but wine was easy to find, since Aunt Clara always kept a few bottles from the cellar in the pantry. I brought everything with me into the dining room and placed it on the table. I had even taken some of Aunt Clara's good china with painted roses and gold rims out of the cupboard to put the food on, since I figured that Miss Lawrence would like it. Then I brought a petunia down from the windowsill to have dirt to pour the wine into. Next I lit one of the half-burned candles in the candelabra on the table and nodded once to Miss Lawrence, who had been watching me all the time—looking a little happier now that help was within sight—and then I closed my eyes and said the words.

"Dear lady in the dining room, please take this meat, wine, and cream cake I have brought to you. Flesh for your flesh, bone for your bones, sugar for your spirit." My voice was shivering a little the first time I said it, but soon—when I found the rhythm—the words flowed more easily, and I lost myself to them again, barely even noticing that I was swaying on my feet. "Flesh for your flesh, bone for your bones, sugar for your spirit, flesh for your flesh, bone for your bones, sugar for your spirit, flesh for your flesh, bone for your bones, sugar for your spirit . . ."

It was much easier to release Miss Lawrence—probably because I wasn't afraid of her, like I had been of Mr. Woods. It didn't take long at all before I felt something like a champagne cork popping in my chest, and then the *asking* was gone and I knew that she was free.

When I opened my eyes, she was still there, though, only now she was definitely happy, because she smiled and did a pirouette under the moose head, which made the pink nightgown billow around her legs. I laughed when I saw it, because she was so sweet. I wondered where she would go now, and what she would do—and what Lily would say if she saw her wandering around. I figured she would yell at me, and that, of course, turned out to be true.

My night hadn't been over yet, though, because the food I had used was all ruined, hidden under a thick layer of mold that would have made Mama shudder all the way down to her toes. I had tiptoed out to the kitchen to get a garbage bag, then silently apologized to the petunia when I threw it in. It hadn't survived either but looked black and as moldy as the rest. I felt sorry for not thinking of what the wine would do to it sooner, but at least I couldn't *feel* it, so I knew that the petunia was gone.

Miss Lawrence, though, had still been there—standing in the same spot as before, only she looked more joyful, and the glue was gone from around her feet. She waved at me, as always, only this time it sent a whiff of upturned dirt across the polished tabletop, so I had known that she was much realer.

I hadn't known what would happen next, though: that Dina would be so upset, or that I would have to feed Aunt Clara. Miss Lawrence hadn't even helped with Mr. Woods, but somehow only made things worse. But even if I had known, I would still have helped her. At least she seemed much happier now that her feet weren't stuck and she could steal Aunt Clara's food. I knew she was angry with Aunt Clara, even if I didn't know why, but I figured that at least this way she got a chance to let her know how she felt. Mama always said it was important to "air out old laundry" to get a fresh start with someone.

CLARA

23

I started my war on the ghosts by escaping them. It was the only logical thing to do. It might not eradicate the vermin that had so rudely invaded my home, but at least it would provide me with some respite.

Or that had been the plan, anyway.

A few days after Cecilia's unfortunate return—when I had realized that she wouldn't just vanish on her own—I got in my car and drove down the hill. There, I parked the station wagon by the side of the road and unwrapped a cucumber sandwich from my lunch. After looking right and left several times, deciding there was no dead lady in sight, I tentatively lifted the sandwich to my lips and was just about to bite down when the slap came, sending the food flying straight across the passenger seat and onto the dusty window. Cucumber slices flew everywhere, and the bread landed on the upholstery, buttered side down.

I wasn't immediately discouraged, though, as I had anticipated some resistance. I started the car and drove again. I didn't stop until I was halfway into town. There was an abandoned house there, dilapidated and falling apart, and I parked my car in the yard. Then I unwrapped the second sandwich I had brought, in the hopes that I was so far away from Crescent Hill that the dead couldn't reach me there. Sadly, it didn't go any better, and soon I was scraping cucumber off the windshield. This time she even showed herself and sat there ramrod straight and grim-faced in the passenger seat, staring straight ahead into the wall of the derelict building.

"Damn you, Cecilia," I said as I put the car in reverse and left the abandoned house. "Is *that* what you want?" I pointed at the building. "Do you want me to go away and leave Crescent Hill to rot? I honestly thought you had more sense than that."

By the time I was back on the road, Cecilia's ghost was gone.

I didn't drive back home, though, but continued into town. There I visited a diner I had driven past many times but never seen the inside of. It had a small staff of tired-looking women in blue uniforms waiting on a drab-looking clientele seated at wooden tables with red-checked tablecloths and ketchup bottles. The air was infused with the scent of old grease. I walked up to the wooden counter and ordered the first thing I saw on the menu, which happened to be a bacon cheeseburger. The sad-looking young thing behind the counter gave me a puzzled look, but if that was because I looked out of place in there, or merely because I looked distraught, was honestly hard to say. Nevertheless, she took my order, and I gingerly picked one of the tables, next to a family of four, who glared at me with disdain when I wiped down the seat with a napkin before slowly sitting down.

My food arrived soon after, and though the scent of meat and cheese made me uneasy, I told myself that this was merely an experiment, and if it should fail, at least I would know that nothing of value had gone to waste.

Thankfully there was some cutlery already laid out on the table, and—taking a deep breath—I lifted knife and fork and cut into the monstrosity before me. The little piece of hamburger and bread glistened with grease as I moved it toward my lips, and I had already opened my mouth—and could smell the cheddar cheese—when the slap came again out of nowhere, sending cheese, meat, and fork clattering to the floor. The family next to me rolled their eyes and the children openly laughed. The sad waitress frowned and took a step closer.

I threw down some money and left the establishment at once, my cheeks burning with embarrassment and anger.

My little act of rebellion had not turned out the way I'd hoped.

In the coming days, I repeated this adventure a couple of times—with just as discouraging results—and the true dread of the situation was slowly dawning on me. It wasn't my house that was haunted; it was *me*.

I *couldn't* escape Cecilia's ghost—and perhaps that meant that I couldn't escape Timmy's either.

As soon as the realization struck me, I decided that I had to *arm* myself. Spring traps would clearly not work on these vermin, but I felt fairly certain that *something* would. I had never been a particularly spiritual person, but I had picked up enough to know that a priest could come in handy when something foul ran rampant in your home. So, on my next venture into town, I drove up to the little white-painted church in Ivory Springs and parked my car.

My plan had been to seek out the priest and—vaguely—describe what was going on. But just as I was about to exit the vehicle, I suddenly got cold feet, because what if the priest agreed to come to the house and then recognized the ghosts? It just wouldn't do if he saw my husband wandering around on Crescent Hill with several ax wounds in his back. Timmy was supposed to have vanished with Ellie Anderson, and as far as anyone knew, he was still living the high life somewhere. It also would be hard to explain just why my former employer came back to refuse me food. Brushing it off as "the folly of the dead" might not be enough. And even if I found a different priest—one from a different town—what if the ghosts suddenly started talking? Just because they hadn't so far didn't mean that they wouldn't. No, it was too much of a risk. I could absolutely not involve a priest. I started the car and drove away as fast as I could.

I stopped by the post office to pick up some sheet music I had ordered for Lily, and then I drove back to Crescent Hill at reckless speed. While I was driving, my mind kept churning, and I realized with increasing horror how this meant that acquiring help for my problem might not be easy at all. Because no matter who I brought in, if the ghosts decided to talk, I was toast.

There was only one open road left to take: I had to get rid of the vermin myself.

LILY

24

Violet had started sneaking down to the basement at night.

And I didn't think she knew that I knew.

It was just luck that I found out in the first place. Or luck and something else: a feeling, or a *knowing,* that had started going off like an alarm clock in my head whenever she was up to something. After Miss Lawrence's return, I had been thinking of leaving my bedroom door open, in the hope that I would hear Violet if she got up in the night, but then I had decided against it because of Mr. Woods. I just didn't like the idea of him seeing me through the open door while prowling the hallway as he did. I worried about Gertrud, too—that he would make her fly through the air and crash into the wall above my bed. I already had problems sleeping because of his knocking, and the only thing that helped was to wear my earmuffs to bed and reread old mystery novels until I drifted off.

My new invisible alarm clock had come in pretty handy then—even though being able to *feel* my little sister was a tad unsettling. But I absolutely preferred it to Mr. Woods. So when I woke up one night about a week after Miss Lawrence had returned, I just knew that Violet had left her room. I ignored Mr. Woods's bleeding face in the hallway and tiptoed down the stairs and—sure enough—could see a light under the kitchen door. I fully expected to find her in front of the refrigerator, looking for meat and bones. She hadn't mentioned another ghost, but that didn't mean that there wasn't any. Violet had stopped telling me things; my lectures had seen to that. I hated that things were like this between us, but I still felt like it had been right to try to stop her. The ghosts were annoying and dangerous, and whatever it was they wanted, they didn't share with us. I honestly didn't see the point of them, besides driving Aunt Clara mad.

Violet wasn't in the kitchen, though, even if the overhead light was on. I tiptoed through the room and peeked inside the dining room, too, but couldn't see my sister anywhere. When I returned to the kitchen, however, I noticed that the door to the basement was pulled tight to the frame but not closed.

This was *very* unusual.

The basement was one of the places Aunt Clara had expressly told us not to go. In fact, the door used to be locked, and the only key that I knew of was with Dina since she sometimes went down there to do laundry. Now it looked like Violet had gotten her hands on a key as well and had snuck down while the rest of us were sleeping.

I got a little annoyed by the sight, but I was curious, too. Although I didn't think of the basement very often, now that the chance was there, I couldn't help but feel pulled in its direction. What in this house could possibly be so dangerous that Aunt Clara had to lock it up? And what was Violet doing down there? Was the dangerous thing maybe so dangerous that she could be in actual danger?

As soon as I thought this, I rushed across the room and didn't even bother to be quiet anymore. I wasn't *too* worried, though, as Dina had told me that the only way my aunt could sleep through Mr. Woods's banging was with earplugs of wax and a hefty dose of sleeping pills, topped with half a bottle of wine.

I pulled the door open, just a little, and very, very slowly. Thankfully, the hinges were well-oiled, or the creaking might have given me away. I peeked in through the narrow opening and saw the wooden stairs bathed in darkness. There was a light down there, though— a golden glow—and if I strained my hearing, I could make out words.

Violet was talking to someone.

"I think I want to be a performer when I grow up. Mama took us to the circus once, and there were girls there who *flew* under the ceiling on trapezes. I would like to fly, I think, and Irpa says that I can, too, if only I practice a little . . ."

Her voice sounded so sweet—so little—and for a moment I thought that she was playing, that she had made up a friend because she didn't have any here. But then I remembered what Violet could *do,* and my heart started racing in my chest.

Whom was Violet talking to?

"I know you can't answer me, but I like to think that you understand me. It would be a little stupid if you didn't, with me sitting here and talking to you . . . It must be lonely down here all by yourself. I wouldn't have found you at all if I didn't get that feeling in my head, so that was lucky—unless you *wanted* me to come and it was you that I felt?" She paused to wait for an answer that didn't come. "I have to go now," she said next. "I have to sleep a little more before breakfast." She laughed like she didn't have a care in the world.

I quickly moved away from the door, went back the way I had come, slipped into the dining room, and waited in the shadows while Violet made her way up from the basement, locked the door—I heard the click—and turned off the light in the kitchen.

I didn't even breathe again before I heard the door to the hall close behind her.

Maybe I should have talked to her then—or *yelled,* as she called it—but I didn't think it would do any good, and I wanted to know what was going on. So instead, I went into the kitchen and sat there on a chair until I figured enough time had passed for Violet to have fallen asleep. Then I made my way upstairs and went back to bed. In the morning I pretended as if nothing had happened, but I kept an even closer eye on her, all while the question of who was in the basement kept popping into my head.

For three more nights, I followed Violet as she escaped the raven room and went downstairs. I didn't do anything but listen, though, and only for a couple of minutes, since I didn't want her to know I was there. I hoped to find out just whom she was talking to—and if she was planning on feeding them—but she mostly just talked about ordinary things, like what soup we had had for lunch and memories of before.

". . . Grandma Fiona made applesauce for us with cinnamon in it, and it tasted like a dream, even if I always liked cherries best. Grandma Fiona's family could make *all* sorts of trees grow anywhere and it didn't even matter if the dirt was poor. I think it was a special talent they had, making things grow like that . . ."

By the fourth night, I had almost convinced myself that it was only make-believe. For once, maybe it wasn't something scary down there, but just a make-believe friend. But that night, as I went to the basement door and pulled it open, I heard the same chanting as before.

"Flesh for your flesh, bone for your bones, sugar for your spirit, flesh for your flesh, bone for your bones, sugar for your spirit . . ."

My heart jumped in my chest, and for a moment it was difficult to breathe. I still managed to gather my courage, though. I took a deep breath, opened the door, and went down the stairs at last, even if I knew that Violet would probably hate me for following her there. It didn't matter. It didn't. I was determined that there wouldn't be any more ghosts running around at Crescent Hill.

At first, all I saw while moving downward were piles of cardboard boxes, broken crockery, and furniture covered in white sheets. The only light down there was one dusty bulb dangling from the ceiling. I finally saw the round-bellied washing machine, which I had previously just heard as it chugged its way through the cycles, and a few drying lines for "intimates" that were strung across the room.

In the middle of it all, Violet sat in a ruined wicker chair, staring at a stained old mattress. It looked like it had been covered up, too, but the sheet had been taken off and lay crumpled on the concrete floor. The mattress looked disgusting. A ragged brown stain covered most of the surface, hiding the pale pink satin underneath.

Red tadpoles squirmed all over the floor.

I startled when I saw the objects placed in front of Violet. There was a gold-rimmed china bowl filled with pieces of bloody meat; an iron pot crowded with chicken bones; an old dusty flowerpot filled with dirt; a lit candle; and a plate with white sugar cubes from the pantry. Violet had pilfered a bottle of wine, too, which had been opened, and some of the wine had been spilled onto the food. The sugar cubes were all soaked through and were a deep burgundy color.

"Violet!" I called, and thankfully she stopped chanting when she heard me. "What are you *doing?*" I asked, even though I knew perfectly well what it was. "No more ghosts!" I raged as my feet hit the cold concrete floor. "Why do you always have to make things so difficult?"

Violet jumped out of the chair. "She *asked,*" she protested. "What am I to do if they *ask?*" She held her hands up before her and looked so very small—and cold, wearing just her favorite nightgown.

"Say no," I snapped. It didn't matter if she thought she did good. I was absolutely certain that Mama and Papa wouldn't have wanted her spending her nights raising ghosts and catching colds.

"But this one is different," Violet argued. "She doesn't even look scary. She has almost no blood on her at all!"

"It doesn't matter, Violet. A ghost is a ghost!" I stopped just before my toes touched the meat bowl and grimaced when a tadpole touched my leg. I didn't feel it, exactly, but it still made me uncomfortable, as if there was something filthy about it. The candle on the floor had already gone out, and the wax had trickled out onto the basement floor, leaving a star-shaped puddle right in front of one of my toes. I turned my head and looked at the mattress and was relieved not to see anyone there.

"Where did you get the key to the basement?" I turned my attention back to Violet. "Did you take it from Dina?"

"No." Violet stared down at her own toes.

"Where, then?" I shivered a little, but I couldn't tell if it was because I was upset or if it was from the chill down there. The air smelled of damp rot, blood, and wine.

"Irpa showed me," she muttered.

"Irpa who?"

"The raven."

"The one in your room?"

Violet nodded and still didn't look at me.

"So 'Irpa' told you how to get the key from Dina?" I prodded.

"No, she showed me how to—oh!" Her face lit up as she pointed at the mattress. "I think she is realer now. Can you see her, Lily?"

With a sinking feeling, I turned my head. At least a thousand cold needles ran down my spine when I saw what had gotten Violet so excited. There was a young woman lying there. She had curly black hair, dimples in her cheeks, and shimmering pearl earrings. She wore only a short white dress that looked like it was made of silk. The garment was spattered with red.

Then, suddenly, we heard a loud bang as the door at the top of the stairs flew open and hit the wall. Someone came rushing down the stairs, two steps at a time—and then she was there.

Aunt Clara.

She stopped when she reached the bottom of the stairs, and her sharp gaze flickered everywhere as she took in the room around her. Violet's cheeks flushed pink—and Aunt Clara saw it.

"It was *you!*" she accused, and pointed at Violet. "*You* brought the ghosts here!"

There was a flurry of motion then upon the mattress, as the young woman rose to her full height and pointed as well, straight to my aunt. Then she gave Violet an imploring look before her mouth opened in a silent scream and she turned around—quick as a flash—to show us the gaping red wound in her skull. It was horribly ugly, glistening and deep. White splinters and a little gray were mixed in with the red.

Violet's gaze shifted from the ghost to our aunt. "It was *you*," she said in a voice full of dread. "You *put* that woman down here!"

CLARA

25

I marched the girls into the dimly lit living room, leaving the specter of Ellie Anderson to rot in the filth in the basement. I honestly shouldn't have been surprised to see her. I should have known that she would appear since the other two were now present. I couldn't *wait* to see just what torment the little hussy had cooked up for me after spending a decade on that mattress.

She shouldn't be here, though. She should be dead and buried—gone and forgotten, as she rightly deserved. The only reason she was not was because of my meddling nieces.

"What have you been doing?" I raged, using my considerable height to my advantage. Violet fidgeted in her frilly nightgown, but Lily didn't look ashamed. She just stood there in her blue pajamas, looking straight back at me.

"What have *you* been doing?" she retorted rudely. "Did you *hurt* that woman, Aunt Clara?"

"I am not the subject of this inquiry!" I shouted, refusing to be derailed. "*How* did you manage to make this happen?" I had placed my hands on my hips and looked at them both in turn.

"I just . . . I . . . They *asked* me to," Violet sputtered. "I didn't mean to, at first, but I had a feeling inside, like I *ought* to—"

"Don't even answer her, Violet." Lily cut the confession short. "She doesn't deserve it. She *hurt* that woman!" The girl was pale and shook a bit.

"Were you in on it, too?" I turned on her. "Did you *know* what was going on?"

"I—" the girl started to say, but then Violet interrupted.

"Lily wanted me to put them back again."

"And why didn't you?" I arched an eyebrow. My heart was racing with fury and betrayal.

"Because they want to be here. They have the same right as everyone else. Just because they're dead, it doesn't mean—"

"They're not here on *vacation*, Violet!" I interrupted her sanctimonious speech. "They're here to make my life a living hell!"

"And why is that?" Lily's voice was ice-cold. "Why do they want to hurt you, Aunt Clara? Could it be because you hurt them first?" I could tell that her breathing came hard and fast, but she certainly stood her ground. Her blue eyes twinkled like polar stars: pinpricks of fire in a freezing landscape.

I shook off the discomfort. "This isn't about *me*," I snapped. "This is about your sister, and how she has ruined my *home*—"

"That woman in the basement seemed *very* sure. She was pointing right at you!" Lily had folded her arms over her chest and did her best to stare me down. I had faced worse than her, though.

"*That woman* is long dead—"

"The mattress was full of blood—"

"You don't know that!" How could she? "All sorts of things can ruin a mattress. I don't even remember what happened to it—"

"That was Ellie Anderson, wasn't it?" My niece was gathering steam and I didn't like it one bit.

"What if it was?" I found it harder and harder to keep my emotions in check.

"Then why is she haunting your basement, unless you did something to put her there?" Lily pressed her lips tightly together and tossed her head, looking so much like Iris in that moment that I could barely stand it.

I gathered my breath and bellowed, "Ellie Anderson was a floozy and a hussy who got nothing more than she deserved! And if you entitled brats had known anything at all about the world, you wouldn't be standing there judging me!"

"You killed all of them, didn't you? Mr. Woods and Miss Lawrence . . . That's why they're so angry. That is why they want to punish you . . . *You* are their 'unfinished business'!" Lily seemed rattled but still kept going, which only made *me* angrier.

"Don't you dare take that tone with me, young lady, or you and your sister might very well be joining them!" Despite all that I had suffered in my life, I couldn't remember ever having been so furious with another person. There she stood, young and carefree, thinking that the world was a crème brûlée just for her; all she had to do was to crack the sugar. She didn't know anything—*anything*!

Violet—inexplicably the root of all my troubles—moved closer to her sister and grabbed hold of the hem of her pajama top. Lily in turn placed a hand on her sister's shoulder.

"Then how are you going to get rid of them?" she asked me. "How are you going to get rid of the ghosts if Violet and I are gone?"

I hadn't thought of that yet. I had barely wrapped my head around the fact that my bushy-haired niece had somehow raised the dead. "How did you do it? How did you bring them back?"

Violet's lower lip quivered. She certainly didn't look very mighty in that moment. She didn't look like someone who could command ghosts.

"I just get these feelings in my head," she said, which made no sense at all. "It's like speaking but without any words. I *know* things."

"You *know* things!" I gave a mocking laugh. "Well, *unknow* it this very instant, and put the dead back where they belong!"

The little brat shook her head.

"Then tell *me* how to undo it," I hissed, waving a finger right under her nose, but the awful child kept shaking her head.

"You can't make Violet do *anything*," Lily snapped. "This is all *your* fault, Aunt Clara. If you hadn't harmed those people, none of this would have happened!"

"If *she*"—I pointed a finger at Violet—"hadn't gone digging them up, nothing *would* have happened. We could have continued on like friends—like allies. But instead you have dropped this *mess* on my porch!"

"I'm *happy* that Violet found them," Lily huffed. "You *should* be punished for what you did!"

"What do you even know about it?" I spat. "A little girl like you . . . You know *nothing* of what a woman has to endure—"

"No, but I do know right from wrong!" The girl lifted her chin, and again I couldn't help but think of Iris. "Mama and Papa taught us that."

I had to laugh when I heard it. "Your 'papa' didn't know shit from pennies—"

"Don't talk about Papa like that," Lily lashed out. Finally, some color had come into her cheeks. "Papa was a *good* man!"

"Your papa was a fool," I sneered. "Just look at what he has done. If he hadn't insisted on that reckless expedition, you two wouldn't be here, and *none* of this would have happened."

It took a beat for Lily to answer; her hand was still cupped around Violet's shoulder and the latter had placed her own fingers on top. "You would still be a murderer," Lily said, in a voice disturbingly quiet and calm. "You would still have killed those people, and at least now someone knows—"

"And what are you going to do about it?" I had managed to collect myself somewhat as well, and stared down at her while my mind kept churning, looking for ways out of this that didn't require giving up the money. "No one will believe a silly girl like you—"

"The ghosts—"

"Are dead, Lily, and dead men can't tattle—that's the beauty of their state."

"But now that they are back—"

"Well, they won't be for long! Your sister will see to that." To my immense satisfaction, I could hear Violet whimper. "You are *grounded*, young lady!" I used my sternest voice and pointed at her chest; my diamonds sparkled almost as fiercely as my anger. "You will stay in your room until you put them back!" Violet started crying, and it sounded like music to my ears. Lily, however, only pulled her sister closer and gave me a look full of disdain.

Our argument was cut short when Timmy chose to appear—drawn no doubt by the friction in the air. Suddenly the cage that hung from the ceiling, holding a taxidermy finch, started dancing back and forth before it promptly crashed to the floor, and all twelve encyclopedia volumes came rushing across the room in quick succession. Volume five hit me hard in the thigh. I screamed with rage and pain and pointed at my youngest niece.

"Get rid of them!" I commanded her.

"And then what, Aunt Clara? What will you do if Violet puts them back?" Lily still stood her ground, despite the piercing hissing in the air and the flying volumes of trivia.

"Then nothing!" I cried. "We carry on!"

"Just like that?" The distrust on her face was stark.

"Sure," I said, and rubbed my thigh. "We'll continue just as before."

But I didn't think the girl believed me. She wasn't stupid enough for that.

LILY

26

I couldn't sleep at all that night. I just lay awake staring into the dark of the owl room with eyes that felt like they were filled with sand. My heart kept racing and my mind kept churning, always coming back to the same awful thing: Aunt Clara was a murderer!

On the other side of the hallway from me, Violet was locked in her room. It wasn't fair, and it wasn't practical. What about food—or when she had to go to the bathroom? Was she lonely in there? Did she cry? I hoped she was asleep. I wondered if there was another key to the raven room, besides the one Aunt Clara had. Maybe Dina could help me in the morning. Everything had become so dark and scary. Did Aunt Clara really want to kill us, too? She had definitely been purple when she threatened us—her whole body had been one blazing flame of danger—so I couldn't help but think so.

Back in the living room, while arguing with Aunt Clara, I had been so angry that it had been easy to be brave, but now that I was alone in my room, the courage had dried up. Fear had come creeping in with the silence and the darkness, and the sounds of Mr. Woods's knocking didn't help. Violet and I were trapped in this house with a murderer, and that thought was bigger than anything else. We were absolutely *not* safe, and I *had* to get us out.

As soon as dawn broke, I slipped out of my room, and—ignoring Mr. Woods's bleeding face—went for the stairs. Mr. Woods wasn't knocking just then. He just stood there in the hallway, staring, so the house was all quiet aside from the faint sounds of morning birds chirping outside. It was silent in Violet's room, too, and I hoped that meant she was dreaming.

Down in the kitchen, the door to the basement was still open. Aunt Clara hadn't even bothered to lock it back up. Probably she didn't think it was necessary anymore, seeing how we all knew the secret of the bloodstained mattress. I pushed it shut, using my hip to make sure it was properly closed, since I didn't want to think of what had happened down there the night before and everything that had happened after. It was just too horrible.

For a moment, I thought of waiting for Dina before setting my plan in motion, but she wouldn't arrive until nine, and I just didn't think I could wait that long. I also worried that Aunt Clara, too, would have trouble sleeping, and that she would come sauntering downstairs much earlier than usual. So instead of waiting, I went to the kitchen counter, where the heavy black phone balanced on top of a thick phone book.

I hoisted myself up to the countertop and sat there with a hand on the receiver while watching the wall-mounted clock slowly tick to seven. Hopefully, this was late enough in the morning that someone would be at the sheriff's office. I didn't even have to look up the number since Dina had listed it among other useful numbers, like the one for a pharmacy and another for a Dr. Smith, on a piece of lined paper taped to the wall. The paper was yellowed and ripped, so I thought it must have been hanging there since Miss Lawrence's days.

When it was a minute past seven, I lifted the receiver and dialed the numbers on the wall. To my relief, a groggy-sounding voice answered on the second ring.

"Yes?" the man grunted into the phone.

"Yes, hi . . . Is this the sheriff?" I asked.

"Sure," his gruff voice sounded. "Who is this?"

"Uh . . . My name is Lily Webb," I replied. "I am staying with my aunt, Clarabelle Woods, at Crescent Hill?"

"I know the place. Did something happen?"

"No—I . . . Not *now,* at least." I took a deep breath for courage before launching into the next part. "I'm calling because I think my aunt maybe *killed* her husband, and other people, too."

The sheriff was quiet for a very long time—so long, in fact, that I thought he maybe had hung up, but then he spoke again. "What makes you say that?"

This was, obviously, the tricky part. "There's a mattress with blood on it in the basement," I explained, "and I think he may be buried in a flower bed."

"Uh-huh." He sounded doubtful and my heart sank. "Why do you think he is buried in the flower bed?"

"I . . ." Suddenly, I didn't know what to say. Did the sheriff even believe in ghosts? "Can't you just look?" I begged him. "I know you think he left with Ellie Anderson, but maybe that just isn't true—and the mattress is *very* bloody."

"Did you ask Mrs. Woods about it?"

"Yes—and she did say that she killed him, or at least she implied it. And that she killed Ellie Anderson, too, and Miss Lawrence . . ."

"Miss Lawrence?" He sounded surprised.

"Yes, so she could get the house—and her money," I quickly explained.

"Is that so?" I could hear the sheriff scratch his head.

"Yes," I said, "it is. And she said that my sister and I would be next if Violet didn't—" I was just about to say "put the ghosts back" but stopped myself just in time. "Can you just come, please? I'm sure you'll find Mr. Woods in the flower bed." Because why else would he be glued there in the first place?

There was another lull before the sheriff spoke again. "How old are you, Lily?"

"Fourteen, but—"

"Are you *sure* you didn't get this wrong?"

"Yes!" I could feel tears welling up in my eyes. "Can't you please just come and look?" If he did and found Mr. Woods, I wouldn't even have to mention the ghosts.

"All right, we'll swing by," said the sheriff, and I did start crying for real then, but only from relief.

"Thank you!" I pressed the receiver tightly to my cheek. "Thank you so much," I croaked through the tears.

I felt a thousand times lighter when I hung up the phone.

I managed to eat some dry toast and drink a little tea while waiting for Dina—and the sheriff—to arrive. The morning seemed strange without Violet there, chattering away, and I wondered if she was awake in her room. I was so tired by then that my hands shook when I lifted the teacup, and I even spilled sugar on the tabletop. All the while, I was listening for sounds, hoping that the sheriff would arrive with flashing lights.

Dina came first, though. At a quarter to nine, she was there, arriving on the red bike she sometimes used. I had been meaning to pretend that everything was fine when she came in—not because I didn't trust her, but because it felt like somehow breaking the spell if I told her about the sheriff. I worried that if I said something about the call, everything would fall apart. I started crying again when I saw her, though, and she immediately dropped her purse and the plastic bag she was carrying and came to wrap me up in her arms, flaming gold all over. She hadn't even taken her coat off yet; it smelled of woodland and cooking grease.

"What is it, Lily? What is wrong? Is it the ghosts?" She pulled a little away to give me a concerned look. "Where is Violet?" she asked before I had had time to reply.

"Up in her room," I sobbed. "Aunt Clara has grounded her."

"Why?" She looked alarmed. "Has she even had breakfast yet?"

I shook my head. "Aunt Clara has the key." I sniffled.

"But why has she been grounded?" Dina asked again.

"Because she brought back Ellie Anderson," I sobbed. "She was down there, in the basement, on the mattress. Aunt Clara hit her in the head with an ax."

"She hit Violet in the head with an ax?" Dina sounded shocked, and several pink flames sprang up on her skin, quelling the golden love.

"No, Ellie Anderson," I explained. "Before—and she killed Mr. Woods, too."

"She did?" Dina's blue-gray eyes went wide. "How do you know that?"

"Ellie Anderson said so, and Aunt Clara, too, afterward."

"What about Miss La—"

"Yes, her, too," I sobbed. "You were absolutely right about that." Finally, I understood what Dina had been thinking all along.

"I *knew* it!" Dina's face looked hard and angry; her nostrils flared and her eyes narrowed, and all the frightened pink flames bled to red. "That gold-digging wretch!"

"You can't tell her that you know," I begged, suddenly terrified. "Maybe she'll turn on you, too."

"But what does Violet have to do with it?" The flames shifted back to worried pale pink.

"Violet was the one who sort of brought the ghosts back," I whispered. "I don't know how she knew how to do it, but she did. That's why she stole the food from the refrigerator. There *wasn't* any fox, Dina. She gave the meat to the ghosts, and this time Aunt Clara caught her."

Dina went very quiet. She retracted her arms and went to stand by the kitchen counter, just staring out into the air. "I suppose we should thank Violet, then, for helping the dead reveal the truth," she said at last. "I just don't know what to do about it. Ghosts can't give evidence in court—"

"But if they found the bodies," I said in a half whisper. "If only they found Mr. Woods—"

We both went quiet when we heard the sound of Aunt Clara coming down the stairs. Her heels clattered against the boards as she entered the hall, though her steps were a little uneven, as if she was limping. Her face looked hard when she peered into the kitchen, and she was orange from exhaustion, like a burning pumpkin.

"Good, you're here," she said when she saw Dina. "I suppose Lily has filled you in about Violet? She left her bed in the dead of night and somehow managed to enter the basement—something she knew was *off-limits*." Her gaze darted between us. "She'll stay in her room until further notice, but you can bring her some breakfast." She gave Dina a nod. "As for you"—her green gaze landed on me—"I expect you to be on your best behavior, unless you want to share in your sister's fate."

With that, she kept striding farther into the house. I just didn't get how she could be her same old self after what had happened. How could she just pretend that everything was fine when *nothing* was?

"Breakfast, Dina," she snapped over her shoulder. "I expect it on the table in twenty minutes—and my mail, too, if you don't mind . . . I suppose you must be at hand as well, to help me eat, with the girl being locked up."

Dina and I looked at each other with wide eyes, then Dina went to the refrigerator to find Aunt Clara's eggs and melon. She made some oatmeal, too, for Violet, and sent me upstairs with a key from her own set. "No dawdling," she warned me with a frightened look in the dining room's direction.

I paused outside the raven room to compose myself, hoping I didn't look too horrible after all the crying and no sleep. I didn't want Violet to know how upset I was. I knocked on the door before fumblingly inserting the key into the lock. The bowl of oatmeal in my other hand was so hot that it hurt.

Before I had had time to turn the key, however, the door just opened in front of me, and Violet stood there on the threshold, still wearing her nightgown and with the knitted blue socks on her feet. I looked from her to the door with surprise—had Aunt Clara forgotten to lock it?

Violet giggled when she saw my expression. "I wanted to tell you last night in the basement," she whispered. "Irpa taught me how to open locks." She held up a black feather.

"Violet . . . ?" I looked over her shoulder to the taxidermy raven on the dresser, but then a movement to my right made me move my gaze to the windowsill, where *another* raven perched—this one very much alive! It shook out its feathers when it saw me, and its eyes glinted oily brown. "Is that ... Irpa?" I asked, no longer even noticing how the oatmeal burned my fingers.

Violet nodded. "She is my friend." She opened the door wider to let me come inside. As soon as I had stepped across the threshold, she pushed the door closed behind me. I couldn't take my eyes off the raven—the sharp beak and the glossy feathers, the *knowing* in its eyes. It didn't have any flames around it, but I didn't always see them either, so that didn't bother me that much.

"How did you—when did you meet her?" I asked.

"Oh, she just arrived on her own." Violet took the oatmeal from my hand and slumped down on the bed. "She knocked on the window with her beak. She is my familiar friend."

"She can talk?"

"Yes—but only in my head." She grinned.

"What does 'familiar friend' mean?" I still stared at the raven, who stared right back at me, cocking her head a little.

"I don't know"—Violet shrugged—"but it's a good thing that she came, though, and gave me a feather to open all the locks, because I *really* had to go this morning."

"But I didn't hear you." I finally tore my gaze away to look at Violet instead. She was already eating her breakfast, blowing on each spoonful.

"You were on the phone, I think." She sounded unconcerned. The raven on the windowsill suddenly took flight and disappeared out the window in a flurry of feathers. Both Violet and I watched her leave.

"She isn't really a raven." Violet gave me a mischievous look.

"No? What is she, then?" I didn't like the sound of that. "Another ghost?"

Violet shook her head. "I don't know *what* she is, but she told me that she looks like a raven so I won't be afraid—isn't that strange?"

"Yes." I shuddered. "But do you think you should have friends that won't show you who they are?" It seemed to me that the longer we stayed at Crescent Hill, the weirder and more scary things became. "Do you speak to her a lot?"

Violet nodded. "Uh-huh. I wanted to tell you about her, but I didn't think you would like her very much, since you don't like the ghosts."

"I like the ghosts better now," I said. "Now that I know why they're here."

Violet nodded, all happy with herself. "It was a *good* thing that they *asked*."

"Aunt Clara is very purple." I couldn't help that fear had snuck into my voice. "And purple means very dangerous," I added. "I have done something, though—something that maybe can save us from—"

Just then, the sound of a car approaching made us both look up. Violet gave me a puzzled look while my heart started racing again. Relief flooded every part of my body.

The sheriff had arrived.

CLARA
27

When the doorbell rang—or rather, chimed—Dina and I had just
finished my breakfast. It had been an unpleasant venture in every respect, as I didn't much like to sit there and gape in front of my overbearing housekeeper, but I was also hungry and hankering for melon,
and seeing how the girl was *absolutely* under house arrest, it simply
couldn't be helped. Dina was not as adept at it as Violet, though, and
kept dripping melon juice down on my chest. It got so bad that I had
to tuck the napkin under my collar to save myself—and my dress—
from further disgrace.

It had been a trying morning already. First, it had been Timmy's
usual shenanigans. Before I had even left my room, the hissing sound
had come rushing like a wind, and the padded stool before my vanity
had come flying across the floor to bar the door. I couldn't just move
it either; suddenly the delicate thing of white-painted wood and
plush purple velvet seemed to weigh a ton. I stood there in Cecilia's
old housecoat and huffed and puffed like a coal-fueled engine, until
the weight suddenly lifted and the stool flew up in my arms with such
force that I stumbled backward and tripped over a chair, hurting my
knee in the process. I couldn't *hear* Timmy laugh, but I felt sure that
he did, as I hobbled out in the hallway. The hissing sound was thank-

fully gone by then, and I could freely curse my thieving husband. I never did that anymore while the attacks happened, as I had noticed how it seemed to make them worse. I had come up with my own theory that Timmy—in death as in life—thrived on the attention he got from others. If I managed to remain somewhat calm and collected when his ghost was around, he seemed to run out of fuel pretty fast. It was hard to do, though—especially when things went flying.

I then proceeded into the bathroom and twisted the taps to fill the bathtub. I even added a little jasmine-scented foam to the bathwater, as I felt I deserved it for putting up with Timmy's antics. Normally, I would have snuck in a couple of secret chocolates, too, in order to really spoil myself—but with the way things were with the food situation, I decided to pass.

I would rather not invite Cecilia Lawrence into the bathroom with me.

I had undressed and was just about to step into the bathtub when I saw it. There she was, peering out from the mirror above the apricot washbasin. I had been thinking about her just then—about her and the girls and what to do about it all—so for the first few seconds I didn't quite comprehend that what I saw existed outside of my own head. But then she waved her little hand at me. It was a friendly gesture, but she didn't seem very pleased; her skin was ghastly pale against the stark red of her lipstick. Her gaze traced the contours of my aging body just as her upper lip lifted in contempt.

I promptly stepped into the bathtub and drew the plastic curtain closed.

"What do you want?" I barked, when I was safely hidden from view. "You cannot *scare* me, Ellie. I dealt with you, remember? You are the one who should be afraid of *me*!"

Of course, I received no answer.

After a few minutes of silence, except for the occasional drip from the tap, I peeked my head around the curtain to make sure she was still there. She was; her smug little face still peered out from the mirror.

"Perhaps it's a good thing that you are mute," I mused, against my better judgment, seeing how I knew speaking to them did no good. But I just couldn't seem to help myself. "What could you *possibly* say to defend what you did? Dallying with a married man? I suppose you've had ample time to think about it since the last time we met. If you had just kept in line, I suppose you would be . . . thirty-six, thirty-seven by now?" I quickly did the math in my head. "The bloom would be about faded, of course, but perhaps you would have had a new husband and children of your own. You should have thought about that before," I concluded, and lowered myself into the water. But the foam didn't smell so nice anymore and my muscles refused to relax. Instead of a luxurious moment to myself, I constantly felt watched—despite the apricot curtain.

When I exited the bath, Ellie was still there, only now she had her back turned to show off the magnificent wound in her skull, right at the center of her cascading hair. I suppose the glistening damage was meant to rattle me, but instead I couldn't help but admire its grisly glory. There it was, in the flesh, so to speak: just what I thought of Ellie Anderson.

"Nice handiwork," I remarked, not as much to praise myself as to irk her. "But if that's meant to prod at my conscience, you should know right away that it won't work. I don't feel bad about what happened back then, and you deserved that blow just as *he* deserved his."

I'd be damned if I'd feel lousy about myself when *she* was the one who had transgressed in the first place. Perhaps she had even *known* what Timmy had planned on doing with my diamonds. I certainly wouldn't put it past her.

Putting on my makeup, however, proved to be a problem with Ellie's ruined head obscuring my view, and when I moved on to my vanity, she was in the mirror there as well—the front of her this time, smiling at me with very red lips. Her eyes looked dark and wild. I opened my jewelry box next, as it had a small oval mirror embedded in the lid, but, lo and behold—Ellie Anderson was there as well. Her bloodied teeth filled the whole thing, and so I had to go without makeup. To compensate, I put on a pretty dress in a purple-flower pattern, but it didn't make me feel any better at all.

I was not kindly disposed then, when I hobbled down the stairs on my damaged knee, cursing my young niece with every step. What on earth had made her do something so foolish as to bring them back, and *how* had she managed it? Just thinking about it gave me a headache. And then—as if to make a terrible morning even worse—someone was ringing the doorbell after breakfast, and I didn't even have lipstick on, nor a smile with which to greet them.

I sent Dina to open the door, hoping that it would be just a traveling salesman, or a neighbor asking to borrow some flour, but that was not to be. My housekeeper looked quizzical and wide-eyed when she came back into the dining room.

"It's the sheriff?" She said it as if it was a question rather than a fact. "He insists that he has to talk to you?"

"Did you let him in?" I snapped.

"Sure," she said, sounding uncertain.

"Idiot," I muttered, and got to my feet. It was absolutely not a good idea to have the sheriff entering my ghost-infested house. What would happen if he saw Miss Lawrence—or Timmy?

I had to get him out again—and fast.

I plastered on a smile before crossing the threshold to the hall; my knee was still aching and I swallowed a grimace. "Harold!" I beamed. "I haven't seen *you* in ages! What brings you all the way out here?"

The old sheriff looked a little uncomfortable. His gray mustache had grown even thicker and wilder since the last time I had seen him. When he removed his hat to clutch it between gnarled fingers, I could tell that his bald patch had spread quite a bit. There are a few advantages to being tall, and seeing the top of smug men's heads is one of them. It generates a certain sense of power.

"I got a phone call this morning . . ." The man fumbled with his hat and lifted a hand to scratch a stubbled cheek. "From a girl."

"A girl?" Something heavy dropped in the pit of my stomach. I had certainly not seen this coming—but then, perhaps I should have.

"Yes." He nodded. "Her name was . . . Rose? No, some kind of flower . . ." He paused while forcing his brain to do a little exercise, while my gaze furtively scanned the room, looking for pale, ghostly faces. "Lily? Could that be it?" He finally hit the mark.

"Oh yes, my niece." I smiled even wider to mask my discomfort. "What did she call you for?" I did my very best to make the question seem casual.

"Well"—the sheriff seemed to be about as tormented as I was— "she suggested that something was going on . . . To be frank, Mrs. Woods, she suggested that *Mr.* Woods is currently to be found in one of your flower beds." He puffed out his chest, but a sheen of sweat had appeared on his forehead. In my own chest, my heart started racing. "I am sorry, Mrs. Woods, but I *have* to follow up on information like this." He suddenly gave up all pretense; his shoulders sagged as he shook his head, and as much as his mentioning the flower bed had rattled me, the sight of his disbelief gave me hope.

"That is very unfortunate," I said, and meant it from the bottom of my heart. "Would you mind if we took this outside?" I lowered my voice. "I would rather the poor girl not hear us talking about her." And it somehow seemed less likely that one of the ghosts would come drifting by if we were outside.

"Listen," I said as soon as we both stood out on the stairs and the door was firmly shut behind us. "My niece is recently bereft, and the poor child has not been herself since her parents died. It's disconcerting, to be honest, all the things she makes up . . . I have been looking into finding a therapist for her, but it's hard with us living so far from everything. I'm *terribly* sorry for her inconveniencing a busy man like yourself—"

"I thought it might be something like that." He looked instantly relieved, gave a good-natured laugh, and fumbled in his pocket for a handkerchief to mop his brow. I thought perhaps I was off the hook—easily and painlessly—but then his face grew serious again. "Of course, I remember the search for Mr. Woods well, and how heartbroken you were back then." His gaze met mine, suddenly sharp.

"Yes, I was. Of course." I stared right back at the man. "It is the worst thing that can happen to a person, losing a loved one to God knows what fate—"

"But why the flower bed, Clara? It's such a specific location. Why would your niece make up a story like that?"

I bit my lip to keep from screaming as the heavy thing in my stomach slowly turned to fury. "Because she has read nothing but old mystery novels ever since she came here," I replied. "She has been filling her head with all sorts of nonsense: murderers and ghosts and whatnot, and being in such a fragile state, her young mind has clearly overloaded. I just let her read what she wanted, as it brought her some comfort, but clearly I should have been more restrictive." I shook my head to express my sadness. "We both know *now* that Timothy's disappearance was no mystery," I reminded the sheriff. "We both know *well* that he left with Ellie Anderson."

"Still . . ." He paused to clear his throat. "No one has actually *seen* the two of them since—"

"Oh, I assume they must have fled the country by now." I did my best to assure him. "With Ellie's ex-husband being as he is, I suppose they have found a better life elsewhere. You are of course more than welcome to take a look at my flower beds," I offered, although it cost me to do so. It cost me even more to add an overbearing laugh. "If nothing else it might put my niece's worries to rest, poor child. I should never have told them about Mr. Woods's disappearance in the first place, seeing how fragile they are since my brother's sad passing. It might not be the best use of police resources, but—"

"No, Mrs. Woods, you are right." He waved his hand in the air dismissively. A mention of costs will often have that effect. "You should look into getting some help for your niece, though. Her spreading stories like that isn't good for anyone."

"I will, Harold, don't you worry about that." My smile was back in place. "Maybe she will even need some medication to help her separate fantasy from reality. I'm terribly sorry about the inconvenience," I repeated. "It's not easy for a childless woman such as myself to suddenly have two charges under my roof—and they *do* need a lot of care, seeing how they just lost everything they had."

The sheriff pressed his lips tightly together and nodded his understanding. "This is clearly a trying time for your family—"

"Oh, we will sort it out." I was still grinning, but the fury made it hard. I meant what I said, though: I would get it sorted!

One way or another.

VIOLET
28

"Furthermore." Aunt Clara waved a finger in the air. The light from the window hit the diamonds in her rings, making them sparkle like tiny rainbows. "I will monitor all your letters, and there will be no more unsupervised phone calls. I will make sure that the phones are all locked up." She sounded very happy with herself, because she didn't know I could open all the locks now. "It's a disgrace, that's what it is!" She looked at us both as we sat on the bed with the empty porridge bowl between us. "What do you think the people in town will *think* if you go around spreading stories like that?" Aunt Clara started pacing the floor, waving her arms in the air.

"It's not stories," Lily protested. "It's the truth. You *killed* those people!"

"Yes, but what good do you think the sheriff can do in this unfortunate situation? How can them finding Timmy's bones *possibly* improve anything? Should they—God forbid—lock me up, you two will most definitely go into foster care and will probably be separated. Is that what you want?" She gave Lily a nasty look, and I could feel my sister shifting on the bed. I wanted to take her hand to give it a squeeze, but Aunt Clara made me think of a dangerous snake right then, and I worried that if I moved she would bite me.

"But you're a *murderer*." Lily looked a little sick. "You *should* be punished," she added matter-of-factly. Mama would have been proud about the way she kept her head.

"Oh, you precious girls with your *rights* and *wrongs*." Aunt Clara continued pacing. She was limping a little, I noticed. "What do you even know about life? Maybe things aren't all black and white, and maybe—just maybe—the departed deserved all that was coming to them."

"Then why are they so angry with you?" I asked, not to make her angrier, but because I wanted to know. "If they deserved it, they wouldn't be so angry, would they?"

Aunt Clara threw her head back and gave a short, barking laugh. "No one likes having their lives taken away," she said when she was done. "That doesn't mean that they didn't deserve it." She paused to look at us again. "To survive in this world, you have to sometimes do things that are unpleasant," she said. "Especially people like you, who have neither a father nor a mother. Who do you think will look out for your happiness but yourselves?"

"Is that what you did?" I asked her, and finally took Lily's hand in mine. "Did you look out for yourself?"

"Yes, Violet, I did—and I am *proud* that I did! It made *my* life better and the world no poorer . . . A woman must be able to take care of herself," she said. "Your grandmother Iris taught me that."

"But what about the law?" Lily asked from beside me, squeezing my hand hard. "There are *rules*—and what about the ones who died? Maybe they, too, wanted to make their lives better." She shook her head as if she couldn't understand it. "Why should *your* life be better and theirs be over?"

"That's just how the world works, Lily. You kill or you'll be killed. Just think about the mice. No one cries over a mouse in a trap, and are human lives truly worth that much more, or is that just something we have made up? We go to war all the time and slaughter one another, and no one even bats an eye! Why should this be any different?"

"It just *is*," Lily said, looking unhappy. "It's the *law*! And I *am* sorry for those who die in wars, too—"

"And the mice," I added. "We are also sorry about the mice."

"But if you *don't* kill the mice, they will overrun your house, eat your bread and shit in your sugar, make your bedding smell like piss, and even gnaw through the cords and set your house on fire. Is that truly what you want?" Aunt Clara bent down and stared us both in the eye—first me, then Lily.

"What does that have to do with the ghosts?" Lily asked. I could feel her fingers relax a little when Aunt Clara finally looked away.

"Everything!" She straightened up. "You are just too young to see it yet."

"But it was Cecilia's house first." I couldn't help but say it. "I think that to her, maybe *you* were the mouse—"

"Oh, keep your righteousness to yourself!" Aunt Clara suddenly bellowed. She towered above us, as tall as a house, with her hands placed at her sides. The diamonds in her ears made rainbows, too. "Why should that useless old hag have everything when I had nothing at all? People who are born to money are *vermin*."

"What will you do to us?" Lily asked in a small voice. She and I *had* been born to money, so did that make us vermin to Aunt Clara? Very probably so, and I *did* feel a little like a mouse just then, in front of a very bad snake.

"It's not about what *I* will do to you, but what *you* will do for me." Her green eyes had found me again. "*You* will undo what you did. You will get rid of *all* the ghosts! I don't know how and I don't care, but *you* brought them here and *you* will remove them!"

I didn't say anything to that, because I didn't know *what* to say. I just stared at the flashing diamonds on Aunt Clara's fingers, swallowing hard all the while.

"When those pesky critters are gone, we can discuss the future," Aunt Clara continued, sounding calm all of a sudden. "Until then, you are at the top of my shit list, and you can *both* consider that a warning!" With that, she strode out the door, slammed it closed, and locked it, too—although that wasn't really a problem anymore.

As soon as we heard her heels on the stairs, Lily turned to me and whispered, "*Don't* put the ghosts back, Violet! If you do, there's less reason for her to keep us around." She looked really scared; her eyes were very big.

I let go of her hand and put both of mine in my lap. I didn't know how to say what I needed to, and it was hard to look at Lily just then.

"I have been thinking of putting Mr. Woods back," I said at last, in a voice that was much quieter than I had meant. "He is making a lot of noise and isn't very nice, and I know how much he scares you. But, Lily." I felt like a mouse again when I looked up at her. "I don't know *how to do it.*"

Lily's eyes widened. "Don't you just . . . *feel* it?"

"No. Before, they *asked* me and then I knew, so maybe if one of them *asked* me to put them back again, I'd know how to do that, too. But no one has asked yet, so I don't know."

"What about the raven?" Lily looked at the empty window where Irpa was before. "Doesn't she know something to help you?"

I shook my head. "She doesn't tell me things with words, just pictures, and when I asked her about it, she just showed me a sword. I don't know what that means."

"Then you must *never* let Aunt Clara know that you don't know how to put them back." Lily's face was very white. "As long as she thinks you can do it, we're safe."

I swallowed hard and nodded, because I *felt* that she was right, and maybe I would figure it out, too, if only one of them *asked.*

CLARA

29

I had had enough. *Enough!* I couldn't stand it for one more minute, being in that house with the ghosts and the red-cheeked traitors huddling together in the raven room. My nieces had ruined *everything:* my quiet life and my peaceful nights—the very house itself! My home didn't feel like mine anymore. It was infested and fouled, ruined by something I couldn't get rid of, and in the midst of all that were the girls, sniggering. Even my dreams of the future suffered, because how could I even *think* about Clarabelle Diamonds when I couldn't even feed myself?

I should've been full of optimism at this point, eagerly awaiting the first finished pieces from Isabella, but instead I was surrounded by deceit and decay. The girls were supposed to be my *salvation,* but instead they had caused a literal nightmare. Instead of giving me the wings I so sorely needed to rise and *soar,* they had effectively grounded me.

And the bills came pouring in: Isabella's fee, and the jeweler's . . . white gold and precious stones. The girls' stipend couldn't cover it all, and I was way too exhausted to forge a new plan. Not even death, it seemed, could prevent my brother from making my life a living misery. The only silver lining I could think of was that if Violet had been the one to summon the ghosts, she could surely send them back as well—to rest, or whatever it was that dead people did. If only that happened, peace could be restored.

It was likewise unfortunate that my nieces knew what I had done. They were only girls, of course, and whatever claims they made could easily be dismissed, but in only a few years' time, Lily would be an adult—a very *wealthy* adult, unless I could somehow strip her of that money—and people would perhaps not be so keen to turn a deaf ear then. My nieces had become *dangerous* to me, dragging up all sorts of nasty things from the past that were better left alone, and I could hardly be faulted for thinking of ways to end my torment. I did not particularly *want* to hurt the girls—it would bring me no joy—but what they now knew could undo all I had been working for. I would lose *everything* if the truth came out, and I could hardly launch my diamond line from prison.

My legacy would become something very different from what I had envisioned.

That morning after the sheriff's visit, I paced my room up and down while thinking of clever ways of doing it. I could set a trap for them in the woods, I thought, and say it was an accident—or I could set a fire, a very small one, and say it was Violet who had been playing with matches. I could also just powder their oatmeal when Dina had her day off and claim that my nieces had run away.

The possibilities were endless—but also quite impossible.

It was the money, of course. I had come to depend upon the pay for their keep, and there was also the sweet hope of more money to come if only I played my cards right. If the girls were gone, there would be no more of anything, and Clarabelle Diamonds would die on the vine. I briefly contemplated working around this fact by taking out life insurance policies on the girls and putting myself up as beneficiary, but then I remembered the ghosts—or rather, the ghosts remembered me. Just as Timmy's infernal knocking started up again, I realized that I had no idea if getting rid of Violet would rid me of the dead as well, and living with *them* was *not* an option.

It was all just such a terrible tangle, and it suddenly felt as if the walls of my beloved home were closing in on me. For a brief moment

I had problems breathing, and all the while Timmy kept banging, while Ellie's pale face stared back at me whenever my gaze grazed the vanity mirror. Cursing and sweating, I found my overnight bag under the bed, tossed it upon the purple bedspread, and went for the phone to make arrangements. I'd be damned if I stayed in that house for even one more minute!

Less than an hour later, I was in my car on the way to the airport, leaving—most of—my troubles behind. I hadn't gotten far, however, before I caught sight of Ellie Anderson's dark eye in the rearview mirror, and I knew better than to even try to stop for a snack. It didn't matter. I had fashioned a plan and would have my little getaway regardless. I admit that I did feel relieved, though, when I had parked my car at the airport and could escape mirrors for a while. I didn't even care if my dress was stained with melon juice, or that my hair was unkempt and my face all naked.

I just wanted to get away.

I felt jubilant when the plane took off and carried me above the clouds. Saying no to the little food tray was no bother either, as it was usually not to my taste, but I did miss the glass of wine I usually had when flying. To invite Cecilia into my little bubble of happiness was not an option, though. What would the man next to me—heavyset and suited—even say if the plastic cup went flying? I comforted myself by thinking of better things to come, and as soon as the plane touched down, I was on my feet, lifting the folded fur coat and my bag out of the overhead compartment, and stood impatiently in line to get to the next part of my ad hoc adventure.

I found a taxi at the airport and was careful not to look in the mirrors while the vehicle wound its way through bustling city streets. Nightfall was not far off, and the neon lights shone brighter, spilling splashes of pink and blue upon the pedestrians lining the streets. The rush of nightlife was not what I had come for, though. I had come to find some peace and to *think,* and I knew just how to make it happen.

The hotel room, at least, was as beautiful as always. Chill air and cool colors met me as I opened the door. The gray carpet was clean and soft, while the curtains in the floor-to-ceiling windows looked reassuringly thick enough to deflect all the light. A large bed made up in blue hues dominated the floor. The room also contained a dresser, a wardrobe, and a vanity set. I promptly covered up the mirror with a robe from the bathroom. Then I lay back on the soft blue bedspread and let out a deep breath of relief.

My stomach growled, though, which was only to be expected, an alarm bell to let me know that the next part of the plan had to be executed. I rolled over on the bed and stretched out a hand to grab the phone. While waiting for the connection, I skimmed the room service menu, twice, and settled on a delectable selection. When the call ended, I finally got up to change out of the melon-stained dress and into a more comfortable purple silk robe, turned the TV on, and settled in to wait.

Sebastian arrived after half an hour, which was high time, seeing how the food was already there, waiting under silver domes that I couldn't even look at, lest Ellie Anderson look back at me in turn. My lover looked as pristine as always in his three-piece gray suit, with a pale pink bow tie and his meticulously trimmed mustache. He had been surprised when I called him to say that I would be in the city that night, but pleased, too, I thought. We often met at this hotel, as he shared his home with his elderly mother and a quarrelsome parrot named Tulip. Ever since Cecilia, I hadn't much liked being around the sick and old. I suppose I'd had enough of it to last me at least a lifetime. Tulip was also both noisy and loud and had a limited vocabulary consisting mostly of curses. Sebastian had adopted the bird as company for his mother, and clearly its former home had been a wild one. I much preferred the taxidermy parrot in my winter garden.

Sebastian presented me with a single red rose as he entered the room. Clearly, he thought this meeting was a romantic one, and I could hardly blame him for that, since he had no reason to think otherwise—yet. When he leaned in to kiss me, I ducked.

"Later maybe," I told him, and moved farther into the room. I dropped the rose on the vanity. "First you have to feed me."

"Oh?" He arched an eyebrow in a playful way, but my stomach ached too much from hunger for me to appreciate the gesture. "With pleasure," he added in a sultry voice.

"Not in an *erotic* way. I need you to help me get sustenance."

"But of course!" He still thought it was some kind of play.

I sat down on the edge of the bed and lifted one of the silver domes to reveal the chicken and assorted greens. I knew that under the dome next to it was a piece of salmon and some fancy potatoes. There was also a glass bowl filled with strawberries and meringue. On a small china platter all by itself stood a single piece of artisan chocolate.

"A little bit of everything." I handed Sebastian the fork.

He did look a little astonished when he settled in and started feeding me pieces of chicken and fish—it was probably not what he had imagined when he arrived, ready for a night of lovemaking. He was far too polite to ask, however, which was just what I had been counting on. The food tasted good, though—it was the best I had had since Cecilia came back—and I savored every juicy mouthful. Sebastian gave me wine, too, trickled it into my mouth, and he didn't even spill one drop, unlike Dina at home.

Three strawberries in, I was sated and motioned for him to put the fork down. By then, however, his politeness had given way to worry. "You seem starved, Clara—what is this nonsense? Are you on a new diet?"

"No," I muttered. "Nothing like that. I just wanted you to feed me, that's all."

"But why?" His large brown eyes looked up at me with worry. "If it's not in an 'erotic' way—"

"Perhaps I *do* have some issues. Maybe sometimes it's hard for me to feed myself, and I need a little help to get it down."

"Oh, Clara." He was instantly all soft compassion; he scooted farther up on the bed, placed his hands on my shoulders, and started gently kneading the steely knots of muscle he found there. I had to admit that it felt amazing. "It's the stress," he said. "I'm sure it's just the stress of everything that has happened lately, with the girls and your brother's death . . . Grief can take all sorts of shapes." He leaned closer and whispered into my ear, "You know I would feed you every day if you would let me."

I caught his kneading hand in my own and whispered back, "I know."

It was the cruelest irony of my life that I had found this nice, clever, and handsome man only after it was too late for me—and through Timmy's betrayal, no less. The first time we had met, I had still been running hot on the fumes from the night of the ax and had wanted to milk the high of its every last drop. That was why I had sought him out: Sebastian Swift, the flustered appraiser I had spoken to on the phone, just so I could see what he looked like, the man Timmy had approached to help him sell my diamonds. I had even brought a few rings along, keeping up the ruse. I had not expected to find a lover, though, when stepping across the jeweler's threshold; had not expected to find a man whose passion even rivaled my own.

He had held my hand in the coming months while the police still looked for Timmy and his mistress. He had showered me with compassion and brotherly kisses; brought me tissues when it all became too much; and had waited, patiently, while the hope of finding Timmy dried up, until he finally made his move. I was already quite taken by then, and could not help but feel a flutter in my chest whenever he was near. In a different story, we would've been a perfect match—but alas, it was too late for me. I had paid with blood for all I got, and despite my best efforts, I no longer knew how to trust.

Sebastian was also a *decent* man, and decent I was surely not. I liked that he thought that I was, though—*decent*. I liked who I was in his eyes. Whenever we were together, I could somewhat forget the crushing of the pills and the honing of the ax, and *be* that woman for a little while. It brought me an immense sense of relief—but of course, I never forgot. I never fooled myself into thinking it could last, or even truly develop. If I brought him too close, I was doomed to slip up, or he would lift the wrong cushion and see what was hidden beneath.

He was better off with his mother and Tulip—it was *safer* for him, with them.

To his credit, though, Sebastian was still here, ten years after we first met. Though I had been clear about my expectations, he still kindled hope. I suppose it was a gift to be loved like that, even if said love was doomed—and even if the woman he *truly* loved was nothing but a mask that I sometimes slipped on.

"You need to relax," he cooed at me next. "Do you want me to draw you a bath?"

I nodded in reply, but then I changed my mind, remembering the large, well-lit mirror in there. It just wouldn't do if Ellie showed up sporting her glistening wounds.

"Let's just stay here," I told him. "Keep working your magic on those knots." I lifted a hand to motion at my shoulders, and he grabbed it and kissed the diamonds on my fingers—to him, they were as much a part of me as the hand itself, and just as worthy of affection. I adored this side of him. "Perhaps I feel a little romantic after all," I admitted, then turned my head to beg for a kiss, and soon we were both at it, tugging at each other's clothes.

For a while then, all was good. Sebastian and I moved in under the covers and had enjoyed each other for quite some time when the first knock erupted. At first, I thought the sound came from the hallway—that some hapless maid was trying to force her way inside to change soiled sheets and mini soaps, but then the knocking sounded again—and again—increasing in strength with every knock. It didn't take me very long to realize that the knocking came from *inside* the room.

Sadly, Sebastian had realized as well.

"What is that?" He stopped what he was doing and looked up.

"Oh, nothing," I murmured, wanting him to continue.

"But it sounds like there's someone *inside* the wardrobe—"

"Nonsense." I tried to laugh, but it came out unconvincing. "There's no one inside the wardrobe."

Then the lamp by the bed started blinking, and the hissing sound came creeping, and then Sebastian sat up in the bed and looked wildly around him.

"What is this?" he asked the air. "Is there a fire?"

I had no idea why he drew that particular conclusion, but I sighed and sat up as well. "I have no idea." I feigned astonishment. "Maybe there's something wrong with the electric—" The room service cart flew across the floor on rickety wheels, crashing into the vanity. A silver dome and several flower-shaped potatoes dropped onto the lush carpet.

"Oh my goodness!" Sebastian cried, and fled the bed. "Did you see that, Clara?" He looked at me, wild-eyed.

"Yes, yes." I sat up under the covers. "Maybe it's an earthquake," I tried.

"Perhaps." Sebastian's voice was shivering, and the bedside lamp kept blinking. He was already reaching for his pants, so I figured that was all the relaxation I would get.

Next, the bathrobe I had so carefully draped over the vanity mirror fell down—doubtlessly guided by my husband's spectral hand—and since I was in clear view, Ellie Anderson came rushing forward, grinning out into the room with bloodstained teeth.

"Who is that?" Sebastian cried. "Do you see the woman, Clara?" He lifted a finger to point at the ghost, who, despite being dead, was clearly both younger and prettier than me.

"Of course I do," I snapped. "The wretched thing keeps following me around!"

I shouldn't have gotten angry, of course. I knew from experience that it was a bad idea. As soon as the words were out of my mouth, chaos erupted: The pillows rose from the bed by themselves and exploded in a flurry of feathers; the rest of the silver domes on the room service cart flew up in the air and clattered down again, while mangled chicken and tomato wedges came hurtling through the room— aiming for me.

"We have to get out!" Sebastian declared while fighting to get his pants back on.

"No kidding," I muttered as I bent to get my robe off the floor. In the mirror, Ellie Anderson laughed soundlessly.

The hissing sound was nearing its crescendo by then, and the dresser drawers started opening and shutting by themselves. The wineglass I had previously drunk from came crashing into the wall above the bed, showering the mattress in glittering shards and missing me by inches.

"Oh, *come on*, Timmy!" I yelled at the invisible man. "As if *you* have a right to be jealous!"

I should not have said that, though, as the glass-enclosed overhead light instantly exploded, adding even more glass shards to the grotesque mélange. I screamed, and Sebastian screamed, and we were both running for the door, picking up items of clothing as we went.

Out in the hallway we both leaned against the wall to breathe. Neither of us was bleeding, I noticed, which was a small miracle. There were no security guards in sight, so it didn't seem like the haunting had caused a stir yet. It was still going on in there, though; we could hear more items hitting the wall all the time. Sebastian looked at me with wild eyes. The fear had all but ruined his complexion; he was white as a sheet under the tan.

"You are haunted," he accused me—or stated the obvious. "Who *was* that in there?"

"Timmy," I grudgingly admitted. "And Ellie Anderson." I sighed deeply. I was clutching the melon-stained dress in my hands but was still wearing just the silk robe. "He seems to have had a change of heart after death." I served Sebastian a story he just might buy. "His mistress has not, though. I think she is jealous of him coming home to me."

"Oh my goodness, are they *dead*?" He shook his head and stared at the closed door.

"Clearly," I said with a snort. "Something must have gone wrong on their travels, or perhaps they both succumbed to some disease. Whatever the reason, they are here now and just won't leave me in peace."

"Have you told the police?" His eyes were round as marbles.

"No, of course not. What would I say? That my vanished husband is haunting me? They would never believe such a story." With some effort, I managed to break through the ire I felt and arrange my face in a sad expression.

"Oh, you poor thing." He briefly folded me into his arms, before letting me go again, brushing tiny specks of glass from his suit.

"I have *never* experienced anything like this," he said next, sounding utterly astonished.

"Well, I would rather not 'experience' anything like it again." I gave him a very dark look.

"But it is proof of life after death." He shook his head. "Perhaps you should call the press?"

"Oh no!" I held up my hands as if to shield myself from the flashes. "I just want them both to be gone."

His mood shifted instantly. "Yes, it is a tragic thing, isn't it? Being trapped on this side." He was still staring at the door. "At least you know for sure that he is dead—so I suppose that's a relief, even if we have suspected it for a while—"

"Yes." I would rather not talk about Timmy's death. "I just wish he would rest in peace."

Sebastian looked at me with compassion. "My mother saw my grandfather once, but it wasn't anything like *this* . . . I suppose you are right, though, and that he *did* have a change of heart. Not that I blame him one bit." The statement was followed by a look of adoration, which I shamelessly sucked up.

"How did your mother get rid of him?" I asked.

"He just disappeared by himself. It was only the once, though, and he never acted like *that*." He pointed at the door with a look of amazement. "Have you *tried* to get rid of them?"

"You mean like with a priest?" I dearly wanted a glass of wine or four, but I didn't think I could find it in me to ask Sebastian for help again.

"Yes . . . or with a medium," he replied. "They are the experts, after all. They can make the spirits go into the light."

"Into the light, huh?" I muttered, just as another crash from inside the room made us both cower. "What kind of light is that?"

"The place where people go when they die," Sebastian explained when we had both straightened up. "Only the people who become ghosts refuse the light, or they miss it when they die."

"How would that even work? How would the medium 'make' them?" This was, in fact, very useful information.

"The medium can talk to them," Sebastian replied. "Sometimes they just need some convincing; other times they need their stories to be heard. A medium can help them with that."

This was *definitely* interesting. "How do you even know all this?" I asked, while picking glass shards out of my hair.

"I saw it on TV." He shrugged. "I'm sure there are plenty of books about it."

I felt a little better then—*even* if I would have to pay for the damaged hotel room.

"The light" seemed to be the answer to my plight, and I knew *just* who was going to help me make it happen.

VIOLET

30

"Sit up straight in your chair, Violet, and focus on the candle flame. Can you do that, do you think?" Aunt Clara stared at me. We were all sitting around the table in the dining room: Lily, Aunt Clara, Dina, and I. Aunt Clara had come home late in the day and hadn't even taken off her coat before she told us to gather up and said she had made a plan. She had decided to talk to the ghosts, she said, and then she was going to chase them to a light. When Lily asked her why she thought they would suddenly start to talk, she said that *I* was going to make them, which I thought was strange, since I had never been able to before. We did as Aunt Clara said, though, and sat down in the dining room, since it didn't seem smart to argue with her when she was so excited.

All five wax candles in one of the candelabras were lit, and we were all holding hands. Lily and Dina had to stretch across the table to make their fingers link. Next to Aunt Clara on the table was a book. It was blue and small, and the front had the title *How to Talk to Spirits* written in big yellow letters. Aunt Clara said she had read it on the plane.

Now we were just waiting for something to happen.

I didn't think it would work since I had no idea how to talk to them and wasn't even sure if I wanted to. Something had happened while Aunt Clara was away that had made Mr. Woods seem scary again.

Everything had been so nice at first, after Aunt Clara and the ghosts had left. Lily, Dina, and I had played cards in the kitchen before we went outside to hang clothes to dry.

It was while we stood there by the clothesline, holding the large wet sheets out between us, that Lily started talking about calling Mr. Skye while Aunt Clara was away, to tell him what was buried at the bottom of the garden. She had been so disappointed that the sheriff had done nothing that I was happy to see that she hadn't given up but was still trying to find ways to tell someone what Aunt Clara had done.

Dina shook her head, though. "You risk undermining your own cause, Lily, if you go to them with just a ghost story as proof. Remember what happened with the sheriff. Mrs. Woods is very good at speaking for herself."

"What if you do it?" I suggested. Dina was an adult, so that would maybe help.

"I wish I could." She bit her lip. "But if something goes wrong, I'd lose my job, and then who would look after you? I just don't want to see you stranded here alone with *her*."

"What if we *did* have proof?" Lily's face lit up like a Christmas tree. "What if we dug up Mr. Woods ourselves and called the sheriff after we did? Aunt Clara isn't here, so she can't stop us." It had been a long time since I had seen her so happy.

Even Dina looked impressed and said, "That's the best plan I've heard in ages."

And so it was decided: We were going to find Mr. Woods's bones ourselves.

When all the sheets had been hung and we had gone back inside, Lily and I changed out of our summer dresses and into thick corduroy pants and T-shirts. Lily put up our hair in ponytails. Dina didn't have anything to change into, so she was still wearing her orange-striped dress, but she had gone down in the basement and brought up lots of shovels and a pickax. She put all the shovels down on the kitchen floor and Lily and I picked one each. Dina brought the pickax, too, in case the ground was hard. Then we started out for the garden again.

It didn't seem scary at all, at first. The sun was blazing from a clear blue sky, and there were sounds of birds in the air. The fresh green grass had grown high by then, and we barely even saw the wizened yellow in the lawn. There were wildflowers, too: daisies and goldenrods, snapdragons and thistles. A thousand pink roses had sprung from the vines that crept across the pavilion. I was happy to see that the plum trees were coming in—plums were Lily's absolute favorite, just like cherries were mine, and we would eat lots of both when we went to visit Grandma Fiona before she died.

We waded through the grass and the flowers until we finally arrived at the bottom of the garden, and Dina put the pickax down. She had a pair of large sunglasses perched upon her nose and her brow was glistening with sweat.

"So where is he?" she asked me.

"There." I pointed to the flower bed in the middle of the crescent, where he had been stuck. It was even more overgrown now, with thistles and nettles. The mossy stones that lined the flower bed looked even more furry than before. "I don't think he is alone, though," I said, since I got a *feeling*. "I think maybe *she* is down there, too."

"Ellie Anderson?" Lily asked, and I nodded.

"That makes sense." Dina drew an arm across her forehead. "She would have buried them together, of course."

"What about Miss Lawrence?" Lily asked. "Is she here, too?"

"No, she is buried at the cemetery," Dina replied. "I don't know how these things work, why Mr. Woods haunts his grave while Miss Lawrence haunts the place she died—"

"They get stuck where they leave their bodies," I said, since that was what Irpa had showed me. "Some do it fast and leave right when they die, while others take some time before they want to go. It makes sense, though. It's hard to leave the place where you have lived all of your life." Irpa had showed me a snail shell when she explained it to me. "Ellie Anderson never even left the mattress before slipping out of her skin."

"Ew." Lily grimaced since she didn't like dead things. "If only we can find a bone or two, the sheriff will have to believe us. We don't have to dig up the whole skeleton." She grimaced again.

I didn't really listen to her, though. Something had changed around us. It was like a shivering *wrongness* had come into the air. I looked around us in every direction and couldn't see a thing, but I still knew—deep inside—that something *bad* was coming. "There's something wrong," I told the others.

"What is wrong?" Lily asked. "You don't have to help dig un-less you want to," she said, thinking I was just trying to wriggle out of it.

"It's not that." I shook my head. "It's just that something feels *wrong*—"

"You can go back to the house—"

"No, it's not that. I *want* to dig, but now I feel like maybe we *shouldn't*." My heart had started hammering hard and fast in my chest, and I got this strong feeling inside as if we *shouldn't* dig. As if we would be doing something *wrong* if we did.

Just then, Irpa came flying above us and landed on top of the pa-vilion. I looked at her, hoping she could help, while cold sweat started pouring out of my body. She showed me an image of Mr. Woods lying on top of the pile of bones, deep in the earth, protecting it with his ghost body. Then she showed me an image of the three of us walk-ing back toward the house with the shovels. "*She* thinks we should go back," I said, still looking at Irpa.

"Who does?" Dina was confused. "The bird does?" She had fol-lowed my gaze to Irpa, and I remembered that we hadn't told Dina about her yet. Lily thought it was too soon after the ghosts and that Dina might be frightened—even if Irpa was much more helpful than the ghosts.

Inside me, another *knowing* came drifting up, like something I had forgotten and then remembered again. "Mr. Woods is afraid that us moving the bones will make him weak, and then he can't bother Aunt Clara anymore."

Just as I said it, a strong wind came blowing in from the woods and rushed through the garden. There weren't any clouds, but the wind just kept coming. I knew that it was him, even though I didn't see him. I just *knew* that he had come back to make sure we didn't touch the bones.

"What *is* that?" Dina looked into the darkness between the trees.

"It's *him*," I said, "and he is very mad."

Dina turned to look at me, but then she had to look away again because leaves and twigs and pieces of tree bark started coming in with the wind. All the while the draft became stronger until it whipped the grass and made the trees sway. Pinecones and dirt hit our faces, and the hissing noise was there now, too, together with the howling of the wind.

"Drop the shovels and get back inside!" Dina shouted. "Get back inside, girls!" she cried again, just as a tree branch came flying from the woods.

We both did as she said and dropped what we held before turning and running as fast as we could. All the while we were being hit with things from the woods: thorny twigs and pinecones, even a pebble or two. Dina came up behind us, crying all the while, "Get back, girls! Get back!"—and we did. We didn't stop at all until we were back in the kitchen.

Once we were inside, I dropped to the floor and just lay there on the cool tiles, trying to catch my breath. Lily, too, placed her hands on her thighs and leaned forward, breathing heavily. Dina leaned against the counter, very sweaty and very pale. When she moved again, it was just to turn around and open a cupboard to take out the bottle of rum. Outside the windows, the wind was still blowing, until—suddenly—it stopped.

The silence was somehow louder than the wind had been. Every-

thing felt like glass around me, as if nothing was really real. It reminded me of the day when we had first learned what had happened
to Mama and Papa. Lily went to stand by the window, looking out,
and after a minute I crawled up to my feet and joined her.

"He didn't want us to dig up the bones," I told my sister.

"But why?" Dina asked. She didn't even bother with cocoa this
time, but drank the rum straight out of the bottle. "Isn't that what
ghosts want? To be found?"

"He doesn't want to go away," I said. "He thinks that if we move
the bones, he will become less real again."

"Why?" Dina asked again.

"Will he?" Lily asked.

"Maybe." I shrugged. "Or maybe because he is so used to having a
body there, he is afraid that he won't be as strong without one. I'm not
sure if Mr. Woods is very smart."

"Certainly strong, though," Dina noted.

"How do you know?" Lily asked me.

"I don't know," I replied. "I just *feel* it."

"I thought the ghosts had gone with Mrs. Woods." Dina came to
stand with us, too, looking out on the ruined garden, where branches
lay scattered everywhere, as if there had been a real storm. The sky,
though, was just as blue as before, with not as much as a single cloud.

I shrugged again. "He must have felt that the bones were in danger.
He loves them very much." I saw a snail house again, an empty one,
hidden deep in the dirt. I suppose I would have felt the same way if
someone wanted to do something to the town house.

"But what are we going to do now?" Lily asked. None of us could
come up with an answer. Digging him up was the best plan we had
ever had, and now we were back where we started. "It was our only
hope." She sounded so disappointed that my heart hurt. "Digging
him up would have been the perfect thing to make people believe us.
I don't even care anymore if Violet and I get separated. It's more important to stay alive."

"She won't *kill* you, Lily," Dina said. "You're far too valuable to her
for that."

"Well, she's done it before," Lily replied, and none of us could argue with that.

So that was why it wasn't a good day for Aunt Clara to talk to the ghosts. None of them had ever attacked *us* before, only Aunt Clara, so what had happened in the garden had been a very bad surprise. None of us were going to tell *her* about it, though, and so we just sat down at the dining room table and held one another's hands.

No one except for Aunt Clara thought it would work.

"I don't think they want to talk," I said when I had looked at the candles for a very long time. "If they did, they would have."

"But how did you reach them before?" Aunt Clara asked. "What was it you had brought with you to the basement?" Her eyes shone about as much as her diamonds right then.

"Food," I admitted after a while. "Things for the ghost to eat—they need that, to be strong."

"Well, should we bring out some food, then?" Aunt Clara smiled in a wicked way. "It said nothing about it in the book, but maybe our ghosts are different."

"I don't know." Something squeezed inside my chest. This didn't seem like a good idea at all, and I wished that I was up in the raven room with Irpa, doing nothing.

"Of course you don't," Aunt Clara sneered. "I would just like to remind you that none of this would have happened in the first place if it hadn't been for you . . . and if *you* won't put them back again, *I* surely will."

"We do have a roast in the freezer," Dina offered, mostly to make her stop yelling at me, I think. "Do you want me to go and get it, Mrs. Woods?"

"Yes." Aunt Clara let go of our hands and I pulled mine back as fast as I could. It was cold and wet from holding hers. "What else?" Aunt Clara looked at me again.

"Wine, maybe? Or sugar?" I didn't *feel* anything, so I was just guessing.

After Dina had risen and gone to the kitchen, Aunt Clara snorted and stretched out her long legs under the table.

"This is what happens when children poke their noses where they don't belong," she said. "And this is the thanks I get for opening my home to orphans. If only you hadn't stepped out of line—"

"Why do you want to talk to them anyway?" Lily interrupted her, which I thought was very brave. I, for one, didn't think I could stand being yelled at again. I felt as thin as paper just then, like something that could rip and blow away.

"I want to make them go into the light," Aunt Clara said, the same thing she had said before. "Spirits aren't supposed to roam around down here; they are supposed to go into the light and be gone." Her eyes were a little wild when she looked at me again. "*You* must surely know that, since *you* pulled them out in the first place." She looked very happy with herself; a smile even spread on her lips. "I suppose you thought you could keep that from me—that I wouldn't find out how it works—but you cannot fool an old fox forever, Violet. I will fix it myself, since you won't." She was still looking awfully happy, which made the squeeze in my chest feel even worse.

Thankfully, Dina came back then, carrying a tray of food, and we all got busy laying it out. There was the roast, a piece of ham, and some bacon on a plate—not one of the nice ones with gold rims, but just a normal blue plate. She also had a glass bowl full of sugar cubes, a jar of raspberry jam, and a bottle of white wine instead of red. I suppose she remembered the mess in the basement and wanted to avoid more stains.

"Well?" Aunt Clara said when all the food was laid out. She reached out her hands again, waiting for Lily and me to grab them. We did it very slowly. "What now?" She looked at me again, as if *I* had all the answers. I didn't want to look at her, though, so I looked at the glistening ham instead.

"Aren't we supposed to say something?" Dina asked. "Shouldn't we call on them or something?"

"Oh yes." Aunt Clara straightened up in the chair. "Spirits," she said in a serious voice. "Won't you come and talk to us? We have brought you food." But the spirits didn't seem to care. "Spirits," she tried again. "Come and have some . . . sugar cubes." She moved a little on the chair, looking a little angry again.

"Maybe *you* should try to eat something," Dina suggested. "Cecilia would come then." She looked very clever when she said it, and even a little mean.

Aunt Clara only glared at her. She was getting angrier all the time, and her face became harder and harder as we sat there around the table, waiting for something to happen.

"You could at least *try* to help," she hissed at me, making it squeeze in my chest again. "This is *your* mess!"

I swallowed hard and just couldn't help it when tears came seeping into my eyes. I hated Aunt Clara so much right then for making me feel so bad.

She seemed to have grown tired of waiting, though, and decided to give it a last try. "Timmy!" she bellowed at the top of her lungs. "Get in here right now!"

LILY

31

Violet's head fell back and her eyes rolled up. I was on my way out of the chair before I could even think, but Aunt Clara yanked me back again, refusing to let go of my hand.

"Sit," she hissed, and I did, but my heart was thundering wildly in my chest and I couldn't stop staring at Violet with dread.

Just as suddenly as Violet's head had fallen back, it came back up and fell down on her chest. Something dark and sticky came tumbling out of her mouth to land on her polka-dot blouse. It was dirt, I realized after a while. Clumps of spit-slick dirt came falling out of her. On the table, the candles started flickering madly, even though there was no draft.

Slowly, Violet raised her head. Her eyes were still rolled back in her head, and her chin was dark with dirt. Just as slowly her mouth opened wide, and then she started to speak, in a very dark and very male voice.

"Clara, you old cow! You always had to get your way." Violet's jaws moved around as if she was chewing, or maybe it was just hard for him to form the words. Hearing Mr. Woods's voice come out of Violet's mouth was almost too much for me, and my vision swam for a moment. I think Dina maybe noticed, because she squeezed my hand right after.

"Timmy!" Aunt Clara sounded giddy. "How good to finally have a conversation. You could have used your words long ago, instead of throwing my possessions around like a petulant five-year-old."

The man inside Violet laughed. It was a very disturbing sound. "I mean to get you, you crazy hag!"

Aunt Clara laughed, too, although it didn't sound very confident. "I won't insult you by asking why, but you have been trying for weeks now and yet here I am—still whole!"

"I mean to take my time," Mr. Woods replied. "I won't rest until your blood has been spilled, but first I want to see you squirm!"

"How utterly dramatic." Aunt Clara was getting back some of her bite. "You *know* that what happened was all your fault. If only you hadn't tried to take my diamonds—"

"Be quiet!" Mr. Woods bellowed, and Violet's small body shook. "*You* took my *life* from me, Clara," he complained. "You took—" Suddenly he stopped, and Violet's face changed. It looked like something was moving quickly under her skin. Again I tried to get up, and again Aunt Clara yanked me back.

When Violet spoke next, it was with the voice of an old woman. "There is no use in fighting this, Clarabelle." She turned her head to look at Aunt Clara. It was almost even more frightening to see Violet like that, moving like our grandmother used to, all slow and careful. "We all get what we deserve in the end, and there is no escaping this time." Her lips curved in an almost gentle smile. "I will make you a prisoner of this house, just as you made me." It was a threat, but it sounded almost sad. "We all reap what we sow—"

"Oh, spare me!" Aunt Clara spat. "Isn't it about time that you went into the light? It's supposed to be there, all white and bright!"

The old woman in Violet gave a cackling laugh. "You can save your breath, Clarabelle. You were a fool to think there was no malice in me. I can be as bitter and cruel as you—just watch me, you dreadful goat! Before I am done, I'll see you gone from *my* house!"

Before Aunt Clara had had time to say anything else, Violet's face changed again. It made me feel sick to look at it, but I couldn't look away either, because it was Violet—my *sister*—and I was supposed to take care of her.

Mama and Papa wouldn't have liked this at all.

"Good evening, Mrs. Woods," Violet chirped as the last ghost came to life. Ellie Anderson made Violet's face look almost normal— but not quite. "It would have been my thirty-seventh birthday today. Did you know that, Mrs. Woods?"

"Nonsense," Aunt Clara growled.

"Yes, maybe it is." Ellie sounded puzzled. "I have *no* idea what day it is, but I like to think that it is my birthday—or that it *would* have been, if you hadn't cut my life short."

"What do you want, Ellie?" Aunt Clara barked. "I have no time for you! If you think that you can scare me—"

Ellie Anderson laughed. "Scare you? Oh goodness, no. I just want you to face the consequences—every time you look at yourself." She still sounded chipper, but also somehow angry. A little more dirt fell out of Violet's mouth.

"Ever the teacher, huh?" Aunt Clara's eyes shot daggers. "If you truly want to celebrate your 'birthday' in style, you should go and look for a light. It's very bright and very white—"

"There is no light for the likes of us. *You* have seen to that." The woman in Violet didn't sound chipper anymore, and something dark had come into her expression. Her eyes had narrowed and her head was lowered. "We cannot willingly march on to the life beyond and let you continue to do as you please. There must be *consequences*, Mrs. Woods, and so there will be no rest for us until you, too, have been killed by unkind hands!"

Suddenly, all the candles in the candelabra went out and the dining room was plunged into darkness. I was out of my seat at once, and this time Aunt Clara didn't stop me. I stumbled through the darkness to the other side of the table while Aunt Clara cursed and Dina fumbled with the matches. I didn't stop before I had Violet in my arms. She was breathing hard by then and was drenched with sweat.

"Violet!" I shouted. "Violet!"

"Lily?" Her voice—her *normal* voice—sounded groggy. "What happened?" she asked, just as Dina gave up on the matches and went for the light switch instead. Suddenly the dining room was bathed in a warm electric glow, and it was the most beautiful thing I had ever seen. There was a smell in there, though, that hadn't been there before, of rank meat and burned sugar. When I looked at the table, it was easy to see why: All the food we had laid out had gone bad. There was a thick crust of green mold on *everything*, and the sugar in the bowl looked like it had melted. Dina saw it at the same time that I did, and she lifted the wineglass to sniff at it.

"Just vinegar now," she said with a grimace. "Are you all right, Violet?"

"Uh-huh." Violet nodded and freed herself from my arms. She used her hand to wipe the dirt off her chin, then looked at her hand with a puzzled expression. "What happened?" she asked again.

"Don't you remember any of it?" I was relieved when she shook her head. It was bad enough that *I* remembered.

"I'll throw this out." Dina looked disgusted as she gathered up the ruined food on the tray.

"Well, that was pointless." Aunt Clara's voice was sharp enough to cut. "Clearly, they won't just go quietly into the light. That means it's all on you again." Her gaze landed on Violet and I shuddered inside when I saw the purple flames crowding her skin. As soon as Dina was out the door, she continued speaking, fast and quiet. "You better make them go away at once, or maybe there'll be a few more ghosts joining their ranks . . ." She rose and strode quickly out of the room, leaving Violet and me behind.

I helped Violet up from the chair and supported her as we walked up the stairs. I had wanted to take her to the bathroom to clean up and then go downstairs to reheat some soup for her, but I never got that far.

As soon as we reached the upstairs landing, Violet turned to me and said, "I don't feel so good, Lily." Then she staggered a little and fell.

I cried out for Dina while bending over her and placing my hand on her brow—it was ice-cold—and pushed my other arm under her shoulders so I could lift her up from the floor. My heart didn't properly beat again before I saw her eyelids flutter and I knew she was alive. She was horribly pale, though—almost like a ghost—and her freckles stood out on her skin. By the time Dina arrived on the landing, I was crying because I was so scared and angry.

"She just fell down," I sniffled when Dina crouched down next to me. "Aunt Clara should *never* have made her do it. Violet is really sick!"

"She's coming to now," Dina said in a voice that was much calmer than mine. When I looked at Violet's face, I could see that her eyes were open.

"Are you okay?" I asked in a voice hoarse with fear. "Are you okay, Violet?"

She gave a faint smile in reply and struggled to sit up, supported by Dina and me. "What happened now?" she asked groggily.

"You fell, Violet! You fainted!" I replied, in that same hoarse voice that I just couldn't shake.

"The affair in the dining room took a toll on you, I think." Dina shook her head. "It's madness what she's doing. Just mad . . . Do you think you can stand up, Violet? Do you think you can walk to your bed if we help you?"

Violet nodded, but I felt furious. "She can't just go to bed!" I cried. "She needs a doctor! Someone has to look at her!"

"It will be fine, Lily." Dina gave me a reassuring smile. "A fainting spell doesn't have to mean that anything is seriously wrong. But if she doesn't recover swiftly and easily, we'll definitely call a doctor—behind *her* back if we have to." She lowered her voice as she said the last part, and glanced at the stairs behind us. We heard opera music coming up from downstairs, though, so Aunt Clara probably could not hear us.

We supported Violet between us as we entered the raven room, and she didn't protest at being manhandled, which told me she had to be feeling really bad.

"Are you dizzy, Violet? Are your legs like jelly?" I fussed while Dina made up the bed. Violet didn't answer, but nodded a few times, so I guessed both things were true. I let out my breath when her head touched the pillow and she could finally rest. I was shivering myself, I noticed, when I sat down next to her on the bed. My hands were shaking badly when I tousled her hair, and I was sniffling again. When I pressed my hand to her forehead, I could tell that it was hot now—like fever hot—even though it had been cold and clammy before. It felt as though she was burning up.

Dina, too, had noticed. "I'll get the thermometer," she said, and started for the door. "I'll bring some cold water, too, and a cloth." She slipped out the door and closed it behind her, leaving me and Violet alone. I sat there sniffling and patting her hand for a while before she finally spoke again.

"I'm so hot," she whispered.

"I know, but it will get better soon." I tried to comfort her. "Dina will bring you everything you need—"

"It's like I'm burning up," she complained, and started wriggling on the bed to get out from under the covers.

"No, lie still," I said, and flung them aside myself, not wanting to let Violet move even an inch if she didn't have to. What I saw, though, made me feel dizzy: In the gap between Violet's plaid skirt and her polka-dot shirt, tadpoles squirmed on the white skin of her belly. There were so many of them, and they moved so fast, darting under the fabric. They weren't big ones like in the garden, but small ones, like normal tadpoles. And all of them were angry red.

"Oh, Violet," I burst out, "there are tadpoles on your belly."

She lifted her head to look down at her body and pulled her shirt up to get a better view. "I don't see any," she said in a faint voice.

"Well, they're there," I sobbed.

"I didn't think you saw any colors on me," she said.

"I don't, but this is different. I don't think they are yours," I explained. "Only ghosts have tadpoles like that—and especially Mr. Woods."

"Do you think he made me sick?" She sounded very little.

"Yes," I whispered, and reached out a hand, letting it hover just above the moving mass. "Maybe I can take them away," I whispered, and was just about to try when Dina came back inside, carrying a tray with a water pitcher, a bowl, cloths, a thermometer, and a couple of pills. Some of the leftover soup was on there as well, in case Violet was strong enough to eat something.

While Dina gave Violet water and measured her sky-high temperature, I paced the floor behind her, much like Aunt Clara had done just a few days ago. My belly was tied up in a knot and I couldn't stop thinking of the tadpoles. I was too afraid to be angry just then, but both Aunt Clara and Mr. Woods were scum in my book. How could they do this to Violet? I knew that saying something to our aunt wouldn't help one bit, but I sure wanted to. Violet looked so very small and pale against the pillow.

"I must feed Mrs. Woods." Dina rose from the lip of the bed. "I'll tell her that Violet is sick, but—"

"I know," I said. "I know she won't do anything. We'll call a doctor, though, tomorrow, if Violet isn't better by then." I wasn't sure if the doctor could help with the tadpoles, but it was good to have a plan.

Dina nodded and smiled. "First thing," she assured me, then unloaded the soup on Violet's nightstand and went downstairs to feed the beast.

As soon as Dina was out the door, Violet turned her burning gaze on me. "Take them away, Lily," she begged me.

"I don't know if I can," I said, wetting my lips nervously. "But I *will* try," I promised.

I pushed her shirt farther up again and watched the quicksilver tadpoles as they darted across her skin. With a strong feeling of distaste, I reached out a hand and captured one of them, holding it up in the air by the tail. It wasn't any bigger than an inch, and it still moved around, twisting under my pinched fingers. It was like a stray flame, I thought. A sick one.

"Did you get it?" Violet asked. "Is it there, Lily?" She looked at my fingers.

"I captured one," I said. "But now I don't know what to do with it."
I looked at the squirming thing dangling from my fingers. It was a
disgusting thing—*vile,* even. And yet . . . Violet was *so* sick, so desperate for my help, and suddenly I knew *just* what to do. Without
even thinking—because then I might gag—I opened my mouth and
stuffed the icky tadpole inside.

It tasted like nothing, but I felt it in there, wriggling on my tongue.
I closed my eyes as it slipped down my throat and tried not to imagine it passing down to my stomach.

"Lily," Violet whispered, surprised, "did you *eat* it?"

I nodded. "It's gone now," I assured her, and I *felt* that it was true.
Somehow, I just *knew* that by eating the tadpole I had made it into a
harmless nothing.

As if my body could freeze it and melt it.

I picked another one from Violet's belly and ate that one, too, and
then, when that went well, I picked another. It took me almost half
the night to pick all the tadpoles and swallow them down, and after a
while, I didn't even think that it was strange or disgusting anymore,
just something that had to be done. Both Violet and I were exhausted
when it was over, and her belly was finally free from squirming things.

"How could they do this to you?" I burst out when the last tadpole
had slipped down my throat. "How could the ghosts make you sick,
after all you have done for them?" I was crying again, but only because
I was tired.

"I know why," Violet whispered. "It was because it happened
wrong. Because the one who *asked* wasn't dead."

CLARA

32

I could not sleep at all on the night following the failed séance, but just lay there tossing and turning on the sheets. I'd be damned if I would just give up and doom myself to an existence as an invalid in my own home, yet that was how the situation seemed at present, seeing how I could not feed myself or even look at myself in the mirror. I could only comfortably leave the house for short periods of time, and without so much as a dab of makeup—and yet that wasn't *all* they had planned for me. The little séance had made as much clear. The ghosts meant to see me *dead* before they vanished. I wasn't hurt by that fact, or particularly furious, as I would probably have felt the same way if someone had slain *me* before my time. And seeing how I had done just that to *them*, I could even empathize somewhat with the sentiment.

It is a powerful thing, wanting someone dead.

I would never forget the euphoric feeling of climbing the stairs to this very room on the night of the ax: the heft of the tool in my hands and the fury that burned in my heart. I remembered pushing the door open and seeing them there on the bed, scantily clad and headed for lovemaking. The feeling of the first swing of the ax as it bit into Timmy's shirt-clad shoulder, followed by a satisfying groan as the man howled and collapsed onto his lover. And the blow that followed, his flesh parting, his blood welling—Ellie Anderson's screams as she squirmed out from under him and tried to run away, but I had locked the door behind me and pushed the key deep into my bra. She was on her way to the window when I hit her in the back of the head. She fell down on the bed in a spray of red. I think Timmy was already dead by then—or would be very soon—bleeding out on the floor.

It didn't take much to kill them at all.

The cleanup, of course, was more of a problem. First, I wrapped them in thick bedding and used Cecilia's little elevator to get them downstairs. Then I dragged them through the hall and out through the front door. That was the easy part, though. Once outside, I found two empty barrels left behind by the lazy gardener, who had stopped showing up shortly after Cecilia died, likely because I had failed to pay the bills. I spent a lot of time hauling each heavy body into its separate barrel, then showering them both in vodka in lieu of gasoline. Then I set the two of them on fire—only they refused to burn.

That was when I broke out the shovel and decided to put them in the flower bed instead. I remember racing against dawn to get the hole deep enough for two wrapped bodies, and then rushing to fill it in again. I even put back the wizened plants and threw out the excess dirt in the woods. It worked, though—it did. The flower bed looked its old shabby self when I was done.

My room had been another case entirely. The mattress had to go, of course, and I fought with the dratted thing for quite a while to get it inside the elevator. Even though I had wrapped it in sheets, the blood seeped through, and I had to retrace my steps with a bottle of bleach to get rid of all the stains. The floor in the hall had been especially bad, where I had dragged the mattress across to get it into the kitchen and down the cellar stairs. The flower-patterned wallpaper Cecilia had preferred for her bedroom was quite ruined with blood, and I had to go into town to get the darkest paint I could find without crossing over to black—which happened to be purple. It did take some cunning to prevent Dina from going in there before the walls were done, but then my husband was missing and that bought me some slack. People are prone to irrational behavior under such circumstances. That was certainly how I passed off needing a new bed that Ellie Anderson had not slept on; I claimed to have burned the missing mattress when the old bed was hauled away. And when all was said and done, the room looked much better than it had before. I never much cared for Cecilia's tastes.

So yes, I knew a little something about bloodlust, but I was not about to let the ghosts have their little revenge. There was a reason why *I* was the one who had won the first time around—and even if they plainly refused to go into the light, I still had my sharpest weapon left. She was currently indisposed, though, or so Lily had told me before I went to bed. Violet was *seriously* ill, she said. She could *barely* sit up in the bed. Lily clearly blamed me for this mysterious illness, since she felt it was the séance that had somehow depleted her sister— and maybe it was, too. But I didn't think it was that serious. There had been a chapter in my book about mediums becoming exhausted and drained, but they bounced right back again with a little rest and water, much like a common houseplant. Besides, she had caused all the havoc in the first place; perhaps some bedrest would do her good— and keep her out of trouble, too.

Perhaps a bout of illness could even sway her to do as I said.

It was a very unfortunate turn of events that the girls who were supposed to be my salvation had made my life such a nightmare instead. None of what I had envisioned when offered the guardianship had come to pass, and I still smarted from Mr. Skye's blatant rejection of my proposal. The girls had means—lots of it. But so far, I hadn't been able to access any of it besides the monthly stipend—and I had paid dearly for that tiny privilege by being imprisoned by the ghosts of my past. It was not fair and it was not right, but I simply didn't know what to do about it all. And the bills kept piling up.

How could I turn this around and succeed? How could I pluck my golden geese without damaging myself further?

There *had* to be a way!

I imagined the jewelry in Isabella's sketches, the glitter and the gleam, and the *want* in me was so strong that I could hardly breathe.

Then—to cool down—I thought about the book again: *How to Talk to Spirits*. There were a lot of references to "professional mediums" in there, and what to expect if you hired one. *Violet* had channeled spirits, right there in my dining room, and even though I hadn't liked what the spirits actually said, could it be that my niece, too, had the makings of a "professional medium"? Might it even be profitable? Slowly, the new thought formed in my brain, shapeless like clay at first, but with the promise of maybe becoming something useful. It was worth looking into, at least, since the girls' fortune seemed currently out of my reach.

With that heartening thought, I finally drifted off, likely due to the sleeping pill more than anything else. And if my dead husband came knocking or messing with the lights, I wouldn't even know it, with my ears full of wax and a sleeping mask on.

The clay was still there the next morning, while Dina scooped melon balls into my mouth, only now the shape had grown some limbs and started looking like something more real. So fascinated was I by this new creation in my brain that I almost forgot to ask after Violet's health, and forgot the answer as soon as Dina said it. Unlike Lily, I had seen many sick people in my days as a nurse—men and women in all stages of illness staggering toward their coffins—and from what I had heard, Violet was nothing like them. Her body had been through an ordeal, that was true, but as symptoms go, fever and exhaustion were mild, and nothing a young body couldn't handle. I honestly wasn't worried at all, and by the time my breakfast ended, I knew just whom I had to talk to in order to set my new plan in motion.

Gail Richards was a fellow nurse, one of the few to work and live in Ivory Springs. We had connected shortly after I arrived in town to work for Miss Lawrence. Besides our occupations, we didn't have very much in common, but sometimes a shared profession was enough to carry you through a lunch or a coffee. Gail was friendly and outgoing and always spoke just a little too much. Unlike me, she seemed to live in harmony with her husband and had raised a couple of dimple-cheeked children in her "rustic" abode in the woods. Not that I had had reason to visit often; Gail much preferred to come to me, being taken with the charms of Crescent Hill. The winter garden especially spoke to her romantic side, and she had often come to keep me company there after Timmy disappeared, sharing countless bottles of wine. I suppose that, had my grief been the genuine article, Gail would have been a rock in my time of need. She was also amply impressed by the fact that my former employer had willed me her estate, for which she credited my outstanding performance as a nurse.

The reason why I wanted to speak to Gail now was that she had often shown a liking for the mysterious and occult. Her house always smelled of Nag Champa incense, and when out of her nurse's uniform, she often sported jewelry wrought into various symbols of dubious origin—most notably the astrological symbol for Aries and a wooden yin-yang. Once, after too much wine, she admitted to being fascinated by UFOs and lamented the fact that she had "missed" the flower-power movement by being just a smidge too old to comfortably fit in. She was still a seeker, though—she had admitted as much—and even though I had thought her ridiculous at the time, her unconventional interests might be just the thing right now.

I figured a surprise visit would be best and entered her driveway at about ten A.M., when I figured that the chances of being offered a meal were slimmest. Clearly, public eating was not on the menu for me at the moment. Coffee was fine, as I could just let it cool, pretending to have forgotten about the whole thing—and all my friends knew I never tasted sugar, so cookies were already out of the question. It was a gamble, but I felt fairly confident that Gail would be at home. She worked mostly nights at a nursing home and never traveled far from her nook in the woods.

Gail's place looked as it had always done, with an overgrown lawn and long-dry garments hanging on the clothesline gathering dust. A couple of camping chairs with bright orange blossoms stood out on her porch, the table between them topped with sad-looking daisies in a teacup. And there was Gail herself, coming out of the house to greet me, probably wondering what guest would be so rude as not to call beforehand. She lit up when she saw me, though, waved, and smiled, before rushing down the stairs as fast as she could, wearing an ill-fitting brown housedress in a material that reminded me of burlap. I checked out her neck and smirked when I saw the yin-yang hanging there. Gail would have the answers for sure.

"Oh, it's so good to see you." I beamed as I exited the station wagon and endured a lengthy hug, which left me smelling like incense all over. Gail's hair used to be brown but had taken on a wizened gray hue in later years, which she seemed not to want to do anything about. It was just as long and unkempt as before, and I made sure not to touch it while we embraced, feeling it was likely to be filthy.

Gail had no boundaries, though, when it came to physical contact. "Oh, it's been so long," she cooed, swaying back and forth with me in her arms. "I have missed you so much, Clara."

"Yes, yes, me, too," I croaked, hoping to get the greeting over with. "It's been hard, you know; the girls take up most of my time."

"Of course, of course. How *are* the little darlings?" She finally let go and looked up at me with her big brown eyes.

"That's actually what I came to talk to you about." I gave her a shivering smile. "We have a situation at home, and I would dearly like your advice."

"Of course! I know all about children," she bragged, while leading me to the porch. "No matter what it is, I'm sure we'll find an answer."

"I do hope so," I said, sending her a pleading look before sinking down in one of the dusty chairs. "It is a peculiar problem—so perhaps it requires a peculiar solution—"

"Hold that thought." Gail held a finger in the air, then she quickly darted into the house and came back out again carrying two cups of coffee. Now that the coffee was actually there, it felt a little dangerous to me. I could not help but picture an undetonated bomb. I had to be very careful not to forget and lift it to my lips out of habit.

When Gail, too, had sat down and all her attention was on me, I sighed and embarked on the sorry tale I had crafted on the road. "I

know you might not believe me," I started, pretending to be embarrassed. "It's such a mind-shattering possibility . . . so highly unusual."
I bit my lip and looked down at my lap.

"What is, Clara? Please, tell me," Gail begged, already seduced by
the mystery.

"It's Violet," I burst out, and took a deep breath. "She isn't like
other children, Gail."

"In what way?" my friend prodded at once. "Is she sick? Is something wrong with her?"

"Oh, I don't know." I sighed deeply and looked away, pretending to
be overcome with doubt. "Perhaps it was stupid to come here—maybe
I shouldn't have said anything."

"Clara, no, please, you know you can tell me *anything*!" She was
ripe now, like a plum in fall. Even if she didn't believe me, she would
absolutely pretend to—enough to help me, anyway.

"Well, Violet, she . . . she speaks to ghosts . . . and believe me when
I say I know how weird that sounds. I didn't believe it myself at
first—I simply refused to—so when she started talking about messages and voices . . . But then I heard my own beloved mother's voice
come pouring out of her mouth, as clear as day, and she died long
before Violet was born, so she couldn't have pretended." I gave Gail a
look that I hoped would convey a mixture of fear and awe. "I never
believed in such things, you know. I was never taken in by stories like
that, but now I have been forced to accept it nevertheless."

"It's the trauma," Gail said, and nodded sagely. "The trauma of losing both her parents must have triggered something inside her. It
happens quite often, Clara. It's not unusual at all."

"Really?" I acted surprised, even though I knew it was nonsense. I
had known a lot of bereft people in my day, and none of them had
spontaneously spoken to the dead. "I had *no* idea that grief could do
that."

"Oh, it absolutely can. It's like the longing for a dead loved one can
make the person touch the border between the world of the living
and the world of the dead." I wondered if she had read that in a book
or if she was just making it up—like me. "Sometimes, like with your

niece, they come so close that they can actually hear the voices of the dead, or the departed can briefly cross over to speak through their lips." Something dreamy had come over her, and I figured she found the whole idea romantic. "What did she say? Your mother?"

I cocked my head and gave a soft smile. "She said that she was proud of me, and that I had done well in life."

"See?" Gail laughed. "Speaking for the dead is a *gift*, not a problem."

"But the speaking isn't really the issue. I accept that this is a part of Violet now, and I would never do anything to discourage her from using her talent—it's just that . . . she so dearly wants to share this 'gift' with the world. She keeps telling me how she wants to give other people in mourning peace through messages from their loved ones. Is that even possible, Gail? Is this a wish I can make come true for my poor bereft niece?" I locked my gaze with hers while waiting for the answer and made my bottom lip shiver a little.

"Well, if she feels so strongly about it, maybe it's like a *calling*," Gail suggested. "And if that is the case, you *must* help her, Clara, because she will feel that *need* in her bones until she answers . . . I cannot imagine it being very pleasant."

"But . . . *should* I help her?"

"Oh yes."

"But how would I even begin? How do I find people in need?" I bit my lip again, hopefully looking insecure.

"Clara, they are all over the place." Gail chuckled, thriving on being the one in the know, and I was very happy to let her shine. "You could look at newspaper adverts—or place one yourself. It's a very common thing to do. The only thing to worry about is Violet's age. Most people who go to mediums would expect someone older— more experienced—than her."

"But my niece is *very* good," I bragged. "I doubt that age has anything to do with it."

"And I think you're absolutely right." Gail sipped her coffee, and I watched her, full of envy. "Some people say that children are more attuned to the unknown—more sensitive, if you like. They are newer on Earth and innocent, while we older ladies are noisy inside, full of clutter and sin." She laughed—and though I bristled at being called old, I forced myself to chuckle, too. "It's just that it might be frowned upon to put such a young child to work."

"It wouldn't be work, exactly—not if it is her calling," I noted.

"But she couldn't do it for nothing, Clara. No one would take her seriously if she just 'gave it away.'" I really liked the sound of that.

"So . . . how much would be enough for her to be taken seriously?" I gave her my widest, most innocent look. The reply I received was less than I had hoped for, but better than nothing, so that was certainly something. And if I could build a reputation for her, the price would double fast.

"Just take it nice and slow," Gail advised. "I might even be able to do you a favor." She gave me a secretive look over the struggling daisies.

I gladly took the bait. "Oh, what is that?"

"I know of a woman . . . a young widow who recently lost her husband. He was as old as sin. Mr. Arthur on the hill—do you know him?" she asked, and I nodded in reply. He had been a piece of work as I recalled it—rolling in money but decidedly unkind, always in disputes with his neighbors. I vaguely remembered reading something about his second wedding in the local newspaper and looking at the pictures of the blushing young bride, thinking that she had done well for herself and wondering if the money had been worth the price. The answer was probably yes.

"I know who both of them are," I said. "Does Mrs. Arthur want to speak with her husband?"

"She does." Gail rolled her eyes. "Though she might not have thought of a medium yet. There's an issue with the will, you see. I overheard the whole story when Mrs. Arthur visited her mother at the nursing home. The old lady was livid after her daughter had left, and I had to give her a little something just to calm her down. Maybe Mrs. Arthur could be a good first customer for Violet," she suggested, and I couldn't agree more. Mrs. Arthur might have friends, too, just as rich and just as much in need as she. Not a bad place at all to get the ball rolling . . .

"But how do I approach her?" I asked. "We can hardly just show up at her door—"

"I'll talk to her, Clara, don't you worry. We're practically friends, she and I."

"Oh, would you?" I pressed my hands to my chest. "It would mean so much," I said. "Violet would be *so* thrilled."

"Of course!" She beamed and threw out her hands. "That's what friends are for! Just be careful so you don't get reported. People are so unenlightened nowadays—they have no respect for sacred callings—and they might confuse your niece for one of those poor exploited children who are put to work against their will."

"Absolutely," I agreed. "That would be a disaster for Violet, who only wants to do good in this world." I sniffled a little and dabbed my eyes with a handkerchief. I wasn't too worried about it, though. As long as my niece put on a good show, no one would complain. I only had to keep it a secret from Mr. Skye.

Finally—*finally*—my golden goose was about to lay some eggs.

VIOLET

33

I didn't think that going to see Mrs. Arthur was a good idea, and Lily didn't either. She had been so furious with Aunt Clara when she came into the kitchen around dinnertime and told us about the appointment that she wasn't even afraid but said it right to her face.

"It's only been three days," she had shouted, "and it's making her sick, Aunt Clara! She *still* hasn't recovered since last time . . . It's wrong and illegal and *bad*!" she had shouted, standing before our aunt, ignoring both the blinking lights in the ceiling and the hissing in the air from Mr. Woods.

"Well, if she dislikes it, she only has to put the ghosts back, and she won't have to do it," Aunt Clara had said, while the lights blinked wilder and wilder.

Lily didn't want Aunt Clara to know that I didn't know how to put the ghosts back, though, so she had just stomped her foot and stood her ground. "The ghosts are here because of *you,* so they are your problem. They have *nothing* to do with Violet anymore."

"Is that so?" Aunt Clara had arched an eyebrow. "Didn't she literally summon the vermin? Clearly, they are her responsibility."

"Violet is *nine*," Lily had cried. "You *can't* put this on her. You were the one who *murdered* them—"

"And would gladly get rid of them again, but I obviously can't, so you see my predicament? At least this way, Violet can make it up to me in some part, since she refuses to put the dead back."

The whole time they were arguing, I sat on my chair by the table and didn't say anything. I was happy that Lily defended me—and terrified of being sick again—but Aunt Clara was our guardian, so in the end it didn't matter what Lily said.

I didn't think it was a good idea, though.

I was much better since the séance night, but I still didn't feel as good as before when Aunt Clara and I drove to Mrs. Arthur's house. Aunt Clara knew it, too, because she pulled over once so she could check my pulse and temperature.

"It won't do if Mrs. Arthur thinks you're sick," she muttered—even though I *was* sick, so it wouldn't just be something Mrs. Arthur thought. I didn't complain, though, when Aunt Clara took out some makeup from her bag and brushed pink onto my cheeks. I just wanted to get it over with. "I will buy you a lollipop later," she said, as if that was supposed to make me feel better. "I hope you're not planning on acting like a sourpuss in front of our client," she warned as she started up the car again. "Nobody likes a sullen child."

"I won't, Aunt Clara," I mumbled, mostly to make her stop yelling at me. It wasn't that I didn't *like* talking to the ghosts—or letting them talk through me—because I didn't remember anything of what had happened on séance night and only knew what Lily had told me. I just didn't want to be sick again and have lots of tadpoles on my belly. Lily hadn't wanted to let Aunt Clara know about that either. She had said that if she knew, she might think that it wasn't such a big deal if I got sick, because Lily could just fix me again.

"You shouldn't let Lily scare you." Aunt Clara stared at the road ahead. Dina had done her makeup that morning and it looked a little weird, with crooked lines of kohl around her eyes. Aunt Clara wouldn't know, though, since she couldn't look in mirrors. "There are countless mediums in this country, all of them healthy and thriving. It's just that you aren't used to it yet. It will get better, just you wait and see."

I didn't know about other mediums, but I didn't think it worked that way for me. I was supposed to help the *dead* when they asked—not the living. Maybe it was different for the others. It was just lucky for me that Lily knew what to do and could pick away the tadpoles.

"Lily is simply misguided—like a watchdog on high alert. I don't blame her, of course, since you *are* recently bereft, but it will do her no good. I suppose she is calling Mr. Skye about now, telling him of our little 'adventure.'" She smirked. "But that won't do any good either. I have already seen to that." She chuckled to herself and I didn't like the sound of it at all. It also made my heart drop like a rock, because I knew that she was right. Lily *had* said that she would call Mr. Skye to tell him what Aunt Clara had done to me. Suddenly, I got very nervous about what my aunt had said to him.

"What if I can't do it?" I blurted out, because maybe if she thought I wouldn't be able to do it again, Aunt Clara would change her mind and take me back to Crescent Hill. "The other ghosts were already at your house, even before Lily and I arrived. But what if there are no ghosts where we are going?"

"Oh, I'm sure you'll find something." She took one hand off the steering wheel to pat mine on the seat, which I hated. "No house is entirely free of ghosts. If you absolutely cannot find anything, just pretend like you do."

"You mean, like . . . *lying*?"

"Well, it would make Mrs. Arthur very pleased if she heard from her late husband. You could just say that he doesn't remember what happened with the will." She paused for a moment. "Not all ghosts are angry like mi—those on Crescent Hill. I suppose they can be happy, too, so pretend to be a happy ghost."

Mrs. Arthur lived in a big white house on the hill not far from Ivory Springs. It looked very pretty but boring, with white columns on the porch. Mama had once said that people who liked to live like that pretended to be Greek gods. Mrs. Arthur didn't look like a goddess to me, though, even though she was very pretty—or if she did, she was a very sad goddess, with puffy eyes and greasy blond hair. Even though she wore a glittering one-piece suit, she smelled a bit like old sweat. I supposed it was because her husband was dead that she had forgotten to take her baths. She did seem happy to see us, though, or to see me at least. She pinched my cheek with long pink nails and called me "the cutest little medium ever."

I didn't see any ghosts, however, when we went inside the marble hall. It was just white, veiny walls and plenty of lilies in tall vases, some of them with black ribbons tied around them.

The living room was just as full of marble, and all the couches were rusty red. A huge fireplace covered most of one wall, and there were arched windows that reached all the way up to the ceiling. When I looked outside, I could see Ivory Springs far below, with its dusty streets and brick houses.

Aunt Clara and Mrs. Arthur sat down on one of the couches, before a mosaic table, where several clear glass bowls had already been put out. I knew they were meant for the wine and the food Aunt Clara had bought while I waited in the car. There was a slab of beef, sticks of toffee, and even a small golden-apple pie. She had said that old men like Mr. Arthur were fond of "traditional foods." I didn't think that the ghosts had to *like* the food, though. It was just there for fuel, like a battery.

"My husband's children from his first marriage don't believe me," Mrs. Arthur said to Aunt Clara. "The lawyer has a copy, of course, but it isn't signed—though I know that Daniel signed the original the week before he died. I was there with him in the room, and we used members of staff as witnesses. I just have to find the signed will, so I need your girl to ask him where he put it."

"Did you hear that, Violet?" Aunt Clara's voice hit me in the back like a rock. "Surely we can do this little favor for Mrs. Arthur." I thought for a moment about saying no—about throwing myself on the floor and screaming. Aunt Clara would *have* to take me back then—and she would be embarrassed, too. But then I worried what would happen next. Perhaps Aunt Clara would send us away, and then we would end up in different places. Or she would send *Lily* away, and then what would I do the next time my belly was crawling with tadpoles?

Maybe Aunt Clara was right, and it *would* get easier when I got more used to doing it. She *had* read *How to Talk to Spirits*, after all.

Aunt Clara and Mrs. Arthur both looked at me. Aunt Clara's foot moved restlessly against the thick white rug on the floor. They had already lit the large brown candle on the table. I didn't feel like I could do anything except join them.

I perched on the edge of a yellow ottoman facing the table, thinking it was close enough. Aunt Clara started fussing with the food in the plastic bag, pulling out the tray of beef.

"Violet's method is a little . . . unorthodox." She smiled with all her teeth when she looked at Mrs. Arthur.

"I thought we were going to hold hands or something," the woman muttered.

"Yes," Aunt Clara said, "that, too. But it's the foodstuff that makes Violet so very effective. Don't ask me why; only the dead know that." She laughed but it sounded fake. "It's nothing dangerous, just a different way of doing things."

"Of course." Mrs. Arthur sounded faint as the meat dropped into one of her glass bowls. The glass had bubbles in it, I noticed, as if it were made of water. Aunt Clara also took out the pie and the toffee and put them into different bowls. Then she poured red wine in the largest one. Mrs. Arthur rose to close the curtains and lower the lights, leaving the whole room misty gray.

"Are you ready, dear?" Aunt Clara gave me a sweet smile that was also very fake. And even though I *wasn't* ready—and my chest still hurt—I nodded. I just wanted it to be done so we could go home to Lily and Dina.

We laced our hands together—Mrs. Arthur's was slick and cold—and then we just sat there for a while, watching the candle flame burn.

"Do you feel anything? Have you located Mrs. Arthur's husband yet?" Aunt Clara asked me after a while. Her foot still moved restlessly on the rug. When I didn't say anything, she turned to Mrs. Arthur and asked, "What was your husband's full name?"

"Daniel," she replied. "Daniel Arthur."

"Think about Daniel Arthur," Aunt Clara said to me. "Try to reach *Daniel Arthur*."

But I didn't know how to do that. I hadn't seen any ghosts at all since we came here, and I couldn't *feel* any either. But I did what she said and thought about *Daniel Arthur*, saying his name many times in my head, while I looked into the flame of the candle.

Then, suddenly, something answered.

CLARA
34

Violet arched her back and her grip on my hand tightened. It looked as if she had had a seizure or been hit by a jolt of electricity. Something came tumbling out of her mouth—that dratted dirt again. I should have thought of that before we sat down in this pristine room. It stained Violet's blue shirt on its way down to the white rug. The girl gasped, and then that uncanny thing happened, where it looked as if something was moving under her skin.

When she relaxed again, Violet had become someone else.

"Where am I?" The male voice sounded from Violet's soft lips. Mrs. Arthur had frozen stiff beside me, and I had to squeeze her clammy hand a little to make the woman speak.

"I . . . It's me, Daniel. You are home," she said faintly.

"Lizzie?" the man uttered, utterly surprised. "Why are you dragging me back?" he chided. "I never asked for that." Even if he sounded a little annoyed, I noticed with some envy how Mrs. Arthur's ghost was not screaming at her or making horrible death threats. Perhaps because he had died of old age, and not because his wife had killed him—even though I felt sure she would have had ample reason to do so.

"I am sorry—I am so sorry, Daniel." Mrs. Arthur sounded like a little girl. I supposed this was how she spoke to her husband while he was alive. Many foolish women fell into that trap and acted much like toddlers for treats, checks, and cuddles—especially if they were the younger second wife. "I wouldn't have brought you back if I didn't have a *very* good reason. It's the will, Daniel. It's gone. The one we signed with the maid and the cook? I can't find it anywhere, and now your . . . children say that it never *existed*." Her voice had veered into a whine.

"It existed," the man said through Violet's mouth. A little more dirt followed the words.

"*I* know that." Mrs. Arthur sounded impatient. "But where is it, Daniel? What did you do with it?"

Violet's lips split into a grin. "I flushed it down the toilet."

"You did *what?*" The woman was halfway off the couch before I managed to yank her back. I had no idea what her plan was, but it might very well have been throttling my niece. When she landed back in her seat, tears came welling from her eyes, making grooves in the layer of makeup clogging her pores. I did feel sorry for her, though. She was the kind of woman who had dedicated her life to securing a certain type of man: old, wealthy, and stupid enough to think that their love was real. Thanks to my mother, I knew these women on sight, and I did not begrudge them their ambition. It took a lot of grit and stamina to marry up in this world—not to mention to caring for an elderly spouse long enough for them to sign their will. It was a filthy job, but it could pay well, and Mrs. Arthur had been close to her payday. The husband was dead and the casket in the ground, so the job should have come to a satisfying end—but didn't.

I certainly understood the tears.

"You are still young," the fool, Mr. Arthur, consoled his crying wife through my nine-year-old niece. "You can marry again, Lizzie, and start another life—and the kids, they *need* it more . . ." I didn't think the prospect of beginning the whole process over pleased Mrs. Arthur one bit, though. The woman was inconsolable and sobbing beside me, and I was just about to call the séance to a close when something highly unexpected happened. Violet's back arched again, and that strange motion under her skin recurred. My belly started to ache when I heard the hissing noise come slithering.

"What is happening?" Mrs. Arthur sounded scared.

Violet turned her head and looked straight at me; her eyes were brimming with hatred. "Clara, you murdering bitch!" Timmy shouted. "So you think you can run away from me? You can *never* run away from me. I will always find you!"

"Get out of here!" I hissed at him. "Get out before I *chase* you out!"

"What?" He laughed. "Are you going to ki—" I slammed my hand down on the wildly flickering candle. It stung badly, but it was worth it, as my long-dead husband shut his trap before he could incriminate me further.

"Oh my God, what was that?" Mrs. Arthur was sobbing uncontrollably, pulling at her unkempt hair.

"Just a . . . *bad spirit*," I assured her. "Put your head between your knees and breathe!" I let go of her hand and rushed to switch the light on.

When I returned to the couch, Mrs. Arthur still sat with her head between her knees, panting loudly. Violet seemed to have regained her senses and looked at me questioningly, no doubt disturbed by our hostess's odd behavior.

"It's nothing to worry about," I told her. "Mrs. Arthur just had a little shock, that's all."

"Why?" Violet asked.

"Because she isn't used to this sort of thing."

"I think it worked, though." Violet was looking at the food on the table, and the thick layer of mold that covered it all.

"Oh, it worked," I assured the girl. It had just worked a little better than expected. I was annoyed at not having considered this. *Of course* Timmy was always around. *Of course* he would do whatever he could to torment me—and Violet was an open channel, ripe to be taken advantage of.

Next time, I silently swore to myself as I helped Mrs. Arthur up from the couch, I would be better prepared. I would kill the flame at once if Violet started to change. I would make sure to stop that thieving bastard as soon as he reared his ugly dead head. I didn't have to change my plans; I merely had to be vigilant.

"Aunt Clara, I think I'm going to be sick," Violet said, before vomiting dirt all over the snowy-white rug.

LILY

35

Aunt Clara came into the owl room and interrupted me midway through Purcell's Prelude in G minor. She ordered me to pack a bag because we were going on a road trip. It was about time Violet and I saw a little of the world, she said—and if I hadn't been so worried about my sister, I might have laughed at that, since we had both traveled a lot with Mama and Papa before and had visited most of the continents in the world. I didn't think Aunt Clara had been to even half of the countries we had.

"What are you complaining about?" she snapped at me. "You always wanted me to 'bring you along' on my travels."

I lowered Gertrud and pointed at Aunt Clara with the bow. "It's not the right time. Violet is still sick." And it was all her fault, too, even though she wouldn't admit it. Violet had been as pale as a sheet when she came back home from that stupid séance on the hill, and her belly had been full of tadpoles again. Some of them were red and angry, and others the azure blue of regret. I had worked very hard to get them all off her, while Violet had whimpered on the pillow. I was still so furious with Aunt Clara that I could hardly *speak*—and now she wanted to go on *vacation*?

"Nonsense." Aunt Clara waved a hand full of turquoise flames in the air, which was very worrying to me, because it meant that she was excited—and it *never* ended well for us when Aunt Clara was excited. "A little fresh air and something new to look at will do her wonders. I admit that the séance with Mrs. Arthur perhaps was a little much when she wasn't feeling her best, but she is young and will recuperate in no time—"

"You don't *know* that!" I told her. "None of us do." How could she be so blind?

Aunt Clara rolled her eyes. "Stop being so dramatic, Lily. She is sitting up in bed now, isn't she? She is talking? Laughing? Violet will be just fine. You can trust me, you know. I used to be a nurse—"

"To old ladies," I protested. "And Violet isn't normal sick, she is *ghost sick,* and none of us know how that works." Against my will, I felt tears pressing behind my eyes. I wouldn't cry in front of Aunt Clara, though. I didn't want her to see me weak, since she'd only find a way to use it against me.

"Well, if she doesn't perk up, we'll just go back home again." She sounded unconcerned. "Be happy, Lily! You'll finally get to 'see something other than Crescent Hill.'"

It was true what she had said about Violet sitting up in bed, and she ate well, too: mostly soft rolls and soup that Dina carried up on a tray. But even though it had been four days since we picked off all the new tadpoles, she was still pale and very, very tired. She fell asleep all the time, even when we were talking—and now Aunt Clara wanted us to leave early the next day to go sightseeing? It didn't seem safe at all.

As soon as the door to Aunt Clara's room clicked shut, I ran to the kitchen and told Dina what had happened. She looked very concerned as she wiped her hands on the orange apron, but she couldn't really help me.

"I will tell Mrs. Woods what I think, of course, but to be honest, I don't think it will make a difference. She will do as she pleases, you know that, and even lie to get her way."

Dina had been just as disappointed as me that the call with Mr. Skye hadn't gone as we had hoped. After Aunt Clara and Violet had left for the séance with Mrs. Arthur, I had rushed to the phone and dialed his number.

"Mr. Skye." I had spoken so fast that I almost stumbled on the words. It was as if a part of me had worried that Aunt Clara would suddenly show up and put a bony hand on my shoulder. "This is Lily Webb, Mr. Skye, and I desperately need your help! Aunt Clara has taken Violet—she is *using* her, Mr. Skye!"

"Wait, Lily, calm down," his smooth voice had sounded on the other end. "*Where* has Mrs. Woods taken Violet?"

"She has taken her to be a *medium* for a rich lady . . . She thinks that Violet has powers, you see, that she can talk to the dead—"

"She does what now?" Mr. Skye sounded both amused and alarmed. "Where are you now, Lily?"

"I'm at Crescent Hill, but Violet is not. Aunt Clara has taken her to speak to the de—"

"Hmm." Mr. Skye had sounded a little strange on the other end. "You know, Lily, I *did* receive a phone call from your aunt earlier today."

"You did?" My heart had started thumping hard and fast in my chest.

"Yes, Lily, I did. She told me that you have had some . . . *difficulties* since your parents' passing—which is understandable and perfectly normal—but she did express some concerns about you hurting yourself or others, and asked for extra funds to get you proper help—"

"No!" I shouted into the receiver. "That's not how it is, Mr. Skye! There's nothing wrong with me. It's Aunt Clara who is taking Violet to visit this lady so she can talk to her dead—"

"Mrs. Woods also told me that you had called the local sheriff to accuse her of *murder*. You know, Lily, if you are unhappy at your aunt's house, you may not be any happier anywhere else, and maybe you should try to give your aunt the benefit of the doubt. She is doing the best she can for you, and though no one can ever replace Ben and Amanda, God rest their souls, she is the closest family you've got now—"

"It's not like that!" I cried into the receiver, although I had already known by then that it wouldn't help. Aunt Clara had gotten to him first.

"Listen, Lily, why don't you ask Mrs. Woods to give me a call? I'm sure we can clear all this up . . . And maybe you *should* talk to a professional, Lily. Maybe you would feel better if they prescribed some medication—"

I had hung up on him then. There was no point, and Dina had been right all along: We were all alone in this, which made it even scarier to be going on a trip with her.

"What if Violet gets worse on the road?" I thought out loud.

"Oh, Lily." Dina came to give me a hug. "This séance business is just awful," she tutted. "And with Violet being so young . . ." She sighed and let me go. "Maybe if I called someone and told them I was concerned—but I would have to leave the ghosts out of it, and that would make things harder. Worst-case scenario, your aunt would find a way to sweet-talk whoever came to check up on you, and then I would get fired, and I would very much like to still be here when you get back, Lily." She looked at me with serious eyes. "I know I haven't done much to help you, but it's not for lack of wanting, and I *do* think it would be worse for you to be here alone, without an ally in the kitchen. That's why I haven't resigned, even if I should, now that I know what happened to Cecilia." She smiled weakly and handed me a linen napkin from a folded stack on the counter so I could wipe my eyes.

"But *why* does she want us to go all of a sudden?" I clutched the napkin in my hand, just in case I had to dry more tears.

Dina sighed again and sat down by the kitchen table, facing me. "I gave up trying to understand that woman a long time ago. She has her reasons, I suppose. The timing is horrific, though, with Violet being so unwell." She shook her head. "I worry that Mrs. Woods is up to something, but I just don't know what to do about it. She *is* your guardian, after all."

"I don't even know where we are going," I complained.

"If only we could prove her crimes, the rest would be easy. If you *do* have to go, you should use the opportunity, Lily. Keep your eyes and ears open, and maybe she'll say something that we can use. Perhaps there's some kind of proof somewhere that we haven't thought of yet." She seemed unconvinced, though, and pink flames of fear had sprung up on her skin.

"Maybe she's going to kill us," I muttered. "Maybe she wants to dump us somewhere far from home." Just the thought of it made my heart race.

Dina took the question seriously and thought about it for a while. "I don't think she will—not as long as the ghosts are around. Just this morning, she saw Ellie Anderson in the silver candelabra in the dining room and it made her livid. Mrs. Woods doesn't want to live like this. She will do whatever it takes to get rid of them, and Violet is the only one who can." We hadn't told Dina that Violet didn't know how; that secret seemed safer kept just between us. "I also think she is after your money," Dina continued. "And if you are dead, there will be no more of that."

Although I knew she said it to comfort me, it was still not a great thing to hear. I had been thinking for a while that Aunt Clara only wanted us because of the checks from Mr. Skye, but it still hurt to hear it said out loud.

Dina must have seen how I felt. "I know it's hard," she said in a softer voice. "But those two things—Violet's abilities and the money—they are *power*, Lily. You have something Mrs. Woods wants, and it's important that you remember that. She won't let Violet get seriously ill or die, because she needs something from her. That's your safety."

"What about me?" I asked in a thin voice.

"If you died, the stipend would be cut in half, and Mrs. Woods needs the money. I have seen the bills come flooding in from jewelers and whatnot. I suppose she is expanding her collection of gemstones. Mrs. Woods needs you, too, alive and well," she assured me, but it only helped a little.

"I wish we could stay here with you instead." I felt heartbroken as I stood there before her.

"Yes." Dina's skin flared with pink. "So do I, but maybe it won't be for long. Maybe she'll grow tired after a night or two on the road."

"I hope so," I said, but I didn't feel it.

CLARA

36

Our little excursion started out wonderfully: The sun was shining, the morning air was crisp, and the girls were . . . if not happy, then at least quiet. The road before us, potholed and narrow, wound between ripening fields and unruly woods, pastures scattered with cows and windmills spinning slowly. Soon enough the dirt road would give way to shiny asphalt, and our trip would begin in earnest.

I was jubilant.

I had followed my friend Gail's advice and placed ads in several local newspapers all over the country, and lo and behold, the replies had come pouring in. I suppose it was the wording the customers—or "clients," as it said in my book—found enticing: *Gifted young medium speaks with voice of departed. Accurate and reliable. Reasonably priced.*

Granted, our last séance hadn't ended exactly the way I had wanted, but Mrs. Arthur had gotten her answer—and she had paid, even if her rug was ruined—though perhaps she didn't care about keeping it pristine after she learned that it wasn't really hers. The vomiting had been unfortunate, but I had confidence that it was a hiccup, something to be expected when the girl was so new to the game. My book hadn't said anything about dirt materializing in the gastric passage, but in my opinion, it was a small price to pay.

I had mapped a route to take us close to where the clients lived, and with what could be made from this impromptu tour, I was reasonably sure that I could pay the rest I owed Isabella and finally hold the first pieces of the collection in my hungry hands. My niece's "gift" would take me one big step closer to Clarabelle Diamonds.

The girls looked comfortable enough in the back seat. Lily had opted to sit there with Violet, even though I had offered her the passenger seat, stating that she wanted to keep an eye on her sister. The latter looked spry enough to me, if a little pale around the gills. Lily had wrapped her in a knitted blue blanket before we entered the car, which gave her an unfortunate resemblance to a bushy-haired blueberry. Lily herself sat next to her, ramrod straight and with eyes that were cold enough to burn. Lucky for me, I wouldn't have to meet that gaze while driving, since Ellie Anderson popped up whenever I stared too long into the rearview mirror. The dead clearly didn't care one jot about car safety.

After a while, the girls' silence started to gnaw at me, however, and I thought I could feel Lily's gaze sear into my neck even through the upholstery. It was out of necessity more than anything else that I had brought her along in the first place. Violet could feed me, true, but I needed a more mature hand for the makeup; it wouldn't do to show up at clients' houses unkempt and barefaced. Besides, she could console her sister if she fell ill again.

"It's going to be a very long drive if you're going to be quiet all the time," I said when three-quarters of an hour had passed and not a sound had erupted from the back seat. "Why don't you play a game or something? I'm sure you did that when traveling with your parents."

It took a couple of minutes before Lily spoke. "Violet is too sick for games."

"Oh, I'm sure she's not. How much energy does it take to count blue cars and red cars?"

"We never did that," Lily said sulkily. "We used to sing songs before, or read a book."

"Didn't that make you carsick?"

"No."

"Violet will be just fine, Lily. Won't you, Violet?"

"Maybe," came her faint little voice. "I'm just very tired."

"See?" I beamed, although they couldn't see me. "A couple of nights' sleep and you'll be as good as new. I've booked a room at a motel called the Pink Dragon. It's supposed to be very cozy." In fact, the rates and location promised me it was not, but they didn't need to know that. It was important that we kept the expenses at a minimum, so the profits from the trip would be as big as possible.

"Maybe there are real dragons there," Violet said.

"You can pretend if you like," Lily replied, using the soft voice she reserved for her sister, which made my skin itch all over. Violet was nearly ten and not a baby.

"Maybe they fly between the rooms," Violet said, "and leave fresh towels at the doors."

"Are all the dragons pink?" Lily asked.

"Uh-huh," Violet's faint voice answered. "Light pink, like the inside of seashells."

"What about their eyes?" Lily continued the pointless exchange.

"They are silver," Violet replied with all the confidence in the world.

It was going to be a very long drive.

"I never went anywhere when I was your age," I cut in so I didn't have to hear more about dragon maids with silver eyes. "We lived far away from everything, and we never had the money to stay away for even one night. If I wanted to see different walls, the only place I was welcome was at my aunt's house—just like it is for you now."

"What was she like?" Lily asked, always so curious about the past.

"Oh, Aunt Laura was a tired woman, always nursing or pregnant. She never knew how to avoid it, you see. Not like your grandmother did, after she had me."

"I don't think Papa ever mentioned Laura." Lily again.

"No, Iris cut all ties when we left. I never learned what became of her."

"Like with you and Papa," Lily said. "You two cut ties as well." Was that an accusation in her voice?

"Just like that." I beamed again and suppressed the urge to look into the mirror. "Sometimes the world takes you in different directions, and it's not useful to hang on to the past. Your grandmother taught me that."

"How was Grandma Iris when you were a girl? Papa told us stories, but only from after she married Grandpa Otis."

"She was vicious, cruel, and not kind at all. She never much cared for me, and after she married Otis, I was only a burden. I'm sure your father told you glorious tales about her legendary Christmas parties and the vacation house by the sea, but you should know that the one person she *didn't* invite was me—her own flesh and blood."

The girls remained quiet for a good long while.

"Why was that?" Violet finally asked.

I lifted my hammer of truth once more and slammed it down, full force. "Because she wanted to erase the fact that she had me. I reminded her of the past, you see—of a life she would rather forget. Iris wanted to pretend that she only started to live the day she became rich Otis's wife, and that nothing that came before that counted."

"Was it bad before?" Lily asked.

"Like you wouldn't believe. We had nothing—were no one—and my parents did their best to rip each other apart." In a flash, I suddenly remembered her again: the little girl rocking on her bed while her mother and father shouted on the other side of the wall. I remembered how I used to imagine that I sat inside a bubble. It was safe in there—it was just me, and no one else could get inside. Although the bubble was as smooth as glass, I imagined that it was made from diamond—the hardest thing in the world, Iris had told me. It was stronger than any steel, and no one could ever touch me in there.

"What happened?" Violet asked. "Did they . . . rip each other apart?" She sounded as if she was about to cry.

"Yes." Again I resisted the temptation to look in the rearview mirror to gauge her reaction. "Iris won."

"How?" Lily sounded tense.

"She killed him. She wanted something better for herself and killed my father to get it. It was ruled a stroke at the time, but she knew better—and I did, too. My father was fit as a horse."

"Was that why she didn't invite you?" Violet asked. "Because you knew it, too?" I was always astonished by the little girl's uncanny knack for picking up on details.

"I always thought so," I admitted. "I suppose I reminded her of what she had done." Pretty Iris, with her cotton-candy hair and silver tongue.

"I thought—I didn't know that Grandmother Iris was like that," Lily stuttered, satisfyingly taken aback.

"No, I suppose not many people knew," I said, "although Otis might have, by the end. He did die rather abruptly, and a lot can be disguised by age."

"Like with Cecilia?" Now there was definitely ice in Lily's voice.

"Just like that," I gladly admitted, feeling amused more than anything else. There was something freeing about saying these things aloud after keeping them to myself my whole life. "What I have done may seem shocking to you, but remember that I learned from the best. My mother taught me many things, but the most important lesson of all was how to take care of myself and never balk at anything to get the life I deserved—just like she did before me."

Lily's righteousness kicked back in. "But did it make her happy, though?"

"Of course it did! Just look at you two, pampered and spoiled. You wouldn't even *be* here if it hadn't been for my father's murder!"

"But are you *sure* that she did it—"

"Oh, I'm sure. He would never have let her go, you see, and it was the only way she could be with Otis. Father and I were nothing but chains, holding her back and dragging her down . . ."

"But it *could* have been a stroke," Lily insisted, so eager to clear the name of a woman she hadn't even met, lest she be tainted by her sin.

"My father did *not* have a stroke," I said, as calmly as I could muster. "Mother knew a thing or two about flowers and herbs—all the women did back then. I suspect she infused his whiskey with foxglove; she always liked those plants the most. Then she bragged to me about how she had 'taken care of it.' Said it was 'for the best.'" Even as I sat there at the wheel, the memory of her words had me fuming. "But Iris got her gowns and her yacht, so I suppose she thought it was worth it. I sure know that *my* sins bought *me* years of happiness, before you two came along." I quickly turned to glare at them. "It's not right what you did, Violet," I continued when my eyes were back on the road. "Dead things should stay dead, and Iris knew that well—which is why *I* had to go, for being a part of my father."

"Is that why you didn't like Papa?" Lily asked. "Because he was Iris's new child?"

"Yes." I slapped my hand against the steering wheel, sending my diamonds into a glittering frenzy. "That is why I didn't like Benjamin. He was still *hers*, while I had been shed like a snakeskin in the grass."

"Papa didn't know that, though." Lily's voice was quiet. "He never knew why you didn't even send us a thank-you note when we bought you Christmas presents—"

"Those little trinkets?" I arched my eyebrows. "They were hardly worth the stamp."

"It's the thought that counts," Lily murmured, but she didn't sound so perky anymore.

"Were you very sad when your father died?" Nosy Violet had regained her voice.

"Yes, I was," I answered. "I was very close to my father—we understood each other, he and I—but I don't begrudge Iris her action. It was the right thing to do, for her."

"Did you cry a lot?" Violet seemed not to have heard the last part.

"I did," I admitted in a murmur. "But then Otis came and whisked us away, and I didn't have much time to grieve after that."

"You were probably not so mean back then." My young niece had no manners. "I can't imagine you as a girl, though," she continued, oblivious to her blunder.

"Why is that?" I asked in a voice hoarse from lecturing. "Do you think the wicked witches and cruel stepmothers in your storybooks just appeared, like that?" I snapped my fingers. "Do you think they were hatched from witches' eggs, or sprung from the devil's brow fully formed? Even women like me, at odds with the world, have a past. We were all girls once—clay to be molded—but not all of us were allowed to grow and flourish as we should."

"That is very sad," Lily noted.

"Yes, isn't it just," I replied wryly. "But if you get nothing, you learn how to take, and that is what I do. If I hadn't taken it upon myself to make my life better, I would have had nothing still, and where is the justice in that when people like you—or Cecilia Lawrence—have far more than you can use just by the right of blood?"

"It's not our fault," Lily protested.

"No," I replied, "but it's not *mine* either. Iris knew how the world worked," I added, "and she was an excellent teacher."

"Papa would have helped you if you asked," said Lily.

"Sure he would." I shrugged. "But I wasn't about to ask him."

"Why not?" Violet squeaked.

"Because when you have nothing, all that is left is your dignity."

"So instead you killed Miss Lawrence?" Lily sounded incredulous.

"Yes," I said, with my eyes still fixed on the road. "Instead, I killed Cecilia."

"But you *had* to know that was wrong," she cried.

"It didn't feel that way," I said.

VIOLET

37

We ate at a roadside diner. The air smelled like grease and tomato sauce, and the floor was a little sticky. There wasn't enough light in there either, because everything seemed gray and dark. There were other people there, but not very many, and small vases with white plastic roses in them sat on all the tables. I suppose they couldn't have real flowers there, because it was so dark. I was happy to be inside, though, and not out on the road, because of Aunt Clara's reckless driving.

Lily and I ordered hamburgers with fries, since that was a thing Mama had said was fine if we dropped cheese and bacon and asked for extra salad, to make sure that we got our vitamins. It didn't taste like much, but we ate it anyway, because Aunt Clara had paid for it and because we were hungry.

Aunt Clara sat next to Lily on the other side of the table and looked at my food all the time. I even heard her belly rumble a little. She couldn't eat in the diner herself because Miss Lawrence would just come and whip the food away. She had ordered a salad to go, so I knew she would want me to feed her when we got to the motel. I felt a little sorry for her and wondered why we couldn't all have waited until the motel, but probably it was because Lily had been so angry in the car and said that it was child abuse to let us go hungry all day.

I would never tell Lily, but I understood Aunt Clara a little bit better after what she had said in the car, about growing up with a mother who didn't like her very much. I had never thought of Aunt Clara as a girl before and figured she must have been very unhappy. She was *still* unhappy, probably, but that didn't make it okay for her to just go around and kill people. I didn't know what to think about Grandma Iris after what she had said. When Papa had spoken about her, she had always sounded so nice, but if Aunt Clara was right, that had just been a lie.

Lily was furious with Aunt Clara after she had made me sick— twice. I was, too, but I didn't know what to do about it other than let Lily fix me again. I didn't remember what had happened at Mrs. Arthur's house after her husband came back, but she had been crying so badly when it was over that I hoped it had been horrible enough that Aunt Clara wouldn't make me do it again. I felt sorry for Mrs. Arthur, though, for losing all that money. Clearly, it had meant a lot to her. She hadn't even yelled at me when I barfed all over her rug.

When Aunt Clara went to visit the diner toilet, Lily and I sat in silence and just watched the other customers for a while. "Do you see the couple over there?" Lily nodded to a woman with dry blond hair and a big-bearded man who sat by the counter. "The lady is very blue. I think she's sick."

"She has a lump here," I agreed, and pressed a hand to my chest where it hurt. "She doesn't breathe very well either." We gave each other a sad look for the woman.

"Look at them over there." Lily discreetly nodded to a family by the entrance. It was a tired-looking mother with two small children who cried a lot while throwing their chicken wings all over the table. "She is pink all over."

"That means she's afraid," I said, feeling sorry for the woman, too.

"I think she is afraid for her kids," Lily said, "because the flames are golden around the edges."

I nodded as we watched the family munch their chicken wings.

"She really loves them." Looking at them made me miss Mama and Papa with a painful twinge. "What does Aunt Clara look like now?"

"Still purple," Lily replied. "But there's some turquoise in there, too—like she's excited."

"What about me?" I asked, even though I knew she couldn't tell. Maybe I hoped it had somehow changed. I would *love* to know what color I was.

"You know I can't see you," she replied. "I think it's because we are sisters."

I thought that was strange, but it made sense, too. It *would* be hard to live together if one person knew what the other one was thinking all the time.

When Aunt Clara came back and we were done eating, we drove through a small town, and Aunt Clara ran some errands. We stopped by a newspaper office and an old-fashioned convenience store before finally driving to the Pink Dragon motel, which didn't have real dragons, but just sad and crumbling concrete walls and a parking lot with plenty of holes in the pavement. It was late by then, and the sky was darkening, making the neon sign on the building glow. There *was* a dragon on it, curling around the letters, but it wasn't really pink—more like red.

Our room had two beds covered in pink bedspreads, thin curtains, and a brown-stained crack in the toilet that made me worry about sitting down too hard. When I went to wash my hands, the water never got properly warm. I could also see black spots on the pink-flowered plastic curtain in front of the bathtub, which made me think of ghost food. Everything smelled like lavender air freshener and rot. Lily turned on the TV and flipped through the channels while I fed Aunt Clara lettuce and tomato wedges from the Styrofoam box. Sometimes Lily helped me by buttering Aunt Clara's baguette.

I wondered what Aunt Clara would do if I decided not to feed her.

When the Styrofoam box was empty, Aunt Clara went outside to make some "private calls" from a pay phone, and when she came back inside again, it was Lily's turn to help her out. Aunt Clara had brought her makeup kit, and Lily had to practice many times, using my face as a model, while Aunt Clara stood behind her and pointed. The brushes tickled, which made me laugh, but that only made Aunt Clara cranky.

"A little more there . . . move the brush a little more like this . . . not so heavy with the lipstick, Lily . . . Violet, please, no grimaces . . ." Her plan was that Lily was going to do her makeup in the mornings so she didn't have to look at Ellie Anderson in the mirror.

So far, I hadn't seen the ghosts at all since we'd left Crescent Hill. The only dead person I had seen was the maid vacuuming our room. She blinked in and out but was there most of the time. She didn't *ask* for anything, though, just stood there in her faded pink uniform and moved the vacuum cleaner back and forth. Probably she didn't even know we were there. I felt sorry for her because vacuuming was boring, and it was a little unfair that she had to keep doing it long after she was dead. I wondered how she had ended up leaving her body while at work, and if she would notice me and *ask* for something if we stayed at the Pink Dragon for long enough.

Mr. Woods caught up with us around midnight. While we lay in the hard beds—Aunt Clara in one, and Lily and I in the other—we heard a rapping on the door to our room. Aunt Clara cursed and hauled herself out of bed, wrapping a purple silk robe around her, but when she looked out through the peephole and opened the door, there was no one there. As soon as she was back in bed, the rapping started up again, and now we could hear the hissing sound, too, and the door to the bathroom started opening and shutting by itself, so we knew who had come to visit.

We were well prepared, though. Lily had packed earmuffs for us, and Aunt Clara brought out the little box where she kept her wax earplugs. The noise really wasn't so bad after I put on the earmuffs. When I woke up again, around three in the morning, Mr. Woods was still there, standing in the corner of the room in his singed clothes and staring at Aunt Clara's bed. I just turned over and hid my face in the pillow, since I didn't like Mr. Woods at all after he had thrown things at us in the garden.

The next morning, Mr. Woods was gone. Lily and I woke up first, and she brushed my hair and braided her own before making us both sandwiches from the bread we had bought the day before. We sat outside on a sunlit bench and watched the cars speed by while we ate. It was very dusty and sad around the Pink Dragon.

"Is Aunt Clara very purple now?" I asked Lily.

"No, not right now," she said. "She is mostly turquoise."

"What about yesterday in the car, when she spoke about before?"

"Silver," Lily admitted.

"Silver means she's telling the truth," I said while chewing—something Mama would have hated if she had been with us.

"Not always," Lily replied. "Sometimes it's just because the person *thinks* it's the truth. It doesn't have to be the *truth* truth."

"Did you ever see colors before Mama and Papa died?" I asked, before taking another bite.

"Once or twice." She shrugged. "I never thought that it was real, though."

"Tell me about it." I wiped crumbs off my chin with the back of my hand.

Lily shifted on the bench and chewed a little bread and cheese herself before she started talking. "I was six or seven, so you were very little then, and we had a red squirrel who lived in an elm tree in the garden. He was very busy and ran up and down the trunk all day, and Mama and I loved sitting by the kitchen window to watch him. We fed him nuts and sunflower seeds from a bowl every day, and Mama called him Fredric. Then one day, Fredric wasn't there, and Mama said she had a bad feeling. We put on shoes and went outside to look for him and found him lying under a lilac tree. It was horrible for us both, but mostly for me, I think. I had never seen a sick animal before, and Mama said she thought he had accidentally eaten poison, which made me feel cold all over." She suddenly stopped, and when I looked at her, I could tell that she was swallowing hard so as not to cry.

"When Mama and I went back inside, you and Papa were there, and he was feeding you mushed banana at the kitchen counter. He saw at once that something was up, and when Mama told him what had happened, he said that we ought to kill Fredric so he didn't have to be in pain. Mama shook her head, though, and said that maybe she could help him, and that if she couldn't, maybe *I* could. I remember that they argued about it, because Papa saw that I was crying and didn't want me to go out there again, but Mama said that she thought I could make a difference, and so I decided that I wanted to."

"Did they argue for real?" Mama and Papa had *never* argued—or at least not when we were there.

"Not in a bad way," Lily explained. "They didn't shout or anything, but maybe that's why I remember it so well—because it was unusual, and because I didn't want Fredric to die."

"What happened next?"

"Mama got some strawberries out of the refrigerator, and a bowl of oranges from the counter, and then we went back into the garden. When we came to the lilac tree, we both kneeled on the ground in front of Fredric—who was breathing just a little and had closed his eyes—and Mama put the berries and fruit down on the ground and made me imagine that we gave the food to Fredric, which I thought was strange, since Fredric ate mostly nuts."

"It's like when I'm feeding the ghosts," I realized.

"Just like that, only no meat."

"Did your food get moldy, too?" I asked.

"I don't remember," Lily replied, which was a little disappointing.

"What happened next?" I had forgotten all about my sandwich by then. I only wanted to hear about Fredric.

"Then Mama made me put my fingers on Fredric's head, close my eyes, and think good thoughts. When I opened them again, I saw blue flames all over Fredric's body."

"Did you tell Mama?" I asked.

"I did." Lily took another bite of her sandwich.

"What did she say?"

Lily squinted her eyes while trying to remember. "I think she laughed," she said. "She thought that Fredric would be all right. We kept touching him for a long while—until the flames turned from blue to orange, and then we went back inside again."

"Just leaving Fredric out there?" I felt sorry for the little squirrel.

Lily nodded. "Mama said it would sort itself out—or not . . . That we had done what we could."

"What happened to Fredric?"

"Oh, he was fine again the next day, and back in his tree. He was there for a few more years before he disappeared for good."

"Did he have any tadpoles on him when you helped him?"

She shook her head. "Only the flames. Now that I know a little more about the colors, I think he was in pain, but that after we helped him, he didn't feel it anymore but was very tired from it all."

I nodded. "That's when the flames turned orange."

"Uh-huh," Lily said.

"I wish *I* could have done something like that with Mama." I suddenly felt very sorry for myself.

"Yes." Lily ran a hand over my head. "I wish you could have, too. I think Mama could have helped us a lot. I think she *knew* things . . . Do you remember how she and Koko sometimes spent hours in the kitchen making little pouches filled with herbs, and braiding weeds into wreaths that Mama said would protect us—like the one on our front door?"

I nodded because I remembered that, too, and how we sometimes were allowed to help. "She gave them to all our neighbors, too."

Lily nodded. "She was always kind to everybody."

"I saw a ghost before, when we were in Bulgaria," I admitted. "He stood outside our hotel room in the mornings and followed us around. I told Mama about it and she said that she would talk to him. I never saw him again after that, so whatever she said, it worked."

"You never told me about that either." Lily sounded a little annoyed. "I never knew that you saw ghosts before—or that *Mama* saw them."

"I didn't see them all the time. And it wasn't like it is now; they didn't *ask* about things then. Did you see the flames any other times?"

"Yes, but that wasn't very often either. The last time before K2 was when Grandma Fiona died." Lily looked like she might cry again. She had loved our grandmother very much, and she never liked it when things died.

"Me, too," I told her. "I never saw a ghost again after she died. Not before Crescent Hill."

Lily's eyes widened with surprise, and she opened her mouth to ask another question, but then Aunt Clara stepped outside the door to our room, and we couldn't talk about it anymore. First, Aunt Clara wanted me to feed her, then Lily had to do her makeup, and then she sent us to the vending machine to get coffee for her and tea for us. When we had carried it all back to the room with almost no spills, she finally told us what was going to happen that day—and nothing was right after that.

CLARA

38

Lily made a terrible fuss, of course, when I told my nieces about the appointment I had made on Violet's behalf. I had always known that she would, but that didn't make it any less tiresome when it happened. She kept shouting about Violet's fragile health and the exploitation of a minor, although the girl seemed as ruddy as ever to me, and what we were about to do was more of an exploitation of the bereft rather than of Violet. Still, her older sister raged like a furious angel inside the terrible motel room and even went as far as to threaten me with the police again. Violet herself just sat on the bed, staring at us both wide-eyed as we battled it out. In the end, though, Lily couldn't do much save accept it when I pushed her younger sister out the door.

I was the guardian, after all.

Out in the parking lot, Violet caused another delay when she paused halfway to the vehicle to wave at a crow in an oak tree. The tree itself looked sick and haggard, growing as it was in the middle of the parking lot; ants crawled on the trunk and the leaves were covered in road dust. The bird looked happy enough, though, balancing on a branch and staring at Violet with its head cocked to the side. Not a crow, I realized, but a raven. Perhaps the girl had developed a fondness for them, living in the raven room.

"Come on, Violet," I called as I unlocked the car door. "We don't want to be late for the appointment."

"I'm coming, Aunt Clara," she called back, but she was still stalling, cocking her head, too, now, mirroring the bird in the tree.

Finally, the spell seemed to have ended, and my niece came running toward the car just as the raven in the tree flew off. It was about high time, too, as I expected her sister to come bursting outside any minute to carry her back in to safety. We just didn't have time for another scene.

I didn't properly relax until we were on the road and away from the Pink Dragon. Lily would be fine. She had plenty of food and water, facilities, and a dozen or so of the mystery books she seemed to prefer, and which she had brought with her from the house. Hopefully, by the time we got back, the drama would have died down. She should *welcome* what I did, truth be told. Violet needed practice, and that was what she would get. Perhaps this could even be a good livelihood for her, somewhere down the line. I sure wished that someone had taken an interest in *my* talents while I was growing up. Not all children had the privilege of being seen like Violet was.

We stopped by a supermarket to stock up on raw beef, wine, and a handful of hard candies. I made a mental note to add the costs to the client's final bill. Then we kept driving toward what looked to be an affluent suburb, crowded with well-kept lawns and tidy flower beds. Violet ought to feel right at home. Instead, she kept fidgeting in the seat next to me, squirming almost, as we drove. I suppose she was worried about another bout of sickness. So was I, truth be told, but hopefully the vomiting had been a single event. I needed the money, so she had to do it; it was as simple as that.

I was deeply relieved when we finally parked the car in Margot Brewer's drive. The girl's worry was contagious and crawled all over me like fleas. Our client's house was large, well loved, and painted white. Flowering bushes crowded around the porch. Miss Brewer— *call me Miss Margot*—had said on the phone that she was a piano teacher, tutoring young students in her home. She had confided that the house had belonged to her parents, so surely if her father was still around, that was where he would be, and the chances of catching him in our little séance were good.

Miss Margot opened the door before we even had time to ring the bell. She looked to be in her fifties. She was short and somewhat squat but had a kindly-looking face and a bright expectant smile. We greeted each other with handshakes—even Violet, although she was still pale-faced and quiet, barely even murmuring her name.

"I know you said that the medium was young, but I had not expected *this*." Miss Margot gave me a questioning look as we filed into her cluttered hall. "She looks like she should be outside playing, rather than spending her time with a musty old woman like me." She said it all in a cheery voice, but it nevertheless held a condescending edge, which instantly soured my mood. We were there to *help* the woman after all, so she ought to be grateful.

"Oh, Violet is very aware of how rare her gift is, and she wants to use it to help others, isn't that so, Violet?" I smiled at my niece, showing my teeth, and she nodded, once. I moved my smile to Miss Margot. "She is a little shy, but she wants nothing more than to help the grieving find closure. She is an orphan herself, you see."

"Is that so?" Miss Margot's eyes widened. "How very sad." She tousled Violet's hair. "Whatever happened?" she asked me, but it was Violet who answered.

"They went to climb K2," she said, "but then they froze to death."

"Really?" Miss Margot's eyes were so wide by then that I feared they would come tumbling out of their sockets. She looked to me for confirmation and I nodded.

"My brother was a reckless sort," I said.

"Well, come in." Miss Margot gestured, then shuffled before us into a living room crammed with overstuffed chairs and overgrown houseplants. A large piano seemed to be the only clean thing in there, gleaming toward us, all polished and dusted. "Sit down." She gestured to a mustard-colored sofa. "I did as you asked." She rushed back out of the room while we seated ourselves and came back again just

as quick, holding an assortment of bowls and plates. "Is there anything else you need? Something of his maybe? I do have a tie and a
picture—"

"That won't be necessary. My niece only needs the kitchenware." It
wouldn't do to stain the woman's coffee table with our bloody beef,
although it looked plenty stained already. Miss Margot and I helped
each other clear space by removing newspapers, knitting needles,
crossword puzzles, and pencil stubs, until the tabletop was somewhat
clutter-free. Then I placed a bowl for the wine and plates for the meat
and candy, while sending the scatterbrained woman on a mission to
find a candle in one of her many drawers. Through all of this, Violet
sat silently beside me, as pale as before. I figured she had some stage
fright. It would be fine, though—it *had* to be. I meant to make as
much as I could off her talent.

Miss Margot finally rejoined us with a green candle in a silver
candlestick, jiggling a box of matches in her hand. "Found them, finally." She grinned at us. "Should I light it right away, or—"

"Let's get out the other necessary items first." I grinned back at her.
"It is your father you want to speak to, right? And he lived here in this
house?"

"Yes—yes." She sounded breathless. "I just miss him so terribly,
you see, and we had an arrangement that he would give me a sign
after he died, but I never got any." She laughed but it sounded false,
so clearly it bothered her. "I thought maybe we had gotten our wires
crossed, and I just want to know if he's all right—" She suddenly
stopped talking as the bloody meat came into view, and looked faint
when it slapped down on her china. She kept her peace all throughout
the rest of the preparations, though, while I poured the candy onto a
separate plate and filled the little bowl to the brim with red wine.
"Now you can light the candle," I said when I was all done.

Miss Margot wasn't looking at me anymore, however. She was
looking at Violet, who seemed even paler and more pained than before. "Are you all right, honey?" Miss Margot asked her.

"*Of course* she is," I snapped. "I would never force my niece to do
anything she didn't want to do."

"Is that so?" She was still looking at Violet, and I had to take several deep breaths to calm the first stirrings of anger that had erupted in my belly.

"You *do* want to check on your father, don't you?" I find it is very useful to remind people of what they want.

"Yes, I do." Miss Margot finally tore her gaze away from Violet, who still hadn't said a single word throughout this exchange. She lit the candle with hands that faintly shook.

We clasped our hands and sat in silence. Violet was staring at the candle but seemed very tense, and her lower lip quivered. This was not good at all. I couldn't keep showing up to these things with a sulking child at my side.

"Think of Miss Margot's father," I said.

"*Arnold Brewer,*" Miss Margot supplied, enunciating every syllable clearly.

"Arnold Brewer," I repeated to my niece, who still hadn't said a thing.

We sat in silence again for a while, and I started thinking about other things—mainly Clarabelle Diamonds and how I soon was to hold the first pieces in my hands. Then something finally happened, and Violet's head abruptly fell back as her whole body tensed, and something came pouring out of her mouth. It wasn't dirt, though, as I had expected, but some sort of clear liquid that bubbled and ran out of her mouth and down her cheeks before it trickled down on Miss Margot's couch. Violet then straightened her head again, and when her shoulders slumped, I could tell that she wasn't herself.

"Margot." Her lips formed the word slowly, as if it was difficult to move her mouth. It sounded more like *Maaahgooo* the way it came out, spoken in a brittle old-man's voice.

"Father!" Miss Margot herself sounded jubilant. "Is that really you?"

"So long ago." Violet forced out the words with some difficulty. "Am . . . so lost," the spirit muttered.

"Yes, Father, you were lost at sea," Miss Margot explained breathlessly. "You fell overboard on the Christmas cruise, don't you remember?" She looked at Violet expectantly.

"I drank the . . . umbrella," the poor man forced out.

"Yes, yes . . . the drinks had little paper umbrellas." Miss Margot had become quite red around the cheeks. "You drank a little too many of them, I think; that's why you fell off the ship." She laughed nervously. "But are you all right, Father? Where you are now?" She composed herself with some difficulty, and tears came trickling from her eyes.

"So cold," muttered the specter. "So lost."

"Tell him to go into the light," I urged, thinking that a message of coldness and loss was probably not what she had wanted to hear, and I *did* want to avoid another unhappy customer.

Miss Margot's gaze shifted from me to Violet. "Father." She wet her lips nervously with the tip of her tongue. "Do you see a light where you are? You must go into the light if you see it."

"There is only . . . salt," lamented the drowned man. "Salt and . . . cod, as far as the eye can see."

"Tell him to go and search for it," I said. "Tell him that it ought to be there."

"You must go and look for it, Father." Some desperation had come into her voice. "Think of all the piña coladas you can drink in heaven, Father. You just have to find the light!"

Then it happened again: Violet's back arched and the strange motion under her skin came back, followed by the first stirrings of the hissing sound. This time I was prepared, though, and let go of the others' hands to slam my palm down on the candle before Timmy could say as much as a word. It felt like plunging my hand right into a pod of stingrays, but at least I shut him up. I did my best to smile and look unconcerned when Miss Margot turned her shocked gaze on me.

"I think it is better if we stop the séance now. I suppose you have a lot to think about." I curled my hand into a fist to hide the damage from Miss Margot's view.

"But the girl," she said, pointing to my niece, who had promptly keeled over on the couch, entirely unconscious.

"Oh, it happens." I tried to laugh it off, although it was certainly awkward. "Such things can happen when one dabbles in the unknown." I promptly moved to sit closer to Violet and pat her shaggy head. "There, there," I muttered, while Miss Margot ran to the kitchen for some water, as if that would make my niece somehow return to her senses faster.

It actually took her quite a while to come around—so much so that I started to grow impatient and worried that I would have to carry the girl to the car. Miss Margot and I had already settled up and were both just standing there, staring at the passed-out girl for *ages*, before she finally stirred. She was drowsy when she came to, and wobbly on her feet, but she didn't throw up, which certainly was a blessing.

As we drove back to the motel, I felt relatively satisfied with the day's excursion. This séance hadn't worked out exactly as planned either, but Violet *had* found the right ghost, and she *had* conveyed a message, which was all I had promised Miss Margot on the phone. Sure, it would have been nicer for all parties involved if the message had been uplifting, but that hadn't been in the cards for Miss Margot. It also would have been better if Violet hadn't fainted, but perhaps a little illness just couldn't be helped. She had bounced back before and would surely do so again.

And Miss Margot *had* paid, too, which was the point of it all— even if the sum was modest. As soon as word started spreading, though, I would see that the price for our services followed suit.

LILY

39

The first thing I did after Aunt Clara and Violet had left was cry—
not because I was sad but because I was so angry. I lay on the smelly
pink bedspread for a good long while, just looking up at the brown-
stained ceiling and waiting for my heart to calm down. Then I tried to
read and watch TV, but I couldn't focus on anything, so in the end, I
just lay there on the bed and stared at the ceiling while my brain
worked so hard that it almost hurt, trying to find a way to save
Violet—and myself. But no matter what I thought of, Aunt Clara was
there like a looming shadow, crushing every plan I came up with.

Before K2, I had thought that all problems had solutions, since
that was what Mama and Papa had said. They had also said that all
ordeals had an end, but I couldn't quite see the end to this one.

On top of all this, my stomach hurt from thinking of Violet and
what was happening to her alone with Aunt Clara, and what she
would be like when she came back. The minutes seemed to move so
slowly. I had left the TV on, and a show about how to make airplanes
filled the screen. I didn't hear a word of what was being said, though;
I was too lost in my own dark thoughts.

When Violet and Aunt Clara finally returned, I was *so* relieved to
see them, but also terrified when I saw how pale Violet looked.

"I fainted on Miss Margot's couch," she told me as she crawled onto the bed. Her eyes when she looked up at me were glassy.

"Oh, Violet." I pressed a hand to her forehead and could feel that it was warm. "She has a fever again," I said to Aunt Clara. "Violet is *really* sick!"

"Yes, yes." Aunt Clara was busy bandaging her hand. She had burned herself, she said, but didn't mention how. "It was an unfortunate ending with the fainting, but Violet did well." She gave a satisfied smile, which annoyed me to no end, seeing how sick Violet was.

"You can never do anything like this again!" I told her. "You can never—*ever*—do it again!"

"No?" She looked up at me, lazy like a cat. "And how are you going to stop me? A few hours' rest, and Violet will be good as new again—"

"No!" I stomped my foot and breathed like a whale. "I won't let you!" I cried, just as the first few tears came trickling from my eyes. I *was* still afraid of Aunt Clara, but I remembered what Dina had said about our power and did my best to stand my ground.

Aunt Clara just laughed at me, though. "I have no time for childish tantrums. If you *really* want me to leave Violet alone, you ought to tell her to put the ghosts back. I'd gladly forfeit her fees for *that*." I didn't believe her, though, since she was flaming liar's green. As soon as she was patched up, she marched back outside to make more "private calls"—setting up new appointments for Violet, no doubt.

I was so angry that I could barely stand it!

I climbed onto the bed and nestled next to Violet, holding her tightly in my arms. She seemed calm, although her body shook from the fever sometimes. I was absolutely sure that her belly was full of tadpoles, but I couldn't do anything about it yet—not before Aunt Clara had taken her pill and gone to bed with wax plugs in her ears.

"Was it really bad?" I whispered to my sister.

"No," Violet answered, "but I don't remember very much. Aunt Clara was a little angry on the way back because Mr. Brewer—the ghost—had been lost at sea, and Miss Margot was really upset because her father was just swimming around down there without seeing any light. But she was happy that we got paid—*even* though I fainted."

"Don't worry about it, Violet." I squeezed her narrow shoulders gently. "This is all Aunt Clara's fault for forcing you to do it in the first place. Remember what Mama used to say about the work she did at her charity? Grown-ups are supposed to *protect* children, not put them to work. She has no right—"

"I would have helped Mr. Brewer if I could," she said. "I would have helped *our* ghosts, too, if I knew how to," she added with a trembling lower lip. "I *can't* when I'm not there, though. I don't even know if they *ask* when they are inside me. It's like I'm not in my body at all, but in a place that is black, like sleep without dreaming."

"I know you would have helped them." I squeezed her shoulders again. "It's like you said: The séances are wrong, because it isn't the dead that *asks*."

"Maybe that's why I become sick," Violet suggested.

"I don't think you're meant to have them inside you," I said. "Just because you can, it doesn't mean that you *should*." I gently sat up to my knees and lifted Violet's shirt up just a little, to see a mass of writhing pink tadpoles there. I supposed they belonged to Mr. Brewer. "We'll clean you up in no time when Aunt Clara has gone to sleep," I said, trying to sound cheery, but feeling as though I was failing.

The rest of the day moved like molasses while we waited for Aunt Clara to go to bed. She had gone into town and brought back a Styrofoam tray of fried fish and chips for us, while she herself ate another green salad that Violet was too weak to shove into her mouth, so I had to do it instead. None of us were happy about it, and the carpeted floor around her chair was littered with pieces of lettuce after. Then I had to remove her makeup using cotton pads and an oily substance. I liked that even less because I had to be so close to her.

"Stop frowning," she hissed at me once, but I just couldn't help it.

All the while, Violet slept on the bed, and I was so worried for her that I sometimes had to go check on her to make sure she was still breathing.

I was so concerned about what I knew we had to do to make Violet feel better that I even slipped Aunt Clara an extra sleeping pill in her coffee, to make her go to bed faster. I hadn't planned on it, but then I saw her pills lying in the bathroom and just couldn't help myself.

She did get tired after that, and took her normal pill, too, which was perfect for us, because hopefully it would make her sleep even deeper, and she wouldn't wake up when we moved around. I had already pretended to go to bed by the time Aunt Clara slumped down in hers, and it didn't take long at all before I heard her breathing change. After that, I waited for a little while longer, then gently shook Violet awake.

We carried the pink bedspread and a pillow with us to the bathroom for Violet to lie on, and left the door open so we wouldn't be surprised if Aunt Clara suddenly woke up. I didn't think she would, though. We could hear from her breathing that she was deeply asleep, and all her flames were white and peaceful, with just a hint of blue from the medicine.

Once Violet was down on the pink-tiled floor, I steeled myself and lifted up her shirt.

"Is it really bad?" Violet asked, and I nodded because I didn't want to lie to her.

"Don't worry," I said quickly. "I'll get rid of them."

Once again, I picked squirming pink tadpoles off my sister's belly and swallowed them whole. It took me hours to get them all off her, and Violet had been quiet and struggling with her breathing all the while, which I didn't like at all.

"What would happen to me, Lily, if you weren't here to take the tadpoles away?" she asked when I was all done.

"I don't know," I said, although my heart had started racing in my chest.

"I think that I would die," she said matter-of-factly. "I think the tadpoles would eat up all the life in me. I can *feel* it, Lily. It's true."

"Nonsense," I muttered, but I felt sick. "How are you feeling now?" I asked, to distract us both from the gloominess.

"Better, but not like I was before," she said, meaning how she was before Aunt Clara started to make her do the séances.

"I have an idea," I said, suddenly feeling a little lighter. "Do you remember what I told you about Fredric?" When Violet nodded, I continued. "Maybe we could try the same thing with you. We still have some apples from the grocery store, and the leftovers from Aunt Clara's salad. Do you want to try?"

Violet nodded eagerly, and I got to my feet and scurried to the main room, where Aunt Clara was sleeping soundly on the bed. But as I passed through the dark room, I suddenly started doubting myself. What if it didn't work—or I did something wrong? What if I made Violet worse? By the time I was back in the bathroom with the Styrofoam box and the two green apples, my heart was racing again. But I didn't *think* I would do anything wrong. Mama had showed me, after all, and if she thought it was safe, it *was*.

I placed the food on the floor by Violet's nest of bedding and filled a plastic cup with water from the tap. Then I sat down cross-legged beside Violet, who was still pale and breathing heavily, even though the tadpoles were gone. I started thinking good thoughts, as Mama had taught me, imagining Violet like she used to be before, all happy and carefree. Then I placed a hand on her brow. Even though I couldn't see her flames, I tried to create the same feeling as I had when Mama and I had healed Fredric.

After we had been sitting there for a good long while, I thought maybe her breathing had become a little lighter, and her brow a little less warm. "I don't feel so bad now," she muttered from the pillow. "I think it's working, Lily."

I couldn't help but laugh, as quietly as I could, because I felt so relieved. "With the tadpoles gone you shouldn't feel sick again either," I reasoned. "Hopefully, this was enough." I removed my hand and looked down at the food: The apples were all wrinkled now, and the lettuce had wilted and curled up. The glass of water was entirely empty.

Violet had seen it, too. "Look, Lily! It *does* work the same way—only with less mold."

"It does." I let out a shivering breath, amazed and relieved at the same time. "I never knew I could do that," I said. Not by myself, without Mama.

"Never let Aunt Clara know," Violet whispered. "She'll only make you go and see clients as well, and then maybe you will get sick, too."

"I don't think I can heal *ghosts*," I said.

"No, but you could heal people. Not that you shouldn't help them, but Aunt Clara will make you do it *wrong*." I didn't like how old Violet seemed in that moment—not like a nine-year-old at all. At the same time, I realized that she was right. Aunt Clara would probably use me in the same way that she used Violet.

"I would never tell her *anything*," I said with a snort. "My birthday is coming up soon," I added to comfort us both, "and then there'll only be *three* more years."

"If we live that long," Violet breathed. I was about to ask her what she meant when she sat up on the bedspread. She *did* look much better: Her cheeks were rosy and there was a sparkle in her eyes that didn't come from fever. I couldn't believe that *I* had made it happen. "Oh, look, there she is again." Violet looked out through the half-open door. I looked, too, but couldn't see a thing. Violet seemed to remember and said, "There's a woman out there—a maid. She is vacuuming all the time."

"Oh no," I said, instantly concerned. "No more ghosts, Violet." We had *just* cleaned her up—

"But this one is different." Violet didn't look at me but at the darkness outside the door, staring at the thing I couldn't see. "She didn't see me before, but now she does—maybe because I'm well again. She is *asking* me, Lily."

"No, no, no." I shook my head. "We don't want another one walking around and—"

"No, wait." She held up a hand. "She is telling me a story in my head. She doesn't want to be *realer*, Lily, she just wants to go home. Not *home* home, but home *beyond*. She says that she worked so many jobs just to have food and a house that all she did in life was work. She worked so hard that her heart suddenly stopped, but she didn't understand at the time that she was dead, so she just continued vacuuming as before. She just wanted to get the job done, so she could go home to her kids and make them dinner. I think she has been cleaning this room for a very long time."

"But what does she *want*?" I hissed, so very worried about my sister.

"To be unglued so she can go." Violet's voice was sad and low. "She doesn't want to vacuum anymore."

"But what if you get sick again?"

"I never did before, when they *asked*."

That was true. "But you're still weak."

"I don't *feel* weak," she protested.

"We don't have any bones or meat," I said.

"No," Violet murmured, rising to her feet. "But this one doesn't need that. She only needs bread and salt, which we have."

"Bread and salt, huh?" I rose as well, and even if I still didn't feel convinced, I went back into the main room and got the half hunk of bread we had left and several small packages of salt from a diner that lay scattered on the table. I *was* curious to see what Violet was going to do with it.

When I came back to the bathroom, Violet filled the plastic cup with water again and placed the bread just inside the threshold. She opened all the small packages of salt and poured them out on top of the bread and around the cup of water.

"Why salt?" I asked her.

"Because it unglues," she murmured, and kept working. We both froze when we heard Aunt Clara turning in the bed, but then she just kept breathing as evenly and calmly as before, so we continued. We didn't have a candle, but we did have a box of matches, and we decided it was my job to keep one burning at all times until the flame went out on its own. I prepared by lining them all up on the edge of the bathtub.

"All right?" I asked Violet before I lit the first match.

"All right." She nodded and placed herself behind the bread. As soon as I struck the match, she started chanting, but it wasn't the same words as before. "Dear maid in the motel room," she said, "please take the bread and salt that I have brought you. The salt is for your spirit, the bread for your soul, salt for your spirit, bread for your soul, salt for your spirit, bread for your soul . . ." She kept going like that until she swayed on her feet—and this time, I couldn't help her if she fell; I was far too busy lighting one match with another and dropping the spent ones down in the tub. There were only five matches left when the one I held suddenly went out, leaving behind just a ribbon of smoke. Violet stopped chanting and slumped against the pink-tiled wall.

"She is gone now," she said, sounding tired but pleased. "I'm happy we got to do that for her."

"And you are okay, too?" I asked her while gathering up the acrid-smelling matches. I noticed that the bread on the floor was covered in thick green mold.

"Sure." She lifted up her shirt. "Do you see any tadpoles?" she asked, and I did not. Her belly was just as it should be.

"It's different when they *ask*," she said, seemingly just her normal self. "And this one was *really* happy not to have to vacuum anymore."

VIOLET
40

Aunt Clara had no idea the next morning that Lily and I had gotten rid of both the tadpoles and a ghost maid in the bathroom. She really must have slept quite deeply not to notice anything, even if she had her wax earplugs in. When Mr. Woods arrived around dawn, she just rolled over in bed and slept on, but that wasn't unusual. Lily and I did almost the same thing, just put on our earmuffs and turned our backs on him. I don't think he liked that much, because he emptied out Aunt Clara's suitcase and strewed her clothes everywhere. But that turned out to be a good thing, because then we could just say that Mr. Woods must have stolen the food as well. It wouldn't be a good idea to admit that we had thrown it out in the night, full of wrinkles and mold.

Aunt Clara looked bleary-eyed, though, when she hauled herself out of bed, and Lily and I weren't allowed to speak before she had had her first coffee, which Lily got from the vending machine. It was almost noon before she decided that the day had begun and told Lily to put on her makeup. Then I fed her crackers, which we also got from a vending machine. They were very dry and salty, and I didn't like them very much.

"You look awfully perky this morning." Aunt Clara sat on one of the chairs of the motel room with her legs crossed and her foot dangling an inch or so off the floor. Her high-heeled shoe was gleaming like a black beetle. "According to your sister, you were close to death last night. Obviously all you needed was some rest, just like I said."

"*This* time," Lily said before I could reply. "*This* time she got better, but we don't know what would happen if there was a next time—"

"Oh, we'll find out soon enough." Aunt Clara sounded very smug, and a shiver of worry rose from my toes all the way up my spine. I *really* didn't want to be sick again.

"You can't be serious!" Lily rose from the bed where she had been sitting next to me and placed herself in the middle of the room. Her brow was wrinkled up with worry. "You can't keep doing this, Aunt Clara! Violet isn't built for it—"

"No? She looks perfectly fine to me," she said—which was true, but only because of Lily. "It's as I have said all along; she only needs to get used to it, and she won't feel those unpleasant side effects any-more."

"She *faints* and *vomits*," Lily shouted.

"I'm not supposed to speak with them like that," I added. "Maybe other mediums are, but I'm not."

"Nonsense," Aunt Clara said with a snort. "It's a goddamned *gift*. And if you truly hate it so much, you know what to do to make it all stop. Put the ghosts back, and you are free—or is it that you can't?" Her green eyes narrowed as she frowned at me.

"Of course not," Lily replied lightning fast. "It's just that we think you *deserve* the ghosts, for making them *be* ghosts."

"And the need to torment me outweighs your concern for your sister's welfare?" Her eyebrow rose in a way that made me aware that she didn't believe us. "I have quite lost my patience with you two. You clearly know nothing of how these things work. *I* do, though. I have read the book, and I tell you that Violet will be fine."

"But she won't!" Lily cried.

"I don't like it," I said at the same time. "I don't like being sick and I don't remember what happens. It's not supposed to be this way!"

"Well, I don't care one jot," Aunt Clara said. "You will do as I say, and that's the end of it." I think she was still a bit tired from the night before, because her eyes were still swollen and she didn't even try to pretend to be nice—or even like us. I wished I could go back in time and tell Mama not to bother with the Christmas gifts.

There was no point in fighting with Aunt Clara, though—not when she had decided and was in a grumpy mood. No matter what Lily and I said, she wouldn't listen, but it squeezed painfully in my chest when we got into the car—leaving Lily behind again to worry alone in the motel room. I hoped she would call Dina and that Dina could make her feel a little better. The only thing that made *me* feel better was that I saw Irpa up in the tree again, and that she made happy noises when she saw me. When the station wagon rolled out of the parking lot, she took flight and followed, which made me feel calmer at once.

I wouldn't be all alone out there.

We drove for a very long time. All the roads were dusty and had plenty of cracked pavement. On each side of us were fields of yellow grass and shrubs with almost no leaves on them. We saw a dead fox— full of smoke—and lots of candy wrappers and soda cans littering the sides of the road. I missed Lily like crazy, because I didn't even know where I was going, and being sick was horrible—though I did feel better now than I had in a long time, thanks to Lily. Sometimes, when I looked in the rearview mirror, I saw Irpa flying behind us, and that was good, because it meant that if something bad happened to me, she could fly back to Lily and maybe show her where I was.

The new client's house was on a small farm set away from the main road. It looked a bit run-down, although the woman who lived there looked spry and happy, wearing a yellow caftan and lots of wooden beads around her neck. Her hair was almost as wild as mine. Despite Lily's complaining about how it was hard to comb through, I liked my hair *because* it was wild—*so* wild that it threw off all the ribbons and hair bands Lily tried to put in it. I wondered if it was the same way for the client—*Samantha Carlsen, call me Samantha*—and if she, too, couldn't take as much as two steps without her shoelaces coming undone. She limped a little, though, and I could *feel* that there was something wrong with her foot. I felt it so much that it was as if *my* foot was hurting, too, and I had to concentrate not to limp myself when we walked over to her house. I didn't want her to think I was making fun of her.

When we went inside, Samantha wanted us to sit down on a brown couch, and both Aunt Clara and I winced when we saw the woven rug under the wooden table. It was made in a fancy red-and-blue pattern, and it wouldn't be good if I vomited on it. Aunt Clara made Samantha roll it up before we started.

"There is sometimes . . . spillage," she explained to Samantha, who gave her a strange look. She had made herbal tea for us, which she gave us in large, glazed ceramic mugs. Mine was brown, while Aunt Clara's was red. Samantha's mug was green. The tea tasted minty.

Aunt Clara had shopped again on our way there, but she had been in a hurry, so all Samantha's mother—who was the ghost we were looking for—would get was a few strips of bacon, a carton of juice, and some pieces of strawberry candy, which she put into ceramic bowls while explaining to the client, as she always did, how my "methods" were "unorthodox." I, for one, was looking at the art on Samantha's walls: lots of rainbows and waterfalls. I thought she had to like nature a lot.

Samantha lit a green candle, and we all held hands as usual, and I was preparing for something to come and knock me away again, but this time, no matter how long I stared into the flame, it didn't happen.

Aunt Clara became impatient and started squeezing my hand really hard. "Think about her, dear," she said in her fake-happy voice. "Think about *Edith Carlsen*." I did. I thought about her for a good long while, and then Samantha let go of our hands to find a picture of a smiling gray-haired woman. After, I thought about her some more, but I wasn't knocked away.

"I'm sorry," I muttered. "She just won't come through."

"Perhaps it is the bacon," Samantha suggested, and shifted on the chair so all her beaded necklaces clattered together. "Mother never much liked it."

"Let's try for a little while longer." Aunt Clara sent me an ice-cold look, but it didn't help, because Edith still didn't come. Not even when we changed the bacon for pickles and tomatoes, and the orange juice for real wine. Edith just wasn't there. Samantha even gave me a brooch her mother had used to hold in my hands—it had pretty blue stones— but it didn't help either.

We just sat there holding hands while the minutes ticked by, and not as much as a speck of mold appeared on the tomatoes.

Finally, Samantha became restless and a little annoyed. It didn't help even when Aunt Clara said, "I swear this has *never* happened before," and, "Perhaps poor Violet is ill."

I wasn't ill, though. I felt just like myself, except that no one came and knocked me away.

We couldn't just sit there forever, so in the end, we had to leave, and I think Samantha for one was happy that we did. The smile she gave us when we walked out the door was very stiff, and so was Aunt Clara's. She was angry that we wouldn't get paid, of course.

When we arrived at the car, Irpa sat on the hood and cocked her head at me until Aunt Clara chased her away. She sent me happy thoughts, though, all the way into my head, which made me dread the car ride back a little less. She also told me why it hadn't worked by showing me an image of Mrs. Carlsen walking through a door.

Despite the good thoughts, the car wasn't a happy place. Aunt Clara looked like an angry bull as we drove along the road. She even made bull sounds, snorting and breathing heavily. She had to swerve not to hit a car that came in the other direction, and I was so frightened that I lifted my arms to shield my face, in case the windshield exploded.

"I should have splurged for beef," Aunt Clara finally said. Her jaws worked hard, grinding her teeth together. "No wonder the lady wouldn't come when all she was offered was supermarket bacon. *I* sure wouldn't have come back for that."

"It wouldn't have helped," I muttered. "She wasn't *there* anymore."

"What do you mean *there*?" Aunt Clara barked.

"She had gone. She wasn't a ghost. I can't talk to them if they're gone."

"Gone? Like to 'the beyond'?"

I nodded. "I think we were just lucky before, that Mr. Arthur and Mr. Brewer were still there. I can't talk to them if they've gone."

"What kind of nonsense rule is that?" Aunt Clara sounded very angry. "Why didn't you mention this stupid quirk before?"

"I wasn't sure before," I said quietly. "This is the first time I didn't find them."

"Well, other mediums speak to all kinds of dead, so I don't see why you shouldn't—"

"It's different for me," I said, feeling angry myself now. "That's why I need all the food . . . I'm not here to help the living; I'm here to help *the dead*." I crossed my arms over my chest and turned my head so I was looking out on the yellow landscape. I didn't say what was on the tip of my tongue, even if it wanted to slip out: *It's* Lily *who helps the living*.

I don't know how I knew that, but I did.

"*Help* the dead, huh? So it's like a *calling* now?" I didn't need to look at her to know she was rolling her eyes. "And you are absolutely certain this isn't some ruse? Something you and your sister have cooked up because you are averse to doing a day's honest work? Perhaps you aren't as innocent as you pretend to be—not as unable to control what unfolds? Perhaps we didn't meet a ghost today because you *decided* not to let it come through."

"No," I said. "She was gone."

"Then why didn't you just lie? Make something up?" She sounded very confused.

"Because I wouldn't even know what to say," I told her. "And I *don't* want to lie!"

"Well, then, tell me one thing, Violet. What use are you to me if you cannot speak to *all* the dead, but just a select few? Why should I bother to keep you and your sister around if you cannot get rid of my ghosts *or* compensate me for my suffering? Why shouldn't I just send you back and let Mr. Skye sort you out? You are likely to be separated, but that's no skin off my nose."

"You need the money," I whispered, still not looking at her. This wasn't a *feeling*. I knew it because Lily had told me.

I don't know exactly what happened then, but the words worked like the tap of a magic wand, and Aunt Clara didn't say any more after that.

CLARA

41

Lemonade was my mantra on the morning following the failed séance, as we readied ourselves to leave the Pink Dragon. *Lemonade, lemonade, lemonade* . . . In truth, I was an expert at making it, having received basketfuls of lemons more times than I cared to count in my life—the latest little citrus being my niece's unwelcome admission the day before. Obviously, she couldn't speak to *all* the dead, only *some* of the dead . . . which already made me dread the next appointment, and possibly the next unhappy client.

I had been furious on the drive back from Miss Carlsen's farm. I had felt utterly betrayed, and not entirely convinced that Violet had been honest with me. It would be just like the two of them to cook up a plan—invent a new "rule"—to pour even more misery on my plate, and I *needed* this to work. I needed the money now more than ever, because Isabella was getting impatient and had even threatened to take her creations elsewhere the last time I called her from the pay phone. She had called me "irresponsible" besides, for commissioning her work without having the funds. She hadn't used the word "charlatan" yet, but I felt sure it was just waiting to be said.

Unless I wanted to see Clarabelle Diamonds slip from my grasp, I needed to find a solution—fast.

And then Violet's admission, as welcome as a turd on the doorstep—
and the failed séance, which had done nothing save cost me a fortune
in diesel. None of this was good.

Not good at all.

The night before had been torturous. Every time the girls laughed,
I winced, and it didn't help at all that Violet was back to her old self.
She was up and down from the bed at least a dozen times per hour,
spinning around and chattering away like a happy monkey.

"Do you think I can be a dancer when I grow up, Lily? Or wait,
they need to lace their shoes really tight, and mine would just fall off
again—but maybe I could buy my own dancing company, and then I
could dance on the stage when it was night and everyone had gone
home . . . Or maybe I could just dance at home instead . . . Or I could
make a bare-feet dancing studio . . ."

On and on it went. It would have been enough to give me a headache if I hadn't already had one. The salad she fed me tasted like tissue
paper, and Lily nicked me with her fingernail when she removed my
makeup, leaving a smear of blood on my cheek.

And all the while, all I could think of was that Clarabelle
Diamonds—my legacy—was doomed, and that all I had to look forward to now was being a prisoner in my own home, with the ghosts
of my past holding the reins, torturing me at every turn.

I didn't think of lemonade at all before I had gone to bed. But this
had always been my pattern: first the despair, then the solution. Because if there was one thing I had learned through all my hardships,
it was that there was *always* a solution, if only one dug deep enough
and were willing to get one's hands a little dirty. This time was no
exception, and by the time dawn arrived, I had a new plan—one that
worked no matter what.

My pitcher was now full of delicious lemonade.

Which is why my mood had lifted considerably by the time we
loaded our suitcases into the station wagon and were finally able to
wave the horrid motel bye-bye. I could tell that my lack of frustration
put Lily on high alert, though, and she kept eyeing me with suspicion as we drove. Violet, however, seemed oblivious, and regaled her

sister with a long and boring story about a red sparrow who laid silver eggs.

"It's good to see you back to your old self," I said, when I had had quite enough of the bird tale. "Being a little sick never hurt anyone. I was often sick as a child myself."

"Did Grandma Iris bring you soup and make it better?" Violet asked.

"No, Grandma Iris was far too busy with her own challenges—my father, for one. She had no time to nurse a sick child."

"What about your father?" Violet asked next.

"He had his own shit to deal with—my mother for one, and the curse of the bottle, too. They had that particular demon in common." I let my eyes roam the dusty landscape as we sped by: dry pastures and sickly trees, a horizon the color of skimmed milk.

"Is that why you became a nurse?" Violet asked. "Because no one took care of you when you were sick?"

"God no!" I laughed, but it came out brittle. "I became a nurse because it was one of the few professions your grandfather would pay for when he wanted me out of the house. I suppose he saw it as a safe bet: There is always a need for nurses, so I wouldn't go unemployed. 'Safe and secure,' he said. 'A good livelihood.'"

"But did you *like* being a nurse?" Violet's relentless nosiness seemed to have recovered fine as well.

"It was work," I said, "but no, I didn't like it. I felt like I had been forced onto that path—and disposed of. It wasn't what I had seen for myself."

"What *did* you see for yourself?" This time it was Lily who asked.

"I wanted to become a jeweler—or even a buyer for a store. I have always liked diamonds best." I looked down at my fingers, the brilliant sparkles.

"But Grandpa Otis wouldn't pay for it?" Violet again.

"No, he wouldn't. I suppose it wasn't *secure* enough." I made the mistake of looking into the rearview mirror for just a second too long, and Ellie Anderson's dark eyes stared right back at me. I quickly shifted my gaze.

"Did you miss your own father a lot back then?" Violet had such a relentless streak.

"Yes, I did, at first—and I was furious with Iris for having taken him away from me, but then I came to understand her better. You see, Ivan wouldn't have been able to offer me *any* kind of education, but Otis did. Iris took care of it, just like she'd said. She *used* Otis to better her own life—and mine, too, by extension. In exchange, he got a beautiful wife and the pleasure of knowing he had saved her, and men like him do like to be the hero."

"He got a daughter, too," said Violet.

"No," I replied. "It was never that way. But he *did* get a son." Chubby, freckled, and mischievous; the apple of his father's eye and the heart's blood of his mother. The golden boy. The seal on their pact. "I don't blame Iris for taking me with her to live with Otis in the city—or for disposing of my father. I realize that sometimes such things just have to be done." What I did blame her for was discarding me: driving me out and making me feel so very unimportant. For not *loving* me, in essence, though I always balked at that word.

"It must have been a bad time for you," Violet muttered from the back seat.

"No, I had a trick, you see." I smiled as I shifted gears. "I used to pretend like I was living inside a diamond bubble with walls as clear as glass, and as long as I was in there, nothing and no one could touch me. Sometimes I would go for days, pretending to be inside that bubble." Whatever Iris threw my way, it simply couldn't touch me. When she complained about my temper, my lack of wit and charm, the bubble would deflect it.

"Do you still sometimes pretend to be in the bubble?" Violet was shaping up to be quite the little detective.

"No," I replied as I changed lanes. "Crescent Hill is my bubble now. I don't need to pretend." Or at least that was how it had been before the girls arrived. "I won't allow anything that threatens me to stay within its walls."

"Is that why you killed Mr. Woods and Ellie Anderson?" Lily's hard voice sounded.

"Just that." I gave a satisfied smile. "I removed them from my bubble. And good riddance to them both."

"Don't you *ever* feel bad about what happened to them?" Lily persisted.

I shook my head, but I didn't look back. "Timmy knew my rules and stepped badly out of line. He wanted to take my *diamonds*—"

"So you think it was *his* fault?" She sounded incredulous.

I shrugged. "One thing my mother taught me is that if you break the rules, there's no one else to blame for being fat."

Violet giggled. "What does that mean?"

"Oh, she had a thing about food." I remembered how I used to sneak down to the kitchen at night to steal sugar and cookies from the pantry, and then how I hid my spoils around my room and other places in the house. I had decided early on that it didn't count if no one saw me, so I used to comfort myself with something sweet every now and then—the only kind of sweetness my life could reliably provide.

I still couldn't bring myself to eat sweet or fatty foods in public and always pretended that I hated the taste, just as Iris had taught me. *Cucumber sandwiches,* she had said. *Cucumber sandwiches and melon balls. With all your other challenges, the best thing you have is your figure.* I suppose she was trying to help me in her way, give me the best possible tools for survival, but that doesn't mean it didn't hurt.

"Your father, though," I told the girls. "He could eat everything he wanted. If he felt like apple pie, the cook would make an apple pie. If he wanted cookies, the cook would make cookies. Then they would all fawn over him and be amazed at how much he could eat. It was a very different life for him."

"Papa was a good man." Lily spoke very quietly.

"He could afford to be." I shrugged again. "There wasn't a thing that he wanted that he couldn't get just by snapping his fingers. I suppose that's why he was so fascinated with dangerous sports. He needed to feel a little more than what his life provided. Waterskiing, diving, parachuting . . . climbing. I suppose the poor boy just needed a challenge."

"It wasn't Papa's fault that he inherited so much money." Lily again.

"Or that he got all the cake," Violet added.

"No," I muttered. "But it certainly wasn't mine either."

They fell quiet for a while after that, so I think perhaps I got to them—or at least had given them something to think about. The peace didn't last for long, though.

"I don't see why we can't just go home." Lily used her whiny voice. "Maybe the next client doesn't have a ghost either, and then you won't get any money." Lily was, of course, well informed about the previous day's fiasco.

"I admit that it's harder now," I said, thinking, *Lemonade, lemonade.* "But all is not lost, and there are still ways for Violet to make it up to me. The world seems to be full of spooks after all, which means that at least some of our clients are bound to have dead relatives on hand. And"—I paused for effect—"I have been thinking of branching out . . . There are people who—like me—are hounded by the dead and have infestations in their homes, so perhaps we could offer our services to them. Even if you won't put *my* ghosts back, perhaps you're more inclined to help our clients with *their* vermin." I was speaking to Violet and forced myself not to look in the rearview mirror to gauge her reaction. "That way we would only have to go to places where we know for a fact there are ghosts, and you would do our clients a valuable service by letting the dead tell them why they are still there. And even if you can't 'put them back,' you can maybe find it in your heart to *pretend* to have chased them into the light?" My conviction that my nieces had been bluffing all along and had no idea how to get rid of the pests had grown both firm and strong. "There was a long chapter on haunted houses in *How to Talk to Spirits*," I added, just to bolster my case.

"That is a terrible idea," Lily said at last, sounding aghast. "Violet will just get sick again."

"And then she will bounce right back," I said, "just like she did last time. We'll stock up on vitamin supplements and carrots. Maybe that will help."

And so, quite pleased, I drove on into the night.

LILY

42

There was absolutely no way we could stay with Aunt Clara; that much was clear after the things she had said on the drive the day before. Now she didn't just want Violet to do séances, but she wanted her to trick people, too! I *hated* what she did to my sister, but I hated even more that I couldn't do anything about it, except one thing: go.

I didn't know *where* to go, though.

Late the night before, Violet and I had been napping in the back seat when Aunt Clara parked the car outside another tired motel: the Silver Star. Violet had started fantasizing as soon as she heard the name, imagining how the ceiling maybe was covered in stars, or perhaps they had seats on the roof so we could climb up and look at the stars, but I didn't think so. I thought it would be just like the last one, and sadly, I was right. The only difference between the Pink Dragon and the Silver Star was the color of the bedspreads, which were blue, and instead of lavender, the air smelled like lemon candy.

Our first night there had been noisy, too, as Mr. Woods came and emptied out our suitcases on the floor again. Then he threw all my Agatha Christie novels at Aunt Clara's head. She shrieked and ducked under the bedcovers while Violet and I ran into the bathroom and closed the door behind us. We sat in the bathtub behind the blue plastic curtain until the shrieking finally died down. I really wished that Mr. Woods's aim was a little better, though, because Aunt Clara escaped the attack with only a couple of bruises on her face, and she deserved so much more.

In the morning, when I did Aunt Clara's makeup, I painted her eyebrows crooked on purpose and was sloppy with the lipstick, too. She did look a little weird, but no one but me and Violet knew, and we sniggered about it all morning. It felt *so* good to laugh again.

It was hard to keep the good mood going, however, when Aunt Clara announced that she and Violet had an appointment. If she found a ghost, I knew that Violet would be just as sick as before by the time they came back, and if she didn't, Aunt Clara would be mad. There was no point in arguing with Aunt Clara, though—it might even make her behavior worse—so I just stood by and did nothing when they left, even if all I *wanted* to do was scream. My stomach tied up in a hard knot when I saw them drive away, but then I saw Irpa outside, pecking at something on the concrete just below the windowsill, and felt a little better—especially when, after a second, the raven took flight and followed the car.

At least Violet wouldn't be alone.

I was alone, though—but this time I knew what to do while I waited. I got out my notebook right away, sat down at the little table in our room, and started making a list of possible places we could go to, but it wasn't very long. No matter what I thought of—my friend Marie's house, or Koko's empty apartment—it seemed impossible that Aunt Clara wouldn't find us. I thought of hostels and shelters, too, and changing our names to live like nomads, but none of it seemed safe from her.

I just didn't know what to do.

Finally, I rose from the chair and fell down on the bed, belly first, exhausted. It shouldn't have been possible for me to fall asleep since I was so restless inside, but maybe spending most of the night in the bathtub had made me extra tired, because I *did* sleep, and while I slept, something new happened.

It started with a feeling as if the bed was shaking—but in the dream, so I didn't wake up—and then suddenly, *I* was shaking, more and more, until I was shaken loose from my body and sped toward the ceiling, face down. I didn't crash into the ceiling, though, but stopped there, just floating and looking down at the room. It was as sad and blue as always, and I looked a little sad, too, lying there on the bed with my braid curled around my ear. My white shirt and plaid skirt were crumpled and stained with tea and ketchup.

I wasn't afraid at all—I suppose I knew it was a dream—but just as I had started wondering how I was going to get down again and slip back into my body, I noticed that something was happening with Aunt Clara's nightstand. There was a faint white color there, throbbing gently around the frame, and a low humming sound in the air, like the one left behind when I played the violin. Once I had noticed, it was as if a string was being pulled inside me, and I rushed back down again, only to wake up dizzy on the bed, back in my own skin.

I just lay there for a while, getting my bearings. My mouth was dry and I had a headache. I got to my feet to go to the bathroom and look for an aspirin, and when I came back out again, carrying a plastic cup of water, my gaze fell on the nightstand. It was a completely normal square piece of wooden furniture that didn't look like much at all, but there was a drawer in it where motels usually kept Bibles. I went to the nightstand on wobbly feet, and with a heart that trembled just a little, I pulled out the drawer.

There *was* a Bible there, but I didn't see it at first. All I could see when I looked in the drawer was a stained old road map. With shivering hands, I brought it out and held it up to my eyes; then I unfolded it completely and put it on top of Aunt Clara's bed. There was a route drawn in red marker snaking across the yellow and green, and when I squinted to look at the tiny letters, I could tell right away that it was *our* route, so it definitely had to be Aunt Clara's map. I looked at it from every angle and traced the red line with my finger, but I didn't really know what I was looking for—until I saw the small blue egg nestled between two ridges on the map, right in the middle of a green swath. I *knew* that shape—I had seen it before, on a map not unlike this one, in the car with Mama and Papa.

It was where Mama's lake house was.

Suddenly, it felt as if my whole body was electric. I studied the map more closely and trailed routes of my own with my finger. I could see train tracks snaking from where we were that ran almost all the way to the lake house. It was a long journey, but not overly so, and nothing compared to the one Aunt Clara had mapped out for us. I sat down on the edge of the bed and drew a different—simpler—map in my notebook and scribbled down all the names I had to remember, before folding the road map and putting it back in the drawer.

Finally, I knew what we had to do.

I was anxious and tense for the rest of the day, but Aunt Clara barely noticed. She kept talking about how the séance had been a success, and how Violet had barely even fainted. Violet herself lay on the bed just as pale and feverish as she was before I healed her, so clearly there *had* been a ghost this time.

"I only spat a little dirt on the carpet," she said. "I didn't vomit at all."

Aunt Clara was so happy that she even let us stay behind when she went to buy food, instead of making us go to another diner. Before she came back again—loaded with hamburgers and a salad for her—I quickly told Violet my plan.

"You just have to be ready," I said. "We have to make the fever go down as much as we can before then, since there won't be any time to pick the tadpoles off."

"She will be looking for us." Violet looked nervous as she lay under the covers, pale-faced and bushy-haired. Even her freckles looked faint.

"Yes, but we have to try." I choked on the last word as I sat beside her on the edge of the bed. "Think about Papa and how brave he was. And think about Mama, who would have *hated* what Aunt Clara does to you—"

"All right, Lily." Her hand came to cover mine on top of the sheet. "Papa always said that you have to try . . ."

". . . and if you succeed, there will be cake," I finished, but ever since Aunt Clara had told us all that stuff about Papa in the car, it didn't sound as hopeful as before. "Do you think you can do it?"

Violet nodded and tightened her lips. "It can't be any worse than this," she said, and sounded almost like Grandma Fiona in that moment—old and aching.

It was definitely time to go.

The jittery feeling continued while we ate, and while Violet helped Aunt Clara eat, and while I helped her remove the crooked makeup. When Aunt Clara turned on the TV, I couldn't even look at the screen because it made me nauseous.

"You are awfully quiet tonight, Lily," she remarked, flaming turquoise all over.

"I have a headache," I replied, and wasn't exactly lying.

When it was finally night, I crawled in next to Violet in the bed and pretended to fall asleep, but instead, I was listening. We had to go between the time Aunt Clara went to bed and the time Mr. Woods turned up, since she might wake up a little when he came, if only to pull down her sleeping mask. I had been hoping to pilfer a few more sleeping pills to make Aunt Clara sleep extra deep again, but she had kept the pill bottle in her purse all night and never left the room after she came back from buying the food. When she went to the toilet, she brought her purse with her. For a moment, I had worried that maybe she knew I had taken some before, but then it wasn't unusual for her to bring the purse along, since it was where she kept her "necessities," so probably it was just bad luck.

I heard Aunt Clara open the little box of earplugs and let out my breath. If she hadn't used those, everything would've been more difficult—and it was hard enough as it was. When Aunt Clara put out the light, I opened my eyes and saw Violet's eyes glinting as they looked right back at me. Neither of us made a sound, almost not even to breathe.

Aunt Clara began snoring after half an hour, but we waited even longer before we quietly rose from the bed. I had already packed our suitcases and hidden brown-checkered pants and T-shirts for us both

under the mattress. We changed as silently as we could, and then
Violet decided to stuff her favorite nightgown down into her suitcase.
She was as quiet as a mouse but slow as molasses, and I had to hold
myself back so as not to show her how impatient I was. My own pajamas lay discarded on the floor, and I wouldn't risk everything just to
bring them with me—but then I knew how Violet was about her
nightgown.

When her suitcase was closed again, I tiptoed closer to Aunt
Clara's bed and found her purse on the floor by her bed. As I bent
down to grab it, I looked directly into her face, and I didn't even
breathe again until I held it in my hand, even though her flames were
blue-tinged white, telling me she had at least taken her usual sleeping
pill.

I snapped open the magnetic button on the purse and very carefully snuck my hand in there to rummage around until I found her
blue leather wallet. My plan had been to open it right away and only
take what we needed, but just about then my courage wobbled, and so
I ended up bringing the whole thing with me as I tiptoed back to
Violet and the suitcases.

I let Violet step outside the door before me, maneuvering Mama's
old suitcase, and then I followed right behind her, closing the door
almost as carefully as I had opened it. Then, finally, I breathed.

As soon as we got to the side of the road and started walking
toward town, everything felt better. The cool night air had never felt
so nice, and just knowing that every step we took was a step away
from *her* made the walk through the night feel a little less long. I
wasn't even scared at all, because the things we were running from—
Aunt Clara and the ghosts—were *so* bad that I felt safer outside than
at the Silver Star.

We mostly walked in a ditch that ran next to the road, so that gave
us some cover, even though the ground was uneven down there, and
we often had to pause because of Violet. She was still weak, and still
hot with fever, even though I had given her another pill before we left.
As soon as we were safely away from Aunt Clara, I would pick all the

tadpoles away and find some bananas or something to make her well with.

I just hoped it wouldn't get worse in the meantime.

The trip to the train station took us about two hours, and by then we were both exhausted. I definitely regretted bringing all the books. We hunkered down in a circle of bushes that grew next to the station and didn't leave it at all other than to check the timetable in the window. Thankfully, the night wasn't overly cold, and I had brought the blue blanket from Crescent Hill and draped it across our shoulders as we sat down on our suitcases, sharing the last of the vending machine crackers. I almost had to force Violet to chew and swallow because she was so weak and said she didn't want any. I knew that she *had* to eat, though. We had already walked for hours, and probably had to walk even more to find the lake house. I finally opened Aunt Clara's wallet, too, suddenly terrified that there would be nothing in there, but there was. There was a *lot* of money in there— *our* money, I reminded myself when I started feeling bad about taking everything.

"Do you think she'll be all right?" Violet asked in a faint and tired voice, probably having thought the same thing.

"Of course she will." I tried to make my own voice sound happy and bright. "Aunt Clara is as hard as a diamond. Nothing at all can hurt her."

"But what will she do when she finds out we are gone?"

"Look for us, I suppose."

"She won't find us, though, will she?"

"No, she won't," I said, although I didn't know that.

As the night dragged on, Violet's eyes became glassier, and when she pushed her suitcase closer and leaned against me to try to sleep, her limbs felt heavy and hot. She really was *not* well, and I felt panicked every time I looked at her; my heart started racing in my chest and cold sweat broke out on my forehead. Her breathing had become more labored, too; I could feel the struggle that went on in her chest when I held her tight. I remembered what she had said about what would happen to her if I didn't take the tadpoles away, and the thought made me feel ice-cold with fear.

"Violet," I said, nudging her awake. She looked up at me with bleary eyes but didn't say a thing. "We can't wait." My voice was filled with dread. "We have to get rid of the tadpoles *now*."

"All right," she mumbled, and begrudgingly got to her feet. "But what if Aunt Clara comes and we don't see her because we are too busy with taking them away—or if we have to run?"

"I don't care," I almost sobbed as I shook out the blanket and put it down on the grassy ground between the bushes. I brought out my flashlight from the suitcase, too, even though I had said I would keep it off to preserve the battery. "Lie down, Violet," I said a little softer. "You can't be this sick on the train." I did my best to sound reasonable and not let her see how scared I was. "It will only draw attention to us."

"Sure." She gave a halfhearted shrug before taking her place on the blanket and pulling up her shirt to reveal a squirming layer of fat and ugly blue tadpoles. They had clearly been gorging themselves on poor Violet while we fled. "Is it bad?" Her voice sounded thin.

"Yes." I let out my breath.

"Worse than before?"

"They are . . . bigger," I admitted.

"They are probably very hungry." Violet sighed.

"Well, so am I," I replied, feeling more angry and less scared by the second. If the icky tadpoles thought they could just *eat* my sister, they had another think coming!

Using the flashlight to see, I started picking them off her, one by one, and stuffed them into my mouth. As usual, they didn't taste like anything, but I could feel them on my tongue like heavy, wriggling garden slugs. I swallowed them down whole, without even thinking about it. All that was important was getting them off Violet. We didn't have any fruit or anything to make her entirely well again, but every tadpole I managed to eat was one less strain on her body.

It took forever, but I managed to eat about half of them before dawn came with a flood of brilliant golden light, telling me that our train would arrive soon. I let Violet sit up on the blanket; she was pale and looked dazed, but she didn't seem quite as feverish as before. While she fixed her clothes, I ate another salty cracker to rinse the tadpoles out of my mouth, even though they hadn't left any taste, just the knowledge that they had been there. As soon as we were on the train, I would buy some nice hot tea.

I just hoped that what I had managed to do would be enough to keep Violet well until we got to the lake house.

CLARA

43

I couldn't believe that they had left me!

Yet there was the bed, all empty, and the ghastly yellow suitcases no longer graced the floor. I sat on the bed in my purple silk robe and just stared out at the room for several minutes, trying to put my mind together.

For all the tension between us, I had never even thought it would come to this.

With a shivering hand, I grasped for the gray phone on the nightstand and dialed a familiar number.

Sebastian answered on the first ring.

"The girls are gone!" I croaked, as soon as I heard his voice.

"Clara, is that you?" His well-modulated voice reached my ears.

"The girls are *gone*," I repeated.

"What do you mean 'gone'?" Worry and urgency had come into his voice. "Did something happen to them?"

"No! They are gone! They left!" I just couldn't bring myself to say it more clearly—couldn't face the defeat in words like "fled" or "ran." "They *left* in the middle of the night," I explained. "They took their suitcases and walked out the door, and now I'm all alone."

"Where, Clara? Where are you?"

I started laughing, quiet and brittle. "At a shitty motel called the Silver Star. I wanted to show them the world!" I gave another—louder—laugh, sharp-edged and tinged with bitterness. "I suppose that's what happens when you try to do right by your family: They spit the kindness right back in your face."

"Clara, they are young. They cannot have gotten far. Do they even have any money?"

I grabbed my purse off the floor, suddenly beset by a horrid suspicion, and rummaged around in its belly for a moment. "They have taken my wallet," I declared.

"Do you have any idea where they could have gone? Maybe they'll try to get back to the city?"

"Maybe." But I didn't think so. Lily wasn't stupid.

"What did the police say?" I could hear Tulip there in the room with him, her constant chatter and whistles. At least *his* charge could be caged. It had to be a relief.

"I haven't spoken to them yet," I answered. "I just called you right away."

His voice audibly softened. "That's kind of you, Clara, but I think the police may be more helpful—or did you want me to come and help with the search?"

"Maybe—no!" He could absolutely not know what I had been up to. "As you say, they cannot have gotten far. Maybe I'll find them on my own." I idly picked at the gauze on my hand, pulling at the edges. The bandage was new; the old one was ruined. I had slammed my hand down on the candle at the séance yesterday without thinking, leaving it smoky and smoldering. All I had been thinking of was keeping Timmy at bay.

"Oh, you poor thing," Sebastian crooned. "You must be *so* worried!"

"Beside myself," I muttered, just as the empty feeling inside slowly started filling up with fury. "I only ever wanted to do right by those girls—"

He tried to comfort me. "They are young, bereft. We always knew that this would take time. It's hard being uprooted like they have—"

"But how are they even going to make it on their own?" I asked, although my greatest worry was for *me*. How was I going to feed myself? "Selfish," I muttered. "They have no care for me at all."

"Clara!" He sounded shocked. "They are just children!"

"I know . . . I know . . ." I sighed and ran a hand through my hair. "I have to find them."

"Yes, you do." His voice sounded mild again. "Alert the police, and then let me know what I can do. I'd be happy to make phone calls to family and friends."

"I cannot believe that they *did* this," I said.

"They are hurting, Clara—but you *will* find them," he reassured me. "They will be back with you again before nightfall, I'm sure."

I, however, was not so sure, but the fury was almost sufficient by then to spur me to action. "I have to find them," I said again, this time far more urgently. "I'll let you know if I need your help." The fury was a bubbling pit, and its thick fumes charged me like electricity.

How could they *do* this to me?

LILY

44

Once we were on the train, everything felt better. With every mile that passed by outside the windows, I relaxed a little more. It was as if Aunt Clara's long, diamond-crusted fingers could reach only so far, and the more distance there was between us and her, the easier it was to breathe. I was still worried about Violet, though, and watched her like a hawk, every rise and fall of her chest as she sat there beside me, her eyes on the landscape flying by outside the window. I knew that she still had a half tummy's worth of tadpoles under her shirt and I was itching to get back to work and remove the rest. I *hated* what they were doing to her.

What Aunt Clara had done to her.

It was warm in the carriage, and after our night outside we sucked up the heat like sponges. The seats were wide and comfortable, with high backs and green upholstery that was as soft as marshmallow—or so it felt anyway, after sitting outside on the ground for a very long time. We bought egg sandwiches and tea with Aunt Clara's money, and then we had a wonderful breakfast while trees and fields rushed by outside. I was thrilled to see that Violet had regained some of her appetite. It was the best food I had had since leaving Crescent Hill—

maybe the best food ever, because there was freedom laced with the egg and lettuce, and relief mixed into the sweet hot tea.

It had also been a very long night.

Violet ate half her sandwich, downed all her tea, and then fell asleep with her head on my shoulder. All those things were good. She was definitely still too sick to travel, but as long as she ate and slept, I hoped she would be all right until I could fix the rest.

All we had to do now was to sit quietly in our seats and get to where we were going without drawing attention to ourselves. I had no idea where Aunt Clara would start searching for us—or how long it would take to sound the alarm if she went to the police—but hopefully she would waste a few hours driving around looking for us. I also hoped that the fact that she had no more cash would derail her for a while.

I didn't want anyone on the train to remember us in case someone questioned them later, but it was a little hard to entirely disappear. Not many people took the train so early, yet two other people, a woman and a man, sat in the same carriage as us, and the red-haired mustachioed conductor kept grinning at us every time he passed by. He was only orange, though, so I didn't think he was suspicious. If he *had* been, he would have been a dark, mossy green.

We had a long train ride ahead of us, so I could probably have slept a little, too, but I couldn't quite let go. Every time I dozed off, I woke right up again, startled and confused, and didn't calm down until I saw Violet there beside me, snoring softly under the blue blanket. Every time the train made a few minutes' stop, I held my breath, terrified that the police would be at the station, demanding to search the carriages. When that didn't happen and we continued on, I slowly let out my breath. I had found a timetable when we entered the train, and with a pen from my suitcase, I crossed out the stops as we passed them. I had put a little star next to Bonewood, which was the station where we would get off. I thought we could walk to the lake house from there, *if* Violet could manage.

She slept for most of the day and only woke up about an hour before we arrived. Thankfully, she looked much better than she had the night before, but still not great, and I really hoped we would find a quick and easy route to the lake house. I was happy that she had woken up, though, since I *really* had to use the bathroom but hadn't wanted to disturb her. My whole body ached when I rose from the seat. We went together to do our business, and bought more sandwiches, too, before we got to our stop. I was too tense to be hungry, but I knew that we needed the energy if we were to spend the rest of the day walking through the woods. I was a little worried about that, since we had never walked to the lake house before, and although I had drawn a map, it wasn't a very good one. I also wasn't great with maps in general, but I didn't know what else to do. Even if we could pay someone to drive us there from Bonewood, it didn't seem like a good idea, with us trying not to get noticed. If Violet didn't feel great, we still might have to, though.

When we finally got off the train, I was still tense, but also determined to see the plan through. I promised myself not to worry or even *think* about things that could go wrong before we were safe at the lake house.

Bonewood turned out to be a small town—even smaller than Ivory Springs—which was good but bad as well, since fewer people would see us, but those who did would probably remember two unaccompanied girls with yellow suitcases. It just couldn't be helped, though; we had to pass through town.

We walked the few streets, between bricked storefronts and dog walkers, until we found a convenience store that was still open, and then we went inside—suitcases and all. Violet had suggested that she could wait outside at the curb, but I didn't think that sounded very safe. I didn't know if there was any food at the lake house, so we had to get supplies, but I did my best to pick food that didn't weigh a lot, seeing how our suitcases were heavy enough already. The store was small and the aisles narrow, which made it hard to get through it without toppling something, especially with our luggage. They did have a pretty good selection, though, so at least we found what we needed. When I saw a crate of watermelons with the fruit, I couldn't help but think of Aunt Clara and shuddered all over. I had loved melon before, but now I didn't think that I could ever eat it again—and especially not melon balls.

I bought bread and cheese, crackers, hot dogs, tea, and eggs. The latter would be a challenge to pack, but we could make several different things with them, so that advantage won out in the end. I bought some pears, too, and cherry-flavored candy, because I thought it would be good for healing Violet. I couldn't say why it felt that way, but it did. The lady behind the counter was friendly enough, but she seemed a little puzzled when she caught sight of our suitcases, so we hurried out of there as soon as we had paid.

Outside the store was a red-painted bench, and we paused there while I looked at my scribbled map. I looked at the houses around us, and the sky above, but I didn't know much about directions, and it was hard to tell where to go.

"Maybe we should ask someone," Violet suggested. It wasn't cold outside, but she was shivering nevertheless, and I worried about her fever coming back.

"No, we can't," I told her. "It was bad enough with the woman in the store. She'll remember us for sure."

"I *said* I could wait outside with the suitcases," Violet replied, not helping at all.

"Well, we already both went inside so there's nothing to do about it now."

"Do you think we should try to fit the groceries in the suitcases?"

"Sure, but not here," I told her. "It'll look strange."

"We already look strange."

"Yes, that's my point." I furrowed my brow and went back to studying the map, even turning my notebook upside down in the hope of finding a clue. I only had to look up to see the woods, but then they were everywhere, surrounding the town in every direction. Tall pines brushed the sky with branches of shaggy green. It was still daylight, thankfully, but I didn't think it would last very long.

Violet must have thought the same thing. "Maybe we have to sleep in the woods tonight." She sounded happy, as if it was an adventure.

"It's better than the bushes by the train station," she added when she caught my dark look. "And it's less dangerous than being with Aunt Clara," she reminded me.

"You're too sick to sleep outside," I told her. "We *have* to get to the lake house before nightfall."

Violet wasn't looking at me anymore, though. Her gaze was on a lamppost—or rather, on top of it, where a large black bird sat perched. Relief instantly flooded my insides.

"Is it Irpa?" I asked, just to be sure.

Violet nodded. "She can lead us to the lake house."

"She knows the way?"

"Yes—if you trust her." She looked at me expectantly.

"Of course I do," I said, and meant it, too. It was wonderful to see a friend in this strange and unfamiliar place.

Irpa took flight, and we followed with our suitcases and bags of groceries. Every once in a while the raven would land on a rooftop to wait for us to catch up, then she would fly off again, just a little bit farther, until we came to the edge of the woods, where we paused to put the food in the suitcases.

As soon as we entered the woods, things became easier because we didn't have to worry about being seen, but harder, too, because of the uneven ground. We walked much more slowly than we normally would, and Violet being Violet had to tie her shoelaces at least a dozen times. All the while I worried that Irpa would suddenly disappear, but she didn't. She was very patient and waited for us in the trees until we caught up, then started flying again. She didn't always follow the trail, though, but flew wherever she liked, so we had to climb across fallen tree trunks and wade through thorny underbrush. I worried about Violet but she didn't complain, just kept walking ahead, following her bird friend.

After about an hour, the sky started darkening for real, and I began worrying all over again, because how were we going to see Irpa in the dark? I had my flashlight—Papa had taught us that you should always have a compass, a flashlight, and a knife—so it wouldn't be completely dark, but it would still be hard to see a black bird. As it turned out, though, it wasn't a problem, because Irpa started croaking as soon as dusk settled, so we could follow her sound instead. Soon, all we could see of her was a faint shadow moving overhead, but we could hear her loud and clear.

"She says it's not far now." Violet sounded breathless as we moved through the dark woods, and I promptly made her pause so I could feel her forehead. When I realized how hot it was, I shuddered.

"It's returning," I told her, and couldn't help that my voice sounded clipped. It was the fear that came roaring back, making me feel queasy with worry. "We *have* to get rid of the rest."

"And we will." Violet nodded. "It's not far—Irpa said so."

"Good." When we started walking again, I was dragging more than carrying the suitcase, and balancing the flashlight in my other hand. All the while, my heart raced in my chest, and I wondered how many pears it would take to completely heal Violet after all this.

How much damage the tadpoles had done.

"I wonder why it's called Bonewood," Violet mused. Her breathing definitely sounded more labored now, and I stepped aside so she could walk ahead of me, just so I could keep an eye out.

"Maybe we can wonder about that some other time?"

"Maybe the trees are made of bone," Violet suggested, just to add some extra dread to the already dark night.

The first sign that we had finally arrived was the sight of the lake between the shaggy trees, gleaming darkly in the light of a pale moon, as still and smooth as black glass. It was so beautiful—and I was so relieved—that I really just wanted to stand there for a moment and look at it, but of course I couldn't do that. Irpa croaked in front of us and we rushed to follow the sound, moving a little faster now, knowing that we had to be close—and then it was there: the house, like a dark presence before us, balancing on the lake's edge with its timber walls and shuttered windows. The bright blue front door looked like an old friend when the beam of my flashlight caught it, and I instantly started crying, although I didn't know exactly why. Maybe it was just because the place somehow *felt* like Mama.

Violet had left her suitcase behind on the ground and walked up the stairs before me. She was already holding her magic feather and inserted it into the lock. Irpa had landed by Violet's feet and cocked her head when we heard the click that told us the door was unlocked.

Nothing had felt so good in my life as when the blue door opened and we could step inside.

❧ VIOLET ❧

45

The lake house smelled mustier than I remembered, but maybe that was because it had been closed up for a long time. The first thing Lily did when we got inside was go around and light all the candles, since it didn't have electricity, or even water taps. Some of the candle wicks sputtered and complained, but most of them behaved, so it didn't take long before we could see the lake house properly.

Grandma Fiona had owned the house before, and Lily said she had gotten it from her older sister, Lois, who had died. Mama had loved her aunt Lois and always talked about how she was an artist who did things her own way. She had even played the violin, like Lily. In the picture Mama kept, she was a tall woman with fancy black hair, smoking a small, slim cigar. Back at the town house, we had a collection of green mugs shaped like goblin heads that Aunt Lois had made, which we used for hot chocolate. Lois hadn't been the first one in our family who owned the lake house, though. Grandma Fiona had told us it was where all of them had lived before deciding to go and grow apples and plums. I could see why they left, since I didn't think the Bonewood should be made into an orchard; it was too wild and wonderful for that. There were a few apple trees around the lake house, though, so I supposed they had tried one time.

The lake house wasn't very big. It was just the ground floor and a loft with two beds built in under the rafters, but there was lots of stuff everywhere: board games, clothes, art, and fishing gear. Almost all the walls had paintings on them, and there were sculptures balancing on the shelves. Most of them were made by Aunt Lois, and it was easy to see they were hers, since they reminded me of the goblin mugs. There were even more goblins in the lake house: blue, green, and brown ones, but also other creatures. I recognized the mermaids, but Lily had to tell me that the other strange clay women hanging on the walls were harpies and dryads. The dryads had twisted, branchlike limbs, which I liked a lot. Even the low ceiling was full of things: weird-looking suncatchers mostly, made from feathers, mirrors, pebbles, and little bones. They made me feel funny inside. Some of them were so long that if you sat on the quilt-covered couch, a feather might tickle your head.

The best thing about the living room, though, was the large fire-place, which took up most of the back wall. We had roasted apples there before, and eaten them with cinnamon. The best thing for Lily was the old violin that hung on the wall, right between a harpy and a mermaid. She stopped to look at it for a very long time, and even ran her hands over it.

The small kitchen was on the other end of the living room. It wasn't a proper kitchen, just a blue-painted counter and a row of cup-boards crammed with Aunt Lois's mugs and plates. There was also a small camping stove on the counter that had to be plugged into a gas canister with a hose. There was no refrigerator, but there was a trap-door in the floor leading to a small space with some shelves to store food. When I was little, I had thought it was exciting to sit on my knees on the floor and reach down in the darkness to find the butter or cheese. I liked the smell down there as well: dirt and something cold, like lake water.

The only other thing downstairs was the bedroom where Mama and Papa used to sleep, in Aunt Lois's old bed, with quilts and blan-kets in all kinds of colors. But when no one stayed at the lake house, all the bedding hung on a line under the ceiling, so it wouldn't rot.

There was an old washstand in there as well, with a porcelain jug and a basin painted with pink roses. The very best thing in there, though, was the collection of photographs hanging on the wall, in different sizes and frames. I went in there to look while Lily built the fire, because seeing all the familiar faces made me feel braver, somehow. There was one of Mama as a girl with Aunt Sarah, sitting in a rowboat in the sunshine on the lake. There was also one of Grandma Fiona, sitting alone on the porch and holding a bunch of apple blossoms. She looked so young and beautiful in that picture, and her eyes sparkled from happiness. Aunt Lois was there, too, her hair almost as black as Irpa's wings, smirking and leaning against the timbered wall. Seeing them all so happy like that, I almost couldn't believe that they were gone. *We* weren't, though, and we were up there as well, in the upper left corner, sitting on the same porch as Grandma Fiona had, sipping iced tea from goblin mugs. I was so small in that picture that I had to use both hands to lift my drink.

I didn't get to look at the pictures for long before Lily called me back into the living room and told me to lie down on the couch. The room felt a little less damp already, and the wood was crackling in the fireplace. I had felt much better since Lily ate the tadpoles at the train station, but I felt hot in my cheeks again and everything ached, so I was happy to get rid of the rest. These ones were blue and regretful, Lily had said, because the ghost lady had been that, too. Lily sighed when she looked at them and pulled up her sleeves. She had cracked the front door open, and soon Irpa came in as well, cocking her head in the door opening and looking so cute that I couldn't help but laugh. When she had jumped around on the floor for a little while, she flew up in the air, sending the suncatchers swaying, and landed on the backrest of the couch. Then Lily started picking tadpoles, lifting invisible things to her mouth. It took a very long time to get all of them off, and I watched the flames while Lily worked, or lifted a hand to stroke Irpa's feathers and tell her how good she had been to show us the way through the woods.

When all the tadpoles were gone, Lily got some of the pears and candies still in the shopping bag and placed them on the floor by the couch, alongside a goblin mug of lake water. She knelt down and placed a hand on my brow, then she closed her eyes. It really didn't take long at all before I started feeling that the sickness had disappeared. It was like how mist rises from the lake in the mornings and hangs there for a while before it is suddenly gone. When Lily opened her eyes again, the pears were all shriveled up, the candy had cracked and was mostly just dust, and the goblin mug was empty. It felt *so* nice to feel good again.

After that, Lily and I ate some of the bread and cheese and drank several cups of lake water. Papa had loved that water—he said it was the best he had ever tasted anywhere in the world. Even the plates at the lake house had goblin faces on them, as small as coins, close to the rim, and none of them looked the same. When we weren't hungry anymore, we went to the bedroom and climbed into the bed. We were both too tired to even take our clothes off. Lily had taken down all the blankets and quilts, and we nestled in under the pile. It was still cold in the room and a little damp, but Lily said that if we lay close together, we would soon warm up. Papa had taught her that.

When we had been lying there for a little while, and I had almost fallen asleep, Lily suddenly said, "Do you want to say good night to Mama and Papa?"

"Okay." I folded my hands and closed my eyes. It *had* been a long time since we'd said good night to them—or their bodies. It just hadn't been very practical while we shared a room with Aunt Clara. K2 was very snowy today, and I didn't even see the red of Mama's parka anymore. They were both deeply buried under a white duvet.

"Good night, Mama," Lily said beside me. "We are at the lake house now. We have left Aunt Clara behind, because she was mean and made Violet sick."

"Good night, Papa." I took over. "We are in the woods alone, so it's good that you taught us all those things about how to make a fire and gut fish."

"We'll be okay, though," Lily said. "I don't know where we'll end up, but we'll be fine." Her voice sounded a little uncertain.

"We'll figure something out," I said, while listening to the howling wind on the mountain. "As long as Aunt Clara doesn't catch us."

We lay quiet for a while after that. I was looking at K2, while Lily probably worried. Finally, she said, "Maybe we should ask our family for help for real? Even if they are gone, maybe they can somehow tell us what to do?"

"Maybe they *are* helping us," I said, and opened my eyes. "Maybe they are helping even if we don't know it. We are *here*, aren't we? Far away from Aunt Clara." And it had only happened because Lily mysteriously found the map and Irpa showed us the way.

"Yes, but . . . maybe they could *say* something, tell us where to go." Lily sighed beside me. "I'd like nothing more than to stay here, but I don't know how we are going to survive alone . . . There's canned food in the kitchen cupboards, but it won't last very long, nor will the money in Aunt Clara's wallet. Besides, sooner or later, the woman at the convenience store will notice two girls coming in alone all the time . . . There has to be *somewhere* we can go that is safe."

"Do you remember Rotger, Lily?" I asked her, because thinking about Irpa had made me think of him. He had been Mama's stray cat who used to hang around in our garden. Mama would feed him every day with fresh salmon and pieces of liver. When I had asked her if we should let him inside, she had said no, that he wasn't that kind of cat.

"Yes. Of course," Lily replied. She had liked Rotger very much.

"I think he was Mama's familiar friend," I said. "Like Irpa is mine."

"Maybe," Lily said after a moment. "He didn't come anymore after K2."

I nodded in the darkness. "He also *felt* like Irpa, only different."

Lily shifted and turned to me in the darkness. "What did you see when Grandma Fiona died?"

"*Her*, of course—Grandma Fiona. Do you remember how the two of us and Mama stood by her bed when she died? I saw her rise up, but she wasn't like herself. I could see through her, for one, and there was something wrong with her face. Also, she was white, like mist."

"She maybe slipped out of her body?"

"Uh-huh," I agreed. "Like the ghosts. But Grandma didn't have any glue coming out of her."

"What happened then? Where did she go?"

"Into Mama," I said, since that's what happened.

"Into Mama?" Lily sounded surprised.

"Uh-huh, and she never came back out again. At least not as far as I could see."

"What was wrong with her face?"

"I don't know." I tried very hard to think back. "Half of it looked sick, while the other half looked as healthy as could be. Younger, too."

"That *is* strange . . . Did you tell Mama?"

"No . . . She was so sad."

"Yes, she was. I sometimes think that's why she agreed to K2—and why Papa insisted on it. He just wanted to make Mama happy again. Perhaps the sadness was even why Mama didn't realize how dangerous it was." Lily went quiet for a while, and when she spoke again, she sounded excited. "Maybe Mama, too, went into *us* when she died? Maybe that's why I see colors all the time, and why you see more dead people? Maybe that's why her family could grow apples and plums where no one else could, because they were special people . . . ?"

"I *hope* Mama went into us," I said, and it did *feel* right. Maybe it was Mama inside Lily who had showed her the map.

"Perhaps she didn't tell us about Rotger, or any of the other stuff, because she didn't think she would die so fast. Maybe she thought we'd have time to prepare. She always wanted us to have *normal* childhoods, and not spend too much of Papa's money."

"We still *saw* things, though," I reminded her.

"Yes, and Mama had Rotger *before* Grandma died, so she must have been special then, too—but maybe it grows stronger when someone dies."

"That *feels* right." I nodded, even if she couldn't see me. "And we are the last ones alive." Everything felt very serious for a moment, while I thought about what it meant. Maybe Aunt Lois was in us, too, and Aunt Sarah. Maybe they were the reason why I sometimes felt like I remembered things that I hadn't ever actually known. "I miss old Rotger," I sighed, when the seriousness started to feel so big that I thought I would maybe cry.

"Yes, I do, too." I could hear Lily smiling. "Even if he wasn't a very friendly cat, and only let Mama touch him."

"What did *you* see when Grandma Fiona died?" I had told her *my* story, so it was only fair that she told me hers.

"It was before, when she was sick. Mama wanted me to put my fingers on her temples, do you remember that?"

"Yes, like with Fredric the squirrel."

"Sometimes when I did that, I could see blue flames on her, and some golden ones, too."

"Gold means love." I took Lily's hand on top of the quilt. "Maybe it made her better, what you did."

"Maybe." I could feel Lily shrug. "After I had done it every night for a week, Grandma asked me to stop, though."

"Why?"

"I heard her tell Mama that it was fine and that she was ready. I didn't understand it then, but now I'm thinking that maybe you are right, and it *was* something I did that helped her stay alive . . . Mama cried a lot after Grandma Fiona told her that."

I squeezed Lily's hand. "Do you think we are witches?"

Lily snorted. "Not like the ones in books. But maybe we are different witches."

"Witches have cats, don't they?" I was still thinking about Rotger.

"Or ravens." I heard Lily smile again. "Maybe we can use magic to get rid of Aunt Clara."

"Maybe," I agreed. "But we don't know *how* to do things—unless someone *asks*."

"Mama would probably have known how," Lily said.

"Yes." I sighed. "But she isn't here."

"But if she is inside us, maybe we can figure it out?"

LILY
46

Morning arrived at the lake house with a blue sky and a blazing sun. The cold from the night before was gone, and Violet and I threw open all the windows to let the warm air inside. It felt like a sign that the sky that had been so bleak the day before was suddenly so clear and wonderful. A nice cool breeze came rushing in from the lake to chase away all the bugs and make the yellow-checked curtains billow like sails, shaking out all the spiderwebs.

We had breakfast on the porch: more bread and cheese, and the leftover pears, too. I had even managed to heat water for tea, although it had taken me a while to attach the hose to the heavy gas canister. I had forgotten to buy sugar at the convenience store, but we found some in the cupboard. It was old and lumpy, but it worked well enough when we hacked pieces off with a knife.

The porch usually had wicker chairs, but they were up in the loft, so we brought out a quilt and sat on the floorboards instead. It was almost like a picnic, I figured, as we sat there with the food between us and steaming goblin mugs in our hands. Over Violet's shoulder, I could see the rippling silver of the lake, and when I turned my head and looked the other way, I saw the old apple trees, heavy with ripening fruit. In just a few weeks' time, they would be ready for picking. I figured we should gather as many of them as we could, in case we ended up spending all winter at the lake house. Grandma Fiona had taught us a lot about the preservation of fruit, and I thought they would keep well in the dark under the trapdoor.

The very best thing about that morning, though, was being somewhere far away from Aunt Clara—and far away from her ghosts, too.

"If we stay, maybe we can fish in the lake," Violet suggested. "We can do that in winter, too, you know. Grandpa George used to ice fish up here, Grandma Fiona told me once . . . and there are plenty of fishing rods upstairs, just standing there in a corner."

"Maybe there's a book about ice fishing in one of the crates," I said, since everything felt safer with a book to lean on. "We should probably know a little more about it if we're going to try it." I took another bite of my sandwich; it was bursting with cheese and crisp slices of pear. Food had never tasted better.

"I don't think ice fishing is that hard. Maybe we could set traps, too." Her eyes went wide with excitement. "Although I don't know if we could kill an animal—could you do that, Lily?"

"No." I shuddered.

"But fish would be fine, wouldn't it, Lily?"

"I don't know, Violet." The thought of killing anything made my stomach churn.

"I think *I* could kill a fish," she said happily. "Especially if I was hungry. If I was *really* hungry, I could probably kill a rabbit, too—for stew."

"We have to chop wood," I said, so we didn't have to talk about dead rabbits anymore. "There's probably some in the shed behind the house. I remember it used to be crammed with firewood before, but probably not enough for a whole winter."

"Maybe that's where the rowboat is." Violet had been talking about the old boat all morning, wanting to take it out on the lake.

"Maybe we can catch frogs from it," she suggested next. "Mama said that some people eat them, but then we would have to kill them first—"

"Fishing is probably easier." I didn't want us to kill any frogs. I didn't want to kill fish either, but I realized that we might have to. "Maybe we can take the train to different towns when we go shopping," I mused. "That way, it'll probably be harder to spot us." And I would much rather buy food than kill it.

"Do you think we can stay here until you turn eighteen?" Violet's voice was suddenly thick with emotion.

"I hope so," I replied, even though I worried that it would be hard. "We'll figure something out," I added, since I really, really wanted to make it work.

Irpa came flying in just as we finished eating. She jumped onto the porch and pecked at our breadcrumbs. The sun caught her magnificent feathers and made them gleam blue and purple.

"Pretty, pretty bird," Violet cooed. She reached out a hand and let her finger trail over the glossy feathers. "She wants to show us something," Violet said. "She wants us to follow her again."

"Is it far?" I didn't want to stray too far from the lake house now that we had finally found it.

Violet stared at Irpa for a while—I figured they were doing their silent talking—and then she shook her head. "She says it isn't far at all."

We got to our feet and left the remains of our breakfast behind on the porch—maybe a squirrel was hungry—and followed Irpa around the house, behind the shed, and into the Bonewood. It was easy to see Irpa against the blue sky; her black silhouette was crisp as she breezed over the treetops. Both Violet and I had put on white summer dresses from our suitcases and enjoyed feeling the warm air on our skin as we followed Irpa through the woods. This time we were on a path that was just slightly overgrown, which was so much better than the hard walk through the underbrush the night before.

Finally, the raven landed in a huge spruce tree, where she folded her wings and settled in, waiting for us to catch up. When we arrived, we saw that she had brought us to a mossy clearing bordered by dead trees. In the middle of the clearing stood a wooden statue. It was old and very gray, but it was easy to see that it was a woman wearing a long dress and with braids in her hair. In her left hand she held a flower or plant that had clusters of round berries and long, slender leaves. I thought maybe it was mistletoe. Her face had become a little smudged over the years, but you could still make out her features. One half of her face was like a normal young woman's, while the other half was shaped just like a skull. I startled when I saw it, and a cold ripple ran down my back, although it didn't look scary, exactly. But it did remind me of what Violet had said about Grandma Fiona's ghost, and I gave my sister a quick look, but she was just standing there, mesmerized by the statue, and if she thought about it herself, she didn't say anything.

The statue lady was staring ahead, into the trees behind us. Around her feet were heaps of bones. Some were small and brittle-looking, while others were bigger and yellow with age. I saw a rib cage there, and some thicker bones, too, that I thought were from a big animal like an elk. In the middle of the bone heap was an open trail where a narrow stream trickled by. It looked almost as if the water came bubbling up from under the lady's skirt. The stream crossed the open clearing and disappeared into the woods. Besides the faint sound of the water, everything was quiet. We couldn't even hear birdsong anymore.

Violet and I had stopped as soon as we entered the clearing, but now we slowly walked toward the statue. The closer we got, the more details I noticed, like the rough-hewn fall of the woman's dress and the blind eyes staring out before her. And then I *saw* her, for real. The lady's outline was covered in tiny flames in all kinds of colors—even black and a deep charcoal gray, which I had never seen before. While I watched in awe, the flames increased in size and strength, and soon it was as if the whole statue was standing in the middle of a bright halo.

"Oh," Violet uttered next to me. "I can see colors, Lily—for *real*."

"Aren't they beautiful?" I asked in a hushed voice.

"Yes," she replied in a voice brimming with awe. "It is the most beautiful thing I ever saw."

"What *is* this place?" I whispered. "Who *is* she?"

Violet slowly shook her head. "Irpa says she belongs to us—or we to her. It's difficult to make out."

"She is wonderful," I replied, although the word seemed way too small.

"Do you think Mama came here sometimes?" Violet whispered.

"Probably." I took a few more steps, still unable to look away from the gorgeous flames. "Why are there bones by her feet?" I asked. "Does Irpa know?"

"She says they are gifts," Violet replied after a while. "Someone asked her for things before, like lots of fish in the lake."

"They *fed* her," I said, thinking about the ghosts.

"Maybe *that's* what Mama's family did," Violet mused. "Maybe they took care of her, and maybe that's why we are special."

I had no way of knowing for sure, but it *sounded* right, somehow.

"I think we should drink her water, don't you?" Violet looked back at me over her shoulder. Her little face looked calm and serene, as if lit up from within.

"Yes." I started moving a little faster across the emerald moss. "I definitely think we should."

We both crouched by the stream, scooped handfuls of cold water, and drank it down. It tasted even better than the lake water: sweeter and more earthy. I think the water did something funny to me, though, because afterward I felt lightheaded and giddy. When I lifted my head, I noticed something glinting high up in a wizened pine, and when I looked closer, I saw that all the dead trees had strange suncatchers in them, just like the ones at the lake house: Feathers, twigs, and pieces of bone slowly danced in the light breeze, so Aunt Lois at least had definitely been coming to the clearing.

"I want to give her something." Violet shielded her eyes from the sun as she looked up at the lady. "It seems a little rude to visit and not give her anything at all."

I looked at the bones. "We don't have any—"

"I don't think it has to be *that*," Violet interrupted me. "I think it could be anything. You could play for her." Her eyes lit up. She got to her feet and brushed debris off her dress. "Race me back to the lake

house, Lily!" She started running. I think she was a little giddy from
the water, too, but it was great to see her so happy after everything. I
let her get a minute's head start and then I ran after her.

When we arrived back at the house, Violet rummaged through the
cupboards and under the trapdoor. She gathered up hot dogs, pear
slices, and the rest of the cherry candy on a goblin plate, and even dug
out a half-empty bottle of plum brandy from one of the cupboards. I
went straight for the old violin, and as soon as I touched the wood, I
knew that her name was Astrid, although I didn't know how I knew
that. Astrid had definitely seen better days, but I looked at the strings
and thought that I could still make her sing, even if it wouldn't sound
anywhere close to perfect.

Before we left the lake house again, I paused to undo my braid.

When we got back to the clearing loaded with our gifts, the sight
of the lady was just as amazing as it had been the first time. Violet
placed the goblin plate at her feet, between a yellow shinbone and
something that looked like a shard of an animal's head. Then she
pulled the cork out of the brandy bottle and spilled it around on the
ground, just like she had done with the cider in the garden; the scent
of the liquor was strong and sweet. Violet didn't have a candle, though,
and she didn't chant anything either, so it wasn't the same thing as
with the ghosts. Also, no one had *asked* her to do anything. I really
liked that thought.

For some reason, I felt self-conscious when I lifted Astrid to my
chin and raised the bow. I had done concerts before, with lots of people watching, but I had never been as nervous as I was in the clearing.
It felt as if someone important was looking at me, even if I didn't
know exactly who that was. I took a deep breath and crossed my fingers in my head before finally letting the bow kiss the strings. I didn't
have any plan for what I was going to play; the clearing wasn't that
kind of place. It was meant for wild things that followed their own
natural rhythm, and so I played like Mama had taught me, with my
bare feet wide apart and my toes buried deep in the moss.

What came out of Astrid was strange and loud—almost not a
melody at all—but Violet, at least, didn't care. She danced around on

the ground before me, sometimes with her eyes closed, as she twirled and jumped and shook her head. I couldn't help but laugh when I saw it. As the music rose and fell, I closed my own eyes a little as well, and again I got the feeling that I might just rise off the ground and fly. It really did feel like I did, too, and when I opened my eyes again, I saw that I hadn't just imagined it: My toes had really left the moss behind and were dangling a few inches off the ground. It didn't feel half as strange as it should have, and I didn't even feel worried at all when I saw that Violet, too, was up in the air, spinning slowly before me, with her head thrown back, her eyes closed, and bliss written all over her face.

We didn't come down again until Astrid told me that the song was over. Thankfully, we didn't *fall* down, but drifted slowly downward until our feet were back on the moss. We both instantly fell over and lay there howling with laughter, me still clutching Astrid to my chest. It was the best feeling in the world!

"I think she really liked that," Violet said, and I knew she was talking about the lady.

"I think so, too," I replied. "Although Astrid should probably get some new strings."

"Maybe there are some at the lake house," she suggested.

"If so, I could come out here and play every day." *If* we could stay.

"I think she's happy we are here," Violet said.

"Well, I am, too." I sighed. Everything was so peaceful and blissful just then that even my toes had curled up with delight.

"It must feel lonely to be out here all alone, with no one to care for her at all." Violet turned her head to look at the flaming statue.

"She isn't alone, though; there are lots of animals in the woods."

"Yes, but they don't *care* for her like we do," Violet said. I assumed she meant our family.

"If we can stay here, we could feed her all the time."

"Yes, we could." Violet still looked happy. Her eyes shone and she had roses in her cheeks. Neither of us cared if our dresses were now dirty. All the food Violet had brought out had grown a thick shell of mold, but for once, it didn't bother me at all.

I glanced up at the sun and saw how far it had traveled. We had been in the clearing for hours, even though it hadn't felt like it. "We have to feed ourselves, too, though." I rose to my feet. "We haven't eaten since breakfast, and it's getting late. We can go back and make food and then bring it here," I suggested, since I didn't really want to leave yet. "Maybe we can bring some candles and lanterns from the lake house so we can stay for a while even after it gets dark."

"Oh, yes, Lily!" Violet jumped up to her feet. "It'll be the best picnic ever," she chirped.

On our way back to the lake house, I felt tired and excited all at once. I couldn't remember the last time we had had such a good day—and something wonderful and magical had happened to us that I hadn't even thought was possible. Even Irpa seemed to share in the joy and flew in wide circles above us, croaking all the while.

Only Violet didn't seem as happy as before, but started dragging her feet as soon as the shed came within sight. "I can *feel* her, Lily," she said. "Aunt Clara is looking for us."

"We always knew that she would," I said, swallowing the hard lump of fear that had formed in my throat. "It doesn't matter, Violet. She won't find us." At least I hoped she wouldn't.

"But she is nearer now than she was before." Violet gave me a panicked look. "I can *feel* her coming closer."

"Are you sure you aren't just afraid? That you just think you—"

"No." An angry wrinkle appeared between her eyes. "I can *feel* it, Lily. She's coming."

A sinking feeling ran through me as my heart plummeted to the depths of my stomach. There wasn't time to think, or even plan. "We have to get back fast, then—to pack!"

We ran the rest of the way, both of us breathing heavily. My heart raced in my chest because I was so scared. We had barely had time to close the door, however, before the sound of cars cut through the quiet of the woods and made us storm to the window to look outside.

"Is it her?" Violet's gaze was wide with alarm.

"Maybe not," I said, clinging to hope. "Maybe it's just fishers."

We both stood hidden behind the yellow-checked curtains, pressed against the wall on each side of the window. When the first car arrived outside the house, I peeked out through the gap between the curtain and the window frame, and my belly started aching when I saw it was a police car.

What I saw next made it hurt even worse, though, because just behind the police car was another car—broad and beige—and I would know it anywhere.

It was Aunt Clara's station wagon.

CLARA
47

I was *seething* when I found them hidden away in that ramshackle cabin, *seething* when I marched them to the car, and still *seething* when we drove away from there. I didn't even know how to begin to voice my considerable displeasure. I hadn't even given the girls time to pack but had thrown all their clothes in the trunk in a jumble. I had retrieved my wallet, though. It had been lying there, just right out in the open, between slices of cheese and a pear on the kitchen counter. I suppose money was nothing to my nieces, seeing how they'd always had too much of it.

"Do you have *any* idea what you have done?" I asked as I slowly maneuvered the car through the thick woods. The dirt road was a disgrace and overgrown from disuse. From time to time, a low-hanging branch would scratch against the car roof. "Do you have *any* idea how utterly humiliating it was to have to go to the police and admit that you had run away? I even had to call your *lawyer*, for God's sake, to ask if you had been in touch—and your parents' fancy friends in the city!" No need for my nieces to know that Sebastian had been the one to make those calls. "Do you think that was fun for me? Do you think that put me in a good position?" I turned my head to look at them, but only for a second, seeing how the road twisted before me. The two of them sat huddled together in the back seat. Lily's eyes were as cold as always, and she did that Iris thing with her mouth again. Violet mostly looked spooked and it delighted me. She certainly deserved it—and more. Not for the first time, I allowed myself to imagine that it was indeed *I* and my meddling with Ben's equipment in the garden shed that had caused their parents' ice-cold demise. The thought was as sweet as honeycomb and felt utterly, unquestionably just.

When neither of my nieces deigned to answer my question, I continued. "You thought yourself so clever, huh, coming up here? As if the lake house isn't on record? It didn't take a genius to figure out where you had gone; it was the only reasonable conclusion. Did you really think I wouldn't find you?" I paused my tirade to breathe. "You think you have it bad, huh, living with me? There are girls in this world with far harsher fates than yours—girls who don't deserve what the world has in store for them *one bit,* while the two of you have made every inch of your beds yourselves, calling up ghosts and what-not! If only you had left the past well alone, *none* of this would have happened!" It was all absolutely true, but I thought it wise to leave out the part where their meddling had actually been to my advantage, bolstering my struggling finances.

Lily finally found her voice and started up her tired old tirade. "Violet gets *sick.* She can't do the séances anymore."

"Well, that is *my* call, isn't it? Seeing how I am the guardian?" I snapped back.

"Maybe," she admitted. "But I think you're doing it wrong. You are supposed to *protect* us, not try to earn any money from us."

"Oh, is that so?" I pretended to be astonished. "I really wish someone would have told me that before! Do you think I'm stupid, Lily?" I dared to look away from the road for another second to crane my neck and scowl at her. "Do you really think that I do not *know* what a guardianship entails?"

"Well, you don't behave like you do," she replied, but the righteousness in her voice had faded, and I took that as a good sign.

"Running away like that." I shook my head. "You two have to be the most ungrateful, entitled brats in all the world! Leaving me to fend for myself when you know how I cannot even *feed* myself, and that it's all because of you! If we're weighing wrongs, it is *you* who have made *my* life a misery!"

"How *did* you eat?" Violet asked, seemingly immune to my accusations.

"I found a way," I muttered, not wanting to share how I had paid a maid at the Silver Star to feed me leftover salad and plain bread—and I would certainly not share how the first maid I had asked had looked at me as if I was a deviant, shaking her head and backing away. Before all that had occurred, however, I had been forced to drive to the bank to get more cash, since my nieces had completely robbed me. Thankfully, they had left the car keys behind, and I always kept my driving license in the glove compartment. Without that stroke of luck, God only knows what would have happened to me, stranded and alone at a run-down motel.

"I told you Aunt Clara would be fine," Lily said to her sister, which meant that at least *one* of them had had the decency to be concerned, which strangely felt like a consolation.

"There is nothing that money can't buy," I said, "but I'm sure you are well aware of that fact. What was your plan, then, Lily? Were the two of you supposed to live up there for *four* years? What about the education that is so important to you? What about your music? I can assure you that no music teacher would have made the trek up there—"

Lily cut me off. "I hadn't decided yet."

"Whatever your parents wanted for you, I'm *absolutely* sure that spending years in the wilderness was *not* on their wish list!"

"Neither was living with a *murderer,*" she informed me. "Or with someone who makes Violet sick, and who thinks about killing us all the time."

"I do *not,*" I lied.

"You do," Lily replied. "Dangerous things are purple, and you are very purple."

"What complete, utter nonsense—"

"How can you *not* think of killing us after what Violet has done, bringing back the ghosts and finding out your secrets?" That, at least, was a fair point. "And where are you taking us now? Back to the Silver Star?"

"No. We're going home, even if I have to drive all night." It was harder for them to escape from Crescent Hill—and easier for me to control them there. Taking them out on the road like this had clearly been a huge mistake.

"You can't keep us cooped up forever." Lily realized my intentions at once.

"No, but I can keep you contained until I can trust you again."

"At least you won't have to do the séances now," Lily said to Violet.

"Maybe I'll find a way," I snapped.

"It won't make Violet put the ghosts back." My niece sounded delightfully worried.

"We'll just have to see about that," I muttered, unwilling to give them as much as an inch. I did have a hope, though, that somewhere down the line, if only I pushed her enough, the girl would come up with a way to do it. It only made sense that if she could bring them back, she had the skills to send them away again, too—even if she didn't know how yet.

As the night darkened around us, I drove on, the fury still lashing in my chest. The anger was almost like a living thing, one that burned and ached.

Iris used to call it monstrous.

I remembered one time in particular. It happened just as I was about to leave for nursing school, and I had pleaded with my mother to let me stay. We had been alone in her bedroom—a pink and frilly disgrace of a chamber that always smelled of spilled champagne and expensive floral perfume. Her clothes were everywhere: Silk, satin, velvet, and lace fought for space on her bed. Some of the dresses were still on the hangers, while shoes with heels pointed enough to kill were scattered on the carpeted floor. On her vanity lay a heap of jewelry, discarded. Her pearls were there, and some diamonds, too. Not the pink one, though. It was still on Iris's finger.

"Please," I had said, although I loathed that word. "I won't be a good nurse, you know I won't. I promise to keep out of your way if only you let me stay."

Iris sighed as she stood before me, wringing her hands. Her candy-floss hair was like a halo around her head, and her pink silk robe draped like that of a goddess. "It's not that easy, Clara. There are other concerns—"

"I know that you don't like me," I said. "I know I remind you of *him* and everything that happened back then, but I won't be any trouble, I swear—"

"Clara." She held up a hand, palm out. "It has nothing to do with *that*." Her eyes narrowed and her brow furrowed. "It's that *anger* in you," she said. "It's no good, Clara. It *scares* me. I just can't trust you with Benjamin—"

"I won't hurt him, I *swear!*" It had been an unfortunate thing that my mother found the half-burned doll I had knitted, stuffed with Ben's soft hair and baby teeth.

"But, Clara . . . I—I just don't *trust* you." Her green gaze slid away from me to land on a silver shoe on the floor. "Maybe you will get better," she said. "Maybe life will mellow you out."

I had been hurt by her words for a very long time, but she had been wrong. Because that anger had served me just fine in life, and God only knows where I would have been without it.

VIOLET
48

While Aunt Clara drove and Lily was angry, I fell asleep in the back seat. It shouldn't have been possible to doze off with everything that had happened that day—and how disappointed I was that Aunt Clara had found us—but suddenly all of me felt heavy and warm, and sleep sort of told me to come, because something important was supposed to happen behind my closed eyelids. It felt almost like when Irpa talked to me, as if someone spoke without words. So, after trying to stay awake for a while, I just gave in to the feeling and let my head roll to the side.

Irpa was in my dream, and she was flying through the Bonewood again, wanting me to follow, so I did. It was daylight in my dream, so it was easy. We didn't go to the lake house, though, but to the mossy clearing with the lady. It was just as sunny and beautiful as it had been before, but now there were lots of apple trees growing where there had been spruces, and there was a wooden fence separating the orchard from the Bonewood beyond. The statue of the lady stood just at the bottom of the garden, in front of the fence, protecting the crops from the wilderness. The bones at the statue's feet were many and fresh. The hem of her skirt was brown with dried blood. The stream trickled merrily, though, and suddenly I realized that I was still feel-

ing that water in me, and that was why Lily and I had floated above
the ground before, and why I had this dream.

I looked at the lady's face. The wood wasn't worn as before but
looked like it could have been carved yesterday. I could even smell the
sap, somehow. The wood was dark, almost red in places, and because
Papa had cut through a branch to show me once, I guessed that the
lady was made of yew. He had also said never to touch the red sap,
because yew could kill you in no time at all—even if the berries were
pretty.

It was then I realized that the lady protected the border not just
between the orchard and the woods but between the living and the
dead as well.

I looked at her face again, the skull part this time, and I knew that
it was me. I was the dead side of the lady. Then I looked at the other—
living—side, and I knew that it was Lily. Then I thought about Mama,
and I knew that she had been mostly the living side as well, and so
had Grandma Fiona. But Aunt Lois and Aunt Sarah had been the
dead side, like me. None of them had been *just* one side, though. Only
Lily and I were just one thing, because we were the only two left. If
we had children—and more than two—it would be more of a mixture
again.

But I knew in that moment, without a doubt, that our family
would always be *special,* because once upon a time we had gone to the
bottom of the garden and sworn to feed the border guard and work
forever in her service, because the lady was *important.* If no one was
there to watch out, the dead would just come and go as they pleased,
and maybe even hurt the living, while the living might refuse to die
and might bring back the dead whenever they liked. The lady dealt
with all of that, though. All Lily and I had to do was aid the dead and
the living when they *asked*—and make sure that the border was sound.

I really wished I had known all this before Mr. Woods had *asked.*

Maybe because I thought about him, they all came then—the
ghosts. Timothy Woods, Cecilia Lawrence, and Ellie Anderson all
stepped into the clearing and walked toward me and the lady. Ellie
Anderson carried a sword in her hands. It looked old and heavy, but

she carried it as if it was nothing. The ghosts looked just as they always did, which was very dead. Their wounds gaped red, and Mr. Woods's singed shirt smoked a bit. They stopped right before me and turned their serious faces my way. They didn't say anything, but I knew in my head what they wanted me to know.

Something bad had happened when they died, and they were *asking* the lady and me to make it right.

A life, they said, for a life.

"The lady isn't here for your vengeance," I said, although I didn't know why. I would normally never use a word like "vengeance." "Ask for release or remain." I would also never normally say anything like that.

The ghosts just looked at us for a moment; their faces were blank and gave nothing away. Then Ellie Anderson lifted the sword to rest against her shoulder, and they all turned their backs again and walked out of the clearing. I thought they were very disappointed.

They cannot ask for that, the lady said in my head. *But that does not mean you should not give it.*

LILY

49

Returning to Crescent Hill was the worst thing that had happened in my life, after K2. I had really believed for a moment that we had made it and were free, so being marched into the car with the police officers watching and sniggering had been like walking into prison without having done anything wrong. My belly ached all the way, and when the car door slammed shut behind me, all I wanted to do was cry.

I didn't, though. I was too angry, and I didn't want Aunt Clara to know how broken and upset I felt. She would probably have loved it, and I didn't think she deserved any joy. All the way back to Crescent Hill, I seethed with angry disappointment. Violet and I had been *so* close, and our time at the lake house had been so wonderful—magical even—which only made it worse to be caught again. All the fear and worry came rushing back as soon as I saw Aunt Clara's face—smiling like the cat that ate the canary—and I hadn't known before then how amazing it had felt not to have to worry about Violet's health, or the angry ghosts, or if we would get *murdered,* even if only for a single night.

Walking up the broken steps and into the hall at Crescent Hill had been horrendous. I nodded a greeting to the taxidermy bear, feeling like one of the stuffed creatures now, doomed to stay at Crescent Hill forever—even after I died. Violet, too, looked sad and thoughtful as we carried our things inside. Aunt Clara hadn't even bothered with the suitcases but had thrown everything in the trunk of the car, next to the ugly black fur coat she insisted on bringing everywhere, even in hot, humid summer.

Dina's smile was sad, too, when she came out to greet us. Her flames were golden and pink. Even though she had fresh rolls and strawberry jam waiting, we all knew that it wouldn't change anything. Violet and I had run as far and as fast as we could, but we had been caught and marched right back.

What was the point in—possibly—being a witch if it didn't make a difference?

I wished that I, too, could have had a dream about the clearing, like the one Violet had had on our way back. She told me about it the next night, while I brushed her hair in the raven room. I got chills up and down my spine when she told me of the border and our relatives, and even more chills when she told me of how she herself was the dead side, while I was the living side. It did make sense, though, with everything that had happened and everything we could do. I even felt a little proud when I thought of how our family had signed up for it, thinking that it was important.

I wondered how much of this Mama had known.

The ghosts made less sense to me, though. Why had they been in the clearing with a sword—and why had they *asked* Violet for something again? Hadn't she given them enough? I wondered if all people who had died—but never left—could go to the lady to make an appeal, or if it was just the ones who had met Violet. I asked her about it, but she didn't know.

None of what she had learned made things any easier for us, though. We were still stuck on Crescent Hill—with Aunt Clara.

Dina did her best to comfort me whenever we sat together in the kitchen, but it honestly didn't help much.

"You'll think of something else, Lily. You're a strong and resourceful young woman, and the day will come," she promised, but it definitely didn't feel like it.

What made everything worse was having to live with the ghosts again. Even if they had been in Violet's dream, they behaved just the same as before. Mr. Woods was still banging on Aunt Clara's door every night, and Dina had to feed Aunt Clara. The latter didn't seem to trust Violet to do it anymore—but I, for one, was happy that she didn't have to. Dina helped Aunt Clara with her makeup, too, so maybe she knew that I had drawn her eyebrows crooked. I felt sorry for Dina, though, who had to do all that extra work, but I was happy she was there, too, making the best of the situation—slipping us treats and making fancy soups that we had never even known existed. She said she was impressed by how well we had done on our own.

I think Dina was disappointed that we hadn't managed to escape, but she was happy, too, in a way. "It would have been extremely hard for you to survive out there alone. Sooner or later, you would have had to get help—and what if something had happened to you at the lake house? If one of you had fallen through the ice . . . It's better to do things properly, and with the right paperwork signed. I swear I will do what I can to help you." Dina meant it, too. She had started jotting down a note every time she felt like Aunt Clara mistreated us—unless it had to do with the ghosts—hoping that it would be useful to show Mr. Skye when the list was long enough.

"That woman should never have had the care of children!" she said. "She only ever knew how to serve *herself*." Seeing how Aunt Clara also was a murderer, that sounded like an understatement to me, but I was happy that Dina chose to stay with us, even if she knew just how dangerous Aunt Clara could be.

We would've been even more lonely and miserable without her.

The only *good* thing about coming back to Crescent Hill was that I could play Gertrud again. It had been fun to play Astrid at the lake house, but Gertrud and I had known each other for a long time, and I had missed her a lot while we were on the road. Her smooth grain and perfectly tuned strings made the days a little brighter, and I swore that if I ever got to leave Crescent Hill again, Gertrud would come with me. She deserved so much better than being left behind.

It didn't take more than a few days, however, before Aunt Clara started talking about séances again. She came into the living room while Violet and I were watching TV and leaned against the door-frame. She had a cunning look on her face that I didn't like, and she was turquoise and purple all over, so I knew that something bad was coming.

"I have been in touch with several prospective clients," she said, "who have houses *riddled* with ghosts—"

"Violet would only get sick," I said, even though I knew that she knew.

"Well, she looks perfectly fine *now*, and with a little practice, I'm sure she wouldn't get sick at all."

"You don't *know* that," I protested. "If you think we're going to just go back in the car with you and—"

"Not *you*." Aunt Clara rolled her eyes. "Goodness, what would I need *you* for—especially since you have proven to be such a flight risk? No, I only need Violet. *You* can stay here with Dina." She still looked smug, and I was too surprised and shocked to say anything at first. "What's the matter?" she asked me. "Cat got your tongue? I thought you'd be thrilled to stay behind and avoid my *loathsome* com-pany."

"But school starts soon," I protested. "You can't travel around with her when school starts."

"Oh, it's a few weeks yet until that ordeal is upon us, and there will still be weekends and holidays—"

"But Violet *needs* me," I cried. My heart ached badly just from thinking of the tadpoles and what would happen to Violet if I wasn't there to take them away.

"As much as a potato needs lipstick." Aunt Clara smirked. "If any-thing, it will be good for you both to have some distance. Violet is not your *child*, Lily, and you have to stop treating her like it—"

"She is only nine, and you're *using* her!" I jumped off the couch to stand before Aunt Clara, shivering all over, but I wasn't the only one who was mad.

"Why should *I* be the only one hurting?" Aunt Clara bellowed, and the purple and turquoise exploded with red. "Why should *I* be the one in pain? I cannot *eat* and I cannot look at my own face . . . and my nights are *torment* because of you! Don't you think the misery should be evenly dispersed?"

"*We* didn't kill those people!" I shouted back, but Aunt Clara only ignored me.

"Violet and I will go," she said in a final, no-nonsense voice, "and there's nothing you can do about it." Her green eyes glittered cruelly. It was then that I knew, deep in my core, what the dream ghosts had wanted, because I felt it, too.

For things to be finally made right, Aunt Clara had to die.

CLARA
50

My new plan of taking just Violet on the road had put a vigor in my step that was sorely needed, seeing how dreadful my life had become, with the ghosts hounding me at every turn, the bills nearly suffocating me, and my nieces pestering me the rest of the time. Bringing them back to Crescent Hill had been the right thing to do, but that didn't mean it was pleasant to live with two sullen girls who glared at me every time I entered a room.

Honestly, what had Lily expected? That I would just let them *go*? That I wouldn't lift a finger to find them when they ran? That I would let my income and legacy go without a fight and just continue to live with ghosts in my house without turning every stone to find the *one* person who could—possibly—solve all my problems? It was a ridiculous thought! *Of course* I would look for them—and as it turned out, I didn't have to turn that many rocks either. For all her cunning cleverness, Lily could be awfully shortsighted. Going to their mother's lake house was ample proof of that, and leaving her behind when we went back on the road would serve as a valuable lesson.

I also looked forward to not seeing her sour visage for several days. Violet could be trained to do my makeup, and she didn't complain even half as much as Lily. Maybe together we could even figure out a way to put the ghosts back, if her sister wasn't there to work against me. I was a little annoyed with myself for having brought Lily along in the first place. Violet would *never* have run if she was on her own. Without her willful sister around, she might even prove to be quite complacent.

The first tour had just been a trial, I decided. The next one would be better.

I spent most of the day after the announcement up in my room with old road maps, staking out a course for Violet and myself. I was done with crappy motels—and maybe if I pampered the girl, she might come around to my side faster. The best-case scenario was that Violet would have such a wonderful time that it drove a wedge between the sisters.

After all, I only needed Violet to fill my pockets and put the ghosts back to rest.

As for Lily, I certainly wouldn't miss her. The girl had always been a nuisance, but after their little prison break, she had been truly insufferable. She walked around the house with a face as glacial as an iceberg. What point she was trying to make with this display was truly hard to tell, but I didn't like it one bit. Perhaps that was why I could not resist taunting her. I'd take an eruption of anger over quiet resentment any day. It is easier to see where an animal will strike if you can see its teeth.

I found myself frequently thinking of ways of removing her from the picture without losing any of my hard-earned—and much-needed—income. If she died, I would lose half the money, so that was out of the question. I had barely managed to pay up to keep Isabella satisfied, but I knew there would be another bill coming due soon. The same predicament applied if Lily lived somewhere else or was put in an institution. I had, however, been thinking a lot about paralyzing agents of late. I was a nurse after all, and fully capable of administering drugs. In the sweetest of my daydreams, the girl was entirely incapacitated, but living at home with her qualified aunt. Perhaps, in a scenario like that, my guardianship didn't even have to end on her eighteenth birthday, when she became very rich. It was a perfect dream, and the only obstacle I could see was finding a doctor willing to sign off on it without asking questions. I was sure I could find one, though—if only I had enough money to offer.

One way or another, I would have Lily crushed under my heel, just as I would have the other one twisted hard around my finger.

LILY

51

The more I thought about it, the more it made sense. The only way Violet could be safe was if Aunt Clara was gone. We had tried everything else, and our aunt was still purple and angry and dangerous. Telling Aunt Clara that I had to come with them because I could fix Violet wasn't an option either, because then she would only make me, too, use my gifts in ways that they weren't supposed to be used, and then maybe *I* would be sick, and there wouldn't be anyone to help me. No, Aunt Clara had to go, and I knew I wasn't the only one who felt this way. The ghosts, too, wanted to get rid of her—so why hadn't they already?

I asked Dina and Violet what they thought on the night after my fight with Aunt Clara, while we were all sitting around the kitchen table eating stew. Aunt Clara was up in her room just then, claiming to have a migraine, which we knew wasn't true. Violet didn't *feel* anything, and she had been liar's green when she said it.

I was just happy to have her gone, though.

"Mr. Woods said that he wanted to see her 'squirm' first," Dina replied to my question. "Maybe that is why. Or maybe her death means the end of them, too, and they don't want to go just yet."

"Mr. Woods is throwing all kinds of things at her," I said, "but none of it really hurts her. It's like he's not even trying!"

"Do you *want* him to hurt her, for real?" Dina's blue eyes were dark, and her flames had turned a worried shade of pink.

"I don't see what other choice we have," I muttered. "Aunt Clara would kill me, too, if she could afford to. I cause her a lot of trouble, and she only needs Violet for the séances." I didn't say aloud what I thought: that Violet, too, might die if I wasn't around to pick off the tadpoles and heal her with fruit and vegetables.

Dina opened her mouth—probably about to say something to comfort me—but then she closed it again. She, too, knew it was the truth.

"She wants to take everything we have if she can," I continued. "*And* she makes Violet sick."

"*Murder,* though." Dina tutted and shook her head. She speared a piece of potato with her fork but didn't lift it to her lips. "It would make us as bad as she is, don't you think?" She looked at Violet and me in turn.

"Is it really murder if a dead person does it?" I asked.

"Yes." Dina gave me a dark look. "But I don't blame you for your thoughts. The situation is dire, to say the least."

I nodded. "But the ghosts never kill her, so maybe there's no point in hoping that they will."

"Maybe we can *ask* them to." Violet looked up from the stew. She had been quiet all through the meal, so it was a surprise to even hear her talk.

"*Ask* them?" Dina sounded puzzled. "How would we do that?"

"They can talk through me." Violet shrugged. "I don't mind if it can help." She gave me a quick, secretive look. We hadn't told Dina that I could fix the ghost sickness. It just felt safer when only we knew. "It is *important,*" she said with a tiny smile, and I knew she was thinking of the lady in the clearing. "And it's the only way. Or the only way that we know of, anyway."

Once again, I *so* wished that Mama and Papa were there to guide us.

"But is it worth it?" Dina looked at Violet with concern.

"I think so." Violet shrugged again. "I don't think Aunt Clara should live anymore." She licked a little gravy off her fork. "She upsets everything."

"I hate the idea of killing," I said, "but I don't think she should live anymore either."

Dina leaned back in the chair and crossed her arms over her chest. "I would take care of you—you know that. I would be happy to be your guardian until you turn eighteen." She was looking at me as she said the last part. "If your lawyer allowed it, of course."

Just the thought of it made my heart beat faster. "I think he would. They wouldn't want us to move around if we didn't have to."

"Would we still have to live at Crescent Hill?" Violet asked with a grimace.

"I suppose it would be yours if Mrs. Woods passed, seeing how she has no other heirs, but maybe we could live at the farm," Dina suggested.

"It wouldn't be as if we moved to a whole new town," I said. "Mr. Skye probably wouldn't mind." At least I hoped he wouldn't. "But what about your husband?" I asked Dina. "Would he want us there?"

Dina smiled. "Joe likes children, and we keep no secrets, so he knows a little of what has been going on around here."

My whole heart swelled just from thinking of how good that would be, but I didn't dare to hope just yet. There was still the question of Aunt Clara, and how we could make the ghosts do what they had promised.

"We *have* to talk to the ghosts," I decided at last. It would make Violet sick, but I could fix that. And it wasn't just about us anymore either, but about doing what our family had *always* done: protecting the balance and the boundary. Not because Aunt Clara had killed someone, because a lot of people did that, but because she forced Violet to be a channel for the dead when she clearly wasn't meant to be. *That* was the trespass, and I *knew* deep inside that the lady didn't approve. It wasn't just the ghosts and Violet and I who wanted Aunt Clara to die—the lady wanted it, too.

"Don't talk to Mr. Woods, though." Violet rolled her eyes. "He is so angry all the time. *You* should talk to Miss Lawrence," she said to Dina. "You and she were friends, so I'm sure she'll talk to you."

Dina looked a little nervous and wet her lips with the tip of her tongue. "I suppose Cecilia is the wisest of them," she agreed. "Mr. Woods was boastful in life as well."

That decided, we finished our stew and started preparing for a séance.

VIOLET

52

As soon as it was dark and Aunt Clara had gone to bed, Lily and I crept down the stairs and out the door. Dina came on her red bike and parked it behind an oak tree instead of in its usual place by the wall. I felt a little sorry for Dina, who had to go home and then come back again, but I was happy that she was there. She knew just as well as us how important this séance was, even if she didn't think we should murder Aunt Clara.

Irpa, too, had come with us to the garden and settled on top of the pavilion, and I waved at her before slipping inside. We had already hidden a basket of meat, wine, and peppermint candy behind the wall. We probably didn't have to hide it, because Aunt Clara never went into the garden, but Dina thought it was best to keep it out of view anyway. Dina had also brought some candles from the farm because we suspected that Aunt Clara had started counting the ones in the dining room ever since she caught me in the basement.

Even though it was still summer, the night air was cold, and Lily and I had put on our sweaters. Dina, too, wore a thick brown cardigan as we settled in the pavilion, where there were still things from the apothecary on the bench: piles of leaves and tufts of yellow grass, a couple of pilfered wine bottles with water and dirt in them, and a small pile of gravel that we had used as money. We hadn't known anything yet back when we played that game. We hadn't known what Aunt Clara had done, and we hadn't even known what *we* could do.

It felt like it was long ago, even if it had been just at the beginning of summer.

The first thing that happened was that Dina lit the candle. It was a big one that could stand on its own, and the flame glowed like a tiny sun among the wizened leaves on the floor. We had been thinking about bringing lanterns, since it was late at night, but then we figured that the more light we used, the more visible we would be from the house, and decided to take our chances with the full moon instead. This turned out to be a good idea, because the moon was very bright, and everything looked like it was dipped in silver.

Next, Dina and Lily placed the food around the candle and splashed some white wine out on the wooden boards.

"It was Cecilia's favorite," Dina said, looking at the bottle in her hand. That was why we had peppermint candy as well; Miss Lawrence had liked them best. I didn't know if the pork chops had been a favorite of hers, or if Dina had picked them because they were what we had, but it didn't really matter. The food was just fuel, but I didn't say that to Dina, because I thought it made her happy to do something nice for Miss Lawrence.

"Are you ready, Violet?" Lily asked.

I nodded. I wasn't worried at all anymore, because I knew that Lily would fix me later. It also didn't feel as *wrong* as before, because this time I had decided for myself that I would let them speak through me.

"You know that you don't have to if you don't want to," Dina said, looking at me.

"But I do." I gave her an impatient look. "I *said* I wanted to, remember?"

"Still, you're allowed to change your mind," Dina said in her calm, light voice, making me love her a little extra just for that.

"I want to," I said again. "I'm ready."

"All right," Lily said, and she and Dina sat down as well, one on each side of me, so we formed a crescent. I wished we had brought blankets or something, because the wood was very cold to sit on, but we hadn't.

We grabbed each other's hands and the other two closed their eyes, while I looked into the candle flame, thinking about Miss Lawrence. It was hard to concentrate, though, with everything that had happened—and also because it was so important to get it right.

When we had been sitting for a little while, Dina started calling for Miss Lawrence. "Cecilia," she said into the chilly night. "Cecilia, if you can hear me, please come to us." Then, when she got no answer, she said, "We call on Cecilia Lawrence . . . Cecilia Lawrence, if you can hear me, please come . . ." She continued like that for a while, and at first nothing happened, but then—suddenly—it did.

LILY

53

I felt Violet's hand go rigid in mine and opened my eyes to see the candle flickering madly.

"Cecilia?" Dina asked, so she must have noticed that something had changed as well.

When I looked at Violet's face, it wasn't the old woman looking back, but someone else—the one we wanted least of all. I could tell it was him by the awful chewing he did because it was so hard for him to speak, and the hatred that burned in his borrowed eyes. All around us, red tadpoles squirmed like terrified maggots on the wooden boards.

"You are not Cecilia Lawrence," I said before I had time to even think about it. "Go away, Mr. Woods. You are *not* the one we want to talk to!"

"No, wait," Dina interrupted. "Maybe he knows something useful."

"Like what?" I gave him—or Violet—a dark look.

Dina chose to ignore me. "Mr. Woods," she said, "how long have you been planning on tormenting your wife before you kill her?" She said it as if it was nothing—as if she was just asking for a marmalade recipe. I was very impressed.

Mr. Woods laughed deep in Violet's throat, and a little black dirt came tumbling from her lips. "Oh, I will tear her apart. She will *bleed* and *ache* like me . . . I'll grind her bones to bloody dust—"

"Yes, but when?" Dina interrupted him. "Will it be soon, do you think?"

The ghost seemed like he hadn't heard her, but just kept making promises he clearly wasn't about to keep. ". . . I'll carve the heart right out of her chest and eat it with salt . . . I'll slit her belly and dance with her intestines—"

"That is all fine and good, but *when* do you expect this to happen?" Dina interrupted again.

"A fork just won't do it," I added. "Maybe you can use something else?"

Just then, something changed in Violet's face. It was the same thing as before, where it looked as if something moved under her skin. She chewed a couple of times more, and then someone else came to settle inside her. Though it still made me feel queasy to look at, I was more prepared this time. I still didn't like it, though, seeing my sister like that.

This time it was the right ghost, so that somewhat made everything worth it. Not only that, but Miss Lawrence was all business when she arrived, and Violet dribbled just a little bit of dirt down on her blue sweater.

"Don't listen to him," she huffed. "He is nothing but a bag of air."

"Cecilia." Dina's voice was suddenly all warm and welcoming; her flames had turned a deep, rich golden. "How I have longed to talk to you," she said.

"Dearest Dina." Miss Lawrence smiled with Violet's lips. "How I have missed you," she said, with just the same warmth. "And how lucky for us all that you are still here, juggling the pots at Crescent Hill."

"But how *are* you, Cecilia?" Worry had snuck into Dina's voice, and a little pink mingled with the gold.

"Oh, we have no time for pleasantries, dear," Miss Lawrence said in her old-lady voice—though I thought maybe she didn't want to talk about it because she wasn't doing that well, running around after Aunt Clara. "We are here to save the children, are we not?"

"Yes." Dina nodded, and I could see that her eyes were glossy with tears, but she was laughing, too. "Yes, Cecilia, we are!"

"No time to waste, then," Miss Lawrence said.

"Why hasn't Mr. Woods killed Aunt Clara yet?" I asked. "He keeps saying that he will—you all do—but you don't."

Miss Lawrence let out Violet's breath. "Sadly, that is not in our power, dear. We may try, of course, but the dead were never meant to harm the living. If they were, they would be killing people all the time, and the world would be a very different place."

"But he throws things at her," I protested. "If only he threw something bigger—or if his aim was better . . ."

"No." Miss Lawrence shook her head, and I noticed that most of her tadpoles were silver now—the color of truth. "He might get lucky, but our power is modest. That is why I can do nothing more than bother her. Also, as soon as we choose a way of doing things, it's hard for us to change our ways. We are much like gramophone records in that respect. We choose a pattern—a groove—and then we're stuck. My groove has to do with food, Ellie's with mirrors, and Mr. Woods—that boastful oaf—is stuck throwing objects and knocking on doors—"

"So, when Mr. Woods says he's going to kill Aunt Clara—"

"It is all hot air. That is simply not in his repertoire." Miss Lawrence shook her head sadly. "And what little we can do is all because of your sister. Without her aid, we would be utterly powerless."

"But what if she *gave* you more power?" Dina asked. The light from the dancing candle flame caught in her whale-shaped earrings and made them shine, white as the moon.

Miss Lawrence thought about it for a moment. "Alas, I doubt it," she said at last, and my heart sank down to my knees. "The dead are not meant to harm the living." Her gaze shifted to me. "*You* must know that better than anyone," she said. "I'm surprised you are even here, talking to the dead, when it clearly is against your nature. Your *sister*, on the other hand . . ." Miss Lawrence chuckled. "She walks just fine among us."

Dina spoke again. "If you cannot help us, Cecilia, what shall we do about Mrs. Woods?"

"I suggest that you get your hands dirty," Miss Lawrence replied in her no-nonsense voice. "Only the living can take care of the living."

"Cecilia!" Dina sounded shocked.

"I have learned a little something since my death," the old woman said with a wry expression. "Like how it's never worth it to waste one's sympathy on those who are black of heart—and make no mistake, Dina, your gifted charges are in *grave* danger from that woman."

"Believe me, I *do* know that." Dina sighed. She was crowded with pink flames now, and also a little silver. "I just don't know how we would do it." She looked very concerned.

"I'm sure the answer will reveal itself," Miss Lawrence replied, which was really no help at all. "We would all very much like to see her die a bloody death, of course—but any unnatural death would do. Then we would be free to move on . . . But I'm sad to say that the key to that blessed event lies with you." She smiled when she saw my grim expression. "Lean on your sister," she told me. "She doesn't mind the dead, nor death itself. She is blessed in that way—unlike you."

And with that, Miss Lawrence was gone. Something moved under Violet's skin again, and she spat another lump of dirt, but no other ghost came to take Miss Lawrence's place. The candle promptly went out, leaving just a smoky wick. I wasn't sorry that no one else had come to speak to us, because the old woman had already told us all we needed to know—which was that they couldn't help us.

I held Violet as she came back to herself. She didn't look good at all but was pale and weak as usual. Clearly, having Miss Lawrence inside her had been hard, and I instantly regretted asking so many questions. While Dina gathered up the moldy food, I cradled Violet in my arms and told her what we had learned. She was just as disappointed as the rest of us by the news.

"At least we tried," she said when she was strong enough to stand. "Papa always said that we had to try."

"Sure," I murmured, but I was too sad to try to cheer her up. I had *so* been hoping that the ghosts could help us, but they were just stuck in their useless grooves and couldn't do anything at all, other than telling *us* to do it.

Violet leaned on me as we staggered toward the house. Dina made up the rear with the basket, and Irpa soared high above us.

"We'll think of something," Dina said in a quiet voice just as we reached the door. "We'll figure out a way." She didn't sound very hopeful. How did you *kill* a person? And how did you do it in a clever way that wouldn't get you caught? Aunt Clara, of course, would know all about it, but we couldn't exactly ask *her*.

Violet and I slipped inside the house as quietly as we could, took our shoes off, and tiptoed up the stairs. She looked feverish by the time we reached the upper floor, but still found the strength to comfort me.

"Don't worry, Lily," she whispered as soon as we had closed the door to the raven room behind us. "I don't mind dead things," she said, repeating Miss Lawrence's words.

I *did* mind them, though, and that was the problem. No matter how much I hated Aunt Clara and realized that we needed her dead, everything in me fought against the idea of taking a life. It went against the rules—not just as in "against the law," but also in a different way, a way that I supposed had to do with me being the "living" part of the lady. As I started picking red and silver tadpoles off Violet's belly, I wished I had been a little more like Mama, with pieces of both inside me. Probably it would have been easier, then, to do what needed to be done.

I was still boiling with unease when I settled under the covers in the owl room and waited for sleep to arrive, and even though I was exhausted from the séance, my mind just kept spinning—fretting and churning, desperately looking for a way out.

Just then, I heard a gentle rapping on the window. At first, I thought it had started raining, but when it didn't go away or even move, I figured that it had to be something else. I got out of bed and tiptoed over, worrying that it was another one of Mr. Woods's tricks, even if he mostly just bothered Aunt Clara. I wasn't prepared—at all—for what I saw when I pushed the curtain to the side and looked out on the moonlit night.

On the ledge outside my window sat a squirrel.

It looked young and had a russet coat; black tufts of hair balanced on top of its delicate ears, and its tail was magnificently bushy.

"Fredric!" I blurted out, although of course it wasn't him.

I moved my head a little to the right to get a better view, and the squirrel did the same thing, mirroring me perfectly. Then I moved my head to the left, and the squirrel mirrored that movement, too.

I laughed at how cute he was.

"Maybe you aren't Fredric," I said, "but maybe you can be Fredric to me, anyway."

Then the strangest thing happened: He answered me. Not with words, but more like a feeling inside. Something in my head just said that, yes, he could be Fredric if I wanted him to be.

It was then I realized that he was like Irpa.

"Are you my familiar friend?" I asked him through the glass, and Fredric told me that he was. Then he said that he would be with me always, until the day I died.

I opened the window to let him inside, but Fredric the squirrel had other plans. He quickly climbed down the wall, jumping between window ledges and pipes, all the while telling me in my head to come, to follow, because he had something he wanted me to see. It didn't even occur to me *not* to do what he asked. For some reason I just trusted him right away. So, for the second time that night, I pulled on my sweater and snuck down the stairs to the hall.

The air outside was even colder than before, but I didn't mind it. Fredric was waiting for me next to the pavilion, and when he saw me coming, he ran toward me on the damp grass and quickly raced up my body to settle in next to the braid on my shoulder. It was so cute that I had to laugh, and also scratch his head.

To the woods, he said then, in my head. *The answer is in the woods.*

And so, to the woods we went, Fredric and I, walking a moonlit path.

CLARA

54

Saturday arrived with a glowing August sun and birdsong in the air. I spent most of it in my room, planning the last details of our trip, and felt wonderful as I hung up the phone, having made the last reservation just in time for dinner.

I stepped out in the hallway with some apprehension, as Lily had been a menace over the last few days—not because she said or did anything in particular, but because of the way she kept looking at me with her eyes narrowed to slits. It was unnerving: annoying and unsettling in equal measure.

The girl looked as if she was about to devour me.

It was Dina's half day off, but she had prepared a delicious piece of venison for meat day, resting upon a bed of wild mushrooms. The meal had kept well in the food warmer, and I even burned my fingers on the plate when I carried it out to the dining room and called for Violet to come help me eat it. The girls had spent the day in the winter garden, where they were blissfully occupied with some new project. They were making suncatchers, Dina had told me, from strings and mirrors and pebbles and such. A silly waste of time, of course, but at least it kept them out of my hair.

Violet came slowly into the dining room, scrutinizing the food. She wore one of her checked skirts and a knitted red cardigan that hung halfway off her shoulder. Clothes were always an issue with her; she wore them all like empty sacks, ill fitting and rumpled.

"What is wrong?" I asked her. "Is the food not to your liking? Not to worry; you won't have to eat as much as a bite."

"It's just the mushrooms." She smiled and shrugged, then climbed onto the chair beside me. "They are cute."

I rolled my eyes. "Well, let's have a taste, then, shall we?" I was already salivating in anticipation. The meat was pink and tender, and the mushrooms smelled of garlic and butter.

"Sure." She was still smiling when she lifted the silver fork. When the first bite landed on my tongue, I automatically closed my eyes to fully savor the tasty morsel. "Do you like it?" Violet asked, looking at me expectantly.

"It is delicious." I wiped my lips with the napkin. "You should try it sometime." There was nothing wrong with encouraging an appreciation for fine cuisine.

"No, I don't think so." Violet giggled, then kept eyeing me as I chewed.

Lily came drifting in when we were halfway through the meal. She stood by the door to the kitchen, leaning against the frame and looking at me with her wolf eyes.

"What do you want?" I barked at her.

"I'm just bored." She sighed and pulled at the arm of her white cardigan. "Violet and I were going to watch TV, but now I have to wait for you to finish your dinner." I had a strict rule about noisy activities at dinnertime.

"Well, meals cannot be rushed," I told her. "It's bad for the digestion."

"Sure," she said, but remained standing there, watching my food with feral eyes and tugging at her braid. "Dina and I picked the mushrooms," she said. "There's lots of them now, in the woods."

"Yes, thank you. I know where mushrooms grow," I said.

"We had mushroom soup before." Lily continued the pointless

conversation. "It was really nice, and Dina made fresh bread to go with it."

"Kind of her," I murmured.

"Yes," Lily agreed. "Dina is very nice."

"Open up." Violet lifted another forkful of mushrooms to my lips. "You have to eat everything," she told me with a nod.

"Did your parents teach you that?" I arched an eyebrow ever so slightly.

The girl nodded again. Her hair had come undone, tumbling out of the ponytail. I hoped I wouldn't find one of the coarse strands in my food.

When dinner was over and done with, the girls planted themselves on the living room couch and watched TV as announced, their suncatchers momentarily forgotten. They both remained there until I chased them out in order to listen to my opera. I could no longer enjoy either wine or secret chocolates, but at least I had the music, which was something. As Wagner's "Ride of the Valkyries" streamed out into the room, I slumped down on the couch and took several deep breaths. Planning a road trip was hard work. There were all sorts of things one had to think about.

Even through the music and the closed doors, I could hear the girls' chatter in the winter garden. I no longer felt entirely easy when the two of them were together alone; I worried that they conspired against me. I couldn't make out any words, though, just murmurs. There was no laughter, but that wasn't uncommon since their failed escape. I honestly quite enjoyed how their unbridled enthusiasm had become somewhat . . . tempered.

They deserved all the suffering they got, for awakening all my secrets.

I dozed off for a while, probably due to the heavy meal, and when I woke up, both the girls and the opera were gone, and there was nothing but silence around me. I didn't feel right, though. My stomach hurt, and I was desperately nauseous. I scrambled up from the couch and only just made it to the pink downstairs toilet before all the delicious dinner came tumbling out of me. I stayed in the bathroom for quite some time, heaving and hurling, before my stomach was entirely empty. It still cramped, though, painfully—and to make everything just a little bit worse, Timmy came to throw his fists against the door.

"Go away!" I yelled at him. "Go away, you thieving troll!" But my husband—always a sucker for disaster—just kept hammering on the door while that awful hissing noise filled the air.

I unlocked the door and threw it open—which did indeed shut him up for a moment—before staggering into the kitchen to find the phone and call a doctor.

The phone wasn't there, though.

The fat phone book was still in place on the counter, but the apparatus itself was gone.

"Lily!" I croaked. "Violet!" Maybe the two of them had taken it away as a joke. "Lily!" I cried again, but my voice was very weak. I stumbled into the dining room, and then farther into the living room, where I fell back down on the couch. My stomach was still convulsing, and for once I was at a loss for what to do. I threw up again then—pure acid down on the Persian rug—and noticed how my thinking wasn't clear; it was hard just to catch and keep a thought.

For a moment, I saw the three ghosts, standing before me in a row and looking down at me. Timmy was smirking as well as he could manage with the bleeding cut on his cheek; Cecilia had folded her hands over her stomach and seemed as happy as the cat that got the cream; pretty Ellie pursed her lips and wagged a finger in the air. That was all I saw before another painful twinge made my body cramp upon the green velvet.

The next time I came to, my nieces were there. They were standing side by side on the other side of the coffee table, holding hands. Both of them stared at me, but neither of them rushed to help me. Lily had never looked more like Iris than she did in that moment; her cold gaze raked over my body like a scalpel, judging every inch.

"It will be over soon," she said in a voice laced with ice. "We gave you a lot."

"What . . . are you . . . talking about?" I croaked.

"Oh, nothing." She shrugged. Violet, beside her, looked down at the floor.

"Get . . . help," I uttered next, with considerable effort.

"No, I don't think so," Lily replied, and then—finally—I understood.

The little fox had tricked me!

If I had had the strength, I would have laughed then, because just as Clarabelle Diamonds slipped forever from my grasp, another legacy slotted in its place—passed on to me from Iris, and now from me to the girls.

Murder ran strong in our family.

"At least you'll be rid of the ghosts." Violet looked up and beamed in my direction.

Lily smiled down at her sister. "Violet has promised that she won't bring you back, no matter how much you *ask*." The girl shifted and tightened her grip on Violet's hand. "It's just like you said, Aunt Clara. Sometimes murder *is* the only way out if you want to make a good life. Thank you for teaching us that."

For a second then, it looked as if the whole girl was engulfed in flames, of all colors of the rainbow—much like the fire in a well-cut diamond. Her sister, too, stood there shrouded in flames, only hers were gray as smoke and black as ink. It lasted for only a second, and then they looked themselves again.

"Violet . . ." I tried one last time to save myself, but the girl only gave me a pitiful smile, and now the ghosts were back, too, laughing and jeering.

"Soon I will see the soles of your feet," Cecilia said. I was stunned to hear her voice at last but figured it had to do with my imminent doom.

"May you rot," said Ellie. Timmy lifted a hand as if to place it on her shoulder, but to my immense delight, she shrugged it off. Their illicit love had clearly not lasted.

Instead, my husband turned his attention to me and toasted the air with an imaginary tumbler.

But I was safe, I was home, in a bubble of indestructible diamond—*soaring* high up in the sky, where no one, ever, could touch me.

✤ EPILOGUE ✤
LILY

Seven months after Crescent Hill burned to the ground, taking our aunt's body with it, Violet and I were back at the lake house. We had wanted to go for ages, ever since the fire, but there had been a lot to deal with since Aunt Clara's death—plenty of paperwork and even statements to the police, though the fire had been ruled an accident, just as we had hoped.

At first, we hadn't planned on burning Crescent Hill, but then it just seemed safer, since the poison in Aunt Clara's body would burn away as well, and it would make it easier for us to live on Dina and Joe's farm. At nightfall on the day of the mushrooms, Violet and I had carried out the most important things—like Gertrud—and then, a little later, Dina had toppled a candle onto the tablecloth in the dining room. It took a while for the fire to catch, but as soon as it did, it moved fast. When the fire truck finally arrived, Violet and I pretended to have just fled the house, and they believed us, too, because we both reeked of smoke and had drizzled hot ashes on our nightclothes. Violet had had to throw away her frilly nightgown after that—the one she got from Mama—which made her very sad.

We had a funeral for Aunt Clara, although there wasn't much left to bury. Her old nursing friends were there, and also a man we had

never heard of before, who said he was Aunt Clara's "special friend."
He gave us each a mourning brooch with lots of diamonds surrounding a golden *C*—and even wore one himself on his lapel. Then he
asked us what had happened to Aunt Clara's jewelry collection, and
when I told him that the diamonds the firefighters had fished out
of the ashes had already been sold, and the money given to Mama's
charity, he seemed even sadder than before. Violet and I gave our *C*
brooches to Dina afterward, saying she could sell them, too, if she
liked. Neither of us liked diamonds anymore.

Aunt Clara had also had a lot of debts, and we had to use most of
the insurance money after the fire to settle everything. It turned out
that she had tried to make her own jewelry line without having the
money to pay for it. The designer she had hired had been very frosty
with Dina on the phone, saying she had waited for ages to get all her
money. I was sorry for that, but I didn't think it was fair of her to take
it out on poor Dina when it was Aunt Clara who had hired her. Perhaps she was just upset that all of her hard work would come to nothing.

When all that was over, Violet and I had spent some time getting
used to our new lives on the farm. It was a big change for us, because
suddenly we lived not only with Dina and Joe but also with a lot of
cows, two cats, and a score of chickens.

We both loved it immensely, though—but not so much that we
didn't still long for the day when I turned eighteen and we could
move back to the town house.

The farmhouse was smaller than what we were used to, and Mr.
Skye had been worried about that, but Violet and I didn't need much.
We had to share a bedroom now, but that was perfectly fine. It wasn't
as if we were cooped up inside all the time, like we had been on Crescent Hill. We went to school every day and had other things to do
besides.

Dina had had a long, serious talk with Mr. Skye after she became
our guardian and explained to him how badly we had been treated by
Aunt Clara. She did it so that he would think twice next time before
dismissing a fourteen-year-old when she called to tell him that things

were bad. Mr. Skye was very apologetic and sent us a bunch of roses, which didn't really help at all, except for making *him* feel better. But at least he no longer thought that I needed medication.

Violet had joined a drama club and spent a lot of time rehearsing, and I had taken up horse riding with some girls from town, since we still couldn't find a music teacher. It was fine, though; it really was. Ever since the clearing, playing had been different for me, like it was something personal that shouldn't necessarily be shared. I still played every day, but I didn't think about music all the time, or daydream about being onstage. Music to me now had become the time when I could let my hair down and truly be who I was. It was also when Fredric would come and visit me, rapping on the window with his little paw. When I had put Gertrud away, he would come inside and cuddle for a while, or we would go for a walk in the woods. I had never thought that I would have long and interesting conversations with a squirrel, but then again, that wasn't *really* what he was. Exactly who our familiar friends were, I still didn't know—though I *had* asked—but I imagined they were something halfway between dead and alive, able to look in both directions.

Riding had filled the void that music left behind. Even if I wasn't very good at it yet, I figured that I could be in time. What I liked most of all was to be in the stable with the animals and take care of them. Nothing felt better to me than to run my hand across a living thing and feel the deep throb of their life within—or even help strengthen it if the animal was sick and no one else was around to watch. I did that in the barn at the farm as well, if one of the cows had an infection or something, bringing with me a bowl of fruit and a cup of water as fuel. Dina knew that I could fix things now and would even ask me to do it.

I had stopped eating meat, too, since I started using my hands on the animals; it just didn't feel right anymore. I couldn't help them one day and then eat them the next, and I definitely liked them better alive. Thankfully, Dina understood and never yelled at me for skipping meals, but helped me set up my own menu instead to make sure I got all the right nutrients.

I already knew, without a shadow of a doubt, that whatever I decided to do with my life, it had to be something to do with animals. I had even talked to Mr. Skye about investing in a wildlife sanctuary when I turned eighteen and was thinking about becoming a vet. It was not what Mama and Papa had planned for me—they had always assumed I would be a musician—but I thought they would have liked my change of heart.

Where Violet would end up was anyone's guess. Things were different for her, because helping the dead was harder than helping the living, it seemed. She was like a light in the dark for them, and they would always find her. No matter where we were or what we did, Violet would often get a distant look on her face, and I knew she was seeing someone dead. She always carried around a hunk of bread, a saltshaker, a candle, and a bottle of water in her backpack, in case she had to help someone move on. I knew for a fact that she had helped a lost janitor in the school's restroom one time, and a farmhand she found milling around in Dina and Joe's barn. Sometimes she visited cemeteries, too, where she would find herself a secluded spot and go at it for hours, until all the bread was gone.

A short time after we moved to the farm, a letter arrived, addressed to Aunt Clara. It was from a woman called Miss Margot, whom Violet and Aunt Clara had met while we were on the road, and she *begged* Aunt Clara for another visit, since her dead father was stuck at the bottom of the ocean.

Violet didn't remember anything of what had happened during the séance, but she did feel bad for Miss Margot, so she and Dina went to see her, just to talk. The problem with Miss Margot's father was that he was at the bottom of the sea, so it was hard to find him to do the salt and bread ritual. Violet hadn't given up, though, and she and Dina had ordered lots of books about mediums and the afterlife to try to figure out a way to coax him to the surface. The two of them also "trained," as they said, hoping to make Violet able to talk for the ghosts without letting them inside her body. The training consisted mostly of Violet staring into a candle, but I knew that the *real* work happened inside her head.

I hoped they could help Mr. Brewer eventually, because it didn't sound fun to be stuck in the sea with only cod for company.

I still worried about Violet, though. I thought that spending so much time with the dead did something to her. We didn't talk much about Aunt Clara and what had happened at Crescent Hill, since neither of us wanted to think much about it, but when we did, it always left me with a bad feeling in my gut. Not just because I had helped kill someone, but because Violet didn't seem sorry for it at all.

"It was a crisis," I said, the one time I confronted her about it. "We did it because she put you in danger and trespassed where she had no business going. She messed up the lady's rules so she *had* to go, but we will never do it again."

"Unless we have to," Violet replied in a serious voice.

"No, we will never do it again. We will never meet another Aunt Clara. There *are* no more Aunt Claras."

Violet looked at me with pity in her eyes. "Lily, there are *lots* of Aunt Claras."

"But we won't . . . *kill* them," I insisted.

"Unless we have to," she said again, slightly overbearing.

Maybe it had been different before, when our family was bigger and the lady's power flowed into more people. Fredric had showed me how everyone born in our family got just a piece of it—even the boys sometimes. Like, one person could see colors, while another one could heal the sick, while a third maybe *felt* things. Then, when family members died, someone else got their gift. Now, with just Violet and me alive, we got everything at once when Mama left, and it was a lot. I didn't think a ten-year-old was ever meant to spend so much time with the dead. Maybe it was because I belonged to the living side that it felt so horrible to me, but I definitely didn't like the idea of my sister being so comfortable with murder—*even* if I had helped commit one.

Still, all through everything, Violet and I had yearned for the lake house. It felt like we had discovered just a tiny bit of what it meant to be in the lady's service the last time we were there, and Violet was worried about her, too, since she didn't get any food. I also think she wanted to see colors again, since she hadn't seen as much as a single tiny flame since the last time we were in the clearing.

Needless to say, we were both overjoyed when Dina finally said we could go.

We packed our bags and loaded them into Dina's small car but left Joe at home because of the cows. Dina was a much better driver than Aunt Clara, and when we had to stop for the night, she booked us into a clean, nice hotel that was nothing like the Pink Dragon. While we were driving, all Violet and I could talk about was how wonderful the lake house was, so maybe Dina was expecting a palace. If she was disappointed by the sight of the old cabin, she didn't say it, though, but just strode right inside and started making it her own by unloading groceries and going through the cupboards. We knew that we ought to stay and help her, but we were both so restless that Dina told us to just go. As soon as all our bags were safely inside, I grabbed Gertrud, and Violet grabbed a box of chocolates, and then we slipped into the woods.

It was spring this time so the ground was wet, and the sky above was bleak, but we didn't mind at all. Irpa was there, too, flying high above us, and even Fredric came to join us as we made the short trek. I wasn't surprised to see him before us on the path, since I had long since learned that he could travel anywhere I was. It was just how it was with familiar friends.

The clearing looked just the same, though, sunshine or not. It was just as green and just as amazing. And there she was: the lady, looking just as beautiful as before, with her face split in half: one side alive and the other one dead. From under her skirt, the water came bubbling, twisting between brittle old bones and a couple of early spring flowers.

Life and death together.

This was why I didn't feel too bad about what we had done to Aunt Clara. I had realized that, sometimes, one thing just had to die for something else to live. Even *she* had believed that, in her way—and maybe that was the reason why she hadn't come back to *ask* Violet for anything, not even when we were wading through the ashes of Crescent Hill.

Maybe she, too, knew that it had been inevitable, and left at once when she died.

I had asked Violet what had happened with the ghosts, and she said that they had gone, too, when Aunt Clara died. Then I asked her what would have happened to them if Aunt Clara hadn't been killed, but had just lived until she grew old and died of a heart attack, and Violet said that they probably would have just continued to mill around at Crescent Hill, looking for a revenge they would never get, so it was good for them, too, what we did. I was especially happy for Miss Lawrence, since she had tried to help us.

All around the lady, flames licked the air, dancing and flickering, making Violet sigh with pure delight.

"Look at that," she said. "Just look at that, Lily. All the colors . . ."

"Yes," I replied, though I admired the other flames as well—those that didn't have any colors, only gray and black. "She looks just like before." I couldn't help but laugh. The clearing was like that—it made you want to smile.

"She'll like the chocolates for sure." Violet started across the mossy ground. "Tomorrow, we'll bring her a roast," she said, "and eggs from the farm—and honey."

"Sure we will." Even if I didn't eat meat myself anymore, I didn't mind if the lady did—or if Violet still loved it.

I crossed the clearing in my sister's tracks, and then—when we were close enough—I put the violin case down by my feet and opened it. "For now, though, she'll get chocolates," I said, just as I lifted Gertrud in the air.

"And music." Violet clapped her hands.

"Yes, music," I said, and started to play.

I kept going until our toes left the ground.

❧ ACKNOWLEDGMENTS ❧

This book went through an unusually long gestation period from idea to finished manuscript. I often have ideas, but most of them never make it because there's always a newer, shinier one to pick. *At the Bottom of the Garden* is different. It survived a temporary burial in a file folder named "Graveyard," rose from the ashes, and became a real book. That is no small feat, and only goes to show that you should never delete anything.

I first had the idea in 2019 but wasn't quite ready to write the story back then, and so it was forgotten until 2022, when I—by sheer luck and happenstance—opened the file and rediscovered Clara, Lily, and Violet. I knew right away that this was still something I *really* wanted to write, and that I finally was in the right headspace to do so. What followed were months of joyful typing and delightful fictional company, so I would like to thank past me for being wise enough to jot down the idea while it was fresh.

I would also like to thank my editor Anne Groell for seeing the potential in the story when it was little more than that initial—once dead—idea, and for her brilliant input, guidance, and faith in the story as it developed. Another heartfelt thank-you goes to the rest of the team at Del Rey, for making me feel so welcome, and for working

so hard for this book. I am likewise very grateful to my UK editor
Wayne Brookes and the team at Oneworld for seeing something special in this novel.

My agent, Brianne Johnson, deserves all the flowers for helping me
shape this wild, unruly story into something more presentable. As
always, thank you for all your wonderful ideas and ceaseless encour-
agement. I couldn't have asked for better support.

This book would probably not exist without Liv Lingborn, with
whom I share a long and multifaceted obsession with wicked women,
fairy tales, and strange little girls in fiction. We have fed each other
book and movie recommendations for years, and endlessly discussed
the importance of subverted tropes. Liv is one of my greatest support-
ers, often my first reader, and this time she even helped me with the
title. Liv, this strange book of weirdness is for you.

To me, *At the Bottom of the Garden* is, at least in part, a book about
death—or about coming to terms with death. The idea was first
hatched following a period where there had been a lot of it in my life,
including both of my parents. Later on, while I was doing revisions, I
very sadly lost a cousin, too, so this book is thoroughly steeped in
death, which is why I want to thank my dead as well, not just for their
lives, but for all that I learned from their passing.

As always, many thanks to my son, Jonah, for his patience and support, and my cat, Tussa, who is probably the strangest little girl of
them all.

© LENE J. LØKKHAUG

CAMILLA BRUCE was born in central Norway and grew up in an old forest next to an Iron Age burial mound. She holds a master's degree in comparative literature and has co-run a small press that published dark fairy tales. Camilla currently lives in Trondheim with her son and cat.

camillabruce.com
Instagram: @camillabruce_writing
X: @millacream

DISCOVER MORE FROM
DEL REY &
RANDOM HOUSE WORLDS!

READ EXCERPTS
from hot new titles.

STAY UP-TO-DATE
on your favorite authors.

FIND OUT about exclusive
giveaways and sweepstakes.

CONNECT WITH US ONLINE!
⊚ 🅵 𝕏 @DelReyBooks

DelReyBooks.com
RandomHouseWorlds.com